THE PRUSSIAN LIEUTENANT

Book One
~ of ~
The Hussar's Love

KARL MAY

TRANSLATED BY
ROBERT STERMSCHEG

THE PRUSSIAN LIEUTENANT

ISBN-10: 1-926676-18-1
ISBN-13: 978-1-926676-18-0

Printed in Canada.

Printed by Word Alive Press
131 Cordite Road, Winnipeg, MB R3W 1S1
www.wordalivepress.ca

WORD ALIVE PRESS
Just Write!

To my Bella Toni.

ACKNOWLEDGEMENTS

I would like to thank my father John Stermscheg, who instilled within me the desire to explore the works of Karl May.

To Ralf Harder, for making the original text available on the Karl May Gesellschaft (KMG) website.

To Annemarie Kramer, who assisted in the editing process.

To Gord and Trish Kell, for their encouragement in the writing process.

To Donna Bjorklund for her proofreading, and to Evan Braun, for his expertise in polishing the work.

To Marjorie Anderson, for her valuable insight and for steering me in the right direction.

To Michael M. Michalak, who supported this work from the outset and believed in this new writer.

To all these people, thank you for your input. It was much appreciated.

FOREWORD

Born in Europe, I was exposed to many wonderful writers—Edgar Rice Burroughs, Alexandre Dumas, and, of course, Karl May. I believe all of us have appreciated the way these gifted authors have opened up a whole new world in our imaginations through their portrayal of life. I have read and re-read many of Karl May's travel narratives and novels and I can honestly say that I have never tired of them. His prolific writings have taken me from the plains of Europe to the endless sands of the Sahara, even to the Rocky Mountains.

As I contemplated this translation project, I felt that I had the time and energy to do it justice, but I was surprised by its complexity. The challenge I faced was in remaining faithful to his original work while conveying the story in modern English. When you consider that much of this story takes place in Paris, where the characters spoke French (naturally!), this becomes all the more apparent. Also, Karl May's novels, interspersed with French references, were penned in German over a century ago and contained a number of idioms largely unknown today.

I also discovered that there were a number of variations of his original work, *Die Liebe des Ulanen*. As I searched further, I realized that the four novels as we know them today (*The Road to Waterloo*, *The Marabout's Secret*, *The Spy from Ortry*, and *The Gentlemen of Greifenklau*) originally stemmed from a series of *Lieferungen*, or consignments in a local newspaper, *der Deutscher Wanderer*. These 108 parts comprised what would later be known as the *Münchmeyer Romane*. They were sold by Karl May to the newspaper and appeared there on a regular basis, running from September 1883 to October 1885.

These stories, which May penned in a style of adventure and intrigue, were well-received by the general public. It's interesting to note that May started his tale circa 1870, and introduced the reader to the central characters, spanning to the second and third generation. The setting was just prior to the Prussian-French War. He then abruptly takes us back to 1814, not in a flashback but in dramatic fashion, explaining how the conflict originated between two particular families. Particularly clever is the way in which May weaved two central and historical figures into the story, Napoleon Bonaparte and Field Marshal von Blücher. The inclusion of these larger than life men added an additional dimension to the plot, heightening the drama faced by the novel's protagonist, Lieutenant von Löwenklau.

I reviewed the 108 parts, made available as a result of Karl Harder's work and the Karl May Gesellschaft (KMG). I chose my translation work by beginning at what would be the chronological starting point, the events taking place in 1814. Although I have perused the later, more commonly known abridged text made available in a four-part series by several publishers, I have followed the original, unabridged version from the KMG. I felt that this would bring the reader into the story at the very beginning, as it unfolds with the lives of the two principal characters, Hugo and Margot. By reworking a few paragraphs, the natural progression of the story then continues into the second book, *The Marabout's Secret*, about 30 years later.

One other detail that should be mentioned is that most, if not all, the subsequent editions to the *Munchmeyer Romane* (published by Karl-May-Verlag or Ueberreuter Verlag) adopted new names for several of the key characters, including our protagonist, the Prussian lieutenant, previously Hugo von Königsau. While doing research, and in consultation with the editor, I adopted the new name of Hugo von Löwenklau. Furthermore, these later editions adjusted the manuscript through the use of chapter headings that were not employed exclusively by Karl May. I have also reworked these to reflect my own work while keeping the story's outline intact.

I often encountered obscure idioms, such as *"Auge und Beine machen"*. Literally translated, this would read as: *to make eyes and legs*. Being unfamiliar with some of these older expressions, I have scoured various sources, including source material on the internet. To my surprise, I often received the answer from an unexpected, yet reliable source: my father. He was quite familiar with them, and after a moment of reflection usually had a quick response. In the modern vernacular, this one would read: *Let's hurry up*, or *Let's get going*.

Karl May often expanded on a thought and "sandwiched" it between several others, ending up with run-on sentences. I recognized that, while this was workable in German, it created long and cumbersome passages in English. To render it more fluent and understandable, I've broken up some of the lengthier sentences.

In other instances, particularly during dialogue, the short, sometimes curt responses seemed inadequate. I found this needed to be addressed, especially with some of Napoleon's discourses. Bonaparte was known for his short, cutting remarks, and while this was fine in German, it lacked something in English.

One example was in Chapter 17:

> *"Highwaymen,"* Napoleon mumbled. *"Know one. Served, but poorly."*

FOREWORD

I rendered this example as:

> *"Highwaymen," Napoleon mumbled. "I recognize a few of them.*
> *They served under me once, and rather poorly at that."*

I was also faced with several nameless figures that were often simply referred to as 'he' or 'she'. I felt that giving these anonymous beings names would enhance their contribution to conversations, making them more complete and interesting.

The many words of an era that have long ago faded into the mists of time also needed to be resurrected and explained to give them relevance. I hope that their use in this story lend it the authenticity it deserves. See the translation notes for details.

Robert Stermscheg
December 2007

TABLE OF CONTENTS

*"Oh, what tangled webs we weave,
when we first practice to deceive."*

-Sir Walter Scott
(1771-1832)

CHAPTER ONE
Marshal Forward

It was the year 1814. The defeated Napoleon was on his way to exile on the Island of Elba. On March 31, the conquering forces, comprised of Austria, Prussia, and Russia, were poised to enter Paris. One man, who had contributed so much to the combined cause, sat on the Montmarte,[1.1] unable to participate in the entry. He was the old Blücher, affectionately known as Field Marshal Forward. He had contracted a fever, resulting in a serious eye infection. Shielding his eyes with the brim of a lady's hat, he could be seen orchestrating the battle for Paris from the hill. While sitting high on his horse during the procession into the city, the brim of the hat protruded from under his forage cap. Fortunately, the pleas of General Gleisenau and the regimental doctor Volzke persuaded him to remain behind.

At last, Blücher's eye infection improved sufficiently, giving him the option of residing in the city. He chose for himself the palace of the Duke of Otranto, on the Rue Ceruti. From his new residence, Blücher wandered about the city, becoming familiar with the historic sites and places of interest. He simply discarded his military tunic, opting instead to wear a plain civilian overcoat. He particularly enjoyed his walks along the tree-lined streets in the vicinity of the Royal Palace, where he could be seen strolling through, unmistakable by his gait and the obtrusive pipe in his mouth.

Blücher often came to Very, an innkeeper in the Tulerie neighborhood where he drank his coffee with milk or refreshed himself with a glass of *warmbeer*.[1.2] On one particular afternoon, several participants were occupying the card room of the inn, engaged in a game of *L'Hombre*.[1.3] Judging from their lively conversation, they were Frenchmen by birth and officers by their demeanor.

At an adjoining table, sitting by himself, was a man in his mid-twenties. He gave the impression of being impartial to the loud boasting, yet he caught every word uttered during pauses in the card game.

The door to the room opened and an older gentleman stepped inside. Though dressed in modest attire, he displayed an air of confidence. He nodded a greeting to the occupants and seated himself at a nearby table. Ordering his customary glass of *warmbeer*, he became so absorbed in its contents that he paid the card players no heed.

There was a dignified manner about the old gentleman, but unlike the players he drew no attention to himself. His head was well-proportioned, yet his large, protruding moustache eclipsed his noble forehead, stately nose, and red cheeks. The strong chin was augmented by blue, piercing eyes that revealed a trusting gentleness and hinted at a sharp, decisive disposition.

He enjoyed the refreshment and asked for another.

While the sun burned relentlessly outside, the air in the inn became sultry. It was no wonder the old gentleman felt the heat after consuming his steaming *warmbeer*. Although all the occupants felt the discomfort, only he decided to shed his overcoat, hanging it on the wall. This simple gesture, though leaving him in shirtsleeves, seemed reasonable to him, though not to the Parisians, least of all the card players.

"Who might this stranger be?" inquired one of the players with displeasure.

His companion nodded in agreement. "Does he think he can come here and show us his uncivilized ways?"

"One thing's clear," another player said. "He's not a Frenchman. A French gentleman would never abandon the rules of decency and reprovingly ignore our good customs. Surely he must be one of those vile Germans! Will those barbarians never learn to behave properly in accordance with good taste? Let me remind you that their military prowess is to control and oppress. Their entertainment is largely crude, and all their customs are tasteless and repulsive."

"Just look at him!" replied another. "He has the appearance of a peasant who presents himself as an uneducated coal worker. He deserves nothing more than to be put out at once."

"Who would dare to stop us?" asked still another.

"Why don't we compel the innkeeper to give this insolent lout's face a slap and throw him out?" the first man asked. "The Germans are nothing but vermin. Like dogs, they deserve a thrashing."

The young man, who had kept his peace, quietly stood up and came over to the card table. "Messieurs, permit me to introduce myself. I am Hugo von Löwenklau, a lieutenant in the service of His Majesty, the Emperor of Prussia. The gentleman about whom you have been speaking is none other than His Excellency, Field Marshal von Blücher. I expect you will retract all your remarks about His Excellency and our Prussian heritage."

The *L'Hombre* players were completely taken aback by the young man's words. They were now aware that the man they had all feared, Field Marshal von Blücher, was seated in their very midst. In fact, this was the very same man who had not only defeated the patriotic forces of France, but also tarnished the *star*, their beloved Napoleon. They mumbled something unintelligible under their breath, scarcely what one would consider an apology. Only the first man, who had likened Germans to dogs, was not to be deterred and uttered a curse through his clenched teeth. He jumped out of his seat and, in a threatening manner, addressed the young officer.

"Monsieur, we did not ask for the pleasure of your acquaintance," he said. "It was therefore inappropriate of you to speak to us, and furthermore, your actions simply confirm that the German people are an inferior race. With regards to this man, it is of no consequence to us whether he be a field marshal or a foot soldier. We do *not* intend to retract a single syllable!"

"May I inquire your name, Monsieur?"

"I am not ashamed of it," the Frenchman replied proudly. "I am Albin Richemonte, Captain of the Emperor's Guard."

"You do not intend to retract your words, Captain?" the young Prussian said politely, bowing formally.

"No," Richemonte said loudly. He noticed Blücher was following the conversation with interest, even while feigning ignorance. "Not one word, not one syllable!" he finished.

"Do you declare then, in all seriousness, that His Excellency is a boor, and the German people are nothing but dogs fit for a thrashing?" asked Löwen-klau, his face expressionless.

Richemonte laughed insolently. "Absolutely."

"Then you will permit me to send you my subordinate, who will make the arrangements to settle this as gentlemen."

"Ridiculous. I have no intention of fighting a duel with a Prussian," said Richemonte.

"Really?" Löwenklau asked. "First you insult us, and now you want to withdraw? If you suppose that we Prussians do not understand the rules of decency, then certainly you have demonstrated by your conduct that you, Monsieur Richemonte, of all men deserve this thrashing. Your lack of proper conduct is deplorable."

Faster than anyone would have thought possible, Löwenklau slapped Richemonte squarely in the face. He followed it up with a second, a third, and a fourth, in rapid succession. The attack was so quick and unexpected that the Frenchman failed to contemplate a defense, much less find time to react. His followers were equally surprised at the speed and agility of the attack. They merely stared at the scene, failing to move a single muscle in defense of their friend.

The Prussian stepped back from Richemonte, who at last came to the realization he had been disgraced. He finally reacted, reaching for the dagger normally affixed to the left side of his uniform. Realizing his error, in that he was only dressed in civilian clothes, he hastily withdrew his empty hand and vaulted himself at his adversary in a fit of rage.

"Swine! You caught me off guard, but now you will forfeit your life."

Though Richemonte threw a punch, it was met in the same instant by a powerful blow which sent him tumbling back, collapsing on the floor. More guests now occupied the card room, many of them German who came to catch a glimpse of the famous Blücher. Löwenklau's lightning-like strike caught them flat-footed and surprised, unsure of whether or not to come to his aid.

The innkeeper, watching from nearby, stepped in, recognizing the severity of the situation. He knew the Germans had been victorious and were the new authority in Paris. He was shrewd enough to realize he could not allow the insult to continue. He quickly escorted Richemonte into a private room, where the reckless captain continued his ranting despite the efforts of his companions to calm him down.

In the lively aftermath, Blücher got up from his table and good-naturedly placed his hand on Löwenklau's shoulder.

"My son, you did that very well!" he said, smiling. "He who belittles innocent people and refuses to give satisfaction deserves his due, which you administered in a most decisive fashion. I heard what that insolent captain said, and by God, I would have given him a good walloping myself, had you not intervened. Your name, my son, is Löwenklau?"

The lieutenant wasn't surprised at Blücher's pointed and blunt manner of speech. It was typical of him. In fact, he felt a great honor to be addressed by His Excellency.

"Hugo von Löwenklau, Excellency," he replied stalwartly.

"Are you are a lieutenant, my son?"

"A lieutenant with the Zieten Hussars."[1.4]

"A lieutenant?" the field marshal questioned. "A man who can deliver such blows, and only a lieutenant? You will become a cavalry master, my son. Come to my office tomorrow morning, and we will bring it about.

"It's damned hot in here, as long as the sun shines. Join me for a little drink of *warmbeer* and remove your *Gottfried*,[1.5] as I did. Come on, my son, don't be reluctant. We're all human beings. By God, I'll be damned if I allow these Frenchmen to strip the flesh from my bones."[1.6]

Löwenklau decided to accept the invitation. He removed his coat and, now clad only in his shirtsleeves, joined Blücher as though they were old friends. The familiarity the old man had placed on him didn't embarrass him in the least. People who knew Blücher, especially his officers, understood his mannerisms. While out walking, the unassuming Blücher occasionally stopped working men on the street and joked amicably about the weather or a particular brand of tobacco. He even lit his pipe on the stub of a fellow's cigar. Such a fellow, unfamiliar with Blücher's idiosyncrasies, usually moved on irritably. Such was the field marshal's way.

Hugo von Löwenklau appeared punctually before the marshal the following morning, expecting to receive his promotion to cavalry master. Instead, he was met by a brooding Blücher.

"Listen, my son," he said, "to this most frustrating story. On the second of April, I abdicated my overall command of the Prussian forces. Almost immediately those penpushers[1.7] thought the old Blücher had nothing more to contribute. Can you imagine that? I told them about yesterday's incident and recommended you for advancement, only to be told there were currently no openings. But I promise you, I'll remember your courage and revisit this issue at the earliest opportunity. Help yourself to some tobacco, my son. A good pipe loosens the tongue, and suddenly I feel like some conversation."

Löwenklau, though disappointed, wasn't the sort to allow such a matter to get the better of his normally congenial nature.

At last, Blücher gave him leave. Although the young officer lived nearby, his journey home was about to take considerably longer than he anticipated.

A distinguished looking mademoiselle walked past. As far as Löwenklau could tell by looking at her back, she wasn't plain-looking. He guessed she probably belonged to an upper class. His eyes assessed the tilt of her head with unusual interest. She had gathered her skirt in one hand, revealing her small delicate feet. Her steady and graceful stride showed she possessed both poise and charm.

Just then, Löwenklau noticed the approach of two officers. By their uniforms, he recognized them as Cossacks. Having caught sight of the young lady, they nodded to each other and, with a knowing look, deliberately blocking her path. Although the young lady wanted to hurry past them, one of the officers grabbed her arm.

"Mademoiselle, aren't you afraid to be walking alone in the city with foreign troops around?" he asked in broken French. "It's only fitting that we accompany you."

She looked at him with large, incredulous eyes. "Many thanks, Monsieur. However, I do not require an escort."

As the young woman spoke to the Russian, she turned her head, allowing Löwenklau to catch her profile. *Ah, such a lovely face. Graceful, tender, and soft*, he thought.

The determined Cossack laughed out loud, keeping a strong grip on her arm. "Perhaps you don't need our escort," he replied. "But we have a custom in our country, where it's unthinkable to leave a young woman without protection. Would you be so kind as to give us your address, Mademoiselle?"

Seeing that the young woman was helpless, Löwenklau decided to come to her rescue. He stepped toward the aggressive Russian, twisting his wrist. With a slight cry, the officer let go of the woman's arm.

"Forgive me, my fellow comrades," Löwenklau interrupted, "but this young woman does not require your escort. You see, she is my betrothed, and I was catching up to her."

The young woman blushed as he uttered his white lie, but she didn't dare contradict him.

"You addressed me as a comrade," the Russian said forcefully. "Are you an officer?"

"Yes, I am."

"Your name, Monsieur?" There was a challenge in the Russian's tone.

"Hugo von Löwenklau, with the Zieten Hussars."

"Ah! A tough bunch. Congratulations on your betrothal, and I ask you to forgive my little indiscretion." The Russian's tone softened noticeably. He was almost friendly. "We saw you on the sidewalk earlier and didn't realize you were a couple."

He may well have had a previous encounter with a Hussar, Löwenklau thought, *recalling we are not to be trifled with.* The Cossacks bowed respectfully and continued on their way.

Löwenklau slipped the lady's arm into his, commencing their stroll down the street. She looked at him and her face was rich with speculation, yet he pretended not to notice. It wasn't until the officers had walked out of their sight that Löwenklau let go of her arm.

"Mademoiselle, I must take this moment to apologize for my daring manner," he said, halting. He waited expectantly for her to respond. When she remained silent, he continued. "You see, I am somewhat familiar with that Russian. Count Mertschakeff is well-known for his audacious and sometimes rude advances. I was certain you would not have been able to repel his overtures, so I took the liberty of calling you my betrothed. It was the only way to protect you from him. Please accept my apology."

The officer looked into her eyes for the first time. They were dark, a mysterious sea wherein he could lose himself for a lifetime. She looked at him with a grateful smile.

"An apology? Not at all," she said. "I owe you my heartfelt thanks, Monsieur."

"May I ask if you have far to go?"

"Only a few streets."

"My wish is not to be a nuisance, Mademoiselle, but when I think of you encountering a similar fate... I would consider it a matter of honor not to abandon you to the next opportunist. Please accept my offer to escort you."

The young woman glanced down the street. Seeing more soldiers ahead of them, she laid her gloved hand on his arm. "I do not wish to bother you, Monsieur, but I see more Russian soldiers ahead," she said. "May I entreat you to accompany me further?"

"With pleasure, Mademoiselle."

As Löwenklau spoke the words, she felt his innocent yet firm guiding hand take hers. She wondered if she had strayed from the rain only to get caught under the eaves.[18] She looked up at him hesitantly, then quickly relaxed. His voice sounded unpretentious and he had such a reassuring look about him.

The couple wandered side by side down several streets, not feeling the need to carry on a conversation. It was the stillness of the moment, with both hearts beating, that surpassed the most poetic prose. It was the natural movement of walking, particularly of turning onto a street, which brought them closer together. During such moments, he was able to feel the warmth of her arm. When they glanced at each other inadvertently, a slight redness spread over her face and she lowered her long lashes. It seemed to him as if he captured some sweet quality out of the depths of her eyes.

When they finally came to a stop at a gate, it dawned on him that the last few moments with her had seemed like hours.

"This is where I live, Monsieur," she said, breaking the silence.

"Then I will take my leave."

As he uttered those words, she detected a suppressed sigh. Her round, expressive eyes lingered on him, conveying gratitude.

"Just a while ago, you indicated that you serve in a Hussar regiment, Monsieur," she continued, feeling drawn to him. "Are you a Prussian?"

"Yes, I am."

"Did you know the Prussians are hated in Paris?"

He nodded. "That is understandable in these times, Mademoiselle, although one should not hate anyone unless one is convinced such hate is deserved."

"You mean to imply that you do not deserve the ill will of my people?"

"At the very least," he said, "I hope I don't merit yours. I am a soldier here because of my duty to my country. I don't hate any Frenchman merely because he is French."

"I believe you, Monsieur. You demonstrated it in the way you handled yourself, which is why I would like to make an exception, a departure from my formal upbringing. I would like to invite you for a visit to our house. If this is convenient for you, I would be happy to arrange it."

"Convenient?" His face shone with genuine delight. His excitement captured the heart of the beautiful girl. "I would be delighted to accept, and look forward to the time of your choosing."

"Please, Monsieur, come tomorrow afternoon at three o'clock. Unless, of course, you are otherwise engaged."

"No," he said. "I will be sure to keep the appointment."

The young woman produced a decorative card and handed it to him.

"Here is my card," she said.

Löwenklau took it, but didn't look at it for a moment. Instead, he looked at her and saw her cast a trustworthy glance in his direction. It was the glance two good friends might have given each other upon parting.

He nearly touched the card to his lips. As he stood in the busy street, he realized the gesture might be perceived as amusing to onlookers. After he had walked a short distance from the gate, he glanced down at her card. In small script, it read:

Margot RICHEMONTE, Rue D'Ange 10

"Richemonte?" he asked himself, slowing his pace until he was almost standing still. *Wasn't that the name of the captain I chastised at the inn? Is it possible they are related? Is this merely an unlikely coincidence?* Although many names appeared similar, he knew the two were not necessarily related.

When Löwenklau arrived at his home, he tried to relax on the divan with a good book. He had difficulty concentrating. The woman's voice kept drifting into his thoughts and, try as he might, he couldn't focus on reading. The letters on the page started to blur and take on a strange, welcoming appearance, as though they were forming themselves into a face both beautiful and charming, just like hers. He put the book away and stood up, pacing back and forth.

I believe this girl is affecting me, he mused to himself. *A French woman, no less! Are French women not depicted as transient, untrustworthy, even disloyal? How can I tell any of my friends about her? I would be laughed at. French women are like champagne, esprit, yes, even Mousseux. They're supposed to be here for our amusement. A Prussian officer seeks more honorable interests!*

Yet despite those things, he couldn't shake her voice.

In the morning, he ate his breakfast almost without knowing what he had eaten. He could hardly wait until three o'clock. He didn't want to admit it, but when he arrived at the prescribed address, he realized he was nearly a quarter of an hour early. He simply continued walking, allowing the time to pass.

CHAPTER TWO
A Parisian Family

Punctually at three o'clock, as witnessed by the chimes of the clock, Löwenklau presented himself at the entrance of *Rue d'Ange 10*. He discovered the first level was divided into two suites. On the right, he noticed the name plaque: Veuve Richemonte.

This must be Margot's mother. Perhaps she is a widow? he thought. The thought occurred to him that Margot no longer had a father. This would explain her more serious disposition. It seemed the aura which surrounded her beautiful countenance sparkled with an earnest approach to life.

The young officer rang the doorbell, and a maid promptly appeared. Upon offering his name, he was readily admitted. Once the maid opened the door to the drawing room, he noticed its stately appearance. Yet, it could not be considered regal. A lady rested on the ottoman, whom Löwenklau supposed to be Margot's mother, dressed in black and her hair already glistening with a touch of gray. The lines on her face were soft, yet carried with them the hint of personal tragedy, so often portrayed in a humorless demeanor. With an almost sorrowful expression, she glanced at the newcomer. As Löwenklau bowed politely, she in turn elevated herself slightly from her resting position.

"I bid you welcome, Monsieur," she said. "I must apologize for my daughter, who is late to arrive. I would, however, like to discuss something important with you first. Please, take a seat."

Löwenklau sat down, aware that her deep and searching glance was on him, as though seeking to penetrate his innermost being. *What an unusual reception. What could she possibly have in mind?*

"I am deeply grateful you took it upon yourself to protect my child," she began. "Margot's wish was that I should meet you personally. I am not sure, however, whether you will be disappointed or not with what I am about to say. No doubt your impression of Parisian society is that it is bright, lively, and easygoing. To a certain extent, you may be right in your assumption. You are a young officer, and share in the desire to be introduced to young ladies. It has become a sort of sport for many, carrying with it the need for young men to congregate and boast of their accomplishments in their clubs. Personally, I have never condoned this sport and have kept Margot far from these cliques. I have done so because I love my child. She has a fine quality about her and I do not want her to be unhappy. This is my heart's fervent desire." She paused momentarily, as though to reflect on whether she had said too much. Or worse, that she had offended the young officer with her straightforward remarks.

It seemed to him as if she had meant to say, *I love my child and do not want to see her unhappy, like her mother.*

"I have fulfilled Margot's wish," she continued. "She spoke with me of the invitation only last night. It might have been perceived as an insult if I had opposed it. Come to think of it, we were ignorant of your own address, Monsieur. Therefore, if you have come expecting to find some entertainment, I believe you will be forced to leave without finding it. This is the matter I wish to speak to you about, and I sincerely hope I have not offended you with my forthrightness."

"Offended?" he exclaimed. "Madame, your concern for your daughter is justified, even admirable, in order to keep her welfare in mind. Officers from all over Europe are the same in this respect. I despise this sport. Like you, I too see people for who they are. I do not assume they are here for my amusement. Since I view life from a more serious perspective, I am encouraged to learn that we share the same ideals. Certainly, this is a difficult time in which we live, and I do not intend to waste one minute of it on meaningless pursuits. I was able to be of service to Mademoiselle Margot, one I was prepared to offer to any lady in distress. Therefore, I do not see the necessity to be the recipient of some special gratitude. I was more interested in the opportunity to meet you. If my presence makes you uncomfortable in any way, then I will take my leave."

He stood up, preparing to leave.

Madame's eyes had a twinkle in them, suggesting his retort was amusing in some way. There wasn't a hint of disappointment in them. She motioned for him to remain seated.

"For the moment," she said, "I am going to assume Margot made the right decision. I find you exactly the way you were described to me. Please, stay a while, Monsieur, and see if you can rekindle the lost art of conversation with two lonely ladies. Is your mother still alive?"

"Unfortunately no longer, Madame. Both my parents are dead."

"That must have been a heavy loss for you. Do you have any siblings?"

"Sadly, no. I remain alone in this world. My best friends are my books, because of their companionship and appeal. Also, I am committed to my regiment."

Madame Richemonte and the lieutenant continued their discourse on the subject of family until Margot at last appeared. She wore a simple dress, but was so alive and alluring that his heart skipped a beat. She blushed as she offered him her hand in greeting. He felt welcome, even pleased that her mother had warmed up slightly. By the ease she seemed to feel toward him, he felt he had gained a measure of her trust.

As he rose to take his leave, she complimented him by permitting him to return the following day at the same time for a second visit. Löwenklau departed, encouraged with the impression the beautiful girl had left on him.

He would have been even happier if he had heard what was spoken about him after his departure.

"This young man is clearly different from many his age, excelling those in his class," Madame Richemonte commented. "Albin could learn something from this young officer. Speaking of Albin, where could he be? We haven't seen him in nearly two days."

In that instant, the doorbell rang.

"Maybe that's Albin now," Margot said. It was evident from her disposition that his visit was not particularly welcome.

"*Monsieur le Baron de Reillac*," the maid announced from the parlor door. The pronouncement made, the man himself appeared in the doorway, and both women realized it was not the man they expected.

He was a thin man, approaching his mid forties, yet he carried himself like a much younger and lighthearted individual. One couldn't call him unattractive, but there was something about his persona which was slightly repelling. He bowed awkwardly, first to the mother, and then to the daughter.

"I rang the bell next door, but received no response. I take it Monsieur Albin is not at his residence?"

"I have not seen him since yesterday," replied Madame Richemonte. She continued reproachfully. "I assumed he had accompanied you in your outings, Monsieur."

"Indeed, Madame," confirmed the baron. "We were away during the day and spent the evening at the club, where we had much to discuss. The overwhelming agreement by many is that the emperor's banishment will not last forever. Some are already inquiring about preparations for his imminent return, and the validity of his current support..."

"Oh, my God! What a careless attitude!" the widow cried. "The victors are still inside our walls and proponents of Bonaparte are already starting to stir things up."

"Don't worry," laughed Reillac. "We are not that stupid. We are cautious in this regard, although in some ways we obviously have not been so clever. Do you believe me, Madame?" There was an emphasis in his tone that made her take notice.

"I don't follow you," she admitted.

"Oh," he replied sweetly. "I only meant that as far as politics are concerned, I can debate with the best. In respect to business dealings, however, I have been far too lenient."

Madame Richemonte coughed into her handkerchief. "Are you here perhaps to discuss business, Baron?"

"Actually, I am not." He cleared his throat, reminiscent of a predator sharpening his claws. "I intended to visit Monsieur Albin. He gave me his word as a gentleman he would be at home at this time."

"His word of honor?" asked Madame. "That is quite impossible."

"Why impossible, Madame? Do you question my respect for the truth?"

"That is not what I meant. If Albin gave you his word, then he will keep it. He is an officer."

The baron shrugged his shoulders. "An officer, of course! Even a captain of the old guard! However, one can still break his word. Are there still officers of the old regime who permit themselves to be humiliated, failing to respond to a challenge?"

Madame Richemonte looked aghast. "What are you implying?" she asked. "Do you mean to suggest that my stepson..." She stopped herself in mid-sentence. It became impossible for her to utter the unthinkable.

"Precisely!" he confirmed, and nodded in a mocking gesture. "He was publicly humiliated."

The widow jumped to her feet. "That is a lie, Baron!"

"A lie?" he said. "How can you think that I would lie about such a matter? Monsieur Albin told me personally, even though it was widely talked about in our club. As the story goes, Albin was seated at a card table with three of his friends. He called all Germans a pack of dogs. He even insulted Field Marshal von Blücher by calling him a lout, unaware that the man himself was present. A Prussian officer took the captain's manner to task, demanding satisfaction by challenging Albin to a duel. Albin in turn spurned the officer and, with a mocking gesture, refused outright. He thereby received the brunt of his insolence in the form of several well-landed slaps to the face."

"My God! What a disgrace!" The widow moaned as she sunk back onto the sofa. One might have expected the anguish of a disappointed mother in her exclamation, but instead it came out as contempt.

"If such incidents occur, then you must accept the likelihood that he has indeed broken his word, Madame," continued the baron. "He promised to await my arrival."

"Then, it is a matter of honor!"

"Of course," the baron agreed. "The club had sponsored a card tournament, wherein Albin was one of the participants. He had his usual bad luck. Having advanced him five thousand francs, he promised to repay me personally no later than three o'clock this date at his residence. It is now five o'clock, yet he is still not present!"

"My God! A gambling debt no less," lamented the mother. "His debts continue to grow, along with his thirst for pleasure."

Reillac laughed ruefully. "You are, of course, correct, my dear Madame. Do you have any idea how much he owes me? I have it all in promissory notes!"

"How could I possibly know the amount?"

He grinned. "Over two hundred thousand francs."

"Two hundred..." The words stuck in her throat like molasses.

Margot, who had been listening, turned pale as a ghost. The baron observed both ladies with a distant, triumphant look.

"That is unbelievable! Incredulous! It simply cannot be!" Madame Richemonte exclaimed.

On hearing these words, the baron simply shrugged his shoulders. His mouth converted to a spiteful grimace. "Unbelievable, you say? Incredulous? Well, let me assure you that Monsieur Albin has expensive tastes. He plays for high stakes and is inclined to shower dance girls with presents, some exceeding ten thousand francs. Having squandered his fortune, he now has no income since the emperor has gone into exile. How his debts could grow to such proportions is no mystery, if you examine his lavish lifestyle."

"I have no idea how he plans to reduce his debt," Madame Richemonte said decidedly. "He is my stepson, though I have already done far too much on his behalf. I have suffered and no longer have the income I once had. Perhaps he can turn to one of his many friends for help. I can do no more! As for you, Baron, I want to remind you that it was you who encouraged and supported him in this madness. If you had not advanced him funds, he would have been forced to live within his means."

The baron's eyes held a peculiar glow. His penetrating glance revealed a mixture of greed, the certainty of victory, and the enjoyment of another's misfortune. "You are mistaken, Madame. Another eager lender would have gladly loaned him funds. By the way, he is the son of your deceased husband, who was my friend. Should I not help, since I am also compassionate toward you, the widow of my old friend?"

"Compassionate with me? When have you ever showed me kindness?" she cried out bitterly. "Just before my husband's death, I mistakenly allowed myself to co-sign his outstanding notes. What did I understand about his financial affairs? I was duped into signing partially completed documents, which were later filled in. When my husband died, you brought all these papers to my attention, stating they were due. I was forced to sell everything of value so I could redeem those notes and evade the debtor's court. You call that compassion?"

"I am not here to address the past, Madame. I am speaking about three notes, which were signed by you, and are now due."

She stared at him, with incredulous eyes. "Three more notes?" she asked. "Which I signed? You must be mistaken. Or perhaps this is another one of your distasteful jokes?"

"This is far from a joke," he replied. "You spoke of papers which had been incomplete, but were signed by you. Let me remind you that there were three such documents when your husband died. Monsieur Albin, having appropriated these, filled them in as required. In exchange, I paid him sums of money, which he collected and presumably spent. These promissory notes were signed in your handwriting, although I have not yet demanded re-payment. Is this not compassionate of me?"

Madame Richemonte managed to stand up. "Do you speak the truth?" she asked.

"The whole truth."

"Has Albin already received the funds?"

"He has indeed. All told, it was one hundred and fifty thousand francs."

"One hundred and fifty thousand francs! Oh my God!" She moaned, clasping her hands together. "I only have an income of two thousand francs a year."

"I will claim this toward the debt, Madame."

Madame Richemonte clearly hadn't expected this response. She looked at him with large, unbelieving eyes. "Then I will go for want, and starve."

"Not at all," he replied even-tempered, shrugging his shoulders. "You will not starve. You will just have to work off the debt."

"Work? But we are already working. Do you think we can survive on two thousand francs a year? We are knitting goods for a local garment shop. Margot delivered the finished work yesterday, only to be accosted by strangers on her way back."

"That is no concern of mine, Madame. Your son, who owes me a considerable sum in notes, swore an oath in regards to his gambling debt of five thousand francs. He has no money. You owe me the sum of one hundred and fifty thousand francs, Madame. I am now asking for payment, intending to redeem the three outstanding notes."

The poor widow clasped her hands together in exasperation. "It is quite impossible! Who gave you permission to pay out such large sums to my step-son?"

"It was your signature, Madame, which allowed me to do so," he grinned. "You are actually mistaken in your belief that you are unable to cover the debt."

"My God, how could I possibly...?"

"With one single word," he finished for her. "With the little word *yes*."

The meaning escaped Madame Richemonte, and she looked inquiringly at him. He took on an air of importance and allowed his leering eyes to wander over Margot's shapely form.

"Let me explain," Reillac continued. "So you can understand me and my arrangements, Madame, allow me to remind you of my former position of head administrator for the emperor's war repository. Those storehouses made me millions. I can offer a young lady a wonderful life, one in which her every whim is looked after. May I remind you also that I had expressed my feelings for Margot while your husband was still alive. At that time, I was rebuffed, with the message that Mademoiselle Margot did not desire my affection. You found yourself in much better circumstances then, but surely you must realize now what a foolish idea it is to marry strictly for love.

"I am now willing to offer a similar proposal. As soon as we are married, and exit the church as husband and wife, I will not only rip up the notes against you, but also those against your stepson. If you decline my offer, then you will be forced to endure the debtor's prison."

He stood up as he spoke his last few words and reached for his hat. "You see that I am being sincere. You may call me hardhearted, or even cruel, but it is of no consequence. Let me speak plainly. I am in love with Margot. She will become my wife, or you will perish in debt. I am giving you a week to consider my offer. On the eighth day, I will return for your decision, trusting you will weigh your options carefully.

"Good day, Madame." He departed, leaving the ladies in no small state of consternation.

Madame Richemonte lay on her sofa and sobbed. Margot sat down beside her and, without uttering a word, pulled her mother's head toward her. Her mother was too preoccupied with her own thoughts to notice the calm on Margot's face. She seemed devoid of any fear. Her mother missed the determination that permeated Margot's whole being, revolting itself against everything Reillac stood for.

"One hundred and fifty thousand francs!" lamented the old woman. "Did you hear that, Margot?"

Margot nodded.

"I don't owe him anything. He swindled me."

"Reillac is a devil, Mama. He has carefully planned the whole thing from the beginning.

"What do you mean?"

"His plan has always been centered on coercing me into marrying him."

"Dear God! Really?"

"Yes!" Margot said. "He found a way to ensnare Papa in his debts, and later seduced Albin into gambling. Look how he made an exhibition out of the promissory notes. Our lives will suffer greatly unless I concede to his proposal."

"You mustn't give in. Never!"

"Oh, but I might," she replied calmly. "I could give him the answer he seeks."

"You're talking nonsense," her mother said, frightened of the implication. "You would be very unhappy."

"No! No, I wouldn't!" replied Margot with such determination that her mother looked at her in surprise.

"No? I don't understand you, child. I know you don't love that schemer!"

Margot shook her head. "Of course, I don't. I despise him. And yet, that's the reason why I'll marry him, Mama."

"You want to marry him because you hate him? You're speaking in riddles."

"Oh Mama, don't you see how sweet my revenge could be?" replied Margot, revealing her thoughts.

"Ah!" said her mother, finally realizing just how desperate her daughter was feeling.

Margot lifted her head and looked at her mother with blazing, almost defiant eyes. Her very being seemed to shake. It was a sign of the pent-up anger directed at Reillac, who had stretched his grubby hands toward her one time too many, thinking he could buy her love with the promise of money. His malice was repulsive.

"He's the devil we have to contend with," she explained. "He's responsible for our poor situation and my father's death. I'm prepared to become his wife just to seek our revenge. He loves me to the point of madness. I have observed his glowering and covetous looks for months now, without giving myself away. I'll become his wife and he'll have to rip up the notes—but he'll never touch me. I want him to succumb because of his desire for me. I'm going to make myself very attractive for him, but only for him, so it will drive him crazy. I want him to cower like a worm in front of me. I want him to plead for every solitary word, an approving look or some act of kindness that he'll never receive. He'll wallow in his torment, and I'll rejoice in his unhappiness."

She spoke in the emotion of the moment, not understanding that the rejoicing she spoke of would be twisted and horrible. She wanted to sacrifice herself for her mother and the debt. Margot mistakenly believed she could remain the master of her own emotions, never realizing the consequences of keeping one man chained to her while another man's love was in her heart.

CHAPTER THREE
An Unexpected Uprising

Lieutenant Löwenklau meandered down the street after leaving the Richemonte home. His thoughts kept returning to Margot. His walk took him past one of the city's many coffeehouses, one that provided an area open to pedestrian traffic. Patrons relaxed here with their coffee or schnapps, observing the hustle and bustle of the passersby. Seeking some refuge, he walked in and chose a quiet seat by the window.

The officer barely sat down when he spotted a familiar face approaching the door. He immediately pulled his seat back from the window to escape the eyes of Captain Richemonte, his new nemesis. Löwenklau noticed that Richemonte appeared to be waiting for someone. He remained outside on one of the seats, close to the open window where Löwenklau sat. Shortly thereafter, another man, whom Löwenklau didn't know, joined him. It was Baron de Reillac, who had just come from the residence of Madame Richemonte.

Although Löwenklau had chosen this coffeehouse for no particular reason, fate seemed to have played a part. The two Frenchmen quickly began a lively conversation, unaware that someone nearby was catching every relevant word. The information Löwenklau gleaned would later dictate his actions profoundly.

"Here at last!" Reillac said angrily.

"I've been waiting for a while," Richemonte replied. "What success did your little visit produce, my dear baron?"

"Up until now? Nothing! I gave your two ladies a week to think things over."

"A whole week? Damn. I was hoping to get some money to tide me over."

"Well, I can still oblige you."

"That's reassuring," the captain said. "How did my good stepmother receive your disclosure about the promissory notes?"

"In the manner most women respond to bad news. At first she refused to believe it, then whined, and finally started to cry. I couldn't stand the damned crying, so I stated my business and left."

"How did my dear sister Margot take it?"

"Her?" the baron mused. "I'm trying to recall what she said. Actually, I believe she failed to utter a single word."

"Do you think our plan will work?"

"Absolutely!" the baron replied with conviction.

"And if they refuse?"

"They'll both take a walk to debtor's prison."

Richemonte smiled. "The devil you say! You're joking of course, Baron. One should not jest about such things, even among friends."

"Friends? *Pah!*" Reillac said, shrugging his shoulders. "You're nothing but a bloodsucker. Your only interest is in yourself, Captain, and certainly not in our friendship. Let me be perfectly honest with you and explain. The only reason I help you out is because of my interest in your sister. When she becomes my wife, I'll cancel your debt, adding fifty thousand francs to your coffers. The promissory notes against your mother will also be torn up. All told, I'll be canceling a debt of over four hundred thousand francs! That's no small amount, regardless of how you see it. Now, tell me, who is the real friend here?"

Hearing this, Richemonte became subdued. "I trust you'll reach your goal, Baron."

"Well, if I don't, you alone are to blame!"

"I? How come?"

"Go and pay your dear mother and sister a cordial visit, one which will really get them worked up! I'm giving you a warning, Captain: should our efforts fail, I will not be so lenient."

"I'm inclined to believe you."

"As you should. You've made my mouth water for a taste of Margot, and I have lived with the consequences. Why should I be concerned about a few thousand francs when you are on the verge of finding out how a poor devil survives in debtor's prison? I advise you to prepare yourself and be firm. By the way, you might exercise more control over your temper."

"What does my temper have to do with it?"

"Well," Reillac said, "they know all about your gambling losses."

"The devil! Who told them about...?"

"I did, Captain."

"You!" Richemonte fumed. "Have you lost your senses? Why should my mother or sister be concerned about my gambling, or for that matter how much I win or lose?"

"Because now they will be much more inclined to cooperate. By the way, they also know about your entanglement with the German officer."

"That, too? Who told them about that?"

"I did, Captain."

"What!?" Richemonte erupted. "Yet you have the nerve to tell me so calmly."

"Exactly. As calmly as when I handed my money over to you," the baron said. "You've created this mess, and apparently have no problem taking my money to bail yourself out. I want to have the satisfaction of openly discussing your affairs. Margot should realize that by marrying me, her offering is cheapened on account of her being the sister of an officer on the brink of financial ruin."

Silence suddenly settled in between the two men. Still listening, Löwenklau expected the captain to explode over this latest insult. That, however, was not the case. Richemonte found himself backed into a financial corner. Although he didn't like the news, he depended on Reillac's money. Therefore, he needed to control his temper. He had to remind himself that Reillac was a means to an end, a solution to his financial woes.

The captain sought for a way to suppress his anger. "Do you think I'm afraid of that German because I refused his challenge?"

"Yes," the baron replied. "That is what I believe."

"Why?"

"Because you dismissed his challenge."

"*Pah!* I'm still going to fight him."

"I don't believe you will get the opportunity."

"Why not?"

"I've heard these Germans are particularly sensitive when it comes to matters of honor," he said. "This lieutenant of the Hussars, what was his name...?"

"Von Löwenklau."

"Right. I don't believe he will enter into another entanglement, Captain, especially since he concluded the first one with your embarrassment. You committed a grave error by refusing his challenge!"

"How can I find another opportunity to redeem myself?"

Reillac shrugged his shoulders. "It would be difficult to predict. In any event, do you require another advance?"

"Yes. A few thousand francs."

"Are three thousand sufficient?"

Richemonte nodded.

"All right then. Let's look after the details, shall we? Tonight you can sign the note, but don't worry, because this time next week I will be your brother-in-law!"

Reillac paid the bill as they both left the coffeehouse.

Löwenklau had listened with great interest, not wanting to miss a single word. It was all becoming clear to him; the baron had laid plans to win Margot's hand by ensnaring her brother, the chastised captain, and driving him to financial ruin. Madame Richemonte, who had been tricked into signing financial papers, was left owing a hundred and fifty thousand francs. Reillac had two well-considered means of obtaining what he wanted, which meant he could *buy* Margot, one way or the other.

What could Löwenklau do? He leaned back in his chair in deep contemplation. In terms of finances, he had only a small sum at his disposal. His estate amounted to roughly the same sum required by the baron, though it would necessitate him selling everything. *If only I were rich*, he mused, *I could pay off their debt, freeing Margot and her mother from this oppression.* Löwenklau walked home, his heavy thoughts constantly returning to Margot and her debt.

When sleep finally came, it was short-lived, interrupted by a vivid dream. In the dream, he saw a massive tower and, in its dungeon, Margot wasted away because of her predicament. It was remarkable how much interest he took from just dreaming about her. If she had been indifferent to him before, she was suddenly considerably more important. Though she had initially occupied his thoughts, the relevance of her wellbeing now doubled or tripled in such a way he knew could easily progress into love. These unlikely and unexpected feelings tugged at Löwenklau's heart.

The young officer awoke at last, happy to be free of the recurring anguish. As he contemplated its meaning, the vision of Margot became ever more magical and alluring. Left with insatiable longing, he impatiently awaited the coming of afternoon. Although the minutes crept along at a snail's pace, three o'clock finally approached, signaling his appointment on *Rue d'Ange*.

When Löwenklau entered the drawing room this time, Margot came up to him with news that her mother was not up for a visit. She had asked to be excused. He gathered her sudden malady was attributable to the baron's recent visit, but he kept the thought to himself.

Though looking pale, he found decisiveness in Margot's face, giving him cause for concern. Her eyes rested on him in friendly contemplation and her speech seemed to be without emotion. He supposed this was more than just her concern for her mother. He looked for a hint of anxiety, which evaded him completely until they discussed matters of the heart. Her face finally showed a trace of warmth.

"Monsieur, I envy you," she said, "for it must be a wonderful feeling to return to one's homeland, knowing you have escaped death on the battlefield, and be welcomed back by a loving wife."

"Don't envy me, Mademoiselle. I'm not that fortunate."

"Really? Don't you have a betrothed?"

"Unfortunately, my heart is my own, not yet committed."

Feeling a little embarrassed, she glanced down. "Does the heart always have to be involved?" she asked him.

"Can you imagine a particularly happy moment that doesn't involve it?"

"I suppose not, though matters of the heart can come in a variety of ways."

He looked at her inquiringly. Her lips quivered and heaviness seemed to weigh on her forehead. "I don't understand you, Mademoiselle," he continued.

"I'm certain of just one thing. One can only be happy in love. Without it, happiness is fleeting and temporary."

"You are mistaken," she replied. "Think of a fierce rage, a burning revenge. To see such enmity satiated must also be fulfilling."

"Absolutely," he replied concernedly. "But it would only be satisfying a devil's happiness."

Margot lifted her eyes, searching his face. "Would you agree with me that even a devil can be happy?"

"Yes, a corrupted or tainted soul could find happiness for a fleeting moment. Perhaps you could give me an example, so I might understand this fierce rage you speak of." Löwenklau really wasn't a bad diplomat. He voiced his concern in the hope she would allow him a glimpse into her oppressive secret. Fortunately, she didn't catch his full meaning.

"Monsieur, I'll try to give you a fitting example," she replied. "Think of a young girl, beautiful, passionate, and full of hope for her future. She possesses all the qualities to be a noble and loving wife. Along comes a conniver who, being captivated by her beauty, is prepared to offer all he has to win her hand. Despite all his efforts, he is spurned. He decides to resort to unconventional means, plotting to win her by trickery. This man works his way into her family, leads them astray, and plunges them one by one into sin and disgrace. He swears he will bring them to utter ruin and humiliation unless they are prepared to meet his demands. The cost is the betrothal of the girl."

"And the girl? What does she do?"

"She agrees to the contract," she said, "to free her loved ones from oppression."

"Undoubtedly she has never loved. Perhaps she possesses such a large heart that she sacrifices herself, determined that she can change the oppressive man for the better."

Her eyes widened. "No! Just the opposite. She wants to punish him."

"Ah! You contradict yourself, Mademoiselle. Initially you said the girl offered him her hand to save her loved ones, but now you claim her motivation was punishment."

"Absolutely!" she insisted. "She wants to punish him, punish him severely. He will catch a glimpse of a heaven he can't ever attain. He will long for drops of refreshment that are pearled upon his lips. Yet, he'll still die of thirst."

"Mademoiselle, this girl is influenced by a devil," Löwenklau said. "You called her good, though in reality the opposite is true. Such a plan can only be concocted in the moment of extreme anger, bordering on hopelessness. No reasonable woman would dare to carry it out. A noble girl would turn her back on such an ill-conceived and doomed plan, the ultimate end being despair and misery. Think of this woman living in misery through the years, all the while exposed to the happiness of those around her. Perhaps she meets an honorable man, whom she could love, but is instead hopelessly bound to her oppressor. She has become judgmental, dishing out her doses of retribution. Is it necessary for her to punish him? Is there not a higher court? Is there not a God who can rescue his precious flock without producing such senseless victims?"

The lieutenant was right, of course. She had come up with her plan in the spur of the moment, filled with disgust for Reillac and faced with her mother's anguish. All he had done was expose the plan that had surfaced from the sea of her despair. He hoped she would be repulsed by it. Amazed at his insight, she realized he understood her, and knew she was speaking of her own situation. Löwenklau, feeling a deep compassion for her, took her hand into his.

"Mademoiselle," he continued, "you paint a terrible picture, one which I laid bare before you. Have you perhaps heard of Dante's hell?[3.1] The woman you speak of not only dispenses her hate, but is also subjected to the same agony herself. There's no such thing as a completely hopeless situation. Destroy this picture, and cast the pieces far from you. It only serves to conjure up revulsion and nightmares."

Margot listened attentively. Her pale complexion slowly waned, only to be replaced by a blush of shame. Still, she made one last attempt to defend herself. "What if there is no other way?"

"How can you say this with certainty, Mademoiselle? People are often shortsighted, many times blind to their circumstances. The small things we grapple with can be next to impossible to accomplish. Those things which seem impossible and exasperating can easily end up solving themselves. How can you dismiss the possibility that wherever there is desperation, aid may be just around the corner? Help can be there disguised, waiting, and often unrecognizable."

"What if people cannot or will not come to your aid?"

"God always provides a way," he said, "one we might not even attribute to Him. He knows the way which leads to deliverance. We only need to trust in Him, and not strive against Him." He saw the change in her face. He had won her over.

"I am grateful, Monsieur," she said, reaching her hand toward him. "Yes, you are a German. A true, genuine German."

"What do you know about Germans, Mademoiselle?"

"They are like children, full of faith and trust," she explained, smiling. "They can also be genuine men, who pray to God and at the same time endeavor to support His plans. One can see the results by the battles you have fought."

The revelation stood well with him, elevating her in his sight. Holding her hand in his, he dared to inquire further. "Was it just an arbitrary example you related, Mademoiselle? Or is it something more personal you struggle with?"

Margot lowered her eyes. She didn't want to lie, especially since he had taken on her 'fictitious' account with such interest and dignity. Should she really burden him with the truth?

She composed herself, replying truthfully, "If it were a true account, could I really come to you in confidence, Monsieur? Would I be ridiculed for my thoughts?"

"I can guess what is on your mind."

Shame crept over her beautiful face. Had he guessed her plight? Her thoughts, although confused, contained words he qualified as devilish. She was ashamed to ask for his opinion because of what he might think of her. Instead, she looked at him inquiringly.

"You spoke of yourself, Mademoiselle. Am I right?"

"Yes, I did," she said, timidly lowering her head. "Will you now pass judgment on me?" She had spoken from the depth of her soul, thinking her contemplation would be repugnant. *What awful things he must think of me!*

"No, rest assured I don't condemn you because of your thoughts. You devised this plan in haste, not taking the time to consider its implications. My first response is to make myself available to you, if only in terms of the advice I can offer. May I inquire further, Mademoiselle?"

"With whom?"

"Only with you," he reassured her.

"Please, feel free to ask me."

"Do you despise the baron?"

Margot was surprised at his insight. "You know of him?"

"Yes, I know of the circumstances, though his name is unfamiliar to me. I must confess two things to you. First, by sheer providence I was able to overhear a conversation conducted in private between two men. One, who is known to me, is an officer in the emperor's guard. The officer called the second man, who I didn't know, a baron. It became clear to me that they spoke of a young lady, whom they were trying to coerce into a forced marriage. Only her first name was mentioned, which coincided with yours, Mademoiselle. So when you related your account, I immediately made the connection. Unwittingly, I became a part of your story. If you place your trust in me, I may be able to help you. By chance, are you related to the officer, a captain of the old guard?"

"What is his name?"

"Albin Richemonte."

"He is my brother," she said, then corrected herself. "My stepbrother actually. But I have lost..." She halted in embarrassment.

"Go on, Mademoiselle," he encouraged. "I'm quite interested in how all this affects you."

"You will think less of me. It was a devilish scheme and I am ashamed to continue."

Smiling he said, "Do not be afraid to continue. I must admit, you come across as anything but devilish."

"I have lost all my respect for him. He brought upon us an endless misery, and is more a stranger than a brother. Albin is the son of my father, and shares in the blame of his death. Be honest with me, Monsieur. You must have your reservations about me now! A sister who cannot stand the sight of her own brother?"

"Not in the least. I am grateful he is only your stepbrother, since I despise him, too."

"Really? You know him as well?"

"Unfortunately, and this is the second item I must admit to you," he said. "Have you heard that your brother had an altercation with a Prussian officer?"

"Yes, just recently."

"Well, the officer and I are one and the same. Had I known you were related, I would have been more lenient."

"You have nothing to apologize for," she said. "You handled the affair as a matter of honor. First on a personal level, and second on behalf of your commanding general. It was your duty. Now, let's part as friends, since there are things I must attend to."

"Pardon me. Are you asking me to leave?"

"I must. My mother is still unwell. Perhaps I can see you tomorrow?"

Although Löwenklau would have gladly continued the conversation and learned more details about the baron and his treachery, he realized she was holding back out of concern for him. He took his leave reluctantly, promising to return the next day.

⚜

Löwenklau took a lengthy walk, still mindful that it wasn't safe for him or his comrades to wander around the city alone at night. There were still those loyal to the emperor's cause who had a deep-rooted hatred for the *newcomers*. It was common at night to hear cries of *"Vive l'Empereur."* It was sometimes necessary to quell the uprisings by forceful means. He returned home just as darkness fell. He spent the evening occupied with his books, though he couldn't keep his mind off Margot's predicament.

It was around eleven o'clock when the noise of a loud racket interrupted his thoughts. Löwenklau opened his window to the sound of angry voices. As he listened, the noise and accompanying confusion escalated to the point that small arms fire could be heard in the night. Although he had witnessed similar uprisings, it disturbed him most when he realized Margot's neighborhood seemed to be the focal point. This reality only compounded his concern. Her mother was sick! He quickly donned his military coat, affixed his saber, and rushed out the door, taking up his pistol.

As he made his way for the Richemonte home, he heard that the French loyalists were trying to stir up the local populace against the occupying force. The situation worsened as he progressed nearer. Members of the French National Guard were scrambling for their posts to head off a possible riot.

When Löwenklau reached *Rue d'Ange*, he found it occupied by rioters. Cries for help were coming from everywhere. He noticed followers of the king were trying to gain entry into the homes of the emperor's supporters. Since no one was willing to intervene, looting seemed imminent.

Shouts and threats of "Long live the emperor!' or 'Long live the Republic!' were bantered back and forth. The likelihood both sides would get into a serious fight was becoming more of a reality with every passing minute. As Löwenklau broke a path through the crowd, he noticed lights on at number ten. Taking this as a good sign, he ran up the steps and rang the bell. The maid, apprehensive at first, recognized his voice and bid him to enter.

"My God!" she said. "We're saved. Come in, quickly. It's good to see you."

She led him through the unlit drawing room, into an adjoining chamber. It contained a lantern, but was otherwise unoccupied. It appeared to be the same room he had seen from the street.

He had barely entered when an adjacent door opened and Margot appeared. Löwenklau was overcome by her beauty. She wore a negligee, over which a housecoat was draped. She must have been asleep when the noises of the tumult had woken her up. She had probably thrown her housecoat over her shoulders to check on the commotion outside without giving any thought to her appearance.

Having only seen him in civilian clothes, she didn't recognize him in his Hussar uniform. Entering the dimly lit room, Margot was startled by the young officer. In the resulting shock, she let her housecoat slip to the floor.

She stood before him like an Olympian goddess. The white negligee hung down to her fine-boned, porcelain-like ankles, displaying delicate feet clad in satin slippers. The negligee had short sleeves, revealing a pair of elegant arms which would have rivaled those of Cleopatra herself. The folds of her garment hugged her body alluringly, the outline of which was clearly visible. Her magnificent breasts, not supported by any brazier, showed a round firmness, such as was common with Egyptian women who proudly wore no corset at all. A strong and fine neck rose above her exquisite shoulders, worthy of supporting such a splendid head. The once plaited tresses were loosened, freeing her magnificent black hair to flow magically down to her hips.

Standing there, Margot resembled a Brunhilde[3.2] as imagined by the eye of a painter who was unable to transfer her beauty and splendor onto his canvas. It seemed so surreal, as though he were in a dream.

Löwenklau wanted to greet her, but was unable to enunciate a single word. He knew she was beautiful, yet to see her loveliness displayed so openly and completely was mesmerizing to him. He recalled her referring to herself as beautiful. She had spoken of her charm, using the expression, 'That which can make a man happy.' Was Margot aware of the vastness and the splendor of her allure? Perhaps not in this very moment! She moved toward Löwenklau with an expression of great relief, oblivious to her scant dress.

"Oh, thank God, Monsieur," she said, approaching him joyfully. "I was so frightened. I'm indebted to you for leaving your post and coming here for our sake, even if only for a minute."

Löwenklau had to compose himself in order to formulate a reply. As he pressed her hand to his lips, he became nearly intoxicated by her beauty. He allowed his eyes to linger on her forearm, then progress to her shapely breasts, barely concealed by the thin garment.

"Only for a minute? I'm here as long as you want me to stay. I heard the commotion from my window, and I came at once. Perhaps the presence of one soldier may aid your cause."

"How wonderful of you to come. We're all alone and I'm afraid the crowd will become more reckless. I won't forget your attentiveness, Monsieur. Let me go tell Mama. It will calm her fears."

"Please, go ahead."

Margot turned to leave, when she noticed her housecoat on the floor. Only then did she realize in what manner she welcomed him. The embarrassment caused her face to turn red. She wanted to pick up her covering, to wrap it around herself, but she realized in doing so she would have exposed herself further.

Seeing her plight, Löwenklau bent down and picked up the housecoat and wrapped it around her shoulders. His hand brushed her warm shoulder as he collected her long hair, allowing it to settle over the coat. It seemed so unreal, as though he was reading it in a fairy tale. He couldn't contain himself. Unable to wait, he took her hands and placed them on his chest, close to his heart. With a longing in his eyes, his words came out in a heavy breath.

"Margot, you are beautiful, beautiful to the point of sin. All this splendor and magnificence is supposed to go to the baron? By God! I would rather run him through with my saber."

She didn't pull her hands back. "Am I really that beautiful?" she replied. "This beauty has cost us everything we owned, our happiness and nearly our future. I wish I was rid of it."

"For heaven's sake, no, Margot!" he said. "You have no idea what you could mean to the right man. I have to turn aside and fight the desire to pull you into my arms and hold you close for the rest of my life. For wherever you are, there's a heavenly bliss." He forced himself to actually turn away from her.

Margot pulled her housecoat tighter and went to her mother's room. She returned a few minutes later, having replaced her housecoat with a more appropriate morning dress. She still felt a little embarrassed.

"Well, Monsieur," she said, smiling, "now I won't be a threat to anyone. My mother sends her thanks. She's still not up for a visit, but... what is all that shouting and noise?" She was about to open the window when he stopped her.

"Please, Mademoiselle" he said, "not here. The light in this room will expose you to outsiders. Let's go back to the drawing room, where it's dark. We can observe from there." Margot followed him deeper into the house.

The tumult on the street seemed to grow more intense. The many voices overlapped one another and the crowd swayed back and forth like a tempestuous sea. As he quietly opened the window, his presence gave her courage to look outside. The window was not very wide, leaving the couple little room side by side. The essence of her soft tender body flowed from her dress and enveloped him. He didn't want to put both hands on the window-sill, an uncomfortable posture in the confines of the small opening, and yet where could he put them? Daring himself to place his one hand around her waist, he felt her wince ever so slightly. But she didn't pull back. He felt the warmth of her body through her dress, as it effortlessly worked its way through his arm. Löwenklau could have traded his whole life for that one wonderful moment without feeling cheated.

The couple watched the commotion below for some time. Suddenly, a nearby gunshot interrupted their solitude. Had it been intentionally fired at the house? Löwenklau bent forward to get a better look. His arm, still clasped around Margot's waist, followed its natural movement. It moved up her slim body, unintentionally touching her breast. He felt her warm breast and gasped, naturally assuming she would instantly remove his hand in anger. To his surprise, she didn't, realizing the accident.

He returned his arm to its previous position, yet placed it more firmly around her waist. She turned her head and whispered to him, "Please, Monsieur, not like that."

Hugo felt the tender breath from her mouth brush his cheek. "Not like what? More like this, Margot?" as he held her even tighter.

"Oh no!" she pleaded. "Shouldn't I allow myself to trust you?"

"Trust me in this moment?" he replied as desire welled up within him. "How wonderful and yet finite this moment is. Are you able to place your trust in me for these few minutes, Margot?"

"For always," she whispered.

He wanted to pull her closer, but she resisted.

"Don't be angry with me, Monsieur. Even though I want to trust you, I can not allow myself."

"Why not?"

"I can not allow it," she repeated. "Not ever."

"Do you hate me?"

In a whisper, she replied, "How can I hate you?"

"Can you love me, Margot?" he whispered into her ear as he pulled her closer.

"No."

He nearly jumped in surprise at her response. "No? Not ever?"

"Never," she said again.

Hugo's arm slid from her waist and he slowly stepped back from the window. He placed his hands on his forehead, taking a deep breath. She heard the disappointment in his breath even as her own heart trembled. Had there been more light, he would have seen her whole being quiver. She waited to see if he would join her again at the window—but he didn't return.

Margot heard shouts from below. "Long live the Republic. Down with the emperor!" Swarms of people were milling about, shouting and fighting. Others taunted them. "Long live King Louis XVIII. Down with the upstarts!" As the three factions continued to clash, shouts and crying were intermingled with gunfire. Though cries of the wounded could be heard everywhere, the clamor continued unabated. The supporters of King Louis gained the upper hand. The unmistakable sound of doors being forced and smashing glass echoed in the street below.

"Hurrah!" they yelled. "Victory to Louis XVIII! Plunder those who support the emperor and kill the Orleanists!"[3.3]

Margot pulled back from the window opening. Löwenklau, resolute and calm, saw Margot shaking with fear.

"Mademoiselle, quickly now, go to your mother and prepare yourself for the worst."

"Oh my God!" she said. "My brother is well known as a follower of Bonaparte."

"Where does he live?"

"Over there, on the other side of this level."

"Is he at home now?"

"Not likely. With all this commotion, he probably stayed away."

They heard voices directly below. "Over here. That's where he lives—the Captain, he lives at number ten..." Angry men were shouting, trying to gain entry below.

"If they would only stay over there!" Margot said. "I'm afraid for Mama."

"If they start over there, surely they will come here as well. Since you have the same surname as your stepbrother, you are tainted with the same brush. We must stop this senseless destruction. Hurry, go to your mother. I will do whatever I can."

As Margot hastened to comfort her mother, Löwenklau heard weak words coming from her mother's room. At that very moment, insistent pounding was leveled against the front door. The maid had fled, leaving Löwenklau alone to deal with what was to come. He took a light, unsheathed his saber, and loosened his pistol. Prepared for the worst, he opened the door. He saw a small group on the steps bolstered with reckless energy.

"What do you want, Messieurs?" said Löwenklau in a firm, commanding voice. Those close enough were surprised to see a Prussian officer. Some drew back a little, but one persistent demonstrator yelled above the tumult.

"We are looking for Captain Richemonte, long known to be a follower of Bonaparte!" one of the men shouted.

"He is not at home," replied Löwenklau calmly.

"It doesn't matter. We've come to pay him a little visit!"

"You've come at a most inconvenient time," smiled Löwenklau. "Really, what sort of valuables can a Bonapartist possess? You will be disappointed, Messieurs. Furthermore, there is a sick woman upstairs, and I appeal to your humanity to consider her well-being."

"Should we go?" one of the men asked.

"Yes," yelled some, but they were drowned out by a resounding "No!" from the rest. The mob hesitated for a moment.

Margot, having left her mother, was now standing in the recess of the foyer. She saw Löwenklau, the light in his left hand casting a long shadow of his tall, commanding form.

"Although I heard some of you utter the words 'plunder' and 'loot,' I'm convinced no follower of King Louis would stoop to this," Löwenklau continued. "We've fought and conquered Napoleon, shedding our blood on the battlefield on your behalf, not to bring you loot and robbery, but peace... Long live King Louis, and long live law and order! Down with cutthroats and murderers! The people of France are not comprised of looters, but of hardworking and law-abiding citizens."

Shouts of agreement drowned out the dissenters. "Long live King Louis. Let's move on. The officer is right." The crowd slowly filed down the steps, eventually leaving the landing.

When Löwenklau returned to the foyer, he found Margot standing there by herself. Her eyes beheld him with pride and admiration. He alone had found the courage to confront the mob. He, the hated Prussian, had taken it upon himself to disperse them from a dwelling which until yesterday had been of no consequence to him. She reached her hands out to him in gratitude.

29

"Monsieur, I give you our thanks. You alone have saved us from a terrible fate. I'll inform my mother the danger has passed."

Löwenklau replaced the light in the foyer after she left. He returned to the drawing room to observe activities in the street below from the window. He heard a slight rustling, sensing Margot's presence behind him. He turned to face her, intending to step aside, but she motioned to him to stay with her.

"Please stay, Monsieur," she pleaded. "There is room for both."

"It is too narrow for two people who cannot love each other," he retorted.

"Please, stay nevertheless," she replied. "The little liberty which you allowed yourself earlier, I can also allow myself."

Margot placed one arm on the windowsill and placed her other arm around his waist, just like he had done earlier with her. A heavenly feeling went through him. Did she guess how much she had hurt him earlier? Was she now trying to make amends? Hugo took her arm and pulled it tighter around his waist. She didn't object.

"Weren't you afraid of those looters, Monsieur?" she asked.

"Afraid? I would have fought them if they hadn't left," he reassured her.

"Oh God! What if they had stormed the door and killed you?"

"Then I would have died a soldier's death. Naturally, I considered the risk, but foremost on my mind was the thought that I didn't want to disappoint you. Had I succumbed to their attack, I at least would have faced eternity with you in my heart."

"Please explain yourself," she whispered.

After a long pause, he replied in a somewhat nervous tone. "My heart and life belong to you alone. Without you, I would become a meaningless machine, devoid of emotion."

She stirred slightly. "Please tell me your Christian name, Monsieur."

"Hugo," he said with as little emotion as he could manage.

"Well then, Monsieur Hugo, why do you wrestle with uncertain dreams which belong in the future? You'll be very happy one day in your exploits."

"No," he nearly blurted out. "I don't think so."

"Why not?"

"Mademoiselle, I would rather not explain, for fear of making you uncomfortable."

"What could you mean, Monsieur Hugo? How can you think this way? You alone are our savior this hour. Please answer my question. Why do you feel you can't be happy?"

"Because, I... love... you, and because..."

She composed herself. "Go on. And because..." she prompted him to continue.

"...my love has not been returned."

Löwenklau took a deep breath, involuntarily brushing his forehead. He looked at Margot expectantly, uncertain of what she would say. She stood before him, looking down, the picture of charm with a touch of embarrassment.

"I'm not permitted to return your love, Monsieur Hugo," she replied sadly.

Löwenklau, ignoring the implication, ventured hopefully, "You're not permitted? If you had the freedom to choose, would you love me?"

"Yes," she whispered, closing her eyes.

"But why? Why can't you love me? Tell me, my dear Margot!"

"Do I have to disclose that?"

"I'm asking you to."

"All right, but not now. Not today. Later."

"Then I'll have to be patient. May I ask you another important question?"

"Go ahead, Monsieur."

Löwenklau unwittingly placed his left arm on her shoulder, pulling her closer, so her head rested on his shoulder. He gently stroked her hair, trying to soothe her.

"Would it be easy for you to withhold your love from me?"

She pressed her cheek against his. "No, actually it would be difficult."

"I'm grateful, from the bottom of my heart, you wonderful, sweet being!" He gently kissed her on the lips. She didn't pull back, responding instead to his kiss. "In the short time I've known you, I've come to love you in a way I can't describe. I feel I can't live without you. Do you believe me, Margot?"

She wrapped her arms around his neck. "I believe you because I feel the same way about you. But we still have to go our separate ways."

"But why? Why? Tell me!"

"It's the same reason I can't love you."

"What if I implored you to tell me?"

She hugged him tenderly. "I find it difficult, very difficult, to answer you."

"Then I'll speak in your stead, my dear Margot."

"Please go on, my friend."

"You believe you can't return my love by becoming my wife because you are bound to the baron."

"Yes. It's because of him."

"What if I can come up with the a hundred and fifty thousand francs?"

"Oh my God! It would be too great a sacrifice," she cried out. "Are you that wealthy?"

"I'll be honest with you, Margot. I'm not what you consider rich, with my sustenance coming from a small estate. It may be just enough to cover the debt, though. I've resolved to sell it all so I can rescue you and your mother from the clutches of that charlatan, Reillac."

Margot, completely speechless, embraced him in the heat of the moment. He felt her heart pounding in the embrace as a deep sobbing took hold of her. While she tried to control herself, it dawned on him how deeply she had been affected by the night's events. He let her release the pent-up emotions, only responding when she had calmed down once more.

"Why are you crying, my love? What's wrong?"

"Nothing, Hugo." She paused. "I'm so happy. I never imagined any man would offer me the entirety of his possessions on my account. How could I ever ask you to sacrifice all this for me?"

"Why not?"

"What would you have left? What could a poor officer subsist on?"

"God will stand by us, Margot."

"My love, you are wonderful." She cuddled up to him and kissed him on his forehead, his eyes, his cheek, and his mouth. She even kissed both his hands. "Am I really worth such a large sum?" she asked him.

He pulled her near, holding her close to his chest. "If I had the ability to convert the few thousand I have into millions, you would easily exceed their value."

The couple stood together, their upper bodies touching, mouth to mouth, for what seemed like hours. The uproar in the quarter slowly died down, moving into another part of the city. Finally, as utter stillness enveloped the quarter the thoughts of the happy couple returned to the present.

"My mother will be so happy!" said Margot. "Should we tell her tonight?"

"Yes, by all means. I know it's a little bold of me, since she doesn't know me that well, but it would alleviate her fears about the debt."

"I'll see if she is still awake."

Margot quietly left the window, returning shortly with the news that her mother had fallen asleep. It made sense to let her rest after the events of the evening.

At last, after countless farewells, they parted company. Löwenklau left, knowing he had lifted Margot's spirits. He started his walk home, full of hope for the future. He expected his mind to dwell on the last few hours, but as so often happens, fate had other plans for him.

CHAPTER FOUR
Chance and Providence

The lieutenant stopped at the next intersection to light his cigar. He hadn't walked far when a heavyset man approached him.

"Wait a minute, friend. Do you have a light for my pipe?" he asked in poor French. Löwenklau recognized the voice of Field Marshal Blücher.

"At your service, Excellency!"

"*Zounds.*[4.1] A German! I didn't recognize you in the dark, though I did hear your saber rattle when you lit that cigar of yours. Who are you?"

"Lieutenant Löwenklau with the Zieten Hussars."

"Ah, it's you. Still not a cavalry master?" he chuckled as he lit his pipe. "I've been running around in this old town hoping to witness some of the revolution, but I haven't been able to see much."

"I, on the other hand, could not escape it, Excellency."

"Really?" he asked. "Come, my son. You must tell me all about it. I know of a little out of the way place where we can have a glass of wine, and maybe a little something extra. You can spill your guts there, and don't worry about the bill."

As the man patted his pocket, Löwenklau could hear the sound of gold pieces. He knew Blücher liked to gamble, although he was known to lose more than he won. Löwenklau supposed he was already on his way to one of those gambling houses. After they walked a while, Blücher stopped in front of an ordinary house.

"My son," he said, "I brought you this far because I think you can hold your tongue and still converse with me about current events. I trust you won't say a word about this to anyone."

"Your Excellency can rest assured I'll be discreet. I don't have a loose tongue,[4.2] and I'll do my best to provide you with some good company."

"Well, I hope that's true. If I find out you haven't been discreet, I'll be disappointed in you."

As Blücher carefully pulled on a cord, Löwenklau heard a distant bell clang. A minute or two elapsed before they heard approaching footsteps.

"Who's there?" called a voice from inside.

"Blücher," the field marshal replied simply.

The door opened immediately and a servant bowed. Blücher didn't pay any attention to him and proceeded to climb the steps. He entered a drawing room full of gentlemen who respectfully rose to acknowledge him. He nodded to them and walked into the adjoining room, failing to introduce Löwenklau. An assortment of wine and spirits were arranged on the table. Blücher helped himself to a wine bottle, uncorking it.

"These Frenchmen are peculiar and damned hard to figure out, yet they do make excellent wine," he reflected while pouring two glasses. "I don't know how that fits together, but I'm so frustrated by it I could pummel them with a wooden ladle. This drink won't do you any harm. *Prosit*, my son." They clinked their glasses, each one taking a sip of the appealing liquid. "Not bad. Not bad at all! Now, my son, sit here and tell me your story."

Löwenklau, obeying his superior, spoke of the uprising and coming to the rescue of the two women. He failed to mention anything about his love for Margot. As he related the tale, several other men entered. They greeted each other politely, respectfully keeping their distance.

Löwenklau finished his report while the marshal eyed him. "So, it was just another uprising," commented Blücher. "Like at Sodom and Gomorrah.[4.3] It seems this little kafuffle wasn't directed at us. Eventually, they even heeded your orders to disperse. Ha! Your actions were honorable, my son. I have to give me credit for that. Tell me now, how did you come to meet these ladies?"

"In the usual way, Excellency."

"Well, how does one meet ladies?" asked Blücher bluntly. It was well known that he liked a good story. He suspected, since the affair involved two ladies, that Löwenklau, in his modesty, had glossed over the personal details.

Seeing as he had to oblige the marshal, he continued. "I met the daughter on the street by chance. Two Russian officers, who were having a little fun at her expense, were detaining her. I took it upon myself to escort her home, and in turn had the opportunity to meet her mother. I must have left a favorable impression, since I was given permission for a return visit."

Blücher nodded, his expression one of amusement. "Yes, those Russians! They pop up like corks from a champagne bottle when they see so much as a skirt. They impeded her progress, you say? How so?"

"One of them grabbed her by the arm."

"*Zounds*! Then she must have been something to look at. Right?"

"I have no intention of denying it, Excellency."

"Ah! I can guess the rest. She captivated you, my dear boy."

Löwenklau shrugged his shoulders, remaining passive.

"It just goes to show you" said Blücher, eying him. "Young people insist on being secretive about small things, as if the matter was of a highly political nature! There he sits, rigid as a Sphinx, and doesn't think the old man is clever enough to grasp the whole situation. Well, my boy, I too was once young and foolish, a real jackass! I ran after the girls like a farmer after his geese, and managed to steal the odd kiss often meant for another. I'm old now and used up like *Methusalem*,[4.4] and yet I'd still rather see a beautiful face than a pair of worn out boots. Rest assured your secret is safe with me. Come, tell me your tale. Let me guess! You fell head over heels for her!"

Löwenklau saw no way of avoiding the questions. He didn't want to lie to the marshal, and even realized that openness with him, as his superior, might be advantageous. "Yes, Excellency. You've hit the mark."

"It's understandable. She's beautiful and you're not bad looking yourself, my son. It's easy to get carried away in matters of love. I have to caution you, though. Kiss her, carouse with her, love her as you will, but for heaven's sake don't marry her."

"Why not?"

"That, my boy, is what I have to tell you," Blücher said. "Look, let me paint you the whole picture. In the beginning, women are soft and smooth, like sweet chocolate melting in your mouth. After the wedding nuptials are over, all hell breaks loose. You can't breathe. You can prance about all you like, just don't make any proposals. Otherwise you'll disappear like ashes from a pipe. You have no idea what women are like!

"Many years ago, I fell in love with an aristocratic lady. I was a raving fool for her. We both liked to gamble a bit, and one evening I won a small sum from her. She was afraid to tell her husband, who she knew would scold her, even though he'd settle the debt. I made the suggestion of canceling her debt in exchange for a kiss. So, what do you think she said? She claimed she would not throw herself at my feet for any trifle sum. The debt was paid and that was that.

"Time passed and I became a general, although I take it she didn't advance much in her financial affairs. Unable to be free of the habit, she continued to gamble. Well, one fine evening we once again ended up at the same table. As you might guess, my son, I won another nice little sum from her. Just like a woman, she stood up and proclaimed to all present that she was now prepared to give me my long sought after kiss, in exchange for canceling the debt. 'Nooo, dear lady,' I replied. 'Times have changed. I've lost my appetite. I'm not going to smack my lips on an old crone just to appease her.'

"My son, you can imagine what a sour face she made. That's the honest truth. At first, women can be as welcoming as honey, but later you're left with a bitter aftertaste. Their smooth faces will give way to tiny lines, then cracks, and even age spots. The wrinkles will come, and they'll lose their hair. The angel turns into a busybody, a tattletale, a dragon, and even a beast, spitting poison and fire. Let me tell you again, fall in love but never get married!"

He eyed Löwenklau. "My son, you look like you've been had!"

Löwenklau broke up laughing. "Excellency, I'm holding my own."

"Dammit, you're holding something back. Have you given her your word?"

"Absolutely!"

"That's even dumber! My poor fellow, I feel sorry for you. Well, is she at least rich?"

"No."

"My boy, you are an ass!"

Löwenklau laughed. "But a very lucky one, Excellency!"

"Well, yes, that's what you think now! Your 'cupid' will quickly turn into a messenger of woe, grabbing you by the neck... and a French lady of all things! Had you considered a first-rate fräulein, there might still be hope. But a Mademoiselle! What were you thinking, my son? You're such an excellent young man. You had only to reach out for any fine lady, but now you've been led astray."

"I know what I'm doing, Excellency. Margot is—"

"Hold it. That's her name, Margot?"

"Yes."

"At least the name doesn't sound too bad. It still doesn't change the fact that she's poor and you have nothing to offer!"

"I've considered selling my holdings," Löwenklau replied without thinking, suddenly realizing this was exactly the piece of the story he'd wanted to keep to himself.

"Sell your holdings? No, my son, if you want to marry her, you have to retain your investments. Your pay is only a trifle, while your holdings exist to tide you over. What would you rely on if this fails?"

Löwenklau looked down, frowning. "You're right, Excellency, of course. I must sell what little I do have, however. I'm compelled to follow through, to offer all I have for the one I love."

"Compelled? That means you are being coerced. By whom?"

"By a newly-made baron. One of my fellow officers told me he was a wartime manager of Napoleon's supplies, and became a rich man through his financial dealings."

"A supplier of goods? Hang it all! Lightning should strike him. All these profiteers are nothing but crooks. How's he connected to you, my son? Did you gamble, owing him money?"

Löwenklau realized he had revealed far too much to remain quiet now. He decided to confide in the marshal, telling him the whole story. As Blücher listened attentively, his expression began to change from one of pure interest to one of concern.

"This is, of course, a totally different matter. Since you're a man of honor, you must fulfill your promise. Your holdings will vanish my boy, but that's the way it is. Yesterday in love, and today an ass! What will you do to obtain the money? You only have seven days until the notes are to be redeemed."

"I'm not worried. Since my holdings are free of any liens, I'm sure any banker would advance me the funds until they're sold."

"Well, my boy, I feel sorry for you. Is this Margot really worth all this fuss?"

"She's worth everything to me."

"Remarkable! Am I permitted to see this lovely creature?"

"If your Excellency commands me, then I will arrange a visit."

"Very well. By the way, have you spoken of this to the mother?"

"No, not yet."

"I see. Are you planning to reveal your plans tomorrow?"

"Yes, Excellency."

"Well then," Blücher said, "come to my residence tomorrow at two-thirty sharp. I'm going to get all dressed up, a real sight to behold! But I'm telling you now, if the lady doesn't make an impression on me, I won't say a word in your favor. I don't want to contribute to your misery."

Blücher rose and walked over to greet a newcomer, whom he seemed to know. The gentleman, who was well-dressed for the outing, had an aura of nobility. Löwenklau noticed costly rings on his fingers. In fact, everything about him spoke of luxury. He was introduced to him as one of the city's foremost bankers. As the three entered the large room, the young officer at once recognized he was among experienced gamblers. The banker went to one of the tables where the game of *Biribi*[4.5] was being played. He asked Blücher to join him, though he saw the marshal saunter to another table.

"Have you ever played the game of *Pharaoh*, my son?" Blücher asked.

"Never, but I've observed it before, Excellency."

"That's good. I want you to play alongside me."

"I've never been a gambler, Excellency. Certainly not with this game."

"Perhaps I should have explained that all who enter here are required to play. I hope you will not disappoint me but play with some skill. Do you have any money?"

"I have a few hundred francs on me."

"That'll do, to start," replied Blücher.

Löwenklau was not a gambler. Though his first thought was to leave, he couldn't do so for fear of offending the marshal. Forced to participate, he vowed to himself not to be careless. As he was introduced to the other gentlemen, he decided to first observe, rather than wager immediately.

Blücher laid one thousand francs in front of him, quipping that he'd quit if he lost the entire thousand. He played with some success. Eventually, Löwenklau felt compelled to play, wagering a small amount. He won, wagered again and, to his surprise, won again. The marshal smiled, encouraging him to continue. Luck was with him, and he continued to win. After about an hour, the young officer won a little over a thousand francs, while Blücher had lost his thousand. The latter stood up from the table, suggesting Löwenklau accompany him.

"My money went to the devil," laughed Blücher. "I've got more where that came from, though. Last night I won a small sum at roulette and I promised the banker I would play again. How much did you win, my son?"

"A little over a thousand francs."

"I'm glad for you. At least my money ended up in German hands. You can join me at *Biribi*. Do you know the game?"

"Only from watching, Excellency."

"That's all right then. I should caution you, though. Entry is a hundred francs, so the stakes are higher. Let's give it a try and see if Lady Luck favors us."

As both men approached the table, Löwenklau noticed it was occupied by the wealthiest players. The banker, who nodded to the marshal, was a skilled and cautious player, while Blücher approached the game as he did warfare. He promptly placed five hundred francs as his first wager, eliciting a smile from the French banker. One could see how Blücher's passion could easily get the better of him. Unfortunately, luck was not with him.

Löwenklau wagered two hundred francs, gaining four hundred. Next, he placed a hundred more on number twelve, winning thirty-two times the amount. Before long, he found himself in possession of four thousand francs. Deciding to pull back half the amount, he worked with the remaining two thousand. His position on the table earned him sixteen thousand francs! After about an hour, the young officer was the winner of a considerable sum.

Löwenklau's natural skill didn't escape Blücher's attention. "Trust your instincts, my son. Tonight's your night."

"Is His Excellency finished?"

"Yes. My money went down the drain."

"Excellency, don't you have any credit?"

"I don't borrow from the French."

"May I offer you an advance from my winnings?"

"Thank you, my boy. I would accept, but to take a loan from your winnings would be bad luck. He who wins should not divide his spoils. I'm convinced you're going to lose from now on. My boy, go ahead and prove me wrong. By the way, how much do you have?"

"About fifty thousand!"

He laughed to himself. "Well, give it a try. It would be gratifying to see you plunder all that money from under the Frenchman's nose."

The dealer signaled that the house would close soon. There was only one other active player left other than Löwenklau. The gambler placed his last one hundred francs on a random number. On a hunch, Löwenklau placed twenty thousand on the adjacent number.

CHANCE AND PROVIDENCE

"Are you aware Monsieur," the dealer pointed out, "that should you win, the house would be obligated to pay you eightfold, or a hundred sixty thousand francs?"

"I'm well aware of this."

"If I may explain," the dealer continued, "the house is currently not at your disposal for the full amount should you win. Would you permit us to remit the balance by way of courier tomorrow morning?"

"With pleasure," replied Löwenklau.

"In that case, let's play."

The bystanders looked on with great interest. The dealer pulled the card and turned it around. Suddenly he turned pale, for it was the number Löwenklau wagered. A unified, exuberant cheer rose up in the room. The only one not participating in the celebration was the dealer. Such a large sum had certainly been lost before, but never won.

The manager approached Löwenklau and asked him for his address. While they exchanged the information, Löwenklau was suddenly struck with the reality that he was the winner and owner of slightly over two hundred thousand francs! Over the course of play, he had appeared calm. Now, as the reality of the situation caught up to him, he was ecstatic! The marshal tapped him on the shoulder, and laughed along with him.

"My God, that was a winning number! That was one in a million, my boy. I'll help you carry your winnings to your residence. First and foremost, though, let's celebrate with some good champagne."

The others joined in, some to celebrate and others to commiserate. Löwenklau took the time to look around him, taking in the luxurious surroundings. He had heard how some members of Paris society opened their private homes to privileged members of the establishment. Everything was provided to the gambler, but of course at exorbitant prices. The dealer, who packed up Löwenklau's winnings, also arranged for delivery of the balance. The marshal was as good at his word and helped Löwenklau carry his small fortune. Blücher actually enjoyed this little servitude. Another man in his position wouldn't have dreamed of becoming a servant to a mere lieutenant.

"Listen, my boy, how do you feel now?"

"I can't describe it, Excellency!"

"I believe you. You had incredible luck tonight. I suppose you realize gambling does have its place."

"I'm certainly no paragon of virtue," laughed the lieutenant, "but I have to say, having gambled once, I'll never do it again."

"Really?"

"Yes, Excellency. I'm giving you my word that I'll never gamble again. I won't tempt fate. I suspect I'd come to regret it. I'm going to enjoy this moment without boasting about it."

"My son, I commend you. Gambling is often compared to a woman whom you can't trust. I've experienced it, but, unlike you, haven't been smart enough to call it quits. In this regard, the old Blücher is a complete ass. Just keep it to yourself!"

"Most of all, I'm thrilled that I won't have to sell my holdings. I can give Margot the one hundred fifty thousand francs and still have a tidy sum left over. I've never felt so ecstatic in my whole life!"

"I congratulate you. When are you planning to give her the money?"

"Tomorrow, Excellency."

"Fine. Take the time to exchange the coins into paper so they won't be so cumbersome to carry. I expect you to keep your word and pick me up at two-thirty sharp!"

"Of course, Excellency."

"You don't think the old lady, her mother, will object to your plan?"

"I certainly hope not."

"And I wouldn't advise her to. A man who offers a huge sum out of love can be trusted with her daughter. Is there no father?"

"Unfortunately not, Excellency," the lieutenant said. "Though, there is a brother." Then, he reluctantly added, "Actually, you've met him."

"What?" he exclaimed. "Where would I have met him?"

"We became acquainted with him under dubious circumstances. He's the one I chastised over his improper comments regarding our Prussian heritage, Excellency."

"Unbelievable! Do you want to become the brother-in-law to that idiot?"

"The stepbrother-in-law, actually," Löwenklau corrected.

"It doesn't matter," the marshal said. "It's still family, even if that braggart is removed ten times over. He'll stoop to the lowest level to gain the upper hand. He's proven it by trying to sell out his own sister. I certainly hope he doesn't cross our path tomorrow or, by Jove, I'll finish what you started so he won't see straight for a week."

"This is my residence, Excellency."

"Well," Blücher said as they stopped walking, "I sure got plucked in Biribi.[4.6] I need to get a good sleep. Good night."

Blücher walked by himself a short distance down the street, declining the offer of an escort to the nearby palace.

Löwenklau turned on the light in his room, spreading out his winnings on the table. He pondered how a sovereign God might have orchestrated the meeting with the marshal. The ensuing conversation strengthened his relationship with him, culminating with an unexpected windfall. He was blessed in being able to cover Margot's debt and still keep his holdings intact. As he lay in bed, he considered how incredibly lucky he had been to win such a large sum. Only the knowledge that Margot would at last be free surpassed the joy he felt at that moment.

CHAPTER FIVE
The Chastised Baron

A t ten o'clock the next morning, a courier brought the remainder of the one hundred sixty thousand francs. Löwenklau took his winnings of gold and silver coins to the nearest banking establishment, changing the coins into more manageable banknotes. He carried in his wallet the assurance his beloved and her mother would not be weighed down with needless worry. Watching the minutes drag by, he anticipated the time when he could head to the marshal's residence. Upon his arrival, Blücher greeted him in his full dress uniform and, true to his word, he was a sight to behold.

"Ah! Here you are, my son," the marshal exclaimed. "It's exactly two-thirty, and time for us to leave on our little errand. I still don't know what I'm going to say. Addressing the troops comes easily to me, but speaking to ladies is an entirely different matter. It nearly gave me a headache going over it, and I still haven't come up with any suitable words. What a sight that would be, the old Blücher standing like a fool, in front of the priest, with nothing to say!"

"Don't worry," Löwenklau laughed. "His Excellency can forge ahead just as in battle."

"It's not so much a matter of me forging ahead as my concern over how this will turn out for you. What's all this talk about marriage anyway? A word of advice, my boy. It's not everyone who can bring the chestnuts out of the fire. I'm in this mess of my own free will, and now I have to see it through with you. Come on, my boy, we should proceed."

Upon reaching *Rue d'Ange 10*, they were admitted by the maid. As soon as Margot heard the door, she rushed forward to meet Hugo with open arms. When she spotted the marshal, she held back, allowing her arms to sink to her side.

"Don't stop on my account," the old man snickered. "I can keep a secret."

Margot was slightly embarrassed. Her trepidation rose when she was introduced to His Excellency, about whom she had heard so much. As they entered the drawing room, Blücher looked around appraisingly. His gaze settled on the young lady.

The marshal tapped Hugo on the shoulder. "My boy," he exclaimed, "I'm satisfied with your choice. Margot certainly is beautiful. God knows my mouth is starting to water just looking at her. Now, here's a woman who won't bring you any shame."

Löwenklau learned that her mother's condition had improved somewhat. She entered the room, still with the look of one who had not completely recovered from a malady. Like Margot, she was surprised to see Löwenklau had not come alone.

The conversation was light and flew from topic to topic. When Blücher learned the two ladies understood German, he prattled on as if they were old friends. Nearly a quarter of an hour had gone by before he got around to explaining his presence. Just as he was about to do so, they were interrupted by the doorbell.

The maid announced the newcomer from the foyer. It was Baron de Reillac.

When the baron entered the drawing room, he hesitated slightly upon seeing the two officers. Reillac was already familiar with Blücher. When Löwenklau's name was announced, he correctly assumed it was the same officer who had humiliated Captain Richemonte at the inn. The baron could find no explanation for their presence other than the obvious one, that they had found him absent next door and had alternatively come to his mother's residence looking for him.

Blücher immediately recognized the Frenchman's name as the swindler who had deceitfully tried to gain Margot's hand in marriage. For his part, he didn't acknowledge the baron's entrance, or his greeting.

"Are you looking for Captain Richemonte?" Reillac inquired.

"Why do you ask?" replied Löwenklau coldly.

"Because of your presence, Monsieur."

"You must be mistaken," the lieutenant said. "The captain made it clear he had no intention of settling our dispute. My presence here is strictly in respect to the ladies."

"Really!" exclaimed the Frenchman. "Do you know each other?"

"Yes, as you can see."

The baron considered the situation. The presence of the lieutenant was likely for the benefit of the daughter, not the mother. Did he have any aspirations toward Margot? A sudden rush of jealousy gripped the baron. He needed to be sure.

"Have you known each other for some time?"

"Is this important to you, Baron?"

"Of course, since I count myself a friend to both ladies present and therefore have an interest in their affairs."

"In that case," Löwenklau said, "I should inform you that Margot and I have known each other for a relatively short time. However, I have the assurance our relationship will span a long time, which can only be broken through death."

The Prussian's intentions and his plan for Margot's future became instantly clear to Reillac. He decided to take matters into his own hands by limiting any further involvement. "Under what circumstances are you involved in the relationship?"

Löwenklau looked at him surprised. "It seems to me you want to know too much about my affairs," he said, shrugging his shoulders.

"Just a little, Monsieur," he replied. The baron brushed aside the sarcastic remark, not to be deterred. "I am concerned for Madame's and Mademoiselle's wellbeing. Any time there is a newcomer in their lives, I naturally make it my business to know of it."

"Really? Are you intending to insult me?"

"Not at all!"

"I dare say you shouldn't!" Blücher blurted out. He had been sitting in an armchair, turned somewhat to the side. The arrogance and the reproachfulness of the Frenchman irritated him, and he felt the need to say something. Madame Richemonte looked at Blücher in fear, feeling powerless in the baron's clutches. If he were offended, he might be much less considerate about her daughter's future welfare.

"What does Monsieur mean by those words?" he asked, looking down at Blücher.

"I mean all sorts of calamity will fall upon you if you keep acting in such an impertinent manner!"

"But Monsieur, I am a nobleman!" the Frenchman called out threateningly.

"A what? What did you call me?" Blücher exclaimed, rising to his feet. "You called me a *Mossjeh!*" He was referring to the word Monsieur, albeit in poor French. "This is unheard of. Unbelievable! I am the Field Marshal von Blücher, the Sovereign of Wahlstatt. Is that understood? You are to address me in terms of His Excellency or Duke, not this *Mossjeh* business! You may wish to be addressed as Monsieur, like other Frenchmen, but I, sir, do not. I'm offended by your cavalier attitude. You call yourself a nobleman? I don't see any sign of it. If you really want to behold a true gentleman, then take a magnifying glass and look over here. I've been a credit to my country, and the family of Löwenklau isn't lacking in its accomplishments either. You, sir, have only recently been elevated to nobility by your deposed emperor. Don't make the mistake of calling yourself a man of nobility before you start acting like one! Your financial exploits are well known, but as for the rest, they have little bearing on the present. I'll send your whole nobility up in a puff of smoke. It's not worth anything to me!"

His words gushed out from underneath the gray moustache with such incredible force that it would have been impossible to interrupt the scolding. Löwenklau smiled inwardly while Margot's face remained expressionless.

Madame Richemonte feared the baron's reprisal, and clapped her hands together in exasperation, expecting the worst.

Reillac jumped out of his chair. "All right! I will address you as His Excellency. Please, would you refresh my memory and tell me how it is you know of my accomplishments? You have openly offended me, and I trust you will grant me satisfaction."

"Satisfaction?" Blücher asked. His eyes flashed with ridicule. "Are you mad? Let's get one thing straight. You were a supplier for the army. That means you arranged for delivery of various meat supplies for the troops. While the poor animals consisted of more bones than flesh, you became a rich man. Perhaps you modeled your intellectual prowess after the sheep, as evidenced by your presumptuous attitude. I suppose the emperor saw fit to reward you with a letter of nobility. You've caused a great deal of unhappiness in this family over your pursuit of the daughter. First, you misled the father, then corrupted the son, and now you burden the mother and daughter with crippling debt. As though this was not enough, you press your position further, bordering on blackmail and threatening the debtor's court and all kinds of misery upon a suffering widow." He spat on the floor. "You have the gall to call yourself a gentleman and ask me for satisfaction? Listen here, *Mossjeh*, I'll be more than happy to give you satisfaction, but not with the saber! Instead, I'll use my whip. Or better yet, a stable broom!"

This was indeed a verbal thrashing, one which the ladies had certainly never witnessed. They came to their feet, expecting the baron in his rage to physically attack the marshal. Löwenklau also slowly stood up, coming to stand beside his superior.

The baron, however, was speechless and white as a ghost. Seething with rage, he would have liked nothing better than to strike out against Blücher. The marshal stood tall and proud, making such an overwhelming impression by his persona that Reillac utterly lost his nerve. Unable to deflect the accusations with lies and excuses, anger welled up within him. Not daring to confront Löwenklau, he instead turned his attention on the ladies.

"You have been talking behind my back," he hissed.

"Not one word," Madame Richemonte cried out.

"But I have," replied Margot bravely.

"Who have you been talking to?" demanded the baron.

"To a real gentleman," she said. "Lieutenant von Löwenklau."

"When was that?"

"Yesterday."

"Really? Are you that acquainted with him, that you would reveal your innermost secrets?"

"That's none of your damned business," Blücher growled. "Let me reply instead, just to show you where you stand in the scheme of things." The marshal turned and faced the Frenchman. "To show you how well acquainted these two young people are, I'll let you in on a little secret. I'm here on their behalf, to obtain Madame Richemonte's blessing."

"What?" Reillac and Madame uttered the question in unison. Madame was still unaware of the discussion that had taken place between the lieutenant and her daughter the previous evening.

Reillac was so taken aback that he thought he misheard. "Madame, can you verify what I just heard and confirm it..." he stuttered.

"Stop whining!" exclaimed Blücher. "There's nothing agreeable as far as you're concerned. Who can say what this man heard? Perhaps his hearing is not up to snuff. To show you I'm serious, you'll become a witness to this betrothal."

"My son, come here," he said, turning to face Löwenklau. "Take your betrothed's hand, and pay attention!" Blücher took both their hands in his, maneuvering the couple in front of Madame. He then placed himself directly in front of her, bowing reverently as though he were standing before His Majesty.

"Madame, the first thing to declare is the love these two have for each other. Secondly, they want to be married. And thirdly, I ask for your blessing on them. If there are any objections," and with this, he looked at Reillac, "I will squeeze his throat so hard that the squeak will be heard by the angels!"

The revelation came so quickly and unexpectedly that Madame Richemonte couldn't find the words to reply. The baron stepped closer before she could formulate an answer.

"I can see this little charade is about to come to an end," he hissed. "Let me remind you that I am not just some quiet bystander. Madame, I implore you to refrain from any hasty decision until I have also spoken." He reached into his jacket, removed his billfold, and with dramatic flair waved the much-bemoaned promissory notes in her face.

"Madame," he continued scornfully, "you have forced me to present these. I demand immediate payment for all debts. If payment is delayed, you will face the consequences!"

"My God!" she replied exasperated. "This is all so sudden. I don't know what to say."

"You don't have to say anything," the baron replied. "Only pay up!"

The marshal regarded him with visible contempt. "Bastard!"

"Was that meant for me?" the baron hissed.

"Of course, *Mossjeh*. Who else? There's only one crook here!"

"We will discuss that later," laughed the Frenchman with an air of superiority. "Now, I demand payment."

"You will get paid," Löwenklau replied evenly, reaching for the papers.

Reillac, however, quickly pulled them back. "Are you intending to pay for Madame?" he asked.

"I trust Madame will allow me to pay the amount owing," confirmed Löwenklau.

The baron laughed out loud. "This is so amusing. Do you have any idea how staggering the debt is?"

"One hundred and fifty thousand francs," the Prussian replied.

"Exactly! You have certainly been well-informed, but do you realize the full amount is to be paid immediately?"

"As I said, I am at Madame's bidding." With these words, Löwenklau removed his own billfold, took from it a packet of banknotes, and placed it on the table.

The baron quickly walked over, opened it, and counted the contents. He failed to hide the disappointment on his face. This unexpected payment, though satisfying the debt, had upset his plans for Margot. "It is the full amount," he slowly managed. "One hundred fifty thousand francs. It is all here."

"Of course it is all there!" replied Blücher testily. "Take your money and disappear from our sight."

These words brought the baron's mind back to the matter at hand. "What do you mean, disappear? His Excellency is using expressions that are inappropriate for cultured individuals."

"You're quite right," replied the marshal calmly. "But don't think for a moment I consider you to be one of these refined and cultured people. You stand below me in rank, much like the way your sheep and oxen stood beneath you. I don't believe for a moment that you treated your cattle with much respect. Now, take your leave."

"You must permit me to stay a little longer. You see, I also have promissory notes pertaining to your son. If he cannot meet the requirements—"

"Then do with him as you please, right Mama?" interrupted Margot.

"I have no reason to feel sorry for him," her mother said.

"There, you heard her," said Blücher to the baron. "Now, surrender the notes."

"Only when I receive the payment from Madame herself, Mon... er, Excellency. I still don't know if she has accepted the lieutenant's offer." The baron played his last card, knowing full well he had lost the game.

"I am completely surprised, Lieutenant," Madame Richemonte replied. "His Excellency has asked for my daughter's hand, on your behalf. I did not think that was possible, considering the short time you have known each other."

Löwenklau put his arm around Margot. "Madame, love is not concerned with time. When it arrives, one is helpless to resist it. I realized right away my heart, and my life, belonged to Margot. She is your only child, and I did not come to rob you, but to bring you joy. God intended to give you a son to complement your daughter, and my desire is to bring you happiness."

"And you, Margot, do you really love him?"

"I love him, Mama," she whispered, hugging her betrothed. "He chose to offer his entire estate for our rescue!"

"Then I cannot accept!" replied the mother.

"You're mistaken, Margot," Löwenklau quickly said. "I don't have to resort to selling my estate after all. Everything changed for the better yesterday, and I will explain later how I came into possession of those funds. His Excellency can confirm that Madame can accept the offer without any harm to my finances."

"Yes, I can," said the marshal. "This extraordinary young man is most capable, and came by it in his sleep. He can give it away or throw it out the window, just as he pleases, without wanting for money."

"But to offer such a large sum, my dear lieutenant!" she exclaimed. "I have to tell you I will not be in a position to repay you."

"I value your friendship more than money. Your approval of our betrothal is worth more than countless millions to me. I ask you to accept the gift I offer so you can satisfy the creditor. Then you can be free from all this worry that has burdened you for so long."

"You're an honorable man, Lieutenant von Löwenklau," she said, offering him her hand in thanks and holding back tears in her eyes. "It might be perceived as ungrateful on my part if I declined your generosity. I accept your offer and give you my only child. In return, I will be proud to accept the role of mother, since you no longer have your parents, and consider myself rich to have gained a son. I see now that Margot was right in her portrayal of you, and I gladly give you my blessing."

She intertwined their hands and blessed them. Margot wrapped her arms around her, tears of joy streaming down her face. Hugo felt he had been blessed beyond measure, a joy for which there was no earthly comparison.

"My children," Blücher added. "Please accept my blessing as well. It may not be worth much, but it will not do you any harm. As for you, *Mossjeh* nobleman, take your money and surrender the promissory notes. Your brief part here is over, and you can exit the stage now. I advise you to leave immediately, or I'll see to it you receive what should have been administered a long time ago."

The baron's eyes flickered with hate. "I suppose you consider this a victory," he said as he pocketed the money. "Don't be too hasty in your celebration. What I strive to accomplish usually comes to pass. Margot has yet to be married to this Prussian, and we don't yet know what the future holds."

"What? Are you threatening us?" retorted Blücher. He stood up and confronted Reillac. "Hold your mouth, boy, or I will shut it for you, you *Mossjeh* reprobate!"

At that, the Frenchman angrily threw the notes on the table and left the room.

❧✠☙

Making his exit, Reillac realized there was nothing left for him to do. And yet, he wasn't about to give up his mission. Reillac, reeling from the rebuke, was already considering ways to avenge himself.

As the baron retreated down the steps, he met Captain Richemonte, on his way up.

"Ah!" the captain said. "It's you, my dear baron. Were you coming to see me?"

"I just left your mother's residence!" he said almost breathlessly, trying to conceal his frustration.

"What's wrong? Did something unpleasant occur?"

"No, on the contrary. Something very pleasant."

"What is it? You don't look calm at all."

"Your mother has just paid me the full amount, to satisfy the debt."

"She paid you?" Richemonte asked, bewildered and disbelieving. "All of it? Unbelievable!"

"Believe it, Captain. I received all my money."

"You can't be serious! Where would my mother get a hundred and fifty thousand francs?"

"From your sister's sweetheart."

"Nonsense. Margot doesn't have a lover."

"In order to satisfy your curiosity, go upstairs and make his acquaintance. I believe they are celebrating right now."

The captain looked at him skeptically. "I must confess you don't look like yourself at all, Baron. Are you sick? Or just possibly going mad? It sounds like you are talking nonsense. Are you suffering from a fever, or something worse? What is happening to you?"

"It is as though I have a fever. I'm consumed with anger... I loathe those Germans. Believe me, it's no fantasy. The truth is, Margot has just become engaged!"

"To whom?" the captain asked.

"You're going to be ecstatic when you hear his name. Take a wild guess, Captain!"

"Don't play games with me. Who is this man?"

"He is well known to you."

49

"His name! Quickly!"

"He is so close. In fact, he has already had the pleasure of touching your cheek, although in a most unconventional way."

Richemonte took a step back. "You don't mean..." he said through clenched teeth. "You are not speaking of that Prussian?"

"Yes, indeed."

"Lieutenant von Löwenklau?"

"Of course! One and the same."

"Is he with my mother now?"

"Yes, indeed."

Richemonte looked appalled. "And he is acquainted with Margot?"

"He asked for, and received, permission to marry her."

"What?" the captain exclaimed, nearly losing his footing. "Baron, you must be in a state of delirium."

"On the contrary, I'm in control of all my faculties. Go and see for yourself."

"Dammit. Are you telling me the truth? I'll have to break up this little celebration. My sister can marry anyone she wants, but not this man. She will have to give me an account of this sordid turn of events and how she came up with the payment."

"It is very simple. Löwenklau provided the funds to pay me."

"So they came from him?"

"From him!" the baron confirmed.

"Then I must go see my mother right now. Here is my house key, Baron. Go into my suite and wait for me. I will return shortly with the news that I have thrown the German lout out into the street."

He ran up the steps and rang the bell, while the baron entered the suite next door. When the maid recognized the son of her mistress, she didn't dare refuse him entry.

"Where's Mama?" he asked curtly.

"In the drawing room, but she has..." She tried to explain, but the captain rushed past her, heaving the door open in his haste.

Löwenklau stood with Margot at the window, while her mother sat on the sofa with... the field marshal. The captain, having ignored the maid's warning, was completely unprepared for the surprise guest, whose mere presence reined him in. He decided to forego his entrance as master of the manor, instead greeting them with a bow.

"You have company, Mama?" he inquired.

"Evidently, my son," she said evenly. "A most welcome visit by His Excellency, Field Marshal von Blücher, and Lieutenant von Löwenklau." With this, she introduced the three men to each other.

Blücher didn't reply, but instead grinned broadly, playing with the ends of his moustache. Löwenklau acknowledged him with a slight nod and, like the marshal, remained silent. Richemonte, feeling rebuffed, seethed with mounting anger.

"I didn't realize you started entertaining German officers," he said to his mother.

"These gentlemen have pleasantly surprised me, Albin. Monsieur von Löwenklau here not only defended your residence, but has also just become engaged to your sister."

"What you tell me is unbelievable. I don't recall having instructed anyone to guard my residence, and therefore have no obligation to him. As far as the other matter goes, I expect to be consulted when it comes to matters pertaining to our family."

If his response was meant as a challenge, she downplayed it. "I'm not going to argue with you," she said. "Unless, of course, I am to understand you're trying to stand in Margot's way."

"And if I don't give you my approval, Mama?" he added.

"Your objection does not change anything."

"I'm going to try nevertheless," he jeered, moving closer to her. "Don't you realize these two men are known to me?"

"Yes, I am well aware of this."

"Did you know they insulted me?"

"No. I believe you insulted them, Albin."

"Let's not argue over semantics," he said. "I understand you're familiar with our discord, yet you invite my adversaries to your house at your pleasure. If that's not enough, you even reward them with the promise of marriage. I oppose your decision and declare the betrothal null and void!"

Margot approached him, pressing her fingernails into his arm. "You don't seem to understand what's going on, Albin. I alone have the right to decide to whom I will give my heart and whom I will marry. You attempted to tarnish my future, and nearly ruined it for our mother. Not only that, but you treated us as chattel to be bargained with at your convenience. You failed in your miserable attempt and we're finally free of the burden. It would be wise of you to concede that the circumstances are different now and that you're powerless to change them."

"Do you really think so?" he laughed scornfully. "Tell me then, to whom does this residence belong?"

"To all of us. Why?"

"No, not to you! Who do you think arranged the lease?"

"You did."

"That's right, which makes me the proprietor. No one has the right to enter without my permission. Gentlemen, I request you leave these premises.

You are no longer welcome guests. I do not want to resort to other means, by having you removed by force."

Blücher couldn't contain himself any longer and broke out laughing. "*Zounds!* That sounded desperate! Imagine, the old Blücher being removed from a premise and charged with being unlawfully in a private dwelling. Listen to me carefully, as I am only going to say this once, *Mossjeh.*"

"I would rather not hear it!" the captain replied.

"Then you'll face the consequences."

"Really! What might those be?"

"That's exactly what I want to tell you now, which may reflect poorly on you later. First, your boasting is absurd. Second, what do your accommodations have to do with me? It is also of no consequence to me if you claim to be the master of your stepsister's fate. However, what does concern me is that you continue to insult me and assert yourself as though you were actually someone of importance! You demand that I leave these premises? My response is for you to leave at once. You openly insulted me, along with the German people. I would only have to say one word to the French provisional government. The adjutant would be bound to institute an inquiry, which would be most embarrassing to you, a low-ranking officer.

"Furthermore, you offended this Prussian officer and denied him satisfaction. The consequences of these actions not only resulted in your embarrassment, but the outcome was also witnessed by many others. I have only to bring this matter to the general in charge of disciplinary affairs, and you will be removed from your position and publicly disgraced. Compared to me, you're nothing more than a dwarf. It's disdainful for me to even get entangled with you. Since you have not shown me that you grasp the situation, I may have to resort to the use of a whip. I advise you to leave us right now or I will be true to my word and start proceedings against you, which will probably result in a dishonorable discharge. The Prussians are still in charge in Paris, and I will be damned if I let an insignificant captain dictate his terms to me in such an insolent fashion. Do I make myself clear?" he bellowed.

The captain hadn't expected such a dressing down by Blücher. He hesitated a few seconds before answering, not wanting to concede defeat.

"Which one of us is a field marshal and which is a captain is irrelevant to me," he countered. "Here we stand, man to man. I am not afraid of you! I repeat this as the brother—"

"Leave us now!" Blücher ordered, pointing to the door.

"As the brother I have the right over my sister—"

"Get out!" the marshal roared. He uttered the words with such a resolute tone that any recourse was out of the question. The two words weren't particularly loud, but the authority behind them penetrated right to the bone.

They conveyed such a decisiveness and finality that it seemed to the Frenchman as though he had been grabbed by invisible hands and pushed out of the room.

He opened the door and departed, reeling from the sting of being disgraced. Full of malevolence, he clenched his teeth to suppress his anger. Once outside, he turned around, raised his fist, and threatened the unseen occupants.

"Don't think I'll forget this. You'll pay dearly for what you have put me through."

CHAPTER SIX
Cloak and Dagger

B aron de Reillac was waiting eagerly for Richemonte's return. When the captain walked into the suite, the baron noticed the agitation on his face.

"There you are. Did they treat you in the same way they did me? It seems the Germans have taken over with little resistance," he said ironically.

"How can you say that?" the captain asked testily.

"Well," laughed Reillac, "you have the appearance of a schoolboy who's been punished. Anyone could tell just by looking at you."

"Go to hell!"

"Is that all you have to say?" Reillac asked, becoming angry.

"Yes, that is all!"

"Before I embark on that journey, I need to put my earthly affairs in order. Here, Captain, are a few papers which I would like to bring to your attention." He produced several promissory notes previously signed by Richemonte, the sight of which only added fuel to the captain's rising anger.

"Since the devil is on his way, he might gather these up as well!" the captain said through clenched teeth, resisting the urge to look at the notes.

"Very well," said the baron. "When they've been redeemed and the amount is paid in full, he can take them any time he pleases."

"Dammit! Can't you wait until I have the means? It's impossible for me to repay you now! You called me your friend. Is it your intention to press me for payment at a time when it's least convenient?"

"Our views in regards to the current circumstances are certainly different. It seems convenient to me to bring our affairs in order today. Why should I wait, since I know you don't have the means to repay the debt? In regards to our monetary relationship, it's fundamental to remember that commitments between friends rate higher than other relationships. I have already been far too lenient with you, my dear Richemonte."

"I can't pay you!" Richemonte said curtly.

"Then you know the consequences!"

"Would you press me that far?"

"Oh, I certainly would!"

"Really?" Visibly shaken, Richemonte paced back and forth. Suddenly he stopped, and with a quivering voice tried to address the issue.

The baron interrupted him by placing his hand on his shoulder. "My dear captain," he replied in a measured tone, "you know I love your sister. I am no longer a young man. I can tell you that an older man's love is totally different when compared to a young man's love. Margot is beautiful. Had I been able to convince her to marry me, it would have been worth it, considering how much this has cost me on your account. The promise of success was the only reason I considered destroying the notes. Since that condition has not been met, I see no reason to honor our agreement. That's all I need to say to vindicate myself, were it ever necessary to justify my actions."

Richemonte, looking stiff and uncomfortable, remained silent, still avoiding Reillac's face. He cast a weary, hopeless glance at the row of houses across the street. After a lengthy pause, he broke the silence. "Do we have to give up all hope?"

"Every one."

"Why every one?"

"Because she's in love with him."

"That German? Dammit! Why did it have to be him? Those two lovers think they have everything in place, but I'm not finished with them yet. I still intend to speak my mind."

"You?" laughed the baron. "What could you possibly say now?"

"Me? *Pah!* Am I not her brother?"

"I'm not disagreeing with you, Captain. Has a will or an order of guardianship been established? No. Even if you were entitled to exert a certain amount of influence over your sister's future, you certainly would not be the man to force the outcome."

"What makes you say that?"

"No one had to tell me. I saw it for myself. The minute you walked out onto the front steps, I could see it on your face—they had shown you the door."

"Yes! They dared to throw me out!"

"Really? So Captain Richemonte takes to the road in fear of the Germans!"

"Shut up!" Richemonte growled. "You too would have met the same fate if you had run into that damned Field Marshal 'Forward'."

"Yes, when Marshal 'Forward' advances, the captain hastily retreats. What do you call that? I call it cowardly."

"Then you're a coward as well!" Richemonte defended himself, visibly offended. "You're the one who has already sidestepped the marshal."

"You can't fault me on that one. Your position as brother is totally different to my position as an outsider. The inference, that you are a coward, might not suit your opinion of yourself, yet there's truth in it."

"In what way? I'd like to know how you've come to this conclusion!"

"How do you propose to eliminate the German? Let me remind you that it was you who evaded the duel with him."

"Dammit! Tell me, Baron, can I or can I not conduct myself in fencing and in the use of firearms?"

"Well, I understood you to be an expert in fencing, and a marksman with the pistol. I wondered why you avoided the..."

"If I avoided the duel, there certainly was another reason. The adjutant general made it clear that none of our officers were to engage the Prussian officers in any sort of entanglements, least of all duels of honor. The consequence of such an action would have resulted in an immediate investigation, and would likely have followed with a dismissal. Are you satisfied?"

"Would the duel have come to the attention of the general's staff?"

The captain shrugged his shoulders. "Do you think the Germans would have remained quiet if one of their officers had been killed by a Frenchman? I would have been dishonorably discharged."

"It would seem that's still your fate."

"Why do you say that?"

"If your debts are made public, they still have no choice but to dismiss you."

"*Pah!* You wouldn't dare approach my regimental commander with your demands of repayment and exposure."

"Dare? Expose? Who's talking about going through the motions of exposure? All I have to do is send for the bailiff, who will bring you to the debtor's prison. That would suffice. As soon as your superiors become aware of your plight, it will become impossible for you to stay in the army."

"Then you will have to contend with an enemy, one you can't easily dismiss."

"An enemy? Who might that be?" laughed the Baron.

"Me, of course!" Richemonte exclaimed self-importantly.

"You? I don't have to worry about you in the least, especially when you're confined behind bars. It gives me little pleasure, though, to have to treat you this way. I would much rather tackle the problem by finding a way around it."

This last remark at least seemed to give the captain a glimmer of hope. Was the baron suggesting a way around their setback? "Then let's find one."

"While you were occupied with your mother and sweet sister," the baron considered, "I was here by myself contemplating a remedy to our present problem."

"Well? Have you found a way out?"

"Perhaps."

"Then tell me!"

"We have to be careful. Are you of the opinion that, had a duel occurred with the German, you would have prevailed and killed him?"

"Without a doubt!"

"I believe you. I've seen you fight. If only there had been an opportunity."

"Are you suggesting I challenge him now?" Albin asked. "It's highly unlikely."

"I was thinking of something else," the baron replied slowly and deliberately. "Isn't it possible he could die by some other means?"

The captain's face turned red. He faced the window and stared out of it for some time, not uttering a word. At last, he turned back to face the baron and approached him. "Are you implying I... should approach him while his back is turned and then attack him?"

The baron smiled at him with an air of superiority, shrugging his shoulders. "I'm not implying anything," he continued. "I'm only suggesting that the road to your demise is a near certainty. That said, should we learn the lieutenant had suddenly died, I would be prepared to tear up half the notes. The rest would follow suit once I was betrothed to your sister."

The captain's brows furrowed and his moustache lifted awkwardly, as if he'd meant to gnash his teeth. It was a look he would repeat often later in life. With his face contorted into this menacing grimace, he spoke in a subdued, barely audible voice. "Your meaning is very clear, although you fail to say the obvious."

"I think we understand each other!"

Richemonte gripped the baron's arm and looked at him with resolve. "Do I have your word?" he asked.

"Of course!"

"Are you certain we will be successful in persuading my sister should this Löwenklau die?"

"Completely certain."

"Then it's settled," Richemonte said. "The man is clearly a German, but foremost my enemy. It is time we did away with him."

"How do you plan to accomplish this?"

"Nothing could be simpler. He will naturally spend the evening with Margot, and go home late at night."

"Most likely."

"The way I see it, he'll head for home but never arrive. The streets are not safe at night these days and anything can happen."

The baron nodded his head thoughtfully, but his malice was clear. He wasn't sure how this would end, though one thing was certain: while the captain was only indebted to him now, by the end of this affair he would be totally under his control.

"I'm satisfied you will do your best," the baron said. "Let me make one suggestion."

"Go ahead. I'm listening."

"There are situations when it's advisable to conceal one's appearance."

"*Pah!*" the captain said dismissively. "Do you think me a novice? I know perfectly well how to conduct myself."

"Well then, we are in agreement."

"I certainly hope so."

"When can I expect results?"

"Let's meet at the coffeehouse. You can expect me to arrive later tonight. I hope to count on you for my alibi. Should it become necessary, it will deflect any embarrassing or accusatory questions which may arise out of this business."

"I remain at your service and hope only that our plan comes to a successful conclusion. *Adieu*, Captain!"

"Farewell, Baron!"

The baron left. He was convinced the captain would fulfill his side of the bargain, through which they would both have a way of getting their personal revenge.

Richemonte remained in his room, pacing back and forth, deep in thought. He finally went into an adjoining room, which he usually reserved for business dealings. The walls were decorated with various weapons he had amassed over the years. He selected a particular pistol and examined it.

This is the best one I have, he thought. *It has yet to fail me. Should I use it? Hmm... it does make a lot of noise. I'd rather avoid drawing too much attention. No, not this one.*

He replaced it, selecting a small caliber rifle. *This one is practical and makes very little noise. However, it's not that dependable. No, I have to be sure he won't get away.*

He replaced this one as well and considered further. At last, he spotted the weapon for just such an occasion. *A Venetian dagger, often used by bandits. A dangerous weapon! One strike and the tip breaks off, becoming embedded in the victim's chest. It would take a skillful surgeon to remove the culprit, if there was enough time. One swift strike and the result would be lethal. This is the one!*

⚜

While Richemonte contemplated the best way to kill his nemesis, Löwenklau was next door with Margot, unaware of the looming danger. She stood by him at the window while the marshal occupied himself in entertaining Madame with his exploits. Always the charmer with the ladies, he certainly fit the bill today. The three were delighted, thoroughly enjoying his stories. Blücher ended his reminiscing with an admiring glance at Margot.

"Take a look at those two, Madame. There they stand, holding each other as though an army were poised to tear them apart. Such is love, and so are those who fall in love." Facing Margot, he quipped, "Don't be embarrassed Mademoiselle. I was once young myself. Now I've turned into an old raccoon that no one cares about."

Margot looked at him. "Excellency, are you implying only the young are able to find love?" she replied cheekily.

"That's exactly what I mean, my child!"

"Excellency, you could be mistaken."

"Do you really think so? Can you prove your point?"

"Of course. It's common knowledge there are ladies who desire to associate with older men. I'm familiar with a few women who share this ideal."

"Indeed," he nodded thoughtfully. "I once spoke to a professor who's quite a famous psychologist. He was knowledgeable about such things and prided himself in delving into people's innermost thoughts. He claimed that young ladies, particularly those in their teenage years, dreamed of men who had already attained their gray hairs. Of course, they change their minds when they fall prey to youthful, cunning suitors. One has to be prepared at all times to step up and snatch the chestnuts out of the fire. Just as I did for your lieutenant."

"So, I'm a chestnut?" laughed Margot.

"Yes! Well... a chestnut to sink your teeth into. I want to... I would like to... Hmm, *zounds*! I'd certainly like to sample this one."

"Excellency, you don't look like the sampling kind!"

"You think not," he replied coyly. "Well, let me prove you wrong. We Germans like to say a laborer is worth his wages. I, on the other hand, have labored tirelessly to bring you two together. It only seems fitting I should receive some compensation. What do you think I would like?"

Margot blushed. She guessed what he had in mind.

"The girl's face is red as a ripe beet!" he persisted. "She knows what my appetite longs for. Is there any hope for its fulfillment?"

"His Excellency hasn't stated his wish," she said, still smiling.

"Very well then. Just one kiss, for all my hard work!"

A mischievous grin spread across her face. "A kiss, from my betrothed?" she teased.

"What! From him? Of course not! What use do I have for another moustache? No, one from you, Mademoiselle! I am certainly no dashing lieutenant who can turn a lady's head, but perhaps you could give me a grandfatherly kiss."

"Perhaps," she replied. "We should first get the lieutenant's permission."

"From him?" Blücher asked in mock protest. "The thought never occurred to me. I managed to conquer Paris and the rest of France without the lieutenant's permission. Why should I now seek him concerning those luscious, beckoning lips? We're wasting time, my dear. Don't worry about him. Now, let me see those luscious lips and I might leave something for him when I'm done." Blücher stood up and came toward Margot.

Blushing deeply, she took two steps toward him. "Excellency," she said. "a kiss from you is the highest honor for a lady. In this regard, I am willing..."

"*Papperlappap!*[6.1] First, I'll give you a formal kiss and then we will see about the rest." He gingerly walked up to her like a servant in the presence of King Louis XIV, placing a soft kiss on her cheek. "So," he said, "that was the honorable field marshal at your service. Now it's Gebhard Leberecht Blücher's turn. He wants to know if he is also worthy of a kiss. What do you say, Margotchen?"

"Oh! He's so deserving, he can get two for the price of one!" She unexpectedly grabbed his face, pulled him forward, and kissed him with fervor, fully on the lips; once, twice, three times in quick succession.

"My word!" he exclaimed. "That was a delicacy I won't soon forget." His eyes glistened with pleasure, filling with sentiment for the young couple. He was still holding her hands. "Did that really come from your heart, you sweet little witch?" he asked.

"Yes, Excellency."

"You've given an old man something to remember for a long time. I won't forget you and when it comes time for you to baptize your first little one, I hope you'll give me the honor of being the godfather. When the old Blücher gives his word, our God takes notice and blesses you in special ways. Even though, being the poor devil I am, all I can really offer is my 'yes' and 'amen'. Well, my business here seems to have come to an end and I have to attend to other matters, which unfortunately won't end in a kiss. Are you ready, my son? It's time we left."

It would have been inappropriate for Löwenklau to remain behind without Blücher, seeing as they had accompanied each other. Even still, he would have preferred to stay with his betrothed.

"If His Excellency allows it," he said, "I'll accompany him. I too have unfinished business to attend to."

"Well, my boy, be quick about your goodbye. Our little visit here is over and I trust you'll resume what you didn't finish next time."

Before they parted, Löwenklau promised Margot he would return in the evening. He bid his farewell to the ladies, who expressed their honor to have hosted the famous field marshal.

The two officers exited the foyer and were about to walk down the steps to street level when the door to the adjoining suite opened. Captain

Richemonte simultaneously appeared from his doorway, also on the verge of leaving, recoiling at the sight of them. For the briefest moment, the captain failed to keep his emotions in check, his face revealing his hatred for the Germans.

"Did you catch the look in the Frenchman's eyes?" Blücher asked his companion once they were out of earshot.

"Yes, Excellency."

"What did you notice?"

"Nothing in particular. He doesn't concern me."

"Don't take it so lightly!" warned Blücher.

"He can't do anything to me."

"Not in an open and honorable sense. However, I didn't like the expression on his face. Do you know what I read in his eyes?"

"Hatred, naturally."

"Hatred and treachery. Mark my words and see you don't underestimate him, my son. This man is a scoundrel and perhaps much worse. He's a menace. It may as well be written on his forehead."

"His Excellency may be right," Löwenklau replied thoughtfully, now taking the encounter more seriously. "Richemonte owes Reillac considerable sums, with the baron consenting to dismiss the debt should he win Margot's hand. This has been their plan all along, and I don't see them changing it. In fact, Richemonte may become more desperate. The baron was even prepared to pay him a fixed amount in cash, though I doubt he would have ever received it."

"Well then, continue with your suppositions. I want to see if that mind of yours is up to figuring this out."

"The baron is pressuring him with those promissory notes. If this information becomes public knowledge, the captain's military career will be at an end and he will have to resign his commission. He will risk everything to avoid such a fate."

"What would be the best way to accomplish this?"

"If Richemonte removed his biggest obstacle, namely myself!"

"Yes, and only then!" Blücher said. "My boy, you're smarter than you look. The captain's eyes leered like a predator's. His whole countenance hinted at an imminent attack. I'm convinced he's up to something. Look after yourself! You are, no doubt, planning to visit your sweetheart later?"

"Yes."

"Make sure you have a weapon with you. I wish you had a *cuirass*."[6.2]

"Why, Excellency?"

"Because a *cuirass* can deflect the first thrust of a weapon. I have a hunch the scoundrel will act maliciously and probably employ a sharp weapon. Promise me you'll prepare yourself and not treat this carelessly."

"I give you my word, Excellency."

"Fine. It would be a shame for you and that wonderful Margot if she suddenly became a widow before her wedding day. I'd like nothing better than to choke the captain until he squeaks. Well, here we are," he said as they stopped in front of his house. "One more thing, my boy!"

"Does his Excellency have an order?"

"An order? Far from it! I just want to know if you're mad at me regarding Margot... damn, what was her last name? Well, whatever it is, you're going to marry her, not I. Anyway, what I wanted to ask you is if you were offended when I kissed your girl?"

"Offended? What does His Excellency think of me? We were both of the same opinion, that it's a great honor for a lady..."

"That's fine, but she's still a spirited little witch! I would have liked to have had her myself, but don't get all worked up over it. At first these angels are like smooth chocolate. Next, they cling like Arabic gum[6.3], then turn into boot polish; bitter and black, so you can commiserate. I hope your girl's an exception. She has a tasty little mouth, that's for sure. Have you already kissed her, my boy? Be honest with me!"

"Of course I have, Excellency."

"Good, then I haven't stolen the first kiss. When did you first kiss her?"

"When I spoke of my love for her," laughed Löwenklau.

"When you declared your love for her," Blücher mused. "Yes, they do tend to get close and hold on tight. They squawk like pigeons. Heavens! If only I weren't such an old goat! Tell me, how did you actually pull it off? What did you tell her, and what did she say?"

"With his Excellency's permission, I'll keep that to myself."

"Hang it all! My son, I can't fault you there. I wouldn't have advised anyone to ask me such personal questions either, especially how I got caught.[6.4] Well, it remains the way we planned. I'll have the honor of becoming the godfather of your firstborn. Make sure there'll be some good wine and a decent pipe for me. Farewell!"

As they parted company, Löwenklau walked to his residence, inwardly smiling over Blücher's inquisitive manner about the way he had declared his love for Margot. He mentally replayed the conversation, taking Blücher's warning to heart. He thought about the captain's face, and had to conclude it contained a menacing, even bloodthirsty look.

The city populace was still reeling from the occupation. The daily reports of minor skirmishes and protests indicated how vulnerable soldiers were to attack. He sent his servant on an errand to a fellow officer, who procured a *cuirass* suitable to repel an attack. The officer smiled at the request, but granted him the favor.

After a while, Löwenklau left his residence again, this time dressed in civilian clothing. His protection consisted of a concealed pistol and the aforementioned breastplate. His precautions also included a change in route, ensuring he approached Margot's house from a different direction.

When he arrived, a lamp burned in the foyer, casting light in the direction of the captain's residence. Noticing the suite's front door slightly ajar, an eerie feeling came over him as though someone inside was watching him. He had the presence of mind not to look closer, for in doing so he would have let the watcher know he had become suspicious.

He rang the bell and was readily admitted. Margot rushed to meet him with a lingering kiss. Feeling the unyielding metal of the breastplate under his coat, she looked up at him with surprise and concern, with her hand resting on his chest.

"What is that, Hugo?"

"Nothing much, my dearest," he replied calmly. "Just a *cuirass*."

"A breastplate? What do you need that for?"

"Don't worry, my love. I picked it up for a friend who's stationed with the Hussars. It was too cumbersome to carry, so I just wore it under my coat."

Not intending to alarm Margot, his words succeeded in removing any hint of concern. He didn't take into account the truth that a woman could often be more intuitive than a man. She could quickly grasp the unspoken, the unseen, something a man only could arrive at after much deliberation. Löwenklau removed his outer coat, the *cuirass*, and his hat while he walked into the drawing room. As he became involved in an animated discussion with her mother, Margot stole the opportunity to speak to her maid.

"Is my brother home?"

"He was there a few minutes ago," the maid said, "but I think he just left."

"Perhaps it was someone else. Go to his suite and check."

The maid was employed to keep house, including the captain's residence. Supplied with a key, she had been instructed only to clean when he was absent. She went next door, returning shortly with the news her brother was indeed absent.

The captain had waited for Löwenklau's arrival, satisfying himself that he would remain with the ladies for a while. Richemonte made up his mind to kill Löwenklau away from the house. He left quietly and went to one of the nearby coffeehouses, intending to spend some time there while waiting for his quarry.

Margot took the key from the maid and, after retrieving a light, went into her stepbrother's suite. Allowing the maid to accompany her, she went directly to Albin's study. She took a cursory glance at the familiar wall, the one which displayed his weapons collection. She spotted an empty nail, but couldn't remember which weapon had hung there.

"Do you also dust these weapons?" she asked the maid.

"Yes."

"Do you know them all?"

"I think so. I have often handled them."

"Think back, and see if you can remember which one hung on this nail."

The maid was surprised at Margot's sudden interest in the weapons, but did as instructed. "I'm not totally certain, Mademoiselle," she replied after a brief moment, still unsure. "But wait! Here are the rifles and pistols, and over there the sabers and knives, and here, ah!... now I recall. There was a unique dagger!"

"A dagger?"

"Yes. The dagger had a black wooden handle and a blade of translucent glass. I have often wondered why one would make a blade out of glass. It could break so easily."

"That's right, I remember now. It's a Venetian dagger. We should leave."

Margot understood perfectly why the blade was made entirely out of glass. As soon as the tip struck a bone, it would break, with the pieces lodging in the wound. Why would her brother have taken this dagger with him today? No sooner had she formed the thought than the answer materialized. She knew he had little regard for others. He was an egotist who wouldn't spare a human life if it stood between him and his objectives. His chief interest centered on his own wellbeing. He had already demonstrated his heartless nature toward Margot when he had conspired with the baron against her.

When Margot returned to her own place, she looked for any sign of anxiety in Hugo's face. She couldn't find a trace of worry anywhere. In fact, his laughter and demeanor suggested he was oblivious to any danger. *Am I the only one to suspect something untoward might occur?* she thought. *Should I warn him and ruin a perfectly good evening? Should I accuse my brother, who is already against my marriage to Hugo, with an act of unproven vengeance? Should I believe Hugo really carries the breastplate for a friend? Does he perhaps have a reason to suspect treachery? Does Hugo choose not to reveal his thoughts for fear of alarming me?*

These questions plagued her mind as she attempted to appear calm and participate in the conversation. Then a thought struck Margot. *If Hugo suspects something sinister, he will have prepared himself accordingly, possibly even to the point of concealing a weapon.*

When the opportunity presented itself, she left the drawing room and went to the foyer. After finding his overcoat, she deftly went through the pockets... and found them empty. Margot barely felt the first pangs of relief when she was struck with another thought. *If he procured a weapon to defend himself, he would probably carry it somewhere accessible, not in the deep pockets of his overcoat.*

Having left the foyer, Margot stepped back into the drawing room and rejoined the others. Leaning up against his shoulder, she absentmindedly slid her fingers down his chest... there it was, in his vest pocket! She felt a weapon, likely a pistol. Margot realized he too was being cautious, and wanted to speak to him about her concerns.

"What do you have there, my dearest?"

Hugo suddenly became aware of her interest. "Oh, that! That's my pistol," he said evenly, trying to conceal his uneasiness.

"A pistol? Why do you carry a pistol?"

"Out of habit mostly. You should know our officers are accustomed to carrying weapons when out of uniform, especially when we're in a city whose occupants aren't always happy to see us."

"Are you just being careful, or are you concerned about something else?"

"Not so much the latter. But we're in a precarious position in Paris. Some of the inhabitants don't much care for us, as we witnessed last night. It's prudent to be careful my love. That's all."

"Are you thinking of a particular person?"

"No, Margot," he replied. It took some effort on his part to come across as being forthright. He succeeded for the most part in convincing her why he had armed himself with a weapon.

"Do you have a personal enemy, one whom you don't trust?" she asked apprehensively.

"I don't think so."

"Are you sure about the *cuirass*?"

"Of course, my love."

"A *cuirass*?" asked her mother. "What about a *cuirass*?"

"Hugo was carrying a breastplate when he arrived," Margot replied. "He put it aside. It's hanging in the foyer, Mama."

"Why the precaution?" she asked, surprised and concerned at the same time. "Is there an imminent danger?"

"I'm not aware of any specific danger," he said, "other than the one that affects all Prussians. It is ambiguous at best. I carried the *cuirass* by coincidence and the pistol in my pocket is from my last outing. There's nothing to be concerned about."

Madame Richemonte felt reassured, but Margot was far from completely satisfied. She decided to keep quiet. She mentally prepared herself for later, though. She possessed a courageous nature and was ready to act on his behalf if necessary. Out of her concern for Hugo, she called her maid, instructing her to take her hat and overcoat to the porter. She left instructions that she might go out later. Only then did she find the time to relax, allowing herself to become absorbed in the present discussion.

It was exactly as the baron and captain predicted. The two lovers, having much to discuss and plan, took a long time before parting company. Löwen-klau started his journey home close to midnight. He took his leave from her mother, who had drawn closer to him in these last few hours. As he put on his *cuirass* and donned his overcoat, he was surprised to find Margot illuminating the way down the staircase, which was customarily the maid's job. They hugged and gave each other a kiss.

"May I come again tomorrow, my love?" he teased.

"Of course, Hugo," she said. "I'll be longingly waiting for you. So please, don't tarry. But I have one more request."

"What is it, my love?"

"Please be careful tonight. I'm concerned for your safety."

Grateful for her concern, he pressed her closer to his body. "Your anxiety stems from the fact that you will miss me, dear Margot," he whispered into her ear. "Your concern reminds me that you find me special."

"No! There is a much stronger reason why I'm concerned, Hugo."

"What is it?"

"I have a feeling you're in danger."

"Don't be alarmed. The streets are fairly quiet. A realistic danger could only come from a personal attack, and I'm not aware of any such peril. Besides, we're not living in Italy and these aren't the middle ages. Assassinations are hardly common."

She shuddered at the thought. Richemonte possessed an Italian dagger.

"Oh, my love," she whispered, "I can't help feeling there is someone that you have to watch out for."

"Who could that be?"

"My... brother."

He felt troubled at the remark. She too had become suspicious. That's why she had shown so much interest in his *cuirass*. She was clearly restless and, now that he listened for it, he detected a slight tremor in her voice.

"Your brother?" he replied. "He comes across as a bramarbas,[6.5] but he's really a coward inside. He won't do anything."

"A coward? No, he has never been cowardly. Once he has made up his mind, he's capable of anything. It's sad to have to speak of your own brother in such a light, but I'm concerned for you. He may not be an assassin, but I can see him inciting others to carry out his purposes."

"In any event, I know how to defend myself, my love. Don't worry. Have a good night's sleep, and dream about me."

Löwenklau took what he supposed was his leave for the night and left the house. Although it was dark, the light from the stars was adequate enough to distinguish objects at a distance. He tightened the belt on his overcoat so it wouldn't be a hindrance to him in case of an attack. He drew his pistol and cocked the hammer, preparing himself just in case. He continued walking, maintaining a slow pace so he could distinguish sounds of being followed.

He would have preferred to walk down the center of the street, though this would have revealed to an enemy that he was prepared. If he remained on the sidewalk, then at least the houses provided a measure of protection. Walking in this way, he was diligent and on guard, aware of his surroundings. The Prussian made it through the first street, retracing his earlier steps. He was halfway down the next street, when he detected... no... rather, he felt a presence behind him. There, in the shadows, he spotted a dark shape that seemed to be keeping pace with him.

There he is, thought Löwenklau. *Just you wait, you miserable coward. I know how to deal with the likes of you.*

Walking slowly, he turned his body around, facing backward, so he could keep a sharp eye on the assailant, who followed him noiselessly.

CHAPTER SEVEN
A Failed Scheme

As soon as Hugo left, Margot hurried down to the porter's room, collecting her hat and shawl.

"Mademoiselle, where are you going at this late hour?" the porter called out to her.

"Not far, Francois. Just around the corner."

"All alone? Reports of uprisings and civil unrest have been everywhere. Allow me to accompany you."

"I'm grateful for your offer, but I have to go alone. There's something I must attend to."

"I understand," the porter replied knowingly. "You want to follow the gentleman."

"No! You're mistaken Francois," she countered. "No decent lady would follow a man to spy on him. Let me through the gate without making a sound. I don't want anyone to know I've left the house."

Reluctantly, he obeyed her wish, allowing her to slip out. She stood near the gate, remaining motionless to become accustomed to the street sounds.

Löwenklau had walked a mere twenty or thirty paces when he stopped. He adjusted his overcoat and pulled something out of his pocket. While Margot scanned the dark street, it seemed her concern for him heightened her awareness. In the meantime, almost imperceptibly, a dark shadow drifted from a doorway and, with almost noiseless steps, crossed the street and followed her betrothed.

That had to be the captain. Her stomach muscles contracted, whether out of fear for her lover or shame that her stepbrother was capable of such an act, she couldn't tell. Margot, having the foresight not to wear her walking boots, wore her house shoes, which had a soft sole that allowed her to step noiselessly.

She followed the two men deftly down her street, and then onto a side street. She could barely hear Hugo's footsteps. However, when they ceased for a brief moment, she pondered. *Has he noticed something? Maybe he's just being careful.*

A few seconds later, he resumed his walk, though it had a different tone now. She continued to listen even though she couldn't understand how it had changed. Then it struck her. *Ah! He's being clever. He's walking backward so he can watch his adversary.*

Forging ahead, Margot spotted the secretive pursuer, who was so absorbed in following Löwenklau that he failed to notice his own escort. Margot wasn't wrong; it was her brother.

❧❧❧

The captain had left the cafe before midnight and was waiting near the gate across the street. He watched the shadows of the people as they played against the curtains of his mother's residence. Filled with rage, Richemonte imagined how much his adversary was enjoying his sister's caresses. Margot was destined to be his saving grace, betrothed to the baron so that he could finally be rid of his financial woes.

"This is the last time you'll be with her," he grumbled. "This dagger will take care of you nicely, leaving my plans unobstructed." He removed the dagger from his pocket and probed the tip with his finger. "Sharp like a needle," he said to himself. *Once it's buried in the flesh, a quick jerk and it'll break, ensuring a painful and unavoidable death. If only the bastard was in front of me now.*

He had to be patient. He continued watching the shadows until he saw the Prussian get ready to depart. After a while, he saw Löwenklau step through the gate and close it behind him.

"It won't open for you again!" he hissed. "The gates of hell will swallow you up first." He would have preferred to yell it out loud to alleviate the rage in his heart. Instead, he was forced to control himself and stay quiet so as not to give himself away. Had it been daylight, one could have seen the bloodthirsty leer in his eyes and the unsightly baring of his teeth, both so characteristic of his outbursts.

He tightened his grip on the dagger and started to follow his quarry, stopping after a few paces. "Dammit!" he cursed. His soles were squeaking on the pavement, making him easy to detect. *Why didn't I think of that before, when I had the time?* Not seeing any other choice, he reached down and removed the boots. *But should I carry them with me? No, they'd be too cumbersome. I'll leave them here at the gate. It's dark enough, but I should find a better place. If someone finds them, it could come back to haunt me. I better be careful and take them with me. If I carry them in my left hand, I'll still have enough mobility to deliver a good thrust.*

He picked up the boots with his left hand and stole across the street, following the lieutenant at a safe distance. In the darkness, he was still able to distinguish his adversary's silhouette.

I'm going to go for his heart, he thought to himself. *Then he'll collapse without making a sound. I'll go through his pockets and remove his billfold and watch. When the police find him, they'll think it was a robbery, instead of murder.*

The captain had covered half of the next street when he noticed Löwenklau stopped walking. He stopped in his tracks. Richemonte had been too preoccupied with greed and on carrying out his plan to notice the subtle change in the tone of Löwenklau's footfall. The city's lack of street lighting allowed Richemonte to close the distance undetected. Not wanting to attack Löwenklau on his own street, he decided to wait for the next one.

The captain quickened his pace and closed the gap to maybe three or four paces. Taking a calculated leap, Richemonte was about to thrust his dagger when he realized Löwenklau was not only alert, but facing him.

"Who's there?" the lieutenant shouted loudly. "What do you want?"

The captain, though surprised, composed himself and decided to press on. He assumed the Prussian to be without a weapon and not particularly skilled in hand-to-hand combat. Furthermore, he surmised he would not be recognized in the dark. What would it matter even if he was? The information would stay buried with the dead man.

"You bastard!" With this short snap, the captain lunged at Löwenklau. The thrust was well-placed, but to the captain's horror reverberated back at him with an unyielding metallic clang. The dagger deflected into Löwenklau's arm.

The lieutenant didn't have to think twice and grabbed the attacker by his wrist. "I'm not going to kill you," he shouted, "but I do want a look at your face."

He pulled out his gun and fired off a shot close to his attacker's face. The blast produced a blinding flash, revealing the surprised face of Captain Richemonte.

"Well, well, the captain! Just as I surmised. Back off, or I'll fire my second shot, and it won't fail to hit its mark!" With these words, Löwenklau pushed the half-blinded assailant away from him, leaving him to stagger away. He was about to turn and continue on his way when two arms lovingly embraced him. For a moment, he thought he'd have to contend with a second enemy.

"Oh my God!" cried out the familiar voice. "Hugo, are you all right? Are you injured?"

"Margot?!" he called out in surprise. "What are you doing here?"

She cuddled up to him. "I saw him stalking after you and I was afraid... I had to follow."

"You saw that? You followed me secretly?"

"Yes. I saw him lurking across the street!"

"My love, that was heroic of you!" Hugo said, pressing her closer. "You've already surpassed my expectations. Do you know who attacked me?"

70

"Yes," she stammered. "The captain." She didn't offer 'my brother,' too ashamed to speak the words. Her concern for her betrothed hadn't diminished, and she asked him for the second time. "Did he stab you, Hugo?"

"He tried, but failed in the attempt." Löwenklau stepped on something lying in the street and looked down. "What's this?"

He bent down and found a pair of leather boots. Richemonte's boots had slipped from his grasp during the struggle. "Ah! His boots!" the Prussian laughed. "This is comical. I'll have to find a way to send them back to him with my compliments."

He took Margot's arm then, dropping the sarcasm. "My love, we have to leave. People will have heard the shot. Look, some are already opening their windows. We should move on." Together, they started to retrace their way back to her place.

"Do you want to go back to my house, Hugo?"

"Yes. You shouldn't walk home alone!"

"I'll be fine," she assured him. "I don't want you to come back in case he attacks you again."

"I don't think he will." The lieutenant grinned confidently. "He took off like a rabbit. If there is a second attempt, then I will shoot, even if he is your brother. We should go Margot, so we're not bothered by onlookers. I'd be forced to explain the incident, and I have no desire to come forward as a complainant against your brother. He's not worth the effort."

"My dearest, are you prepared to forgive him?"

"Yes, but I do want a word with him."

"Don't do it. He's still a dangerous man!"

"Don't worry. I'll make sure there aren't any reprisals."

Some of those who opened their windows expected to see more action. Others were annoyed at being awakened by what looked like a gun-toting boor just out for some fun. Löwenklau placed his right hand on Margot's shoulder and drew her left arm around his waist. They walked quietly together, grateful for having escaped the deadly encounter.

Margot felt something warm and wet on her hand. "My God!" she cried. "You've been wounded! Show me your hand, Hugo."

He obliged and she examined his arm. "You're bleeding from the upper arm!"

Although the breastplate hindered any serious injury, the tip of the dagger had penetrated the tunic, leaving a wound behind. He hadn't felt anything since the attack.

"Hugo, hurry! I need to examine it more thoroughly," she said, her voice tinged with alarm. "I hope it's not serious."

"No, not at all," he said calmly. "The blade only deflected off my arm. I think it's minor."

"It's a good thing you wore the breastplate. He could have killed you."

Trying to contain her fear, she quickened her pace. They arrived at her house, and she signaled the porter to open the door. Instead of opening the gate from his room, Francois came himself.

"Has anyone entered since I left?" she asked him.

"Yes," Francois replied haltingly.

"Who was it?"

"Mademoiselle, I'm not supposed to disclose that."

"Who forbade you to tell me?"

"The same person."

"My brother?"

"Ah, you already know! Well then, I won't reveal anything if I tell you it was he."

"Is he at home?"

"No. The captain seemed to be in a hurry."

"Did he leave already?" she pressed.

"Yes," the porter said. "When he first showed up, I thought it was you, Mademoiselle. Since I like to serve you personally, I went outside. That's when I recognized the captain."

"What did he say?"

"He gave me five francs and warned me not to tell anyone he'd been at home. He must have had a little adventure."

"How do you know?"

"Well, I was quite surprised to notice that... that..."

"What? Please continue!"

"I'm not sure if I can tell you, Mademoiselle. He warned me not to say a word."

"I would think you would make an exception for his sister."

"True," he admitted. "The light was poor, but it looked like he wasn't wearing his boots. He was standing in his socks! I couldn't believe my eyes, but as he mounted the steps, I saw it was no mistake. Something must have happened."

"Did he spend much time in his suite?"

"No. Perhaps just a minute, long enough to put on a pair of boots."

"And then?"

"He came downstairs in his new boots and nodded to me, leaving the house in a hurry."

"Which way did he go?"

"To the right. I found the whole thing rather puzzling. I paid attention to his footfall, even though he tried to walk quietly. I heard him turn to the right."

"I appreciate your candor. Please keep this to yourself."

"Mademoiselle, you know of my devotion to you," he said. "If you were not his sister, I wouldn't have mentioned a thing. A porter has to be discreet. You can depend on me!"

"We hope so," Löwenklau said. "Here's a little something for your discretion." He reached into his pocket and gave the porter a gold piece.

When Francois saw the shining metal coin, he bowed deeply. "You are very generous, Monsieur," he replied. "Such a reward is seldom seen. You can trust me implicitly."

The porter accompanied them with an unusual formality. He was convinced the young couple had also experienced something unusual. The Prussian officer had just left a short time before, and Mademoiselle had secretly followed him. When they entered the upstairs foyer, Francois returned to his own room and examined the gold piece.

Sapperlot! he mused to himself. *At first I thought it was a twenty franc piece, but now I see I've been rewarded with at least forty francs! This is grand, extraordinarily grand. One doesn't make such a generous gift to a porter unless it's because a lady is present. Perhaps this German officer is taking up the conquest of Mademoiselle Margot, in the same way his fellow countrymen have forged ahead in France. Well, the way I see it, he's a good man and she's an exceptional lady. They suit each other perfectly, even though I would've liked to see her with a French gentleman.*

He admired the gold piece for a little longer, then secured it in a secret compartment and continued his internal monologue. *He left, and she followed him secretly. Something out of the ordinary must have occurred. It seems likely their adventure was somehow connected with that of the captain. Well, I suppose it shouldn't concern me.* Fortunately, he failed to notice Löwenklau had been wounded, or his musings would have continued.

Meanwhile, the two lovers were assembled before Madame Richemonte. Margot was quietly telling her about their harrowing experience.

"Dear God, could it really be true?" the distraught mother said. "Could my own son be capable of such an atrocity, even murder? How could he succumb to this cowardly act, attacking Hugo in the dark? And you, Margot, you placed yourself in great danger."

Margot occupied herself by bringing in water and linen strips. She prepared makeshift bandages, all the while finding herself still participating in the conversation. She accepted her mother's gentle reproach. "Really?" she replied. "You find it difficult to accept that Albin is capable of such an act?"

Madame Richemonte replied in tears. "Unfortunately, I should confess I've often thought him capable of such a crime. He who mistreats members of his own family is often capable of removing any obstacle from his path, particularly those who are in his way. Still, I find it difficult to believe he was involved."

"Then look at his boots. They're over there."

"Perhaps they belong to another man."

"No," she insisted. "The porter noticed him come home in his socks."

"It may be a coincidence," Madame said. "Though I can't explain how a captain of the guard could return home without his boots."

"Then I'll call for the maid. She's acquainted with his personal things and will certainly be able to identify his boots."

"No, no! The maid shouldn't become involved in this. Margot, hurry up. Don't you see the lieutenant is losing more blood?"

"Dear God, yes! I have to clean it first and then apply a bandage. Come here, my dear Hugo. I'm worried the wound is more serious than we thought. I will put on a temporary bandage and send for a doctor."

"Don't worry, my dear Margot," Löwenklau replied with a good-natured smile. "It's probably nothing more than a small cut. It shouldn't present much of a problem."

"Then please remove your shirt. Mama will allow you to undress."

Madame Richemonte left the room as he removed his upper clothing. He removed the *cuirass* and the jacket; its sleeve was as bloody as the shirtsleeve. They could distinguish the mark where the dagger's tip had impaled on the polished metal. Without its protection, the dagger would have surely penetrated to the heart. Margot rolled up the sleeve. She became pale out of concern for him, yet her hands didn't so much as shake.

She cried out in horror when she saw the wound. "Dear God! This is a deep wound! Isn't it dangerous?"

"Oh no, dear Margot," Löwenklau told her. "It looks worse than it actually is because of all the blood. Take the sponge and clean the wound. Then you'll see right away how you're mistaken."

She followed his instructions. The concern on her face made her look even more beautiful. How soft and tender were her hands. Every moment with her provided a glimpse into his future with this lovely girl. He didn't even look at his wound, focusing his attention instead on Margot, on her reddened cheeks, her taut mouth, and the pearly white teeth between those full lips. The expression in her eyes alternated between tenderness and deep compassion while she dealt with the bloody wound. The wound was finally clean and ready to be examined.

"You're right, it's not as large as I first thought. Thank God!" she said. "But isn't it deep?"

"No," he said. "The tip broke off when the dagger struck the metal. Most of the energy was spent and the stump deflected into my arm."

"Why are you bleeding so much? Was an artery punctured?"

"If that were the case, then you would have seen something quite different. The broken dagger just extended the wound, breaking some small veins."

"It must be very painful!"

"I'm a soldier," he said, matter of fact.

"My dear, Hugo, I wish I could carry that burden for you."

Hugo wrapped his healthy arm around her and pulled her close. He looked deeply into her dark, moist eyes. "Is that how much you love me?"

"My love for you is never ending," she whispered.

"Really?"

"Of course! Believe me, Hugo." She kissed him repeatedly on the lips. Then she fashioned a bandage. Ten times, twenty times... he lost track of how many times she asked if he was in pain. Each time he sought to lay her fears to rest, reassuring her he was all right.

CHAPTER EIGHT

A Devious Servant

The captain ran to the coffeehouse in his new boots for his prearranged appointment with the baron. Reillac arranged for a room so they could discuss the events without interruption.

"Well?" the baron asked. All his hopes and anxiety rested in this one syllable. His eyes glowed like those of a lioness, eager to find out if her returning mate was successful in the hunt for his prey.

"Wine!" Richemonte replied, equally short. His features conveyed far more than his voice, a mixture of stress and excitement.

"Well, then!" exclaimed the baron, taking the order for wine as a positive sign. "Success it is! He who calls for wine must have earned it. Am I right, my dear captain?"

"Yes, it was a damn dirty job," Richemonte said deceptively.

The baron didn't catch the underlying meaning, assuming the attack had gone as planned. "Then let us celebrate with the best wine." He called for the waiter and made his selection.

Both men were quiet, preoccupied with their own thoughts until the wine arrived.

"Let us drink to our little venture. Now, tell me all about it!" Reillac said.

Richemonte, who downed his glass in one gulp, replied bitterly. "You look pleased that my little 'job' went off without a hitch."

"Of course!"

"What if you were mistaken?"

"*Pah!* You're just trying to stretch me out a little, like on a rack,[8.1] then surprise me with good news. You can't fool me. I pride myself in being able to read people. Your entrance and your posture at the table suggest to me that you've completed our objective just the way we planned it."

"You may be right, although there may be others more knowledgeable in judging one's outward expression. I have just embarked on a difficult task, although the outcome has yet to be determined."

"I trust you were successful in delivering a good thrust!"

"Of course, I was," replied the captain, irritated at the implication. "But the best thrust can miss its target."

"Then it wasn't your best effort. Rather, a poor attempt."

"Let me rephrase that. Even the best thrust can be parried or come up against an unforeseen obstacle."

"I would think human flesh would pose little resistance."

"True, but a *cuirass* is damned solid!"

The baron looked uncomfortable for a brief instant. "You don't mean to tell me our quarry carried a flak jacket?"

"That's exactly what I mean. I'm not making this up."

"From what I know, Löwenklau is an officer in the Hussar regiment, and only those in the horse regiment typically wear such protection."

"In any case, he was wearing one!"

Reillac searched the captain's face, while motioning his hand in a dismissive gesture. "Ah! You failed in your attempt," he replied in a nearly insulting tone.

"Unfortunately."

"Are you trying to downplay it?"

"Of course not. I wouldn't consider it!"

"Really? Surely it must have occurred to you. You plainly didn't strike at him, or perhaps you simply avoided the confrontation altogether. Maybe you were spineless, and now you seek to excuse yourself by claiming he carried a *cuirass*."

Richemonte's eyes flashed with anger. His lips twisted upwards angrily, revealing his teeth. It was this outward sign, like an animal baring its teeth, that became his trademark in his latter years. He stood up with a menacing look.

"Baron!" he exclaimed. He uttered just this one word, but it conveyed such a rage, it actually scared Reillac. He recoiled and leaned back against his chair.

"What is the meaning of this?" the baron demanded.

"If you dare accuse me once more of cowardice, I will demonstrate my courage most expertly on your own person, something which only a *cuirass* could repel!"

"Are you threatening me, Captain?"

"Yes," he said, sitting back down.

"Well, I object to this sordid treatment!"

"*Pah!* Your objection won't help your cause in the least, especially if you choose to affront my honor in this way."

"Are you sticking to your claim that Löwenklau was wearing a *cuirass*?"

"I don't give a damn whether you believe it or not!" the captain replied acidly.

"What would have possessed him to wear one? It's incomprehensible to me."

"Exactly. Unbelievable, but true!"

"Do you think he had a premonition of the attack?"

"I don't know, maybe. Go and ask him!"

Reillac wasn't about to back down. "Or is it customary for German officers to wear such devices under their military coats, to protect themselves against possible ambush?"

"Ridiculous! Only someone unfamiliar with military customs would think of such a thing."

"Why's that?"

"Because a soldier is only allowed to wear clothing and arm himself with weapons that are approved by his superiors," Richemonte explained.

"Ah, really?"

"Of course. If a Hussar wore a *cuirass*, it would be proof he was afraid to go into battle. It would severely tarnish his honor and reputation."

"I didn't realize that."

"There's an underlying thought," the captain began, "that suggests you're not the great judge of people you claim to be."

"You have a sharp tongue, Captain. I forbid you to use this tone with me. What are you driving at?"

"Even if the Hussars had permission to wear a *cuirass*, let me point out one obvious point: they'd have no need of it, since the war is over."

The baron shrugged. "Then how did it occur to him to obtain and strap on a *cuirass*? We're living in relative peace, especially tonight."

"Yes, it's unbelievable. Could he be so astute? He's only a German!"

"Are you implying the Germans aren't perceptive?"

"Absolutely!"

"I'm surprised at you!"

"Well," Richemonte said, "how clever can a barbarian really be?"

"Just go and observe the North American Indian," the baron suggested, "or other uncivilized cultures. There you'll see ample proof of their shrewdness, which would surprise even you."

The captain admitted, "You've got a point."

"Perhaps we've been wrong in referring to the Germans as barbarians."

"We shouldn't get sidetracked with these nuances. They'll only distract us from our goals. We should stick to what is relevant."

Reillac couldn't have agreed more. "So! Are you serious, you did your best? And Löwenklau got away?"

"Yes."

"Hang it all! All because of the *cuirass*!"

"Only because he wore one!" replied the captain grimly.

"That's too bad. Tell me what happened!"

"He was, just as we surmised, with my sister. He left the house very late."

"Were you waiting nearby?" the baron asked.

"Yes, across the street."

"What weapon did you choose?"

"My Venetian dagger."

Reillac smiled. "Such a dagger is a formidable weapon. When did he leave?"

"It was nearly midnight. I followed him on foot."

"Did you meet up with him in *Rue d'Ange*?"

"No. I wanted to avoid that," replied the captain. "However, I caught up to him on the next street. Just imagine my surprise when I noticed he was walking backwards."

"Backwards? Toward you?"

"No. He walked ahead, but he was facing me."

"Dammit! Very peculiar."

"Yes," Richemonte agreed. "He must have been expecting me."

"So he heard you approach and prepared himself for an attack."

"There's no way he could have heard me coming. I had removed my boots."

"Were you in your socks?"

"Yes."

Reillac came to the only reasonable conclusion. "Somehow, he was alerted to our plan."

"I'm almost inclined to believe it. But how? Who could have told him? I certainly didn't!"

"And me least of all. I haven't spoken of it to anyone."

"Neither have I."

"Then it's a mystery how he could have prepared himself for the attack," the baron said. "Maybe you accidentally uttered your intention when you were with your mother and the marshal."

"Far from it. You know yourself that we didn't discuss it until much later, after I had left my mother's residence."

"Unbelievable! Go on. I suppose he was prepared to defend himself. Did you consider delaying the attack when you realized he was wearing a *cuirass*?"

The captain shook his head. "Not at all. Perhaps it would have been better if I had avoided the entire encounter. It would have left him in doubt about my intentions. I didn't even see the *cuirass* in the dark. He called out to me as I lunged at him. I struck at his heart with all my might, but the dagger deflected on the metal and the tip broke off. That's when I realized he was wearing a *cuirass*."

"He should go to hell! Wasn't there a more suitable part of his body to strike, such as his throat?"

"No. It never came to that. I only had the one chance. Suddenly, there was a struggle and he gripped my arm. And then, the strangest thing happened. Someone showed up, one whom I would have least expected."

"Who?"

"Take a wild guess."

"How should I know? Who was it?"

"You will be astounded—my sister."

The baron was speechless. "Unbelievable," he said again.

"Then seek her out and confirm what I just told you," the captain replied sarcastically.

"How did she happen to follow him?"

"I'd certainly like to know."

The baron considered this bit of news. "This confirms they were both worried about his safety. Margot followed him secretly because of her concern for him."

"It's the only explanation that makes sense."

"So then, she runs after this German ape," exclaimed the baron angrily, "while I'm disrespectfully turned away. I have to find a way to upset their plans. What happened next?"

"Naturally, I had to flee so I wouldn't be recognized. Had I persisted, I would have been detained since people were starting to take notice of the noise in the street."

"Do you think you were recognized?"

"No, not then," he lied. "Perhaps later."

"Really, how come?"

Richemonte explained. "I had removed my boots earlier and carried them with me. I lost them during the skirmish, though, and fled without them. Later, Löwenklau must have found them and Margot might have recognized them as mine."

"How careless of you," Reillac said. "Wasn't there a place you could have left them?"

"No, I didn't want to leave it to chance that someone would come across them."

The baron looked down at his feet. "How come you're wearing boots now?"

"Why do you think? Did you expect me to come here in my socks?"

"Then where did you get them?"

"They're mine. I ran home and picked up this pair."

"Hopefully without being detected."

"No," the captain said. "That damned porter personally opened the door and must have seen me in my socks. I commanded him not to tell anyone."

The baron laughed derisively. "That was clever of you. Very clever indeed! You expect him not to blabber it to the first person he sees?"

"I gave him some change to keep his mouth shut."

"Ah! How much did you give him?"

"Five francs," Richemonte said.

"A whole five francs?" laughed the baron, incredulous at the thought. "Heavens! What a large sum! Well, Captain, I don't know whether to laugh or feel sorry for you! It was a mistake to get the porter involved, but you're powerless to change it now. Did he see you leave?"

"Probably."

"Well, he probably spilled his guts to your sister when she arrived at home. What do you plan to do when they confront you tomorrow?"

"Confront me about what?"

Reillac could hardly believe the other man's stupidity. "Naturally your sister, her mother, certainly Löwenklau, and perhaps even the police, will want you to give an account of your actions."

"I'm going to laugh in their face."

"They won't be able to do anything," the baron assured him. "Because I'm your alibi. You've been with me the entire evening!"

"What if you have to swear an oath?"

"Then I will swear. We are in allegiance in this matter, and we have to support each other. I'll see to it no blame falls on you, but that's as far as I'll go."

The captain understood him well, though he didn't let on. He refilled his glass, finishing it off again nearly in a single gulp. "What do you mean?" he asked.

"We've come to the end of our business arrangement."

"How come?"

"You failed to complete your task," Reillac said, "and you find yourself in a precarious position. I will stand by what I said earlier. You can depend on me for your alibi. However, nothing has changed in terms of your outstanding notes. I'm obliged to tender them tomorrow."

"Ridiculous!"

"Why is it ridiculous? There's only one way to eliminate the German, and that's through his death. You were unsuccessful in your attempt, and I doubt you will get a second opportunity."

"Who says so?"

"I do," the baron said. "Besides, he's been warned and next time he'll be even more careful."

"That's where I disagree with you," said the captain.

"In what way?"

Richemonte began his explanation. "Let me point out that I'm a better judge of people than you think, Baron. My dagger did deflect off his protected chest, injuring his arm. I felt it go in. Do you think my sister will let him go home while he's bleeding? She'll most certainly insist he come back to her house so she can examine and dress the wound."

"Hmm! You may have something there," Reillac said thoughtfully. "However, we're here, and he's at her house getting treatment."

"If I know Margot, I guarantee that's where I'll find him. It's quite simple."

"When do you think he'll leave?"

"Probably not too soon."

The baron mumbled something inaudible, staring ahead into space.

"What are you thinking about?" Richemonte asked.

"I just had an idea."

"What sort of an idea?"

"Is this door shut, so we will not be overheard?"

Richemonte looked behind him toward the door. "Of course," he replied.

The baron leaned over the table with a malicious look in his eyes. "Do you want him to just walk away?"

"Absolutely not! I want him to feel he is safe now, impervious to further attacks."

"Will he be on his guard?"

"It doesn't matter."

"Perhaps he will report you to your superiors."

"If it suits him."

"It's possible he will leave Paris and get away."

"This will not happen so quickly."

"Well," the baron went on, "I've heard rumors of a quick departure of the Prussians."

"All the more reason to act quickly!"

"That's more like it. But when?"

Richemonte merely shrugged. "Tomorrow, the day after, whenever it suits me. I'll think it over."

"Captain, tomorrow or the day after tomorrow will be too late. Now is the time to strike!"

"Well, you're in a hurry!"

"Because this is the best and quickest option."

"Do you realize what it will take to get it done?"

Reillac offered his companion a slight smile. "No more than a little perseverance."

"That, I have. Who will arrange a suitable opportunity?"

"I will," was the baron's short answer.

The captain was clearly surprised. "You?"

"Yes, I will," replied the baron.

"I don't think I understand what you're saying."

"Well," Reillac said, "it's really quite simple. If the man dies today, then he can't confront you. I'll rip up the notes and Margot is free to become my wife."

"But what about the *cuirass*?"

"We will resort to a firearm."

The captain remained unconvinced. "The question remains, will it penetrate the metal?"

"I was thinking of a shot to the head."

"That would do it, but with considerably more noise."

"We won't be out in the open."

"Hold on," Richemonte said, as though finally grasping the baron's proposal. "You said *we*. Are you implying that we'll do this together?"

"Yes!" the baron said. "I must have Margot at any price. I'm consumed by her beauty and am prepared to offer much to possess her. I now recognize this would be difficult for a single man to accomplish. Therefore, I'm willing to accompany you."

"Does this mean you'll assist me?"

"Yes."

The captain looked at him with surprise. In that moment, he also realized the reason that compelled Reillac to accompany him personally. "Oh, I see. You'll just come along as an observer, to make sure I'm up to the challenge. Am I right?"

Richemonte had guessed correctly, but the baron didn't want to infuriate him a second time. "Not at all," he replied. "It's much easier to finish him off with a well-placed shot to the head rather than in a knife fight, an inferior weapon."

"That's exactly what I thought," replied the captain.

"I'm convinced you won't miss. If I do accompany you, it's not because I doubt your ability. I simply want to be sure of our success."

"Do you want to see it for yourself?"

"Yes, of course."

The captain laughed. "I find it too risky," he said. "We would have to stop each passerby and look into his face. It would draw too much attention to us. And when the right man came along, we would give our intention away and he'd have the time to muster a defense and get away."

"It's not that complicated, Captain."

"I'm not following you. Do we need to see him up close?"

"Of course! Not just a fleeting glance. I intend to illuminate him."

"Are you crazy?"

"Not entirely," Reillac said. "You see, I have a little pocket lamp,[8.2] which should do nicely."

"Anything else?"

"Yes. I have a pair of double pistols. There aren't many passersby at this time of night. We can wait and listen for his approach. We don't know which route he'll take, but we can wait near the entrance to his residence. This way, he'll walk right into our hands."

"Will your lantern shed enough light?"

"It should be enough! When he comes, I'll open the lamp shield momentarily, and the light will hit his face. We'll have both our confirmation and a sure target. You take the pistol, and I hold the lamp. While I expose his face with the light, you take your shot."

The captain thought about the scenario for a few moments. "Not a bad idea. But won't he see us?"

"Actually, we'll be in the dark. The light will briefly blind him, so he won't distinguish anyone. Best of all, he won't be able to make an accusation since he'll be dead."

The captain mulled it over in his head. Things were moving too quickly. The unsuccessful attempt had barely passed and already the baron was concocting new schemes for him.

"And afterwards...?" Richemonte asked, trailing off.

"Naturally, we'll have to hurry back to my house. We will have an alibi."

"I doubt it. Your servants will notice we have just returned home. They'll know we have been absent."

"You underestimate me, Captain," Reillac said. "I'm not as foolhardy as you might suppose. My servants currently believe I'm in my study, because I left a light on. No one has access, not even my valet."

"Do you have a secret entrance?"

"Naturally."

"I take my hat off to you, Baron."

"Like I said, one never knows what can happen. By the way, I've taken part in other nocturnal excursions. It has been beneficial when my servants are able to confirm in all honesty that their employer has been home all night."

"Will you really rip up those notes?"

"On my honor!"

"What about the sought after sum," Richemonte asked, "after the engagement has taken place?"

"You will receive it. I'm giving you my word of honor."

"All right," the captain said, sticking out an open palm. "Here is my hand."

"Excellent! And here is mine."

They shook on it. Once again, the staff threatened to break over Löwenklau's head.[8.3]

"We don't have any time to lose, Captain!"

"Right! Go and fetch your lamp and the pistols, while I head to *Rue d'Ange*. I'll be on the lookout."

"Where do we meet?" the baron asked.

"Under the archway, across from Löwenklau's residence."

"Good. How long will you be?"

"No longer than five minutes," Richemonte said.

"Give me ten. Signal the waiter, so I can pay."

Richemonte didn't have far to go to get back to *Rue d'Ange*. It was already late and the street was dark and empty. Only his mother's suite showed some light. He noted shadows moving behind the curtain, and spotted the form of a man near the window.

There he is, he thought. *This gives me time to prepare. He won't be so fortunate the second time! This time his luck has run out.*

The baron didn't have far to go either. He arrived at his residence by way of a back lane. He used his passkey to open the gate in the rear wall and walked through the garden to the back terrace. Four massive pillars were joined by wooden slats, leaving the impression they could support more than just the vines that hung from them. Reillac climbed up to the top and knocked on a window. After a moment, the window opened from the inside.

"Is that you, Baron?" a voice inquired.

"Yes, Pierre, it's me. Are you blind?"

"I'm sorry, Monsieur. It's dark tonight. I couldn't see you."

"Stand aside so I can come in."

"Should I turn a light on?"

"No!" the baron snapped. "Let us proceed to my study."

He climbed through the opening and they walked into his study, which was already lit. The décor gave the impression of the room belonging to a man who possessed the finer books and first editions not for reading pleasure but as a means of flaunting his wealth.

It was clear that Reillac hadn't entered his residence quite as unobtrusively as he had suggested to the captain. The servant was definitely his confidant, whom he trusted in all respects. Pierre, his valet, wore gray pants, complimented by a velvet vest and white scarf. Like his master, he was tall and lean. His face betrayed a mixture of deception and cunning. This man was evidently schooled in all sorts of disciplines and possessed the skill to come across pleasantly in social graces, even while detesting them.

"Monsieur, you're back early," he commented.

"Yes, but only temporarily."

"Do you require more money?"

"No."

"I thought the captain, after having done his *job*..."

"...wanted to be compensated immediately?" the baron interjected with a hint of laughter. "No, Pierre, he made a mess of it, failing miserably in his attempt."

"Idiot!" the valet exclaimed contemptuously. He clearly intended to show his master his disapproval. He knew he could have done a better job himself. Pierre's relationship with the baron was built on respect and courtesy and he enjoyed a measure of trust with his master, particularly concerning sensitive issues.

"Yes, an idiot!" agreed the baron.

"One thrust, one solitary thrust! How much easier could it have been, Monsieur?"

"I must allow him a little latitude," Reillac said. "The German may have been forewarned, and therefore carried a metal breastplate under his coat."

"*Morbleu!*"

"Yes, the dagger was unable to penetrate the *cuirass*."

"Then a firearm is the only option."

"Absolutely! Where are my pistols?"

"There, in the bureau. Are you considering going yourself...?"

The baron nodded.

"Cannot the captain carry this out alone...?"

"Evidently not," Reillac said. "He needs someone to encourage him. Are they loaded?"

"No, Monsieur."

"Then load one for me, but carefully!"

"Monsieur! Think of the risk to yourself!"

"Don't worry about me. There's no real danger. It's been arranged. We won't be suspected."

Pierre seemed genuinely concerned. "Are you certain?"

"Yes, don't concern yourself about me. If necessary, we have an alibi."

"Of course! You have been at home all evening," he replied astutely. "What about the captain, what is his story?"

"He's been with me all night."

"Fine." Pierre opened the bureau, removed the box containing the pistols, and commenced loading one of them.

"Where is the small lamp?" the baron asked.

"Right here, in the drawer."

"Good. Light the wick."

"Very well, Monsieur," Pierre replied. "However, one can't always predict..." He seemed to enjoy responding in unfinished sentences. In this particular situation, it was appropriate to leave certain matters unsaid.

"Just make sure the window is closed, but not locked."

"Really? For what purpose?"

"It's possible the captain will accompany me. He doesn't need to know you are aware of my plans," the baron said. "Quickly! Finish with the lamp. I don't have much time." Reillac took the loaded pistol and waited for Pierre to light the lamp.

"I only hope it turns out well!" the servant mused.

"Why shouldn't it?

"Oh! The devil often has his dirty paws in our best laid plans."

"Evidently we'll have that honor ourselves, by playing his role," laughed the baron.

"And yet, still...! Monsieur, I don't care for the Germans. I would rather polish that Prussian away with ten bullets instead of one. If I were in your shoes, I would have settled the matter in an entirely different fashion."

"A different fashion? Tell me," the baron asked.

The valet, with an air of self-importance, puckered his lips and kissed his fingertips. "In a very different fashion," he replied.

"I'm familiar with your gestures, but I still don't know what you're getting at. Out with it!"

"Well, let me state the obvious. I'm in love with a certain Mademoiselle, but she doesn't reciprocate my love. There's an easy way for her to be persuaded to become my wife."

"What is that, *mon ami?*"

"I'm implying she will plead with me to become her husband."

"Pierre, you're not being very clever!"

"Perhaps. But neither am I stupid, which I can attest to by my reputation."

"So, tell me," Reillac said, "how would you persuade her?"

"I would invite her over for a visit."

"Would she accept?"

"She would even come into my sleeping quarters, Monsieur!" His face adopted a lascivious expression.

The baron laughed briefly. "You're putting me on!"

"On the contrary, I'm convinced of it!"

"You're speaking deliriously."

"Oh, I'm in perfect control of my faculties."

"You don't know Margot!"

The valet pursed his lips knowingly. "I don't need to know her preferences. It all depends on the manner in which she receives my invitation."

The baron allowed himself a little more time, giving Pierre greater attention. Intuitively, he felt Pierre had a specific plan in mind. "What would be your ways and means?"

"It all depends on the circumstances," Pierre said, obviously in contemplation. "Has Mademoiselle ever visited her betrothed at his residence?"

"I don't believe so."

"Monsieur, didn't you say Blücher is an admirer and supports the newly formed couple? It suggests the lieutenant must be in good standing."

"Probably."

"Then perhaps the marshal could invite both of them to his residence for a visit?"

"Of course," Reillac said. "In that regard, I've heard how Blücher invites the lower grade officers, often on a whim."

"Then we have an opportunity."

"I still don't understand what you are getting at."

"*Eh bien!*" the valet exclaimed. "All we have to do is procure an adjutant acting on behalf of His Excellency, the field marshal. The adjutant, dressed in a 'borrowed' German uniform, attends to Madame Richemonte's residence and presents an invitation from the marshal. It basically proclaims that Mademoiselle Margot has been invited to dine with the field marshal. Naturally, her betrothed is also invited, but won't be able to pick her up. The marshal, not wanting to spoil the surprise, sends his adjutant in a carriage to get her."

"Scoundrel! Now I get your drift."

"Fabulous, isn't it?"

"I detect a problem, however. A rather large problem."

"Which one, Monsieur?"

"If her mother is not invited as well, it would seem discourteous and perhaps even suspicious."

"Didn't you say, Monsieur, she hasn't been feeling well lately?"

Reillac nodded. "Yes, of course."

"Then this is the excuse. The adjutant simply has to convey the marshal's regrets in not being able to visit with her mother, due to her illness. This should suffice in removing any suspicions."

"Absolutely."

"Well," Pierre continued, "I also happen to know of an unethical alchemist who's not opposed to making some money on the side. He would be willing to sell 'things' to his friends for a good price. Of course, these things are unavailable to the average customer."

"Do you consider yourself included in his circle?"

"I'm privileged to be a long standing member," the valet grinned. "He has a very potent potion. Just sprinkle a few drops into a handkerchief, hold it close to a lady's nose, and rest assured she will quickly lose consciousness."

"Villain!" the baron roared with delight. "Have you ever tried this 'perfume'?"

"Yes, with her gracious permission," replied Pierre cynically.

"On a lady?"

"Naturally! It would have been wasted on a man."

The baron could hardly hold back his grin. "You are, and remain, one devious fellow."

"Why thank you, Monsieur!" Pierre replied sarcastically.

"You may continue."

"Mademoiselle will be alone with the adjutant in the carriage. He administers the perfumed handkerchief at an opportune time."

"You, you are a piece of work. By God! Continue."

"You are too kind."

"Does she faint immediately?" Reillac asked.

"Immediately!"

"For how long?"

"About half an hour."

"Does it cause her any ill effects?"

"On the contrary," Pierre reassured him. "She awakes as though from a long nap, fresh and alert."

Reillac liked the sound of this new plan. "And then? Where does she wake up? At the marshal's palace?"

"That wouldn't serve your interests."

"Where else then?"

"Naturally, right here."

"Ah! How devious."

"Monsieur, she'll wake up wherever it pleases you, be that in your foyer, in your study..."

"Listen, your plan shows a lot of promise, however it's too improbable."

"Why improbable?"

The baron regarded him respectfully. "I don't think it's workable."

"I don't agree with you, Monsieur."

"It would be too difficult to hire an adjutant in uniform."

"That wouldn't be necessary."

"And why not?"

"I know of a young man, who, for the small sum of two or three hundred francs, would quite willingly wear a German uniform."

"Could he play the part?" Reillac asked.

"Oh yes, he's an accomplished actor."

"He would have to speak and comprehend German."

The valet smiled, having already thought through this little detail. "He does so fluently."

"He would have to keep it confidential."

"Of course he would."

"Can you vouch for him?"

"Completely!"

The baron paused, thinking it over. "You must have a lot of trust in him. If any of this leaks out, I'd be forced to dismiss you from my employ! Do you understand?"

"I understand," he said, nodding, "but you needn't worry about this young man. You see, he's my son."

The baron stared at his servant uncomprehendingly. "Your son?" he asked. "But you have never been married. Or am I mistaken?"

Pierre shrugged his shoulders, coughing, somewhat embarrassed. "I have never lied to you, Monsieur. Although I have never married, I'm still this young man's father. Everyone has to live with their own regrets, Monsieur!"

"Fine, you don't have to explain yourself to me. Does he know you're his father?"

"Of course. I'm the one who paid for his upbringing. His mother is no longer alive. She was of German descent, which is why he speaks her language as well as French."

The baron was so smitten with this new plan that he completely forgot about his appointment with the captain. He paced back and forth, considering the merits of the proposed plan, while Pierre observed him with a bemused expression.

"Did you make her unhappy?" the baron asked.

"Unhappy? Not at all! She was a German woman, and was quite happy to fall into the arms of a Frenchman."

"Is your son in Paris?"

"Yes."

"Is he available at a moment's notice?"

"At any time. He's currently without employment."

"Good," Reillac said. "What about a coachman? Where could we get one who will keep his mouth shut?"

"Not to worry. I've considered this already and I know of one whom I can trust completely. Namely, myself."

"Ah! I hadn't considered you. You are an absolute rogue. Where could we get a carriage?" the baron asked. "I couldn't possibly use my own!"

"I know of a middle man who could rent one to us."

"Is he to be trusted?"

"It's of no importance. He's not going to know what we plan to use it for."

"What makes you so certain he'll rent it out without any questions?"

Pierre shrugged. "No problem there. We're old friends from long ago. I still see him on occasion when I'm on holidays."

"Well then! I am going to consider your proposal. It gives me a golden opportunity should my present plans not work out. The doubts I previously had have vanished. Of course, there is one other obstacle."

"Which one?"

"How to bring Mademoiselle inside my house."

"Oh, that!" Pierre said dismissively. "Through the garden."

"Someone might notice."

"Not at all. In your foresight, you will arrange to release the servants early. That way, there will be no witnesses."

"Of course, you're right. This is plausible after all. How do we get her to wake up?"

"That part should be interesting, to say the least."

Reillac's face darkened somewhat. "On the contrary. What will she say? Will she scream or put up a fight?"

"Probably not. I expect she will be bound and gagged."

"Hang it all! You have thought of everything—just like a kidnapping. But I'm no bandit!"

"Nevertheless, you are still a careful man, Monsieur. You can remove the restraints later."

"What if she doesn't keep quiet?"

"It'll be in her best interests to do so," Pierre pointed out "She'll return home later as though she had dined with the marshal. Her betrothed will find out it wasn't true. She won't be able to tell him where or how she had spent the last few hours. This would surely cause a rift between the two lovers and Monsieur would have free reign with her."

"Pierre, you really are a devil in disguise," Reillac said. "Your plan is most attractive. I'll have to give it some serious thought. However, for now— *Parbleu!* I have to leave. The captain is waiting for me!" He concealed the pistol and the small lamp, preparing to leave via the window.

"Monsieur," questioned Pierre. "Are you really going to shoot the German?"

"Not I!" replied Reillac with a devious grin. "Richemonte will."

"Then you'll be his witness?"

"Of course."

"All right," the valet said. "Please don't place yourself in a dangerous situation. Things can go awry, even with the best laid plans."

"I'm well aware of this, Pierre, and I promise to be careful. Just don't lock the window. If both of us show up, remain in the adjoining room until I call for you. Good night."

CHAPTER NINE
Nocturnal Adventures

The baron left Pierre in the study, exited through the window, and climbed down the veranda's lattice work. He hurried out through the back gate to meet with the captain.

"My God!" Richemonte exclaimed when Reillac finally showed up. "You took an eternity to get here!"

"I couldn't get here sooner," the baron lied. "I had to wait for a pair of lovers to leave the street."

"Damn those lovers! I've been waiting for almost three-quarters of an hour."

"Did he come already?"

"No, but he could be here any minute. Did you bring your lamp? It's so dark; it's like peering into a sack."

The baron pulled out the lantern. "I have it right here."

"What about the pistol?"

"Yes, here it is. Take it."

"Is it loaded?"

"Yes, both chambers."

The captain, not completely trusting Reillac, carefully examined the pistol by touch to get a feel for it. Meanwhile, the baron stepped back into the recesses of the archway and lit the lantern's wick. Satisfied it would burn, he closed the cover and put it in the outer pocket of his coat so he could have it ready at a moment's notice.

"We should wait on the other side of the street," the captain said, pointing to a building across from them. "He lives over there."

"Just a minute. We have to discuss our exit, and possibly a quick withdrawal."

"Right," Richemonte agreed. "One can never tell whether or not things will go wrong. In case they do, you promised to furnish me with an alibi."

"Not a problem. You'll stay with me overnight, as though we've been together all evening."

"If something unexpected happens, we can make a hasty retreat to your house."

"Yes, but not via the front entrance," Reillac said. "Do you know the back lane?"

"I think so."

"My garden is at the rear. There's a small gate in the wall, and it's the only way to get in. If we have to separate, we'll meet at the gate." He looked around at the empty street warily. "We should go now."

They quietly crossed the street and settled into the dark archway of Löwenklau's building, lying in wait. After a few minutes passed, they heard the distinctive sound of approaching footsteps. They cowered under the archway where they couldn't easily be spotted. The captain readied the pistol as the baron reached for his lamp.

"Pay attention!" Reillac advised him. "He's coming. When he stops to ring for the porter, I'll bring out my lamp and shine the light in his face. You hold the barrel up against his temple and fire. He'll die instantly."

They listened expectantly as the steps drew closer.

"It's probably not him," whispered the captain. "The footsteps don't sound like those of a soldier. Of course, we should be ready just in case. If he continues past the gate, we'll know it's someone else."

The man in question approached slowly. The assailants' heartbeats quickened from anxiety, though it quickly turned out to be for naught. The stranger walked past, oblivious to their presence.

After a short pause, the captain relaxed. "I was right," he said. "But I was hoping that it was him."

"Why?"

"It would have all been over!"

"Are you suddenly afraid?"

"*Pah!*" Richemonte spat. "Don't be ridiculous. Why are you still questioning my abilities?"

The pair fell silent again, waiting impatiently. Nearly two minutes elapsed before they heard another round of approaching steps. The captain listened attentively, cocking his ear. "It sounds like a soldier approaching, maybe even an officer. I'll wager on it," he whispered.

"Good, you're knowledgeable in such matters. If he stops, I'll use the lamp. Just make sure you don't shoot until we verify it's him."

The strong military footfall came closer. Just a mere ten steps, then eight, six, four, and finally he came to a stop. They couldn't see what he was doing, but they thought he looked up toward the upstairs window. The captain elbowed Reillac, who produced the lantern and opened the small cover. The man's form was outlined in an instant as the bright light illuminated him while the two perpetrators crouched unseen in the dark.

"*Zounds!*" the man cried out, peering at them. "What in damnation are you two doing here?"

The two men were shocked, their hearts sinking at the familiar bellow. Instead of facing Löwenklau, they were face to face with Field Marshal Blücher.

The baron was first to react, hastily closing the lantern's cover to conceal his identity. He did so awkwardly, actually exposing the captain for just an instant. Richemonte, who was holding the pistol and ready to fire, allowed the barrel to waver, terrified at how close he had been to firing at the old marshal. Fortunately for him, the light only exposed the pistol in his outstretched hand, and not his face. Blücher was too experienced a soldier not to spot the gun and, to his credit, had the fortitude to avoid making a critical error. The two culprits, still speechless, failed to respond to his inquiry.

Blücher was forced to repeat himself. "I'm asking you who you are. State your business!"

The captain composed himself. "We're night watchmen," he answered.

"Why are you standing there?"

"We're waiting for our replacements."

"All right then. Show me your face. Open the lantern!"

Carrying out the order would have brought them both dire consequences, but the baron was quick to come up with a solution. The lantern had a small slide, through which he could reach in and extinguish the wick. A slight movement was all that was required to put the light out.

"Right away!" the baron replied, depressing the slide. He lifted the lantern just as the light went out.

"Damn!" he said, doing his best to sound surprised. "It just went out."

"Don't worry about it," Blücher said. "Good night." With this, the marshal turned and continued his walk down the street.

As soon as he was far enough away, Richemonte cursed. "Dammit, the marshal! Who could have predicted it?"

"He was attired in civilian clothes! You were right, though. He was certainly an officer."

"Baron, do you realize the mistake we just made? I should have shot him."

"Heavens! What on earth for?"

"France would have been avenged by his death!"

"You're right!" Reillac allowed. "I feel the same way, especially since he's favored Löwenklau over me."

"Hang it all! I was such an idiot. I shouldn't have let the opportunity pass me by."

"Look at it this way," the baron said. "Had you fired at Blücher, Löwenklau would have escaped. Let's not lose sight of our main objective."

Neither one wanted to admit that it had been Blücher's compelling personality and vocal authority that had kept them at bay. They both felt it. The old man's influence alone had lowered a hand brandishing a loaded pistol.

"Do you think the old man believed we were night watchmen?"

"It didn't sound like it," Reillac said.

"He wanted a closer look at us. Your idea to extinguish the light came at exactly the right moment. He would have recognized us otherwise."

"No doubt. This all seems surreal. I want to be certain he went home."

"Why?" the captain asked.

"If he went inside, then all's well," Reillac explained. "However, if he went further down the street, we'll know he became suspicious and maybe even guessed our actual target."

"Then listen!"

The two men listened for the sound of footsteps, but the street was utterly quiet. "He must have gone home after all," the captain said. "I don't hear him anymore."

"Damn! We were talking when we should have been listening. I want to be sure."

"But how?"

"That's easy. He always has two guards at the gate. I'm going over to inquire."

"All right. What if Löwenklau comes in the meantime?"

"Then don't hesitate to give him a bullet. Or better yet, both of them. I better hurry."

He sauntered over to the palace gate like a man casually returning from the local bar. He spotted the two sentries, alert and on duty, and approached them. "Good evening," he said in greeting. One of the guards acknowledged him in broken French.

"The gentleman who just returned," the baron said, "was he the field marshal himself?"

"Yes."

"Did he turn in?"

"Yes."

"Thank you, *messieurs*," he said and began walking back toward his compatriot's hiding place, satisfied. He bent over and promptly relit his lantern so as to be ready for their intended victim.

Although relieved for the moment, the conspirators should have known better than to get too comfortable. Fate was not on their side.

❧✠☙

The old Blücher had indeed become suspicious, though he was too clever to let it show.

They pretended to be night watchmen, the marshal thought privately. *I'm going to get to the bottom of this and throw a wrench in their plan. One held the lantern, the other a pistol. Scoundrels! More likely they were waiting to ambush someone. But whom? Could it be the lieutenant? No, surely not!*

I warned him, though. Is it possible he's still with the girl? Could be. After all, lovers pay more attention to the beating of their hearts than the ticking of a clock.[9.1] *If he's still at her house, I'll have to act quickly. I'll send someone over to them, but who? No one here knows the house.*

He paused to consider the dilemma, then came to a suitable conclusion. *I'll have to go myself!* Turning around, he was struck by yet another thought. He hit his forehead with the palm of his hand. "And you call yourself a field marshal!" he muttered. "What a mistake that could have been."

If you walk past those two scoundrels, he pondered silently, they'll be tipped off and grow suspicious. But if I go the long way around... Damn, what if they've already caught on? They may have noticed my distrust of their story. More than likely that scoundrel let the light go out on purpose. If they supposed I suspected anything, they would have to satisfy themselves by inquiring after my sentry.

Listen Blücher, you still possess some smarts. You could have been a detective. Just wait, you two can't fool me. I'll fix it so you get an X instead of a U.[9.2] *I'll make sure you turn red and blue, blushing like an old woman's nose at Christmas.*[9.3]

He quickened his pace, closing the remaining distance to the palace gate. The guard heard him approach. "Halt!" the voice called out. "Who goes there?"

"Hold your horses!" Blücher said. "It's me."

"Who is it?"

"Who do you think it is?" he challenged.

"That's no name. No one can enter without permission."

"I'm impressed with your tenacity, but you must know the old Blücher, right?"

"We know of him!"

"Well, then! Have a peek under my cap."

"It's too dark out in the open. Come under the light."

"Fine, my boy. You're hard to fool!" Blücher came forward a few paces into the light, allowing the sentry to distinguish his features. "Well, come on! You doubting Thomas, use your *Pince-nez.*[9.4] You're not going to look too smart without them!"

The guard recognized the marshal right away, though he didn't seem to be flustered in the least. He was used to the marshal's idiosyncrasies and no doubt realized he would have been punished for allowing him to walk through without being questioned.

"Well?" Blücher asked. "Do you recognize me?"

"At your command, Excellency!" he replied, as both soldiers presented arms.

"Listen, put your rifles away. Now, can I come in or do I have to find somewhere else to spend the night?"

"His Excellency may pass."

"Well done, lads! You had your way with me and now I'm going to show you I, too, can be stubborn. I think I'll fetch my cap and go for another escapade. Pay attention, men! It's likely someone will come and pump you for information in a few minutes, no doubt to see if I returned to my quarters. Make it clear to him that I turned in. Understood?"

"At your command, Excellency!"

"Very good," he said. "Keep those eyes open so the hoodlums don't come after me. Well, you've certainly done your duty tonight and deserve something. Here, have an eight groschen piece."[9.5] He reached into his pocket and presented a pair of coins.

"Pardon, Excellency," one of them replied, "but one cannot accept presents while on duty. I would have to report it to His Excellency!"

Blücher patted him on the back. "You're a smart one. Nobody is going to pilfer your horse while you're on it, that's for sure. Come tomorrow morning at nine o'clock and see me. Instead of the eight penny piece, I'll give each of you a *ducat* and a ration of tobacco. Of course, you'll have to make a report that I tried to subvert you. Understood?"

"At your command, Excellency."

"Good. Make your report or, God help you, the devil will do summersaults at your expense!"[9.6]

He walked away as quickly as he could manage, realizing he'd remained a little too long with the sentry. Blücher had been gone only a short time before the baron showed up inquiring after the marshal. He got his answer, albeit according to the marshal's own instructions.

Blücher made a slight detour so the bandits wouldn't see him. He came to *Rue d'Ange* and found the lights still on. He rang the bell, and was admitted by the porter. Realizing he didn't have any time to waste, Blücher climbed the steps two at a time and crossed into the foyer. Footsteps approached, and Margot's head appeared in the open doorway.

"Who's out there?" she called into the darkness.

"It's me, my dear fräulein," Blücher said.

She nearly dropped the lamp at the sound of his voice, though she still opened the door to admit him. "Excellency? You've come at a late hour!"

"Please forgive my intrusion. Is the young man, Löwenklau, still here?"

"No, Excellency. Do you wish to come in?"

"God be gracious! When did he leave?"

"Only two minutes ago!"

"Dammit! He'll run right into their trap. Good night!"

Blücher stormed down the steps, ignoring the lady's pleas for an answer. He ran out, stopping only when he hit the street.

"Bad luck!" he murmured under his breath. *Now what? Which way do I go? Right or left? Let's see. I came from the left and would have seen him. He must have gone the other way.*

And that's how Blücher, the celebrated field marshal, found himself running back down *Rue d'Ange*, taking it upon himself to warn a single lowly lieutenant as he retraced his way back down the same street. Eventually, he came to a stop as an idea came to him. Nearly out of breath, he listened carefully until... there, in the distance! He heard the firm, steady gait of a soldier. He knew immediately it had to be Löwenklau. There was no time to lose, since Löwenklau was almost back to his residence.

Blücher cupped his hands to his mouth and shouted, "Löwenklau! Halt! Turn around! They're after your hide!" In the same instant, Blücher saw the illumination of a lantern, followed by the sound of two rapid gunshots. "My Lord!" the old man exclaimed, breaking into a run again. "Those devils got to him first!"

In a matter of seconds, Blücher covered the distance to the gate, where the imposters were 'keeping watch'. There was no one to see. While probing in the darkness, he came across two discarded objects. He bent down, not sure what he had stumbled across. As soon as he handled them, he recognized the lantern and spent pistol.

"That's my boy!" he shouted, relieved. "He didn't meet the devil after all!"

Blücher took the time to catch his breath as a few soldiers carrying lanterns hurried over. They belonged to his palace contingent. Having heard the shots, they must have been sent to investigate.

"Over here, boys!" Blücher called.

A corporal illuminated him. "Excellency, did someone dare to shoot at you?"

"No, my boy, not at me or you, but at another. Take a good look around with your men, and see if there's a Hussar lieutenant a little worse for wear."

"A lieutenant from our Hussar regiment?"

"Yes, most worthy Corporal! Stop asking me questions! Get your arms and legs moving[9.7] and keep your questions to yourself."

Although they searched the entire area, they couldn't find a trace of Löwenklau, not so much as a drop of blood.

"Excellent news!" said a relieved Blücher. "Come here, Corporal, and show me your lantern."

The soldier complied, raising his lantern. Blücher took it, allowing its light to illuminate the objects.

"What is this, Corporal?" he asked.

"A lantern," the soldier replied dutifully.

"Good, my boy! And this here?"

"A pistol, Excellency."

"Very good. I'm impressed with your knowledge of physical science and armaments. When I resign my commission, you can apply for my position of field marshal. Return to the barracks and lay your ears on the bunk[9.8]. We've done all we can."

His men obeyed. Blücher wasn't at all surprised the shots hadn't generated more commotion. The Parisians had grown accustomed to nightly disturbances. As stillness returned to the street, he turned his attention to the two sentries at his gate.

"Do you still recognize me?" he asked.

"At your command, Excellency!"

"Well, did someone approach you?"

"Yes, Excellency!"

"Did he inquire if I had retired for the night?"

"Yes, Excellency!"

"Did you allow him to leave?"

"Yes, Excellency!"

"Good! What about the pistol shots? Do you know where they came from?"

"They came from down the street."

"Did you notice who fired them?"

"No, Excellency. We cannot leave our post. However, we did see two men run right by us."

"You're both good lads," the marshal remarked. "I'm not going to lecture you, otherwise you'd have two reports to make tomorrow. So, two men ran past here you say?"

"Yes, and a third was after them, Excellency."

"Really? Was he pursuing them?"

"It seemed that way. Over there, by the second gate, there..." The man trailed off.

"There what?"

"There he stopped, Excellency."

"The foolish lad! Why would he do that?"

"He, er... he removed his boots."

"His boots? Heavens! The fool removes his boots instead of running after them. Well, he deserves to get a few smacks where it hurts!"

"Then he ran after them!"

"Ah, just as well! What's the use in that, running with your boots in your hands?"

"Pardon, Excellency! He left his boots behind and called out for us to watch them."

"What? Keep watch over his boots? Did he go mad?" Blücher asked. "What next? Maybe he wants you to present arms in from of them. Ridiculous! Maybe Field Marshal von Blücher's honor guard will have to pay tribute to the muddy boots of the first fellow who happens to come by. If I get my hands on him, I'll teach him a lesson he won't soon forget. I'll brow beat him with those boots, that's what I should do!"[9.9]

"But Excellency, he gave us his name!"

"That, too? What insolence! What did he call himself, this madman, this *Urian?*"[9.10]

"Lieutenant von Löwenklau!"

"Lieutenant von Löwenklau," he repeated slowly, enunciating each syllable. "Well, that explains it. What an old ass I've become. I should have seen it! The higher one moves up in rank, the more foolish one becomes. Especially with the rank of field marshal. Did he really give you that name?"

"Of course, Excellency!"

"Did he run after them?"

"Yes, Excellency."

"A clever man! The culprits can't hear his steps anymore, because he's now after them in his socks. They foolishly think they have evaded him and let their guard down. This way he will catch up to them. Did he say whether or not he'd been wounded?"

"No," the guard said. "He was in a rush."

"Then he must be alive. Look after those boots. My boy, go over there and fetch them!"

"Pardon, Excellency, but I cannot do that!"

"What? Why not?"

"I'm not permitted to leave my post."

"Dammit, that's true. Well, if there's no other way, I'll fill in, like old Fritz on guard duty. Give me your rifle, my boy! I'll cover for you while you get them."

"Excellency, this won't work either."

"*Zounds!* Now what? Why won't it work?"

"His Excellency is out of uniform, dressed in civilian clothes."

"You're right again! Listen, my son, you really are not a bad sort. You know your regulations better than I do—which doesn't surprise me in the least, since it's been fifty years since I learned them. What's your name?"

"August Liebmann."

"Very well, my dear August, come to me in exactly twenty-five years and recite these regulations. You'll have your chance then to boast of your accomplishments. Now, I have to fetch those boots. Where are they?"

"At the second gate."

"Fine. You can put yours there, too! I might as well do the rounds and collect any stray ones. Just wake me up when you need them, lads!"

True to his word, Blücher collected the lieutenant's boots, placing one under each arm and returned to the sentry.

"Lieutenant von Löwenklau will naturally return and inquire about those reeking sauerkraut tubes of his. Just tell him I collected them and he is to present himself at my residence immediately, in his socks, even if I'm asleep. Do you understand?"

"At your command, Excellency!"

"Good night, August."

"Good night, Excellency!"

CHAPTER TEN

Margot Investigates

W hen Blücher appeared earlier at *Rue d'Ange*, expecting to find the lieutenant, Margot was utterly surprised by him. When he'd uttered his parting words, a sudden fear enveloped her.

"Dammit!" he had said. "He'll run right into their trap!" He had run down the stairs as though just learning of a looming catastrophe. *What could this danger be? Who were the scoundrels he referred to?* Her betrothed had already been exposed to danger once that day, and now, possibly, he was again. *Should I wake Mama and the maid? No, they wouldn't be of much help, and end up just worrying about the outcome.*

Margot paced back and forth across her room. She became restless, unable to find even a semblance of peace. She had to go out for some fresh air. She decided to go to Hugo's residence to see if his light was on. He had clearly described his apartment to her, and she was sure she'd be able find it in the dark.

Margot put on her hat and wrapped a shawl around her shoulders. The porter was taken aback when he saw her walk to the front door, wondering why she was about to leave for the second time that night.

"For God's sake!" he said. "Mademoiselle, what happened that you have to leave so late?"

"Nothing, Francois. Just open the door!"

He saw the paleness on her face. "Who was the gentleman who rang earlier and then left in such a rush?" he inquired. "He couldn't wait for me to open the door fast enough."

"Field Marshal von Blücher."

"My God, then it must be very important. You should hurry." He let her out onto the street.

Margot knew Hugo had turned right, and so took the same road. She hadn't gone far when she heard the sound of pistol shots in the distance. She paused for a moment, gripped with fear. *Were those shots connected to the danger Blücher alluded to?* she reflected. *They seemed to have come from the area where Hugo lives.*

Gripped with fear, Margot ran to the end of her street and turned the corner. She saw lanterns far down the lane and hurried toward them. They disappeared from view just as she stopped, finding herself in the vicinity of the residence Löwenklau had described to her. She searched for a light, but there wasn't one. Had Hugo come home, he probably would have lit a candle. In the absence of such a light, her concern worsened.

As she tried to figure out what to do next, the sound of voices further along the street came floating toward her. She turned and hurried toward the sounds, hoping she might find some explanation. As Margot came closer, she heard a loud verbal exchange.

"Good night, August!" a deep baritone intoned. She immediately recognized the marshal's voice. If she had any doubts, she was reassured by the sentry's reply, "Good night, Excellency."

Margot came to the gate and approached the sentry. "Was the field marshal here?" she asked.

"Yes."

"I must see him at once!" She tried to enter the gate, but he blocked her path with his rifle.

"No one is allowed entry!"

"But I must see him!"

"Come back during the day and make an appointment!" he said sternly.

Blücher reached the landing and was about to climb the stairs when he heard a commotion. He stopped to listen. He could hear a woman's voice and the firm refusals of the sentry, advising her to return in the daytime.

"What is it now?" he called back.

"A woman, Excellency!" said the sentry, who had no qualms about standing his ground to the opposite sex. He was of a different sort, one that made no distinction between a lady or woman, a girl or fräulein.

"A woman?" he questioned. "Nothing more? Send her away! I'm not going to give an old frump audience at this late hour."

"But she looks young, Excellency!" the guard yelled back.

"Young?" the marshal asked. "Don't be fooled, August. They all claim to be ten years younger—get rid of her."

"She insists that she is acquainted with His Excellency."

"What? That cannot be true!" Blücher replied, slightly embarrassed.

"She says that Your Excellency had just paid her a visit."

"That's a damned lie!" the marshal retorted. "I don't make social calls to women at night. Give her a good smack for suggesting such a thing!"

"She says I need only say her name—Richemonte."

"Richemonte? My word! Are you insane, my son?" With these words, he quietly returned to the gate, still carrying the boots under his arms. He recognized Margot immediately.

"August, you are an ass! You've got to be the biggest camel that wanders the Sahara, looking forlorn and confused.[10.1] Look here! Anyone can see this is no woman!"

The poor sentry looked helplessly at the marshal. "But, Excellency—"

"She's not a Madame either. Take a closer look."

"At your command!"

"Hold your tongue! August, where did you get the bright idea to portray a young Mademoiselle as an ordinary woman, you confused raccoon?"

"I beg your pardon, Excellency, but she is not a man!"

His retort momentarily stunned the marshal and he reconsidered. "You're right about that!" he exclaimed. "A lady is still a woman. But don't you see, my son, there are only Madames and Mademoiselles in Paris. Had you told me there was a Mademoiselle here, then I wouldn't have told you to send her away. Since you came to the conclusion on your own that she is actually a Mademoiselle, I will be compassionate and hold off on giving you another lecture. Don't take it to heart, my boy." He chuckled to himself.

In the meantime, Margot had approached him, pleading with her outstretched hands. "Forgive me, Excellency! My concern for Hugo didn't leave me any peace. I had to come. On my way over here, I heard shots..."

"Ah, Mademoiselle, there's no need for you to apologize," he replied. "I interrupted you by appearing at a very late hour, and just as suddenly departed, failing to give you any explanation. It was not very gracious of me. Please, come with me upstairs."

Blücher escorted her upstairs into a well lit and comfortable drawing room that had most likely served as a parlor at one time. The Rococo furniture was made from the finest rosewood. The cushions and pillows were embroidered with the most luxurious silk. She saw costly vases and clocks, exquisite rugs, and draperies. On the base of an enormous clock rested a bootjack. An old leather pouch filled with tobacco hung on a statue of Venus, and proudly displayed on a costly Persian bedcover was a pair of military boots. A priceless gold casket was filled with broken pipe stems, but worst of all was the entire floor, which was littered with maps, reports, and discarded envelopes of various sizes.

"Mademoiselle, this is my study," he said matter-of-factly. "Take a seat and tell me what's troubling your heart."

He stood in front of her, still carrying the boots. Even though she worried about Hugo's fate, she couldn't help but smile at the old soldier, who seemed to have nearly transformed himself into an old shoemaker.

"Your Excellency's visit this night brought on a terrible uneasiness, one I couldn't shake. Did it have anything to do with my betrothed?"

"Yes, of course. I wouldn't have come to you otherwise."

"In that case, please tell me: is Hugo in danger?"

"Hugo? Hm! Who's that?"

"Lieutenant von Löwenklau's first name is Hugo."

"Well then," Blücher began, "Yes. He was in some danger, Mademoiselle."

"Dear God! Was it serious?"

"They shot at him a little."

Her eyes widened fearfully. "Why, this is terrible!"

"Yes, they were waiting for him at his gate. There were two of them."

"What did they do to him, Excellency? Oh please... please, tell me quick!"

She went pale, leaving Blücher in a state of consternation. He concluded that the best way to reassure her would be to show her one of the boots, pulling the left one from under his arm.

"Do you recognize this jackboot?" he gestured with the left boot.

"No," she replied in surprise.

"Well, maybe this one then?" he said, showing her the right boot.

"No, I don't."

"Hmmm. That surprises me. I would have thought the sight of them would bring you some comfort."

"Those boots? Excuse me Excellency, but I don't understand."

"These jackboots speak a language of their own, one which should be familiar to you. We have them, the boots that is, which is the main thing. He will come to fetch them in good time, and probably in his socks to boot." He snickered at his own pun.

Margot started to feel embarrassed. She couldn't make any sense out of the marshal's ramblings, speaking as he was in riddles. "Your Excellency, please, whom do you mean?"

"Well, Hugo naturally."

"Hugo? Ah, now I understand. Do these boots belong to him?"

"Yes."

"Ah!" She blushed, though still bewildered. "How did he come to...?"

"...to possess these? Oh, that's easy. Every officer under my command has a pair just like them."

"No, no! I mean how did Your Excellency acquire his boots?"

"If you think I borrowed them from him, you're mistaken. They were lying at the foot of the gate."

"But how did they get there?" asked Margot, more confused than ever.

"He put them there and instructed my sentry to keep an eye on them," he said, then added, "Probably both eyes."

"Excellency, I still don't understand why he put them there in the first place. How do these facts relate to Hugo being in danger?"

"Very closely. Two men, hidden under the cloak of darkness, were standing near his gate. They had intended to kill your lieutenant, but he managed to evade being shot, which is still a bit of a mystery to me. He took off on foot, pursuing them. I suppose he took his boots off so they wouldn't hear him chasing them. He left the boots in my care. Or, more accurately, in the sentry's care, but that would be splitting hairs."

"What? He followed them alone? How careless of him!"

"Don't worry, my dear *Margotchen*," he said affectionately. "If we have his boots, then we'll be sure to get him, too. He probably wanted to see who the villains were."

"I already have an idea as to their identity."

"Really, you have suspects?"

She nodded. "Yes! Surely one of them must be the same person who stabbed him earlier tonight."

"Stabbed him? Tonight? Heavens! Stabbed him where?"

"In his arm."

"Oh, then it wasn't too serious?"

"They were aiming for his heart!"

"Donner and Doria![10.2] They meant business."

"If he hadn't worn the metal breastplate, he would be dead by now."

"Ah, he wore a *cuirass?*"

"Yes," she said. A fellow officer loaned him one."

"Good! So, he was sensible enough to wear it. Who was the perpetrator?"

"My God! I find it almost impossible to tell you."

As she spoke, realization seemed to flood over him. "Ah! Now I have an inkling who is behind the attack. I want to reassure you that you can be open and honest with me. Perhaps I can help you, as well as your lieutenant. Please tell me everything, but first I need to fill my pipe. I think better with the aroma of a good pipe filling my senses with a deep, burning inhalation.[10.3] Once my pipe has found a comfortable place under my moustache, I can give you my undivided attention." Blücher filled one of his favorite pipes and lit the contents. Seating himself on the couch, he motioned to Margot to seat herself on a divan and continue her tale.

≪✠≫

Elsewhere, events surrounding Löwenklau could best have been summed up as anything but ordinary. He had spent a considerable amount of time with Margot and felt he'd stayed perhaps too long before departing. Her mother had offered him a spare room for the night, so he wouldn't have to go home in the dark a second time. Both ladies feared another reprisal was possible. He had declined their offer and finally started his journey home.

Margot had accompanied him to the gate. She made only one request of him; to be careful on his return, due to the omnipresent dangers on the street. Resolving to be vigilant, he didn't discount the possibility of a second attempt on his life. If that turned out to be the case, he knew they would employ a more formidable weapon, likely a firearm. Repelling such an attack would be more difficult. For this reason, he resolved to walk in the middle of the street. His enemies were probably concealed near a gate, making detection difficult.

By the time he approached his residence, a thought struck him. If they wanted to be certain of ambushing him, what better place would there be to hide than near his own gate? The lieutenant slowed his pace, his eyes trying to pierce the darkness.

He came to within four or five paces of his gate when he heard a loud cry. "Löwenklau! Halt! Turn around! They're after your hide!" He recognized the marshal's voice right away, and in particular his tone of warning, which he would undoubtedly have had a good reason for employing.

Löwenklau was about to turn around when a beam of light escaped from a nearby lantern. He correctly assumed the light was meant to expose him, by presenting a clear target for a pistol shot. He threw himself to the pavement, and not a moment too soon. The decisiveness of that pivotal instant saved his life. He hadn't hit the ground yet when he heard the loud rapport of a pistol. The bullet that had been meant for his head sailed harmlessly through the air above him.

"He threw himself to the ground! Light up the ground!" an urgent voice rasped.

Although he barely heard the voice, he recognized it as Captain Richemonte's. For a second time, the light revealed him, and in a desperate move he rolled his body to the side. A split second later, another shot rang out, this time missing him by only centimeters, striking the pavement beside him and ricocheting away.

He decided to change tactics from avoidance to action. The shooter had used up both barrels. What if he had another pistol? Löwenklau didn't have to think twice. He jumped to his feet and lunged at his enemies. His fist connected with the nearest one, who stumbled and dropped his lantern, immediately abandoning his partner and running down the street.

Hugo grabbed the remaining culprit. "This time you won't get away, you villain!" he called out.

Löwenklau tried wrestling him to the ground. The captain dropped the spent pistol in order to defend himself better and grabbed him by the front. Once again Richemonte came across that strange feeling of striking metal.

"Coward!" the captain hissed. "Stop hiding behind that metal plate!"

The Frenchman gripped his arm, aiming for the wound he had inflicted during the first attack. Löwenklau cried out in pain.

"Ah! I've found the vulnerable spot!" his enemy taunted.

The captain used both his hands and concentrated with all his might on the weak spot. Because of the pain, Löwenklau had no choice but to let go of his assailant. As he freed his injured arm, his adversary gained the advantage, broke free, and jumped to the side. Löwenklau lunged ahead, thinking his enemy was still in front of him, but missed him in the darkness and stumbled. The captain abandoned the assault, the sound of his footsteps echoing down the street.

Without hesitating, Löwenklau took off in pursuit. He started to run, but quickly came to the realization that it would be folly to chase his assailants in the dark, whose steps he couldn't hear due to his own. As he stopped to remove his boots, he noticed he was near the gate to Blücher's residence.

"I'm Lieutenant von Löwenklau! Keep an eye on my boots!" he called out to the sentry, tossing them out onto the street.

Hugo then continued on after his enemies, who had, by this time, gained a considerable lead, even though he had lingered only a moment. Fortunately, luck was with him. He could still hear the footfall of their boots. Being in excellent shape, he felt he could close the gap. Although the breastplate was a nuisance, he held out and started to cut into their lead.

Out of instinct, he stopped to listen. He was right to do so, for their footsteps started to separate. Quickly, he had to decide which one to pursue. One went into a side alley while the other ran on ahead. The alley wasn't paved, which would make it difficult for him to follow, so he decided to head straight.

Following the second man, he noticed the figure ahead taking a sudden left. He followed suit, but stopped at the next corner, turning left, and repeating the maneuver at the next intersection. Finally, stopping to catch his breath, Löwenklau tried to gain his bearings. When the footsteps started to fade, he cautiously proceeded.

It dawned on him that this was the same alley the first man had ducked into. He had to be careful, assuming that the two men had probably planned to meet here. He slowly groped his way forward and discovered the narrow alley had a high brick wall on the right and a lower garden wall on the left. He slowly crept forward, then stopped when he thought he heard a noise nearby.

There it was, on the left wall, likely a key turning in an old rusty lock. *There must be a gate in the garden wall*, he thought. He slowly felt his way along the wall. When he neared the gate, he heard whispering.

"Well, that went smoothly!" a man said sarcastically, believing they had eluded their pursuer.

"It's your fault!" said the other.

"Mine? How come?"

"Your thrust was inadequate, and you demonstrated poor aim!"

"Well, how can I aim properly when you can't light up the target? Why did you have to abandon all and run? We could have finished him off together,

I couldn't do it alone! You called me a coward, and now you can have it back, twofold."

"I wouldn't have considered leaving you if the unexpected help hadn't arrived."

"Help? Help from where?"

"Didn't you hear someone calling just as I was about to open the lantern?"

"Yes. Who could that have been? It ruined everything!" The voice paused. "Tomorrow is another day. A postponement is not a cancellation."

"True. We should go inside. This isn't the best place to make revisions to the plan."

"How are we going to get in? Through the door?"

"No! My servants would see us. They still believe I'm at work in my study. We'll climb up on the veranda and go in through the window."

"Is it open?"

"Yes. Come on."

The voices faded into the night. Had they left? Löwenklau had to be sure, and so he remained perfectly still. After a few minutes, he detected a distant noise, consistent with a window being opened. He decided to follow them.

The lieutenant knew he had to become familiar with the layout of the house. He felt his way along the wall. The wall was taller than he thought, with its top out of reach. The large stones had gaps, though, that provided sufficient handholds, allowing him to climb to the top without difficulty. Satisfied there was no one in the garden, he quietly climbed down the other side. It was no ordinary undertaking for him to enter these premises.

If they confronted him here, it would certainly be a fight to the finish. As a soldier living in Paris, one of the occupying forces, pursuing French citizens, albeit his enemies, he wouldn't be shown pity, least of all mercy. He was standing in the garden, though the darkness prevented him from seeing where he was. Relying on touch, he felt his way toward the house. Following the wall to the center of the courtyard, he finally came to the veranda they had mentioned.

This must be where they climbed in, he guessed. *If it supported their combined weight, it'll support mine. I have to try.*

The officer felt the lath pieces and cross members, managing to pull himself up. Once on top, he carefully examined the deck to see if it would carry his weight. Deciding it would, Hugo quietly crept to the window. Although he found it locked, he reasoned that it must have been the one they used. Peering into the darkness, he noticed an adjoining door which led to a brightly lit room. Two men were pacing back and forth, caught up in an animated conversation. Each time one came near the door, he could be seen and heard, allowing Löwenklau to catch portions of their conversation.

Aha! It's the captain and the baron! I should have guessed, he thought. They both appeared agitated, judging from their gestures and the heated discussion. Unfortunately, he only caught small segments of the exchange.

"...yes, that's the best!" he heard the captain say.

"...and if I get her without blemish," the baron replied. "I should pay the same..."

"That should speak for itself, because if I don't agree, nothing will come of it..."

"Well then! All right. I suppose... our original agreement... and you'll be my brother-in-law, and one should consider... "

"If it is successful, then they'll look in vain... especially that damned Löwenklau who..."

"The main problem..." the baron said. "If we are able... the time he usually comes... it should come to pass... or else it'll be too late..."

"I'm going to make certain inquiries tomorrow," said the captain, "...and be of service... resistance at least..."

"I will find a way to break the... and count on your help," said the baron. "I expect to find... Margot's honor is at stake... thus it remains that... I'm counting on it."

They abruptly closed the dividing door. The light went out and the conversation moved to another room. Löwenklau waited for a while longer, without results. He successfully retraced his steps. The garden shed was higher than the alley, allowing him to climb the wall with relative ease. He realized it would be to his advantage to be able to find this small alley and its narrow gate again in the daylight. He made a mental note of a few features so he would be able to locate the house again later.

As he walked back, Hugo thought about the conversation he'd overheard and its implications. He recognized they had concocted a new plan, but it wasn't clear to him what it entailed. He had caught only bits and pieces and was trying to make some sense of it. The captain was going to make inquiries, Margot's honor was at stake, and they planned to overcome her resistance. But all of this didn't amount to anything conclusive. The only certainty was that it was to be carried out soon.

Löwenklau soon came to his street and the marshal's palace. He returned to the place where he had left his boots, but found them missing. He walked over to the sentry to make inquiries. Due to his quiet footsteps, they didn't hear his approach until he was nearly upon them.

"Stop!" the sentry called out. "Who goes there?"

"A lieutenant with the Prussian Hussars," he replied. "How long have you been here?"

"Not quite an hour, sir."

"Were you given a pair of boots?"

"No, sir."

"Were you not told that an officer would return?"

"Of course, Lieutenant."

"What name were you given?"

"Lieutenant von Löwenklau."

"I am Lieutenant von Löwenklau."

After a quick pause, the sentry responded. "The lieutenant is expected immediately at his Excellency's reception hall."

"Really? At this late hour?"

"Yes, right away, sir. We are to inform the lieutenant not to go home."

A momentary embarrassment settled in. "*Sapperlot!* I don't have my boots with me!"

"His Excellency has them inside."

"Were they confiscated?"

"I don't know, but we were told to advise the lieutenant to present himself immediately—in his socks!"

"Well then, let's proceed!"

He entered and climbed the stairs to the foyer. Another sentry stood in front of the drawing room.

"What are you doing here so late?" Löwenklau asked.

"I have been ordered to await your arrival and to advise his Excellency."

"Ah! So he is expecting me?"

"Yes."

"Then advise His Excellency that I have arrived!"

The subordinate ducked inside and returned a few minutes later, advising him to enter. The lieutenant nodded curtly and closed the door behind him.

He went forward three steps, then made the required bow upon catching sight of the marshal. Blücher was near his desk and the smell of pipe tobacco was everywhere. Situated on the table was a costly Japanese platter, which the marshal had used to collect the ashes. Sulfur sticks and matches had been left haphazardly on a silver tray.

"Well, well, what do we have here?" Blücher asked, feigning surprise. "You enter my drawing room quietly, like a rogue. As if my money is not safe with your sticky fingers. Heavens! Just look at you, my boy. You don't have any boots on!"

"At your service, Excellency!"

"Well, where are they?"

"They were unexpectedly appropriated by His Excellency's sticky fingers!"

Blücher smirked, and held up his hand in a mock gesture. "Just keep your jokes to yourself. You know, I usually forgive the bad ones, but the good ones told at my expense usually merit solitary confinement!"[10.4] He continued, trying to sound serious. "In all my recollection, it has never occurred to me that a lieutenant should present himself without wearing his boots! It's highly irregular!"

"It's even more puzzling His Excellency should command a lieutenant to appear in mere socks."

"Listen, my boy! That was a bad joke, and I won't hold it against you. Don't make too much out of it. Now that your socks are out in the open, I can think of someone who would appreciate them more. Look at those socks, my son! They're dirtier than a pair of muckers worn by a horse handler. Your toes certainly look healthy enough. Go to the wardrobe and collect your boots!"

Löwenklau obeyed and opened the wardrobe. There they were, situated alongside His Excellency's gold and silver harnesses. He took them out and put them on in front of the marshal.

"Well now," the Marshal replied heartily, "this is the Hugo I remember. Go to the other door and knock!"

Löwenklau did as instructed. The door opened immediately, and he was struck with surprise at what he found inside.

"Margot!"

"Hugo!"

They embraced, not in the least embarrassed by the marshal's presence. The old man pulled on his moustache and contorted his face in all sorts of grimaces.

"Yes," he finally said, "these two sure are wrapped up in each other! What about the old Gebhard Leberecht? Who is going to pay any attention to him?"

"I will!" Margot replied.

She walked up to him fearlessly and embraced his neck, kissing him tenderly on his cheek.

"Girl, this is going about it the wrong way. Didn't Hugo teach you any better than that? Come here, my pretty one!" He pulled her closer and kissed her on the mouth. He then turned to face Löwenklau. "If you object, then report me or give me a smack! I'll have you know I spent several hours with your little witch. She completely captivated me, so we came to an arrangement, that it would be more fitting if you were the general and I the lieutenant."

Hugo sat down beside her and, with Blücher catching every word, began to recite his adventure. Blücher didn't interrupt, instead pacing back and forth, smoking his pipe with the fervor of an erupting volcano. Löwenklau was thorough in his report, leaving out not even the smallest detail. Margot leaned her head on his shoulder and started to cry, happy to have him back, safe and sound. To her, it seemed the great field marshal had become much more than a trusted friend. He was more like a father, in front of whom she could be herself and not hold back her emotions. When Hugo came to the end of his story, Blücher let out a groan.

"Unbelievable! Your only brother," he said to Margot. Turning to Hugo, he asked, "What will you do, my son?"

"Strike them down when I find them!"

"No, that wouldn't be acceptable. I forbid you, understand?"

"But, Your Excellency—"

"*Papperlappap.* I promised her!" he said, pointing to Margot.

Löwenklau looked with tenderness into her moist, beautiful eyes. "Margot, are you serious? Do you want me to show leniency...?"

"Hugo, he's still my brother!"

"All right! What about this Baron de Reillac?"

"Him, too. I don't want you to keep entangling yourself with him."

"She's right. It's the best way," Blücher replied, moved with compassion for the young couple. "Didn't you know Rebecca also heaped burning coals upon Herod's head?"[10.5] The lieutenant couldn't suppress a smile. The marshal noticed his snicker and feigned embarrassment. "What are you laughing at? Was it just peat instead of coal?"

"It must have been chunks of coal, Excellency, because the top of Herod's head was almost entirely consumed. Actually, I would find it difficult to let the baron go. He doesn't concern us, and we don't owe him anything, but he will still regard us as an enemy for life."

"Can you deal with him without it affecting my brother?" asked Margot.

"It would be difficult," Löwenklau admitted, "but if we don't deal with them now, we expose ourselves to their next blow. You remember what I overheard. They're already scheming some new, dastardly plan."

"I have the answer, my boy," said Blücher. "Instead of rendering them harmless, I would much rather protect you both. Either solution leads to the same result. What would you think if I arranged for you to go to Berlin, my boy?"

"But Excellency, how can I leave Margot behind without my protection?"

"Not at all. I've already discussed this with her. Madame Richemonte has a relative in Belgium. Both ladies will leave on an excursion tomorrow, and no one will learn of their whereabouts. Once there, the ladies will be safe from the offences of those scoundrels."

Löwenklau was struck by the brilliance of the plan. "That's a great idea, Excellency!" he said, smiling. "If we're able to carry it out, we'll avoid prosecution and also escape the reprisals that would naturally follow."

"Of course it's a great idea. You've already witnessed the old Blücher playing detective. Your part is to accompany the ladies to their destination and then proceed directly to Berlin. I'll fill you in later with the details. Of course, you'll have to assist me in preparing the necessary documentation."

"At your service, Excellency!"

"Good! Now take your leave and escort your lady home, which is becoming of a good gentleman. Come see me punctually at nine o'clock. We'll need the whole day to complete this, and later in the evening we can meet again. To ensure nothing else befalls you tonight, I'll send an eight-man detachment along, whose job will be to escort you back safely to Madame's house. Here's the order, my boy," he said, passing the lieutenant a piece of paper. "Hand it to the duty sergeant. Now, good night my children! And when you kiss each other, keep the noise down. It tastes much sweeter when it's quiet and tender."

They left with their newfound escort, eventually reaching the Richemonte residence without further incident. The porter opened personally.

"Excuse me, Mademoiselle," he said. "Were you with Marshal Blücher?"

"Yes," she replied.

He made a reverent bow to her. When she departed, he reflected, *He can't be just a lieutenant. More likely an incognito prince. Why else would those two be held in such high esteem by the marshal? I wish them all the best, even for Margot to become a princess.*

Margot was overwhelmed with the events of the last few hours, and felt the need to wake her mother. Madame Richemonte was initially stunned to hear about the danger the young lieutenant had barely escaped and that Margot had been brave enough to go out into the street a second time. She was able to calm herself only when she learned of the night's successful conclusion.

The suggestion to visit her Belgian relatives was well-received. She had often been invited for a visit, but had been unable to accept. Feeling both of them would be received with open arms, she quickly penned a letter to her acquaintance and announced their plans. Löwenklau promised to look after the letter.

They felt the packing of their goods and other necessary arrangements should be done as quietly as possible, deciding to give notice to their maid just before they departed. After their arrival in Belgium, mother and daughter would find a suitable time to travel to Berlin so the couple could plan for the upcoming wedding. For this reason, they chose not to bring furniture and other cumbersome items, but rather planned to sell them locally. Blücher indicated he would make the proper arrangements to protect the privacy of the two ladies.

While Löwenklau was occupied with the marshal, mother and daughter had many items of business to arrange in order to reduce their burden on the day of the trip. Madame's health had suffered of late, particularly out of concern for her stepson. It came as no surprise when evening arrived and she found all her energy was spent. She decided to lie down again to regain some of her strength for the journey ahead.

"Do you think the marshal will pay us a visit?" Madame asked Margot.

"Either that or he'll invite us formally to attend as guests at his palace, Mama. I'm sure he said we needed to meet and go over some of the details."

"If he shows up, then I'll come down to meet him. Should he send an invitation, you'll have to convey my regrets, as I'm not up to a lengthy visit. Perhaps I'll find some time tomorrow to bid him farewell and thank him for all his kindness."

CHAPTER ELEVEN
A Mademoiselle Disappears

It was getting dark and Margot had just lit a lantern when she heard the rattle of a carriage stopping at the gate. The bell rang downstairs a moment later. She went down to look for herself.

A young officer was waiting for her when the porter opened the door. He was dressed in a Prussian uniform, adorned with a sash indicating his rank as an adjutant.

"Excuse me, Mademoiselle," he said, bowing deeply. "Am I at the correct address, the Richemonte household?"

"Of course! Please come in, Lieutenant." She led him into the salon and asked him to take a seat.

"Pardon, Mademoiselle, but I must carry out my obligations before I can attend to your request. Is Madame Richemonte ready to accompany us?"

"Unfortunately, no. She is not well."

It seemed, for the briefest moment, that a look of satisfaction crossed the officer's face, one that didn't draw Margot's notice.

"I am sorry to hear that," he replied regretfully. "Do I have the honor of meeting Mademoiselle Richemonte?"

She answered with a slight bow.

"Then allow me to congratulate you on your betrothal. I have come on behalf of his Excellency, the Field Marshal von Blücher. His Excellency is pleased to invite both ladies to his residence for dinner. Since the gracious lady is not feeling well, may I suggest she dispense with the ordeal of a late visit?"

"Thank you, Monsieur. Having anticipated an invite, we already mutually agreed that it would be best if my mother declined. Please, allow me one minute to inform her. Is Lieutenant von Löwenklau with His Excellency?"

"Of course."

"No doubt he is awaiting my arrival. I will not require any more time to get ready. I will be right back."

When Margot walked into the adjoining room, the masquerading officer took a few moments to look around the room. *Sapperlot! What a surprise*, he mused. *I thought I would run into a problem, one that could only be remedied by the most skilled diplomacy. Instead, everything is going according to plan. She was expecting a car-*

riage to pick her up and is even dressed for the evening. Her mother has already decided not to go out. If that isn't a miracle, I don't know what is! As long as that damned Löwenklau stays out of the way, I will have succeeded!

Margot reappeared a mere two minutes later, declaring she was ready to depart. Since she knew the marshal was unpretentious in welcoming guests, she dispensed with fussing over her appearance. Her outfit was modest, yet outwardly pleasant. It was simplicity that elevated her beauty. Even the alleged ordinance officer took notice, casting an admiring glance her way. She looked refined and distinguished, and yet also held the charm of youthful innocence. The swindler felt a momentary pang of conscience, settling into a deep regret over what he was about to do.

She really is beautiful, he thought. *So bright and chaste. Too bad this wonderful creature is destined to become a sport for the crusty old baron. It's a damned shame! If my father weren't employed by him, I would have thought twice before consenting to help the baron in one of his schemes. If only he were younger and more appealing. I feel sorry for what's to become of her.* He gestured with a bow, indicating he was prepared to escort her. Margot started her journey, not realizing its true significance.

The carriage was waiting at the gate. Pierre, the baron's valet, now attired as a coachman, sat disguised on the buckboard. The officer opened the carriage door, allowing Margot to climb inside. He followed suit and, after closing the door behind him, they embarked on the short trip. It was already dark outside, and the odd lantern was lit on the street, though their sparse arrangement was not sufficient to light the way. The ordinance officer began a lively conversation in an effort to distract Margot from watching where they were going. Had she been paying attention, she would have noticed the coach turn onto the street where Blücher resided, yet continue past the palace. Nonetheless, something within Margot became alert. Like every person, she possessed an inherent trait that allowed her to accurately sense the passage of time. By her own reasoning they should have arrived by now.

"Monsieur, shouldn't we have arrived already?" she asked.

"It would seem so, Mademoiselle," he replied. "I just noticed the coachman take a slight detour. Let me have a closer look, to see if I am right." He peered out his window, leaving the impression he couldn't distinguish anything. He looked across to the other window. "If you please, Mademoiselle, I will take a look from your side." As she moved back from the window to allow him room, she was suddenly and forcefully pressed into the corner of the coach.

"Dear God! What is this? What are you...?"

Margot was unable to speak another word. While a handkerchief clamped down over her mouth, a strong unpleasant odor emanated from it and invaded her nasal passages, sapping her strength. Out of desperation, she tried to repel her attacker, but in her powerless state she wouldn't have held off even a child, much less a grown man. A few seconds later, she lay unconscious on the floor of the carriage, hostage to the unfriendly officer.

"Ah! That was easy enough," the actor whispered into her ear. "I would have expected it to be more difficult. Now, allow me to take a small reward that wasn't part of the arrangement." While the carriage continued moving, he slid over to her motionless form, lifted her head gently, and pressed his lips against her exquisite mouth. Suddenly, he found himself overwhelmed by the strong odor of the narcotic substance. It nearly took his breath away.

"Damn," he muttered to himself. *I can't do it! I just about lost consciousness, as she did. Too bad! I suppose it would have been short lived anyway,* he thought as the coach brought them to a stop.

The carriage reached the alley and turned into it, stopping at the prearranged gate. The gate door opened inwardly, revealing the presence of two eager men: Baron de Reillac and Captain Richemonte.

"Well! Did we succeed?" the baron asked his valet.

"I'm not entirely sure," Pierre replied from his lofty perch.

"Not entirely? Hang it all! You must know if she is inside."

"She is inside the coach, though it remains to be seen if the 'perfume' did its job."

"We'll find out right away," the baron said, reaching for the carriage door. His senses reeled as he immediately detected the substance. "Well, did it work?" he asked impatiently.

"Completely," the actor said from inside.

"Then let's get her out." Reillac reached for Margot's unconscious form while the captain stepped in to help. "Here is your money," Reillac said, pressing a small purse containing the ill-gained wages. "Now return the carriage." The actor pocketed the payment and sat down in the carriage.

"How much time do I have before I need to return?" Pierre asked.

"Just until you have returned the coach. I may need you soon."

"It may take me a while."

"How come?"

The valet shrugged, gesturing to the carriage. "We have to sanitize the interior. The narcotic's aftertaste can linger for quite some time, and we wouldn't want it to be traced back to us."

"All right! How will you disinfect the coach?"

"I have all the required items with me. We'll go a little ways out of the city and pick a secluded field where we won't be disturbed. But it will take some time. We should return by midnight."

"Go on, then! I'll handle the rest."

The carriage rolled down the alley, disappearing from view into the darkness.

"Monsieur, please carry your sister," the baron said to Richemonte. "I will open and close the doors."

Richemonte followed the man's instructions and carried Margot upstairs to the library. This was accomplished without detection, as Reillac had had the foresight to grant most of the servants an evening off. The one or two who remained had been sent on minor errands. Once upstairs, the captain positioned his sister on a chair.

"I think we should tie her up," Richemonte said.

"Tie her up? Do you really think that's necessary?"

"I do. She'll probably make a fuss when she revives."

"*Pah!* We can deal with that by placing a gag in her mouth."

"Fine, but we better tie her arms so she won't be able to remove it."

The baron regarded her menacingly. "Look at her! She's as pale as a corpse."

"I hope she's all right and didn't succumb to the narcotic," Richemonte said, his eyes conveying a peculiar glow.

"I certainly hope not, for your sake."

"That sure would put an end to your plans."

"And yours as well!"

"It doesn't matter that much to me," the brother said dismissively.

"I doubt that. If it were the case, I wouldn't become your brother-in-law, and there wouldn't be any need to rip up the notes."

The captain replied with a fiendish smile, baring his teeth. "Oh, I'm not afraid of them anymore. They no longer have a hold on me."

"Really? Why is that?" asked the baron, paying more attention now.

"It's quite simple. You now have control of my sister and I'm asking for the notes in exchange."

"She is still not my wife."

"Whether she is or isn't, the outcome depends on your own cunning."

"True," Reillac allowed, "but things can still go awry, regardless how well it is planned."

"That's no longer my concern, Baron!"

"I don't understand you, Captain. I gave you my word that I would destroy the notes once Margot and I have been married. I'll fulfill my end of the bargain, but only when the condition is met."

The captain shrugged his shoulders. "If that makes you happy, then keep those papers," he replied. "As far as I'm concerned, they've already been ripped up."

The baron glanced at him in surprise. "What do you mean?" he asked.

"Do I really have to explain it to you?"

"Humor me, please."

"Do you know the penalty for kidnapping?" Richemonte asked.

"Oh, I see what you're getting at..."

"Do you know the consequences of forcing a lady's hand in marriage?"

The baron's face turned red with anger. "Go to hell!" he spat. "Do you think you can frighten me?"

"No, that isn't my intent. I merely wish to point out that I'm faced with the same predicament."

"Are you threatening me?"

"Not in the least! I merely want you to realize that the notes no longer have the same hold on me they once did."

"I intend to present them," the baron said, "should my plans concerning your sister hit a stumbling block!"

"Then tender them, for God's sake! But know this, you'll not receive any payment."

"Then prepare yourself for debtor's prison, Captain!"

"And you as well, Baron, for criminal proceedings!"

"*Sapperlot!* Now I get it. Would you really report me to the authorities?"

"Without question."

The baron contemplated that for a moment before continuing. "You have the ability to be a formidable adversary. Yet you forget about one important point."

"Which one?" asked the captain, genuinely curious.

"You're implicated in all of this."

"Prove it!"

"Well, you're here with me."

The captain laughed at him contemptuously. "How do you intend to prove my complicity?" he replied. "Have I ever spoken to your valet about our plans?"

"No."

"Or with his son, the infamous ordinance officer?"

"No."

"Or with anyone else, for that matter?"

"Certainly not! However, both of them have seen you near my carriage!"

"Of course. But they still can't prove I was aware of anything. I have planned my part carefully from the beginning, so as not to be implicated later. Only Margot will learn of my involvement. I hate her and I want her to know I am seeking my revenge."

"Captain, you are a dreadful man!"

"Yes, well, we are both equal in this respect," he replied coldly. "Look at her, Baron! I get the impression she'll wake up soon. The glow has returned to her cheeks. We need to tie her up."

They tied her to the chair with cloths and placed a handkerchief in her mouth, making her incapable of screaming.

Elsewhere, on his way with his father out of town, the disguised actor found himself contemplating his prior thoughts at the Richemonte residence. *As long as that damned Löwenklau stays out of the way, I will have succeeded.* He certainly would have been surprised to learn that the one thing which he feared most—the discovery of their plot—hung on one man's efforts.

◈✠◈

Löwenklau spent the whole day at the palace with the marshal, making plans for the upcoming journey. With the onset of evening, the room darkened and Löwenklau reached up, pulling down a fedora Blücher had absentmindedly tossed over an arm of the chandelier. He lit the candle, brightening the study once again.

Both men continued to work hard, engrossed in their paperwork. Blücher prepared instructions from himself to Löwenklau in written form. Some of the documents were standard correspondence, while others contained information of a more sensitive nature. All were to be delivered in person upon Hugo's arrival in Berlin.

"There's a rumor," Blücher began, "that His Majesty and his entourage are planning a trip to England. It'll be nothing more than a fanfare of their exploits in saving Europe from Napoleon. Naturally, I'm included and dare not refuse the King's entreaty. I fear I'll be dragged around for weeks, a reluctant witness to the spectacle. It'll be some time before I have an opportunity to return home. I'll require a reliable man, one whom I can trust, to, in effect, act as my eyes and ears. He would keep watch and inform me of the circumstances upon my arrival. I too have to contend with enemies, some lesser and some greater. Do you understand me?"

"Absolutely, Excellency!" Löwenklau answered, smiling knowingly.

"Well, I see you haven't fallen down, my boy.[11.1] This is why I've chosen you and know I can be candid. Tell me again, what happened to Napoleon?"

"He was banished from France and confined," Löwenklau said, humoring him.

"Confined where?" asked Blücher, feigning ignorance.

"On Elba, of course."

"Wonderful!" exclaimed Blücher sarcastically. "I had no idea at the time what kind of place this Elba really is. I hadn't ever heard its name prior to his banishment. Now, tell me, what do you make of it?"

"It is a small island."

"Yes. But what is unusual about it?"

"It has an open coastline."

"Exactly, my boy! An island without cliffs, bulwarks, or reinforced walls. This so-called *bonahomier*[11.2] can leave at his pleasure! Where is this little island located?"

"Near Italy."

"Yes," the marshal confirmed. "It's very close to the Italian coastline where this emperor is worshiped. Who can make any sense out of this decision? Hang it all! They should never have allowed him such freedom. Instead of Elba, they should have dumped him in Mount Vesuvius. There he would have felt some heat, much like he gave us. I'm telling you, I don't trust him. Mark my words—he's coming back!"

"I agree with you, Excellency. He has a large following in France. They'll not only look forward to, but even celebrate, his return."

"I believe you," Blücher said. "We soldiers have labored hard to remove him from power only to be undermined by pencil pushers who have left the back door open so he can slip back in. These idiots like to play with gunpowder and think they won't be blasted to pieces. They form a congress for world peace, take a chunk of one country, a sliver from another, and apportion it to a third. Before they get their act together, Napoleon will suddenly rise up and rap their knuckles. What will happen then, my son?"

"They'll be calling, 'Where is the old Blücher?'"

"Yes, they'll be calling for the old man to get them out of a bad predicament. What these 'political tailors' cut up, stitch, and patch, the old Blücher will resolve with one thrust of his saber. This is why I need to keep my eyes open and send you in my place, to keep a semblance of reason in the Prussian aristocracy. Naturally, we'll correspond on a regular basis. If you can't make any sense of my letters, it would be better to burn them in a fire than show them to one of those bootlickers.

"Now, let's try to finish. I still have more instructions that need to be put into correspondence."

Both men worked into the evening. At long last, Blücher put the last stroke on the last piece of paper. "Finally!" he exclaimed, satisfied. "Put your quill in the oven, throw the ink well against the wall, and stuff those papers in your coat pocket. I'm tired of all this paperwork. Now, go to your Margot and tell her to bring her mother along for a little visit. We still have things to discuss."

Löwenklau didn't have to be told twice and he quickly carried out the order.

It was already dark. As he was about to turn into *Rue d'Ange*, he met a carriage coming his way. Much like him, the driver seemed to be in a hurry, but Löwenklau was too preoccupied with his own thoughts to pay him any heed. He had no idea that this very carriage sped away with his beloved Margot, kidnapped and unconscious.

When he reached the residence, the maid admitted him.

"Is Mademoiselle Margot at home?" he inquired by way of greeting.

"No, Monsieur. She just left."

"Oh. Where to?"

"She's on her way to the field marshal's palace."

"Really? How curious! Did Madame accompany her?"

"No."

"Did Mademoiselle go alone?"

"I believe an officer was with her."

Löwenklau was taken aback. "What kind of officer?" he asked. "A German one?"

"I'm not sure. Madame would probably know."

"Please, announce my presence right away!"

Madame Richemonte was surprised to hear Löwenklau was in the foyer. Upon admitting him, she responded to his inquiry. "Margot drove to see the marshal, my dear lieutenant."

"When was this?"

"Just a few minutes ago, in his carriage."

"I met a carriage on the way here. I heard a German officer came with it."

"Yes. An ordinance officer from the marshal!"

"An ordinance officer? Impossible!"

"Perhaps he was an adjutant?"

"Still unlikely."

"Lieutenant, the marshal sent an officer to collect us for a dinner at his palace."

Löwenklau felt as if his heart had skipped a beat, but managed to keep his composure. "Did you get his name?"

"No, I didn't. Come to think of it, I didn't even see him."

"Were you not also invited, Madame?"

"Yes, but I'm still not feeling up to a visit. Therefore, I excused myself, sending my regrets."

"Ah! Then I must apologize for my mistake."

"A mistake?"

"Yes, I didn't realize the marshal had the foresight to send for a carriage. I came on my own to collect you both. Please excuse my haste."

"Well then! My dear lieutenant, would you be so kind as to personally give my regards to the marshal for his thoughtfulness? Perhaps I will have time to see him tomorrow before we depart."

Löwenklau assured her that he would and left the house. A growing uneasiness crept into his thoughts as he made his way back across town. Fearing they had fallen prey to a new, deliberate plot brought on by the baron and Captain Richemonte, he ran all the way back to the marshal's palace, arriving red-faced and out of breath.

"*Zounds*, where have you been?" Blücher asked. "Is something wrong?"

"Is Margot here, Excellency?" Hugo replied.

"No, I thought you would bring her along."

"His Excellency didn't send for her?"

"No."

"No carriage?"

"None whatsoever."

"No ordinance officer with a carriage?"

"No. What's going through that brain of yours?"

Hearing these answers, Löwenklau was forced to accept the inescapable conclusion. "I fear she has been abducted!"

The marshal jumped out of his chair. "A thousand devils!" he called out. "Kidnapped? Are you out of your mind?"

"Certainly not, Excellency. I must leave at once!" He turned toward the door, intending to make a hasty exit.

"Hold on and turn around this instant!" Blucher said, calling him back. "Don't you realize, you dunderhead,[11.3] that you have to remain until I dismiss you! What's all this fuss about Margot? If someone has concocted a devilish scheme, then you can't just storm out without a plan. You have to handle this with wisdom and deliberation. Do you get my drift, my boy?"

Löwenklau realized the old man was right and forced himself to calm down. "Margot has been abducted, Excellency!"

"Yes, I know. You already told me that much. But how?"

"Just a short time ago, a carriage pulled up to Margot's house."

"Ah! Accompanied by an officer?"

"Yes."

"What kind?"

"I don't know. Madame didn't see him. He identified himself as an ordinance officer..."

"Sent by me?"

"Yes, with an invitation to dinner from His Excellency!"

"Damn!"

"Madame excused herself," the lieutenant went on, "sending her regrets because she felt too tired."

"Which means Margot went alone."

"Evidently."

"Where to?"

"That part isn't clear, but probably down the street." Löwenklau could hardly contain himself. His voice betrayed his concern for Margot. Blücher began to pace back and forth across the room.

"It's all a damned lie, a heinous plot without equal. I never sent a carriage. She has been abducted, but by whom?"

"Who else but Baron de Reillac."

Blücher seemed forced to agree. "*Zounds!* It has to be him. And her sweet stepbrother is probably an accomplice!"

"No doubt, Excellency!"

"Where did they abscond with her? If we only knew!"

"I think I can guess."

"Really?"

"Yes," Löwenklau said. "Unless I'm mistaken, I believe I know just the place."

"This is good. Very good. We could surprise them in the act."

"My best guess is they brought her to Reillac's house."

"Why do you suppose that?"

"They were plotting something last night. Excellency, do you remember what I overheard?"

"What?"

"A new plot. The captain wanted to make inquiries. I believe their plan was to abduct Margot all along!" He made a fist and prepared himself to storm out the door. "Yesterday, I heard they wanted to force Margot into a marriage with the baron. Now I know how they plan to accomplish it. Can His Excellency guess the means?"

Blücher stepped back a pace. "Damn!" he said, his eyes glowering as he spoke. "Could it really be possible?"

"I'm convinced of it."

"I'll make mince meat out of both of them!"

"Please give me leave. I have to go and find out if I'm right!"

"Give you leave? What for? You're not going anywhere without me. Do you have any weapons on you?"

"Not on me, Excellency."

"Then grab a couple of my pistols for yourself. Do you think we can find the baron's house in the dark?"

"I took great care when I left so I would recognize it again."

"All right! We will overpower them!"

Blücher affixed his saber and removed two pistols from the wall. He was excited, as though he were about to go into battle. Löwenklau didn't want to lose valuable time, and yet he hesitated.

"Excellency, your saber will be too cumbersome."

"Why do you say that?"

"Because we'll need to climb a high wall, followed by a veranda."

"Very well. I'll leave it at home. Are two of us enough?"

"I don't know. It depends on the circumstances."

"Then we'll appropriate two or three hardy boys from the guardhouse."

Löwenklau paused and mulled things over in his head. "Excellency, one problem will be gaining entry into the house. It's still a private residence, not a military target."

"No problem. We'll just climb the lattice and smash the window. Just like that, we'll be in. *Basta!* What could be simpler than that?"

"True, but we'll be breaking into a private dwelling!"

"If it was up to me, we would have dismantled all of France!"

"Excellency, we need a good reason to enter by force."

"The villains have the girl," Blücher blustered, getting caught up in the moment. "That's good enough to absolve us from any wrongdoing."

"If we could only prove she's there! We'll need the proper authority to search the house."

Blücher stopped to reconsider. "You might be right."

"Think of it, Excellency. Field Marshal Blücher charged with unlawful entry into a private French dwelling..."

"Damned embarrassing!"

"All of this in occupied territory. There may be serious repercussions, even bloodshed."

"You're right, of course. We'll need special help."

"I have an idea to handle this in an orderly and legal way."

"In that case, Margot better get set to wait twenty years. I'm all too familiar with the wheels of justice. They grind at a snail's pace. Even a snail is like a swallow compared to the swiftness of justice in this country."

"Yes, I know."

"Well, let me hear your idea."

"We simply go to *le maire des arrondissements*," he said.

"Ah, the district magistrate. Good thinking! If Blücher goes looking for his help, he wouldn't dare throw up any obstacles."

"My thoughts exactly, Excellency. We'll explain the baron's involvement in this affair. To satisfy himself, the official will have to accompany us and conduct a thorough search of the house."

"Fine. But he's still a Frenchman, so he might drag his heels."

"We'll flatter his intellect and embellish his powers of observation."

Blücher nodded respectfully. "Good. I suggest we take a few soldiers in uniform. This should make it official and leave an impression—"

"Yes, Excellency," the young officer interrupted. "We'll position them on the veranda, out of sight. They'll have to be ready to act on our signal and may even be in a position to observe something."

"That's a good idea. Finally, we have a plan. Do you know the magistrate's address?"

"Yes. It's adjacent to the small alley."

"This should work, and we won't lose any time. Here, take these two pistols," he said handing over a pair of weapons.

Both armed with a pistol for each hand, they proceeded to the guard's quarters. The marshal's unexpected arrival created a significant stir. Those who were present instantly jumped out of their bunks, coming to attention.

Blücher surveyed the scene with a quick glance. He approached one of the soldiers. "You there! Soldier! Are you not the August with whom I spoke to yesterday?"

"At your service, Excellency!"

"Did you make your report?"

"As you commanded!"

"Were the details made known to you?"

"Of course!"

"What was the judgment?"

"A reprimand, Excellency."

"Of course, a written reprimand," Blücher said. "This reproach is all thanks to your diligence. Well, my good August, you can take pride in the knowledge that you have reported the old Blücher and saw him chastised. They will be impressed! Why didn't you collect your money?"

"But, Your Excellency—"

"But what?"

"It would have left the impression that I was in need."

"*Zounds!* August, you're a proud one. You have distinguished yourself greatly, and I have to say I'm impressed, you old Swede. That's why I'm going to give you an opportunity to earn a commendation. Are you fit enough to climb?"

"At your command, Excellency!"

"Even climb over a wall?"

"Of course!"

"Very well. Round up three more men who are also accomplished climbers. You won't need your rifles, but make it quick. I'll explain the rest later!"

Within a single minute, the four soldiers were assembled and ready to go. Leading the team to the alley, Löwenklau halted them at the small gate.

"We are searching for a lady in distress," he explained. "We surmise she was brought here against her will. You are going to climb this wall quietly and without detection, making your way into the courtyard and continuing to the veranda. There, you will climb the latticework, one at a time, to the top. We'll enlist the magistrate's help, coming in through the front entrance. It's very important that you remain hidden until we call for you. If you have to," he added, "then force your way in through the window."

"Exactly," confirmed the marshal. "As soon as I call 'August, get in here!' I want you to immediately force your way through the window."

Though flattered at the marshal's confidence in him, August Liebmann was no fool. An idea suddenly came to him. "Excellency," he asked, "did the lady come in a coach, or was she forced to walk?"

"She was driven in a carriage. Why?"

"About fifteen minutes ago, a fine-looking wagon came down this very same alley."

"A fine-looking carriage? *Sapperlot!* How do you know this?"

"I saw it for myself, Excellency. The duty officer sent me on an errand. I saw the carriage turn in, just as I came up to the magistrate's office."

"Well, August, I commend you. Do you have a girl of your own?"

"No, Excellency."

"If I had a daughter to spare, I would offer her to you. Now climb that wall, you rascals," the marshal ordered, "and don't let anyone see you do it!"

CHAPTER TWELVE
Blücher's Justice

W hile the four Grenadiers took great care to climb the lattice without detection, the two officers walked into the magistrate's office. They asked for an appointment and were readily admitted to his inner office, where they found him at work. The magistrate, who was seated at his desk, was so absorbed in his work that he failed to look up in response to their greeting. He simply nodded his head to acknowledge their presence, busying himself with the task at hand.

Blücher coughed to get his attention, but when the magistrate kept writing, he whispered to Löwenklau, "How would you say 'simpleton' in French?" he asked.

"*Benet*," Löwenklau answered quietly.

Blücher nodded in satisfaction and stepped forward. "You there, Monsieur *Benet*!" he said.

The magistrate jumped out of his seat as if a snake had bitten him. "What did you call me?"

Blücher good-naturedly placed his hand on the politician's shoulder. "Do you speak any German, my friend?" he asked.

"Of course, I do!" he said, nodding proudly.

"Well, had I known, I would have called you *Einfaltspinsel* instead." Either way, he was calling the man a simpleton.

The magistrate moved the spectacles further up his nose. "Monsieur," he replied haughtily. "What gives you the right to...?" He stopped in mid-sentence as he looked up at Blücher. A gradual recognition came upon him. His facial features started to convey the unmistakable look of apprehension.

"Ah! My son! You finally seem to recognize me," Blücher said in a friendly tone.

The magistrate responded by bowing deeply. "I'm honored by His Excellency's visit. How may I be of service?"

"To begin with, my son, I require you to show us more respect in all future encounters. We came to discuss serious matters, not to gaze at the back of your head. Do you understand me? Incidentally, I want to know if you could spare us a little time."

"I remain at your service for as long as you like!"

"Well, I only need a little time, though I do require you to accompany us."

"Where to?"

"Are you acquainted with a certain Baron de Reillac?"

"Very well. I have the honor of being his brother-in-law."

"His brother-in-law? Hm! How are the two of you related?"

"His sister is my wife, Excellency."

"Speak of the devil! Now I understand why you came across as such a simpleton."

At first, the magistrate pretended not to be offended by the old man's spiteful words. However, Blücher's latest indiscretion stung his pride so deeply he had to retort. "His Excellency is forgetting that I am an official."

"Oh, that's right! It was a simple oversight. I mistook you for a statue, but then I realized you are the magistrate. It's a good thing you reminded me."

"I am still at your service," the rebuffed official replied.

"Fine. Get your hat, put on your *Gottfried*, and accompany us!"

"Accompany you? Where to?"

"We need to pay your brother-in-law a little visit. Where else?"

"For what reason?"

"All in good time, my son."

"If His Excellency would allow me to comment, I need to know the purpose of this visit."

Blücher continued to look down at him. "Allow me to reiterate. You'll be advised of it once we are at his residence. Are you coming or not?"

"Actually, I don't need to accompany you."

"Then stay if you like, my good man. I will send for you."

"Certainly, if you please."

"Well, I just happen to have a quarter of a million troops at my disposal. I'm sure I could convince a few of my boys to drag you out of your little office."

"If his Excellency puts it that way," the man quickly replied, "I certainly can't refuse the invitation—"

"That's fine! Come along then. Your work here is finished."

The magistrate removed his cloak and retrieved his coat and hat, declaring himself ready to accompany them. Once outside the office, they kept him in the middle as they walked to the baron's house.

Blücher didn't waste any time and addressed the magistrate. "Monsieur, no doubt you have heard I'm an austere man. I'm usually congenial in nature, but I get downright ornery when it comes to matters of wrongdoing. I've come to you for help since you are the official representative of the police."

"For what reason?"

"A young lady has been separated from her mother!"

"Ah, did her lover abscond with her?"

"No, it's far more serious than that. She was taken against her will."

"Really? A kidnapping? That is serious. Who is this poor girl?"

"Mademoiselle Richemonte."

This seemed to give the magistrate a momentary pause. "Are you referring to Captain Richemonte's sister?"

"Yes, indeed. Do you know the captain?"

"I have seen him once or twice at my brother-in-law's house. When was she abducted?"

"Roughly half an hour ago."

"Do you know the culprit?"

"We suspect him to be your brother-in-law."

The magistrate stopped in his tracks. "Dear God. My own brother-in-law? The baron?"

"Yes, the newly made baron."

"Why would he do this, Excellency?"

"Because he is a villain and quite capable of such an atrocity."

"Pardon me, Excellency, but I can't bear to listen to such accusations. How could a relative of mine...?"

"*Papperlappap!* The fact that you two are related is of no relevance to us. Your brother-in-law is intending to force Mademoiselle Richemonte to become his wife. What is even worse is that she doesn't love him. Take a look at this fine and upstanding gentleman," Blücher said, pointing to Löwenklau. "He is a dear friend, an accomplished officer, and furthermore the Mademoiselle's betrothed. Last night, your brother-in-law and this Richemonte fellow ambushed my officer on the street not far from his own residence. They fired at him with a pistol, yet were unsuccessful in their attempt to kill him. This is when the determined baron concocted a plan to kidnap the girl."

"Unbelievable!"

"Do you doubt me?" the marshal asked. "Dammit, if the old Blücher said it, it's the truth. And if that weren't enough, he audaciously usurped my own noble name to carry out the scheme. He used an imposter to collect the lady on the pretext of dining with me. Instead of coming to my residence, she was driven to the baron's house, where we suspect she is being held."

"Excellency, this whole story is simply inconceivable. I know the baron to be—"

"A rogue, am I right?" interrupted Blücher. "This is where we are in complete agreement."

"I intended to say the opposite."

"Well, you will not get far with me there."

"The whole thing sounds so preposterous, that I—"

"*Monsieur le maire!*" thundered Blücher. "Don't be delusional in thinking my sole purpose is to bring my entire army to France, occupy Paris, and then merely entertain minor officials with fables. When I see something and disclose it, then you can damn well count on it!"

The magistrate did his best to subdue himself. "What do you want from me?"

"Your brother-in-law resides within your jurisdiction. Is this not so?"

"Of course."

"Well, we intend to conduct a search of his house."

"Dear God! Are you serious?"

"Very serious. I don't want this search to be some secretive affair, but a most public one."

"Am I to assist you in this undertaking?"

"Naturally! I respect the laws of the land, Monsieur."

"I must declare to His Excellency that a search is out of the question."

"Really? Please elaborate."

"Certain requirements are necessary to facilitate a search and to enable due process—"

"We have all the due process we need," Blücher said, interrupting again. "To conduct a search, we only require two elements!"

"No, much more!"

"*Papperlappap!* The first requirement to a house search is the house itself, and the second is to have one who will search it. *Basta!* The house is here and so is the searcher. In fact, we have several at our disposal. There is no valid reason not to search."

"With all due respect, I must abide by my original decision."

"Then stick to your decision, but it will not hamper ours. Will you be so kind as to accompany us to your relative's house?"

"Actually," the man replied reluctantly, "I'm far too occupied with my work."

"Then work an hour longer, Monsieur. As far as the Germans go, we've had to work many long hours on your account. Where is the house, Lieutenant?"

"Over there, Excellency!" Löwenklau said, pointing down the street to the baron's home.

Most of the lights were out. The marshal approached the entrance and rang the bell. The gatekeeper appeared and promptly opened the front door.

"Does Baron de Reillac reside here?" asked Löwenklau.

"Yes, Monsieur," came the reply.

"Did he go out?"

"No."

"Is he engaged with anyone?"

"I believe Captain Richemonte is with him."

"Anyone else?"

"No one else, Monsieur."

"There you are! We all heard it!" said the magistrate, relieved.

"What did we hear? We have heard nothing!" Blücher said, pushing the magistrate up the steps to the foyer. "Do you really think we are as foolish as you Frenchmen? They wouldn't be so stupid as to tell the porter they had just abducted a girl. Honestly man, where are your brains? We'll find out soon enough where they have hidden her. Lieutenant, ring the bell!"

While Löwenklau and Blücher were making their way to the magistrate's office, Margot began to stir, waking up from the deep stupor. She glanced around, trying to regain her bearings, and found herself in an unfamiliar study. She tried unsuccessfully to recall how she had arrived here.

Margot involuntarily tried to touch her head, as though she were contemplating something. For some inexplicable reason, she was unable to move any of her limbs. As her eyes adjusted to the dim light, she realized her hands and feet were bound and her mouth was covered with a cloth. Then it all came back to her. She remembered the ordinance officer that had picked her up and administered the 'perfume' she was forced to inhale.

She allowed her eyes to roam about the room, but no one was there. Where was she? A cold fear gripped her, causing her to shiver. She heard a noise behind her. She couldn't move her head, though it proved unnecessary when the one making the noise came into view.

It was her brother. He crossed his arms and looked at her. Margot closed her eyes so she wouldn't have to look at him. It struck her that the whole invitation and subsequent carriage ride had been a ruse. She was certain she had become the victim of a clever plot. The perpetrators had tricked her into accepting a ride with a questionable conclusion at best.

Albin looked at her with amusement and spoke scornfully. "That's what you get for choosing a German brute."

She was unable to reply. Having the desire to play cat and mouse with her, he partially removed the handkerchief. She took a deep breath. The clean, fresh air did her good, purging the trace amounts of the narcotic.

"Are you enjoying the fresh air?" he continued. "It's too bad my presence fouls the clean air."

Margot kept her eyes closed. She wanted to prepare herself and discover his intentions before responding.

"Isn't it a shame you have to spend your precious time with me instead of sitting down to a nice dinner with Blücher and your soldier boy?"

She remained silent.

"Well, that's all in the past. From now on, consider yourself someone else's property."

At last, he got the response he was looking for. "Whose property?" she asked.

"Don't you know?"

"No."

"Why, the baron's!"

"Ah! Him! Did you help him?"

"Of course."

"My God! My own brother!"

"My God! My own sister!" he repeated mockingly.

"Does Mama know I'm here?" she asked, suddenly concerned for her mother.

He laughed out loud. "Her? Know about it? Are you crazy?"

"She'll find out soon enough!"

"Of course, she will. That's the idea."

"When?"

"Whenever it suits you."

"I'm not following."

"You'll understand right away. Look!"

In that instant, the baron leaned over the chair and kissed her on the lips. Margot hadn't been aware that he was standing behind her. She called out for help, but was stopped by her brother.

"Hold it!" he warned her. "Don't scream! If you do, I'll pull the gag back over your mouth. Believe me, it will only make your situation worse!"

"Who touched me?" she asked, shaking with a combination of fear and loathing.

"It was me," the baron proudly admitted, walking out in front of her so she could see him clearly.

"Shame on you!" she cried out. "So you are the villain I can thank for all this trouble."

"Complain all you want!" he grinned. "You're under my control now. I'll find a way to tame your ways."

"No, never!"

"Really, you don't believe me?" he asked. "Let me tell you what awaits you. I'm in love with you, but you insist on pushing me away. I pleaded with you, cajoled you, and even threatened you—all for naught! Now I've been forced to resort to the only means left to me. You'll become my wife today—in fact, this very evening. You better get used to this place, because you'll be here a long time, however long it is before I decide to release you. You won't have any honor and you'll certainly never belong to anyone else. Consequently, you'll plead with me on your knees to remove the disgrace you find yourself in. In time, you may even become the baroness, but that will depend on my good pleasure."

"You're a devil in disguise," she managed contemptuously.

"Yes, well, I'm the devil and you're the angel. This should be a charming union."

"Never!" she blurted out. "God will protect me!"

"I wouldn't believe that if I were you. God has far more important things to do than concern himself with the little problems of our Margot. Today, you will be as good as my wife."

"I'd rather die," she whispered.

"Well, it won't come as fast or as easy as you might think. You will eventually get used to my tenderness and enjoy life's pleasures again."

Margot turned as pale as a ghost. She searched his face with trepidation. "You can't be serious, Baron?" she asked. "I don't... I can't love you."

"You'll find a way to love me."

"Have some compassion! Think of my father, who was your friend, and of my poor mother, who has already suffered so much."

"Your father is dead, and your mother doesn't concern me anymore. However, I'll be most pleased to welcome her as my mother-in-law."

"Won't you consider the all-knowing God?"

"All-knowing?" He laughed. "He'll witness some very interesting nuptials."

"God will insure that evil doers are punished."

"I'm not afraid of His punishment."

She shuddered. The man really was a devil of sorts. She turned to appeal to her brother. "Please, take up my cause, Albin. You're my brother."

"Ridiculous!" the captain replied. "When did you last concern yourself about my welfare?"

"Albin," she said reproachfully. "You know very well how we pleaded, worked, and suffered on your account."

"It was all for a good cause," he said without pity. "The baron has agreed to rip up all the promissory notes when you become his wife. As a good sister, it's incumbent of you to freely give him your word. You have to make a decision now. I'm asking you: are you going to give your consent or will we have to insist?"

She realized she couldn't expect any mercy. "I won't become his wife," she replied firmly. "Whether of my own free will or by coercion. God will protect me."

Margot thought about what Löwenklau had told her yesterday when they were together in the marshal's study. Hugo had climbed the balcony and overheard her brother and the baron devising a new scheme. Even if he had only caught parts of it, it should suffice to lead him to rescue her. Although he hadn't been entirely clear on its significance, he certainly wouldn't doubt it now. Hugo would eventually attend to her mother's residence, bringing the invitation, or perhaps even being accompanied by the marshal himself. In any event, they would learn of the deception soon enough and reason that she had been abducted by Reillac. It only remained for them to find out where they had hidden her; whether in his very own house, or at another location. If the latter proved to be correct, her hope of being found was slight.

"Well, I see you've made your choice. She's all yours!" the captain said. "Baron, I deliver her into your custody. Do with her as you please."

"Albin!" she pleaded. "Don't allow it. Please, don't abandon me!"

"*Papperlappap!*" he said, shrugging his shoulders.

"Think of our father!"

"Oh! He's just as responsible in making me the reckless person I've become. The influence of his memory won't help your cause in the least."

"Dear God! What else can I say?" she lamented. "You're both despicable. Less than human even."

"Not at all. I'm very human," the baron said. "Let me prove it to you. My heart is capable of making a human response." He came closer, intending to kiss her.

"Get away from me, you villain!"

He puckered his lips, emphasizing the obvious. Unable to move her head, and left with no other means to defend herself, Margot spat in his face.

"There! You disgust me!" she cried out. "At least release me from my restraints so I can show you what I think of your conduct."

"No, not now!" laughed the baron, wiping the spittle from his face. "You certainly have a strange way of wanting to be kissed. I'm going to gag your little mouth to prevent a re-occurrence."

He replaced the handkerchief over her mouth. The porcelain color of her skin was visible above the collar of her dress, making Reillac desirous. He started to kiss her neck, aware that her whole body winced in disgust. As he surveyed her lovely features, he felt desire well up within him again.

"Is she truly mine?" Reillac asked the captain.

"Do you intend on keeping this our little secret?"

"Of course."

"Very well, then."

"*Merci!* I'll give you one promissory note for your kind deed."

"Only one?"

The baron, laughing out of spite, turned to Margot with a saucy look. "I'll dispense with the rest after the wedding!"

"What if it doesn't get that far?"

"She'll change her tune soon enough."

"I mean, if you happen to change your mind, Baron."

"Me? Impossible!"

"Oh, I could think of instances where a former love loses its appeal."

"In that case, I would still consider our arrangement as though your sister had in fact become my wife."

"Then let me have the first note!"

"I have it in my bureau drawer," Reillac said. "First, we need to move her to a more secure room."

"Where to?"

"I have a small room, accessible through a secret entrance, where she should be quite comfortable. She'll be as secure as though she were in Abraham's bosom."

Opening the hidden door to the secret room, Richemonte noted it was the same room where the two had plotted her abduction.

❧✠☙

The four Grenadiers huddled together outside on the veranda deck. Having managed to climb up undetected, they were now patiently waiting to observe anything of interest.

"It's damned boring!" one of them whispered.

"Just like sentry duty," replied another.

"Stop complaining!" August said. "We have to be alert and keep an eye out for the missing girl."

"Well, where is she?" asked the first man.

"Inside the study naturally, where the voices are coming from. Be quiet or else we won't hear a word."

"It would have been better if she were with us."

"Ridiculous! I don't want to get tangled up with a French woman," said August.

"Why not?"

One of the men paused, then admitted, "I fell in love with one on Tuesday."

"Really?"

"She fell in love with me, and I took her home."

"Congratulations," August offered.

"Hold your tongue! When I came to see her on Wednesday, I found her with another man."

"Was he her lover?"

"Of course," the love-struck man said. "He's a garbage collector."

"What next?" August asked.

"She charmed me again on Thursday."

"That was dumb of you."

There was no point in arguing the insult. "On Friday, she took yet another man home."

"What did he do for a living?"

"He was a panhandler."

"How awful for you!"

"And on Sunday, there—"

"Did she use her charm on you again?"

"Nearly, she's sort of pretty, but..." The soldier's voice trailed off as he perked his ears. "Listen, do you hear voices?"

All four of them strained to catch something audible.

"Did you hear that? It seemed like I heard a woman calling," said the second.

"Should we barge in?" the other asked.

"No! You're answerable to me," replied August. "Blücher let me pick my own men, and even allowed my name to signal the entry. I don't want to disappoint him. Now shut up, I see some movement!"

The hallway door opened, and then the inner one. Margot, who was still bound to the chair, was carried in by two men. They put her near the window, close to where the four Grenadiers were concealed. They whispered their observations to each other.

"For God's sake! Don't let them see you!" said August.

"She's bound to the chair."

"They gagged her mouth!"

"Heavens! She's beautiful."

"Yes, and we only have a glimpse of her."

"Who could those two be?"

August raised a hand, cutting them off. "Listen. I think I recognize them!"

"Where from?"

"Could they be those two villains from last night, who shot at our Lieutenant Löwenklau?" one of the men asked.

"Hmm, you've got something there."

"What about the girl? Could she be the one who came to Blücher's palace last night?" August asked. "You know the one. He chastised me for not being able to distinguish a woman from a Mademoiselle?"

"Are you sure?"

"Yes," he said. "I see her clearly now. Don't you recall? We escorted her home with the officer."

"Sapperlot! What should we do?"

"What are they intending to do with her? Run her through the wall? Look, a hidden door! If only we could have seen how they opened it," the third man whispered.

August grinned confidently. "I saw it," he replied.

"Really? How did they open it?"

"All in good time," he said. "I'll report it to Blücher."

❧✠☙

The baron and the captain disappeared into the hideaway with their prize, but returned shortly empty-handed. They closed the door behind them and walked back into the study. The baron opened one of the drawers, removing a hidden compartment. He handed Richemonte one of the notes. The captain snatched it out of his hand, read it quickly, ripped it to pieces, then stashed them away carefully in his pocket.

A distant bell rang outside in the foyer, causing the baron to look up.

"Who could that be?" he asked.

"Perhaps it's your manservant?" Richemonte suggested.

"Possibly. Wait here while I check."

Reillac hurried through several rooms and came to the foyer. He expected to see his valet, but instead saw his brother-in-law on the front stoop. His two companions, Löwenklau and Blücher standing to the side and out of the light, went unnoticed for the moment.

"Oh, it's you," Reillac said. "Why are you here at such an unusual hour?"

"I've been entreated to introduce two gentlemen," the magistrate replied.

"Really? Who?" Reillac walked out into the main part of the foyer and immediately recognized his guests.

"Baron de Reillac!" said Blücher curtly.

"Yes! What can I do for you, Monsieur?" the baron asked.

"Just wait and see," Blücher said under his breath. "Is Monsieur Richemonte with you?" he added, slightly louder.

"Yes, he is," Reillac volunteered somewhat reluctantly.

"Anyone else?"

"No."

"We'll have to make sure."

The baron stood in his way. "Please, my good man. This is not a good time for a cordial visit."

"Well, it is for me, old boy!" the marshal said, simply shoving him aside. "You're about to find out what this visit is all about."

The baron, caught off guard, had no choice but to admit the two newcomers into the house. He was pleased he'd had the foresight of moving Margot into the secret room. They would have caught them in the act had they arrived only a few minutes sooner. What did they want? Did they suspect Margot was in the house?

"Where is the captain?" asked Blücher.

"In my study."

139

"Then we shall meet him there. Please, lead the way!"

When they entered the study, Richemonte was just as surprised to see the guests as his accomplice had been. The captain did a good job of concealing his rising panic, though. He exercised tremendous control over his emotions. His instinct told him that this meeting would require his complete resolve to extricate himself from a possibly dicey situation.

"Captain Richemonte, His Excellency, Field Marshal—" the baron managed by way of introduction.

"That's fine," interrupted Blücher. "Don't burden yourself with formalities. We're already acquainted with each other! Where is Mademoiselle Margot?"

The old marshal didn't beat around the bush, preferring rather to confront his enemy with guns blazing.

"At home, I should think," replied the captain.

"Ah! At home!" Blücher nodded thoughtfully, while looking around the room.

"Excellency," commented Löwenklau. "Do you smell something?"

Blücher inhaled the stale air. "What a repulsive smell. It reminds me of ether! Lieutenant, I believe they have drugged her!"

"If the slightest harm has come to her, God help them!"

"Now, tell me, Baron," the marshal began, "what have you done with Mademoiselle Margot?"

"Excellency, I find it most peculiar that I am being asked a question about a certain lady's whereabouts. Lieutenant Löwenklau should be the one to supply that information."

"He has done so."

"Then why this inquiry?"

"The implication is that the lady will be found here."

"Really," smiled the baron. "I have not had the pleasure of entertaining the Mademoiselle."

Blücher pressed him further. "Does that statement include today?"

"Naturally."

"May we verify this for ourselves?"

"Excellency, are you questioning the word of a gentleman?"

"Absolutely!"

"Are you calling me a liar?"

"Yes."

"What an insult, Monsieur! I resent that. I only admit reasonable people. I certainly cannot allow disrespectful people to search my house at will."

Blücher approached him. "What did you say, you *Changeur?*[12.1] You have the gall to call us disrespectful? The devil's the only one who can make any sense out of your hospitality. I'll show you a different side of respect, and another, and another!"

If the baron expected merely a verbal exchange, he was sadly mistaken. Instead, Blücher pummeled him with several well-placed slaps to his face, as though he were ringing a bell.

"Excellency, for God's sake!" the magistrate protested.

The captain looked like he was about to lunge at Blücher, but was stopped in his tracks by the appearance of two pistols, both held by Löwenklau.

"Stop!" the lieutenant commanded. "Anyone who touches His Excellency will be shot on the spot!"

The baron was so overtaken by the speed of the onslaught that he failed to defend himself. Only when Blücher backed off did he contemplate a reprisal by holding up his fist. His feeble gesture was met by the muzzle of a pistol.

"Down with your hand, you reprobate," Löwenklau said.

The baron lowered his arm, staring like a madman. He saw the determination in Blücher's face, realizing that he would shoot.

"Gentlemen, please, such a scene!" objected the magistrate. "Permit me to voice my opinion. Excellency, this is highly irregular and unusual..."

"*Pah!*" Blücher interrupted. "I don't find anything irregular here. Quite the contrary! This man," he pointed to Richemonte, "recently received a thrashing from the lieutenant for his audacious behavior. It only seems fitting therefore that the baron receive the same. Indeed, there are instances when only a proper form of discipline will suffice."

"Your Excellency, you are armed with pistols!"

"Of course, but only as a precaution. Last night, one of these two men shot twice at my lieutenant, while the other illuminated him with a lantern. You have to be on guard around such people."

"What slander!" the baron said.

"Outright lies!" said Richemonte.

Blücher turned to address the magistrate without looking at the two men. "Well, there you have it. Not even a chastising is sufficient enough to bring these two back to reason. They remind me of an apple which has become so foul it gives off a rank smell—it is beyond hope. Since they were unable to kill the groom, they have devised a new plot by attempting to overpower the bride. Rest assured, we will find Mademoiselle Margot."

The baron composed himself and appealed to the magistrate. "Jules, you're an official! If you are reluctant to carry out your duty, I will make a formal complaint to your superior. If these two foreigners don't remove themselves immediately from my house, I'll protect myself against any future attacks from them. I intend to retaliate with any means at my disposal. We should leave now, Captain!"

Although he turned to leave, Blücher threatened Reillac by lifting his pistol. "No one leaves without my permission," he said.

"Excellency," complained the magistrate, "this has gone too far!"

"Ridiculous! I know perfectly well how far I can go," Blücher bellowed. "I have a feeling I'm going to go even further."

"What you mean is that you're going to search this house regardless," said the magistrate.

"Exactly."

"Even while you're armed?"

"Even then."

"I object, and I need to inform His Excellency of all the consequences should he continue."

"It doesn't matter."

"Very well," he said. "I'm washing my hands of any blame."

"As far as I'm concerned, you can wash them in milk and honey. Now, can we proceed?"

"Since you're forcing my hand, I must comply. I declare as the chief magistrate of this district that His Excellency, Field Marshal von Blücher, has made the allegation regarding a young lady who has been brought here against her will. The inference is that this lady is currently confined within these premises. I will now direct a search of all these rooms, but absolve myself from any responsibility."

"I will assume full responsibility," Blücher added.

"Very well. Lead us!" the politician instructed Reillac.

"I expect to be excluded from this fact finding mission," the captain said.

The magistrate gave Blücher a questioning glance.

"He will remain with us," Blücher insisted. "Lieutenant, do not let either one of these men out of your sight!"

The search covered all the inhabitable spaces of the house. It was carried out with great care and diligence, and yet yielded no results. They returned to the study without finding a trace of Margot. The baron and the captain displayed triumphant looks on their faces.

"I'm going to demand satisfaction!" hissed the baron.

"As will I!" Richemonte added.

The magistrate simply shrugged his shoulders. "You certainly have the right. I too have been mistreated and will try to salvage my downtrodden honor. I must request that the two Prussian gentlemen leave this house."

"I demand an immediate and unequivocal compliance," the baron contended.

Blücher laughed out loud and turned to face Löwenklau. "Look at them, my son," he said. "How puffed up they have become. Let's wait and see if they will ask for forgiveness later. Come on!" He made a motion to return to the rooms which had just been searched.

"Hold it!" interrupted the baron. "My patience has come to an end. I forbid you to come in here a second time!"

"Don't get yourself all worked up," said Blücher. "All of you will nicely come along, or you will regret it later."

"But," the magistrate attempted, "Your Excellency—"

"Hold your tongue! Forward! All of you, get in there or I'll shoot!"

They obeyed and followed him into the study. Blücher once again faced the magistrate. "Are you convinced that the one we have been searching for is not in this house?" asked Blücher.

"I will swear to it," replied the official.

"Well, I haven't seen anything either. However, I suspect the baron and his bosom friend have been playing games with us. Therefore, I want to ask someone who is probably smarter than the magistrate." He paused, then called out, "August, get in here!"

With those words, Blücher unlocked and opened the window. The four Grenadiers jumped into the study. The magistrate was astonished, while the other two looked downright fearful. If the soldiers had been concealed for some time, then they would surely know the truth, dashing their hopes. Once again, the captain tried to make his way to the door. Löwenklau stopped his advance by pointing the pistol at his head.

"Stop! Get back!"

"Ah!" Blücher commented calmly. "The boys want to leave our little get-together without permission. I would advise them to stay a while longer. All right, all three of you, into the corner!"

"What, me too?" complained the magistrate.

"Of course! I conquered Paris after a lengthy siege, and I can certainly keep three slippery frogs in confinement. Forward!" Holding his pistol out in front, he prodded them into the corner.

"Close the window, boys!" he instructed the Grenadiers. "Now, three of you cover the door and, since we have those three *Mossjehs* corralled, it is your turn, August. Were you paying attention?"

"Yes, Excellency! I saw her."

"Saw whom?" Blücher asked.

"The Mademoiselle," the officer clarified, "who is not to be confused for a woman."

"*Zounds!* Are you sure? Where is she?"

"Over there, Excellency!" August said, pointing to the far wall.

"Over there? But that's a wall."

"Yes. She is hidden behind the wall, Excellency!"

Awareness dawned on the marshal's face. "Aha! A hidden room. How do you get in?"

"There is a hinge on the floor. Just bend down and depress it."

"How do you know that, my boy?"

"I paid close attention, sir, just as His Excellency instructed." The Grenadier was positively beaming.

"Soldier, friend, deliverer, my good August, if your words bear truth, then you're worth your weight in gold."[12.2] Blücher walked over and examined the harmless looking hinge. He depressed it, and instantly the hidden door opened, revealing the inner room. It was too dark to see inside, so Blücher ordered one of the Grenadiers to fetch a lantern. Löwenklau took the lantern and stepped into the dark while the rest carefully watched their 'charges' in the corner.

"My God!" Löwenklau called out in disbelief. "Margot!"

"What's happening?" called Blücher.

"She is bound to a chair!"

The marshal turned to the Grenadier. "August!"

"Excellency!"

"See if you can find some ropes. Then tie up these two hoodlums nice and tight, even if their fingernails turn blue."

This was music to the soldiers' ears. They fashioned ropes from the nearby curtains and both villains were tied up in no time.

"Come here, Monsieur, and assess the situation," beckoned Blücher to the magistrate.

The magistrate complied and accompanied Blücher into the small room, where they both beheld an unusual sight. Margot was still tied to the chair. Although Löwenklau had removed her gag, he was hugging Margot.

"Finally, finally!" he exclaimed. "You have no idea how desperate I was for you, Margot!"

"No more than I was, Hugo!" she whispered tiredly but happily. "I could hear you searching."

"Really? From in here?"

"Yes, I heard every word."

"Were you able to hear us while we searched the rest of the house?"

"Yes," she said. "When you left, I thought it was all over for me."

"My poor thing, how you must have anguished over your fate."

"Just then, all of you returned," she said, smiling.

"Did you hear how we discovered the hidden door?"

"Yes. Everything is all right now, Hugo."

"Oh, no! It's not quite all right!" the marshal interrupted. "Er... Lieutenant, aren't you going to untie her?" he laughed.

The two lovers were so overjoyed that they hadn't thought about the ropes that still bound Margot to the chair. As Löwenklau cut them, Margot jumped out of her imprisonment, and rushed over to the marshal. She picked up his hand and kissed it.

"Excellency, I am very grateful to you!"

"For allowing you to be abducted, my dear girl?" he joked.

"Oh no, because I've been set free!"

"You're mistaken, my dear daughter. It was your very own man who came through. I had no idea where to look for you. He at least had some suspicions."

"Hugo would not have been able to pull it off alone," she said. "Who would have listened to him?"

"Ah, you mean the flurry of activity when the old Blücher wants something done. Well, this is true. However, your lieutenant is quite capable and he would have found a way. Tell me, how did those two manage to abduct such a fine lady and imprison her in this house?"

Margot recounted her ordeal from beginning to end. She spoke loud enough to be heard by all, including the two prisoners who were lying bound in the hallway. Were they contemplating their atrocious behavior as she unraveled the story of their despicable conduct? Margot didn't conceal one detail, not even the fact that the baron had kissed her.

"What? He kissed you?" asked the surprised marshal. "Where?"

"Once on the lips and then repeatedly on my neck."

"I'll teach them both not to take advantage of a beautiful lady!" While her account had left no small impression on the marshal, he was beside himself, barely able to contain his outrage. "I have a mind to bring this to a quick conclusion. Löwenklau, find a sentence to fit this heinous crime. I cannot seem to come up with one at the moment."

"I could strangle them both!" Löwenklau replied through clenched teeth.

"Great! Let's choke a little life out of them. It'll serve to remind them how we held our breath when we didn't know what had happened to Margot."

"Excellency," said the magistrate, raising his arms in protest. "Please consider that only the law can justify handing out punishment!"

Blücher threw him an irritated look. "Keep your comments to yourself, you *Mossjeh*," he said testily. "Let me remind you how much your laws accomplished when we wanted to search this house. And what did the man of the law find? Nothing! I'll become the laughing stock if I turn them over to you. I suspect they would even be rewarded for their treachery."

While the magistrate contemplated Blücher's words, Margot took his hand in hers and pleaded with him. "Excellency, please allow good to overcome evil!"

"Yes, yes... I know. He is your brother, and so on. Just like before. Am I right?"

"Yes."

"But things are different today. The occupation of the city carries with it more stringent laws, including a new severity for such transgressions—the death penalty."

"Oh my God!"

Margot pleaded and begged with the marshal until, at last, he relented. Löwenklau remained silent. One part of him sided with justice while the other sided with his love for Margot. Still, he loathed contradicting her.

"I cannot allow them to leave without some sort of punishment," replied the marshal doggedly. "They kidnapped a French citizen, shot at a German officer, and insulted me. They deserve the death penalty. One word from me and they will be hanging from the gallows tomorrow morning. However, I'm not going to grieve you, Margot. Despite their actions, I will spare their lives."

"But not their freedom?"

"Let me think it over!"

Margot started to plead with Blücher again. He was powerless to resist her entreaty and finally gave in. "Hang it all, girl!" he exclaimed. "I cannot seem to oppose you. All right, I will grant them their freedom. But if you demand one more iota of me, I'll change my mind and hang them tonight!"

After Margot obtained all she wanted, she stopped pleading. Blücher secretly nodded to Löwenklau, as a sign that he wasn't about to give in entirely. He had something in mind.

"I still have a few regulatory matters to conclude and they are much too boring for a fine lady. Löwenklau, why don't you take Margot home? I'll follow as soon as I am done here."

"To your residence, Excellency?"

"No, to her mother's. I want to see her as well."

Löwenklau didn't hesitate and made a motion to depart. Margot thanked the Grenadiers first, and then they were on their way. Blücher waited until they left before beginning his inquiries. He wanted to deal with the matters quickly and expediently.

"I'll dispense with reports and regulatory matters and get to the heart of the matter. No doubt you two scoundrels heard me promise Mademoiselle Margot to grant you both your freedom. I'll keep my bargain under two conditions. One, you tell me the truth, and two, you won't hold anything back, or by God, I'll promise you on my honor as an officer that you'll be hanging come sunrise."

The two villains were convinced it was in their best interests to answer his questions.

"Now then," started Blücher, "who was the imposter that played the part of the ordinance officer?"

"The son of my valet," replied Reillac reluctantly.

"Who was the coachman?"

"My valet."

"Ah, and where is he now?"

"He must be at home. I heard him come in during the search. No doubt the porter informed him of the new guests."

"Really? Did he withdraw because of our presence?"

"Probably."

"Well, it's time for a chat. I will call for him." Blücher went to the study and pulled on a bell ringer. Shortly after he rang, a man appeared, dressed in a servant's uniform.

"Who are you?" Blücher demanded.

"The valet, Monsieur," Pierre replied.

"Good. Your master has been waiting for you. Where is your son?"

"Downstairs with the porter."

"Go and fetch him. The baron requires you both."

The 'actor' came upstairs, naturally dressed in his everyday clothes. Blücher met them in the drawing room and escorted them to the study.

"Is this your valet?" he asked the baron.

"Yes."

"And this other one, is he the son?"

"Yes."

"Very well, I'm glad you're all present to witness my verdict."

Only then did the valet realize he had been summoned into a trap. Looking around at the Grenadiers, he saw that an escape was out of the question.

Blücher faced his Grenadiers. "Men," he began mischievously, "you carried out your assignment to my complete satisfaction. Therefore, I'm inclined to grant you a little fun. If only we had a switch at our disposal."

August stepped forward, replying with a smirk on his face. "If His Excellency would permit, I'll have a look around and perchance find a suitable walking stick or two."

"*Sapperlot!* Go and have a look, my boy!"

August didn't have to be told twice. In a short time, he collected all of the baron's walking sticks.

"How did you make out, August?" asked the old man.

"Very well, Excellency, especially with these three bamboo rods!"

"Fine," he said approvingly. "Let's get started. To begin with, we have a valet, who became a coachman and enticed his son to play a part in the abduction. He will get forty strokes for his part. Tie him up and cover his mouth. I don't want to hear him whimper."

The valet was bound and gagged. After he received his forty, it was his son's turn.

"This one here masqueraded as my ordinance officer. He has the propensity to become quite the cheat. He will receive forty as well."

The sentence was carried out. Next, Blücher kicked the captain with his boot.

"He's already bound. Don't gag him, because I want to see if a captain of the old guard can hold his own. He planned to sell his own sister and fired at a Prussian officer. He gets sixty strokes. They must be sound ones so that he won't get up for a while. I'll be content in knowing he won't be capable of plotting anything adverse in the near future. Get to it, boys!"

Receiving sixty blows was no small matter, and yet the captain withstood the pain without uttering a single sound. When the Grenadier finished, Richemonte's lips were bleeding and his eyes were bloodshot. Although he kept quiet, he shot the marshal a glance full of hatred and vengeance.

Then, Blücher's attention came to the baron.

"This man abducted a girl and conspired to kill a Prussian officer. He is also deserving of sixty blows. As a reward for his rude behavior toward our dear Margot, he will get another twenty. Do not spare him either, boys!"

The magistrate kept his peace until now, reasoning that since he was the baron's brother-in-law, he should at least say something on his behalf.

"Excellency, permit me to pose the question: does your authority extend to the baron?"

"You question my authority? If you don't hold your tongue, I'll show you how far my authority extends, even over the magistrate of this district! Don't provoke me. These three deserve a much greater punishment, *Mossjeh.*"

The Grenadier gagged the baron's mouth, fearing his self-control wouldn't be on par with the captain's. He received the eighty strokes without let-up and the matter was settled.

"Well, our work is done and we can leave," smiled Blücher. "These four *messieurs* should be satisfied with us, since we didn't cheat them out of a single blow. The magistrate can remain behind and tend to their needs, perhaps with a soothing salve, although I doubt it would be as effective as what we meted out. If my brand of justice is not to his liking, then I'm prepared to bring charges against all of them before the criminal courts, which can dispense their own punishment. Well, good night all."

The marshal left with his Grenadiers. He led them back to the palace where they returned to their regular duties.

"Listen, my good August," Blücher said before they parted, "you and your men have rendered a most noble and timely service. Present yourself tomorrow morning, and each one will receive five *Laubtalers*[12.3] and pipefuls of tobacco totaling the number of blows dispensed. By the way, how many were there?"

"Two hundred twenty," replied Liebmann quickly.

"Hmm, that is quite the quantity of tobacco to pay on their behalf, but I don't mind. You've earned it. If that *benet* of a magistrate had opened his mouth once more, I would not have hesitated to let him have it as well. But then I would have run out of tobacco. Good night, boys."

Blücher continued on his way to Madame's house, content with the knowledge that he had rescued a couple from disaster. Being able to dish out his own brand of justice gave him immense satisfaction.

CHAPTER THIRTEEN
Two Villains Unite

Over a year had passed since that eventful evening in Paris. A new ruler had come to power in France and the occupying forces pulled back. Blücher made his trip to England, where his many accomplishments were greatly celebrated, and when he returned home, he was received with no less fanfare. He still had to contend with some well-positioned political enemies, but he was always remembered as the great Marshal Forward in the hearts of his people. The marshal carried a grudge within him against those politikers who had given Bonaparte so much leeway. He knew exactly what all his Prussian armies had gone through to tame and depose the dictator who had dared to confront the modern world and the audacity to label the Germans as *cochons*, pigs.

In 1815, the Congress of Renown took place in Vienna, only to be saddled with the problem of how to resolve the outcome of the war to everyone's satisfaction. Many compromises were made and a certain feeling of bitterness permeated the discussions. Too much power and land entitlement had been turned over to the French, minimizing the hard fought advantages of the Prussian Alliance. Blücher sided with this overall opinion and commented, "I fear that France will become vocal again, and boast in her accomplishments. Those of us who fought the hard campaign have been lured into a peace that is neither lasting nor secure." He continued his warnings, making his proclamations to those who would listen. He did his best to keep the Prussian army fit for battle, ready to march on short notice.

Napoleon had been deposed, but he had thousands, perhaps even millions, of followers who were left behind. Despite his defeat, his talent and charisma continued to shine. His soldiers and many other supporters esteemed Bonaparte like a god. One famous poet, Heine, said it best:

What of my concern for my wife or child?
Let them beg, let them go hungry.
I have a more noble cause, in mind
My Emperor, my Emperor is in exile.

Napoleon knew the situation all too well and decided to use it for his gain. He wasn't a man to play the role of deposed emperor for too long, yet he made one critical error. He escaped Elba too soon, not realizing some of the occupation forces were still in France. Furthermore, the ambassadors of the concerned nations were still assembled in Vienna and required little prodding to come to a resolution—to renew their fight against Bonaparte. The fragile peace was suddenly interrupted with the news that Napoleon had left the little island on February 27 and landed with an armed force in France.

The undertaking had the appearance of a romantic adventure, which soon blossomed into a full-scale uprising. Napoleon, who made it to Paris in a few weeks, was once again emperor of all France. Bonaparte quickly spread the news that he desired peace and had no hostile intentions. Concluding that all of Europe would unite against him, he prepared himself, in the shortest time, to repel any invasion, whether from the Belgian or the Netherlands borders. His old followers wasted no time lending him their support, including two well-known Bonapartists: Captain Richemonte and Baron de Reillac.

Both of these men had gone through a difficult time. The chastising they had suffered under Blücher's hand, or more accurately under the Grenadiers' wielding of bamboo rods, had kept them out of commission for many months, though eventually their wounds had healed completely. During their recuperation, their combined hatred of the Germans had only grown stronger. The thought of carrying out some form of personal reprisal against Blücher had become a constant, burning obsession. Just as the first news of Napoleon's return spread, they found their physical wellbeing improved to the point that they considered offering their services to the emperor.

Baron de Reillac was reintroduced to Napoleon, and was immediately enlisted to provide supplies to the first army corps, under the command of General Drouet. Richemonte had intended to enlist with the old guard but, due to Reillac's recommendation, was given a company of the new guard instead. A complement of the old guard had been set aside to facilitate a quick attack. The new regime, however, decided to incorporate them into regiments and battalions of the new guard.

The captain received his orders to leave Paris in the morning. He sat in his favorite coffeehouse, enjoying his breakfast. Reillac, who was occupied with supply problems, had promised to meet him there. He kept his word and made his appearance, although somewhat later than expected. The two men, humiliated and chastised by Blücher, shared a common bond in their hatred toward him and were thus inclined not to be harsh toward one another. In fact, commonsense told them to remain quiet about certain events. This compelled them to view each other as confidants, though neither one would have gone so far as to call the other a friend.

On this particular day, Reillac arrived with a singular expression, one that immediately registered with the captain.

"What news do you bring?" Richemonte asked.

"Something so trivial it would normally compel me to settle the matter on my own, if I were a member of the military contingent," the baron said. "You know General Drouet, of course?"

"Yes, naturally."

"I mean his preferences."

"Not entirely."

"One of his penchants happens to coincide with mine. He's a confirmed enemy of Blücher."

"Is that so?"

"He has just been informed that Blücher has left Berlin, taking his forces through Cologne. It has been rumored that he will set up residence at Lüttich, where he will also establish his headquarters. It's an opportunity to create a little havoc, or perhaps even a daring raid."

"Is there a specific plan?"

"Possibly. The general will no doubt entertain your involvement in his campaign."

The captain's eyes lit up. "Then I will head over!"

"Yes, go ahead. Do you want my recommendation?"

"Absolutely."

"This may prove to be your best opportunity. By the way, I won't remain in Paris for long."

"Are you planning to join the army corps?"

"Yes," Reillac said. "The general feels my personal presence would be an advantage to him. I'll be at his side to resolve issues quickly."

"Then you won't be in a position to make much money," laughed Richemonte.

"Perhaps. Now, here's another disclosure, one of a personal nature. Your sister—"

"Ah!" Richemonte exclaimed. "Have you finally managed to track her down?" he said scornfully. "I would very much like to pay her a little visit."

"I've just received correspondence from Berlin. There's still no news of Löwenklau's marriage."

"Has their passion for each other diminished?"

"Not likely!"

"Anything is possible."

"No, you're on the wrong track," the baron said. "This Löwenklau is clever. He'll have kept her address a secret, fearing of our long overdue reprisal."

"I would do almost anything to learn of her whereabouts!"

"No more than I would," Reillac said. "I couldn't sleep last night. While I lay there pondering matters, an idea struck me."

"An idea? Ah! Since it's such a rare occurrence for you, perhaps you feel it necessary to boast?"

"Stop with your jokes! I have a feeling something good may come of it."

"What have you come up with?"

"We've spent a lot of time and energy on inquiries to find your sister's address, so far without success. Now, tell me, my worthy captain, doesn't your mother receive rent for her residence at *Rue d'Ange*?"

"Certainly."

"Through whom?"

"The banker Vaubois, I believe."

"Then this man must have her address in order for him to forward the funds to her."

"Heaven and hell! This has to be it. I'm a complete idiot for not having thought of it myself. I'll go to the bank right away!"

"Hold it! Let's consider this carefully. What if your mother strictly forbade the banker to give out any information? She probably warned him about us."

"You're right. We have to find another way."

"Fortunately, I have found one. One of my maids has a daughter who has a connection to a local bank."

"Do you find her attractive?"

"Certainly, but calm yourself. I'm not a threat to her."

"Something to do with the age difference?" Richemonte suggested with a laugh.

"Not in the least. In fact, it's her boyfriend who works for the bank."

"Ah, perhaps the Vaubois bank?"

"Unfortunately, no. I've established a good rapport with her," the baron continued, "and I'm sure I could persuade her to ask her friend for a favor."

"Let me guess—"

"It'll be quite easy. The young clerk goes to the Vaubois bank and makes an inquiry concerning the account."

"What if they should ask for a reason?"

"He replies that he hasn't been given one because he has been entrusted with a number of inquiries on behalf of his bank."

"What if they show reluctance in giving out the desired information?"

"Then he advises them the matter is of importance because of time constraints."

"You may have something there," he said. Suddenly, an unwelcome thought occurred to him. "Dammit! I have to depart tomorrow. I won't have the time to look into this."

"Why not? The clerk is scheduled for a visit at noon today. I expect to speak to him while he visits with his girl. It's eleven o'clock now. If I leave right away, I'm convinced I can arrange it. We will meet here tonight. If I'm successful, I'll have the address with me!"

"Excellent! Please hurry, Baron!"

It wasn't necessary for the captain to urge him on since the baron had already plucked up his hat and walking stick. Reillac paid for his beverage and left quickly. Richemonte remained behind a little longer, reflecting on their conversation. He finished his coffee and left for his appointment with General Drouet.

General Drouet had a brutal nature and was well-known for his clever and enterprising exploits. Despite his boldness, he maintained his composure and didn't succumb to rash decisions in the heat of the moment. If a goal could be achieved through daring or cunning, he always chose the strategic way. Although he was absorbed in making final preparations for his troops to leave Paris, he found the time to admit the captain. With a quick, penetrating glance, the general appraised Richemonte.

"Have you seen any action in Spain, Captain?" he inquired.

"Yes, General, under Suchet."

"Suchet, you say. He's a capable strategist, perhaps the most brilliant man in the Spanish campaign. We had to deal with raids conducted by small pockets of resistance. No doubt you're accustomed to fighting small skirmishes."

"Indeed, General."

"I'm sure you will agree with me that victory can be affected by matters which are often relegated to secondary importance, such as knowledge of the terrain, the mood of the inhabitants, etc. One cannot ignore such important considerations. They often come to impact the outcome of large battles. We will be going to the Netherlands. The two opposing marshals in charge there are Wellington and Blücher." He paused for a moment, then asked, "What is your impression of Blücher?"

"I hate him with a passion. He can go to hell, for all I care."

"I would like to accommodate, even expedite, his departure," laughed the General while throwing Richemonte a sinister look.

"I wish I had the resources to make it happen."

"Do you know where the old *bramarbas* is currently located?"

"In Lüttich, I believe."

"Correct! Captain, I'm eager to learn what precautions and military measures he has undertaken. This can be accomplished under the right circumstances."

"Surely there must be a few good men around," the captain suggested.

"Perhaps I can count on you to be one of these men?"

"I certainly hope so."

"You were recommended to me," the general revealed. "What would you think of a side trip to Lüttich and the surrounding area?"

"It could prove to be very fruitful, if not a little risky."

"Also very dangerous."

Richemonte set his jaw determinedly. "I'm not afraid of Blücher."

"A corps commander by the name of Bülow has set up his headquarters near Lüttich. He should not be underestimated."

"Then I will be on my guard."

"I would especially like to learn about the layout, troop movements, and the enemy's plans. The main thing is to glean everything pertaining to Blücher."

"I won't disappoint you."

"Do you know Blücher well?"

"Yes."

"Does he know you, too?"

"We have met a few times."

Drouet considered that carefully. "A meeting could prove awkward."

"Certainly not for me, but perhaps for him."

"Well, we will hear about your plans later. You don't have to worry about being recognized. Unfortunately, I cannot make my instructions any clearer."

"I can guess what you are implying, General."

"Perhaps you can. Do as you think best," his superior said. "No doubt your trip will require expenses. May I inquire if you are with means?"

"Unfortunately, I am not. I'm living on my meager military pay, which I have yet to receive."

"Ah, that is embarrassing. Here, take an advance from me." The general pressed a roll of coins into his hands. "When I learn of good reports, I'll compensate you further. *Adieu,* Captain!"

When Richemonte returned to his residence later, he opened the roll, finding five hundred francs inside.

Only five hundred francs for Blücher's head? By God! He's worth more than that, he mumbled to himself. *Let's wait and see if I can earn a bit more.*

It was late in the afternoon when the captain arrived at the barracks. He was informed by the colonel he was being granted a three-month holiday. On instructions from the general, Richemonte was furnished with three months wages, to be paid immediately. He received a sealed letter, along with the sum, which he assumed probably held specific instructions for his 'mission'. As he walked out of the barracks, the captain was too proud to admit to himself that he was being sent out—as a spy!

155

He went home and examined the contents of the sealed letter. It bore a number of documents, including identity papers and passes bearing different names. The one common element to them all was his physical description.

In the evening, Richemonte visited the well-known coffeehouse, finding the baron was already present, waiting for him.

"Were you with the general?" asked Reillac.

"Yes."

"Did you receive any instructions?"

"I've been ordered to take a holiday for several months. Plus, I was handed several good documents for my journey."

"Congratulations!"

"Baron, I resent you mocking me at a time like this!"

"Pardon me. That wasn't my intent." He took a moment to regard Richemonte's expression, which was considerably tamer than it had been earlier that day. "Why the sour face?"

"Well, what good is a holiday if I can't make use of it? The general seems to think I'm a man of means and only paid me a three-month salary," Richemonte said, failing to disclose the advance he had been given by Drouet.

"That's too bad! I, too, have nearly depleted my personal resources."

"That may be, yet you have the best business contacts at your disposal. I, on the other hand, have none."

"You're right," the baron admitted. "I'll advance you another thousand francs if you promise to pay your sister a visit on your return trip."

"*Zounds!* Did you find her address?"

"Yes."

"Was it difficult?"

"Not at all. The clerk merely asked for the information and he received it right away."

"Where has she been staying?"

"At the Jeannette estate, near Raucourt."

Richemonte frowned. "I'm not familiar with Raucourt. Where is it?"

"In the Argonne forest, not far from Sedan."

"Is it close to my proposed route?"

"Yes. You'll need to adjust your itinerary, but only very slightly. I would be grateful if you could drop by for a visit and report back on my personal interests there."

"Of course," the captain agreed. "Anything for a thousand francs."

The baron laughed. "Surely you didn't think I'd forgotten?" He paused to consider his financial situation. "I need to see how much I have on me."

"I know you have your priorities."

"Hmm," he murmured. "I've already committed myself to more than I'd like. I had to place my entire fortune along with my credit to satisfy the demand of military purchases."

"You must stand to gain a considerable profit, though."

"Not as much as you might think, Captain. If the emperor succumbs to the Prussians again, I'll be facing financial ruin."

"Then the thousand which you're about to give me shouldn't have much of an impact on your resources."

"Of course not! Here's the money for your trip. Make sure you keep me informed."

The captain nodded. "Of course. Where should I write you?"

"I plan to stay here for the time being. I'll make sure your letters follow me via military dispatches. *Adieu*, Captain."

"*Adieu*, Baron."

The captain smiled to himself as he departed the coffeehouse. He had managed to come into the possession of a thousand francs through the clever fabrication, ensuring he would be well-prepared for the perilous journey ahead.

CHAPTER FOURTEEN
The War Chest

It was three weeks later when a young man wandered along the muddy road toward Sedan. Bouillon, a village along the way, sat cradled in the deep gorge of the Ardennes near the river Semos. Its name was derived from the famous knight Gottfried von Bouillon, once a renowned fighter who'd helped in the capture of Jerusalem during the crusades. The day was wet and stormy and nightfall was approaching fast. The downpour, undeterred by the looming darkness, continued to fall in buckets. In the rain, the road was hardly distinguishable from the muddy fields around it, a dark, sticky track reluctantly yielding to its solitary weary traveler. Although he was tired, he quickened his pace when he spied the lights of Bouillon in the gloomy distance. He decided the hamlet would be a good place to spend the night.

Looking for an inn in the pouring rain, he barely recognized the large wooden wineglass adorning the doorway of a nearby building. When he walked inside, he found the lower room lit by a torch but devoid of guests. The innkeeper and his wife, both advanced in years, were the only ones he could see, sitting at a dirty table. The traveler greeted them politely, though he didn't receive much of a response.

"May I dry my clothes on the hearth?" he inquired.

"Help yourself," the proprietor replied quietly.

"Is it possible to get something to eat?"

"We have a little milk and some bread, but that's all. We're poor people," the man said. "Where are you headed?"

"Considering the weather, I wasn't planning on going any further today."

"Were you hoping to stay the night?"

"Yes, but I didn't want to impose on you."

"Where are you from?"

"Paris."

"And where did you come from?"

"Lüttich."

"Dear God!" the woman exclaimed. "Those Prussians have occupied Lüttich."

"Yes, I know," the traveler said. "I managed to elude them."

"You did the right thing. They're looking for a fight, for which the emperor will rap their knuckles. What sort of work did you do in Paris?"

The traveling man smiled. "I'm a musician."

"Really? And yet you aren't carrying an instrument?"

"The Prussians took my fiddle," he explained.

"Then you must know they're nothing but a bunch of robbers and thieves. The emperor will quickly eliminate them. Do you have an identity card?"

"Sure."

"Let me have a look. We're not allowed to provide lodging to anyone without a valid pass. The town official made it very clear."

"Why's that?" asked the stranger.

"Because the land is full of Prussian spies."

"That seems like a dangerous line of work."

"I've heard the pay is good. Meanwhile, we honest people are suffering from hunger."

"Is Bouillon that poor?"

"Before the war began," the proprietor said, "our town was already struggling. Since then, things have only gotten worse. It's all because of the military strong box."[14.1]

"What strong box?"

"You haven't heard about the stolen war chest?"

"No," the traveler answered. "As I said, I'm not from around here."

The old man eyed him. "What did your parents do, Monsieur?"

"My father was a poor weaver."

"Ah! Another poor weaver. The town is filled with poor weavers." Looking the stranger over, the man decided to take him at his word. "I'm inclined to trust you. You have an honest look about you."

"Well, I would like to think so."

"Put some wood on the fire and I'll tell you the story of the missing strong box."

The stranger did as he was told.

"Did you want the milk and bread now?" the old woman asked.

"Yes, please, if it's convenient."

"Would you be so kind as to show us your pass?"

The young man reached into his pocket and produced a tattered book, which he handed to the old woman. She gave it to her husband, and left the room to prepare the simple meal.

The innkeeper took a pair of old spectacles from a drawer and gingerly placed them on his nose. He slowly paged through the book, grunting to himself with satisfaction. "You must have traveled all over the country, Monsieur."

"Yes, all over," the stranger nodded.

"I can tell by all the stamps in your booklet. Even though I can't read them all, it appears to be in order. Am I right?"

"Yes, it's all correct and up to date," replied the stranger, mildly amused.

The old woman came back in, placing a can of milk on the table and a few slices of bread beside it for dunking. This was their entire evening meal. While the stranger dug in, she questioned her husband about the young man's pass. "Does everything check out?"

"Yes. There are names and stamps."

She appraised the stranger again. "He seems to be poor, but a good sort," she whispered.

"Yes," he agreed.

"They even stole his fiddle," she added empathetically.

"Such a shame. I feel sorry for him."

"Dear, should we?"

"Yes, I think so."

"Good. Do you want to tell him?"

"No, you can tell him. I know you enjoy it."

"Listen, Monsieur," she said, smiling and turning back to the stranger. "We weren't sure about you at first."

"Yes," he replied amicably. "I noticed you were quite reserved."

"Fortunately, you've convinced us you're not a vagabond."

"I certainly am not, dear mother."

On hearing these last few words, she threw her husband a proud look, for no stranger had ever spoken to her so politely. "This is why we decided you should sleep in the hayloft," she said.

"In the hayloft?" he replied, a little disappointed.

"Yes, we don't want you to sleep where we normally put strangers."

"I'm grateful for your hospitality. Where do guests usually sleep?"

"In the goat pen."

"Really?" he said incredulously. "In the goat pen? Do you still keep goats?"

"Two of them. Unfortunately, we only have leaves for bedding and they're a little damp. We don't want you to catch a cold. Did you like the milk?"

"Very much, thank you!"

"It came from our two goats," she said. "Come now, husband, don't you want to tell our guest the story of the stolen strong box?"

"Of course! But I can't seem to get a word in edgewise."

"Tell him the story. I'll be quiet."

"Yes, go on!" encouraged the guest. "You've aroused my curiosity."

"Oh, it's nothing much, Monsieur. Have you heard anything about the fearsome Blücher?"

"Quite a bit."

The proprietor nodded as he launched into the tale. "Last year, Blücher crossed the Rhine with his forces, coming as far as Toul, which lies to the south on the far side of the mountains. He sent one of his generals, Prince Schisch-something—Schisherbatoff, I think—with a complement of ten thousand men toward Void and Ligny. Our boys were protecting a large military war chest that was destined for the war effort. The Frenchmen were too small in number to pose much of a resistance. Their chief concern was to safeguard the strong box."

"That goes without saying," the stranger interjected with a knowing smile.

"They couldn't risk moving it over open ground to the Marne River."

"Probably because the Prussians had too much cavalry in the area."

"Yes," the husband said. "A young captain made his way with about half a company in an attempt to go through the mountains toward the Argonne Forest."

"Didn't the enemy notice their attempt?"

"Apparently not. They slipped through."

"And did they secure the chest?"

The storyteller shook his head. "Unfortunately, no. The rest of the story is a tragic tale. The men were suddenly attacked during their march, with shots coming in from all sides. Ambushed, the soldiers fought back bravely, but twelve fell the first night. The second night, another twelve men succumbed."

"Who was responsible for the attack?"

"We weren't able to find out. Even if you had come to the site of the ambush, you wouldn't have been the wiser."

"Probably not."

"After four days of fighting," he continued, "only ten men were left standing guard. On the fifth day, only six men remained, and only four men on the sixth day. The last survivors came to Bouillon with the strong box, asking for our help. Since we're not soldiers, we feared we would get caught up in the battle. Therefore, not wanting to be killed like the rest, we fled into the hills."

"No one would blame you."

"The following day, we found the bodies of the four soldiers not far from here. They had been shot and the strong box was gone. After a few days, the German troops left the area. In the meantime, a French reconnaissance troop was sent to search for the missing war chest. They blamed our villagers for the entire matter, and as punishment we had to pay them compensation, which left us all in the poor house."

"That's a tragedy all right. Did you find any trace of the infamous strong box?"

The proprietor shook his head. "No, not a thing."

"Was any inquiry conducted?"

"What do you think, Monsieur? At first we suffered through the long war and then we faced a season without government. Now, we finally end up with a government that doesn't count for much. No, nothing has changed."

"Perhaps the culprits were the remnants of a Prussian company?"

"I don't think so. They were too familiar with the layout of the land."

"Perhaps robbers or highwaymen?"

"That's more likely," he acknowledged. After a brief pause, he went on. "I've said more about this tragedy than I planned. Tell me, are you going directly to Paris, Monsieur?"

"Yes. Why do you ask?"

"Maybe you'll have the good fortune of seeing our great emperor."

"No doubt!"

"I wish I could go in your stead. Are you by chance taking the road through Sedan?"

"Yes," the stranger said.

"Will you be stopping in the village of Raucourt?"

"Possibly."

"Then don't fail to visit the Jeannette estate."

"Jeannette? Why should I stop there?"

"Because that's where the prettiest girl in all of France lives."

The stranger smiled at the claim. "Come, come. Are you enraptured with the youthful looks of a girl?"

"Yes," the proprietor readily admitted, "and what honest Frenchman wouldn't be? Of course, I do so honorably."

"Is her beauty that enticing?"

"I'm no savant, as you can tell by looking at my old wife, but everyone talks about the girl—"

"What did you say?" his wife interrupted, unable to contain herself. "What can you see by looking at me? What did you mean by those remarks?"

"If I were a savant, then I would have married a pretty one!"

She laughed good-naturedly. "Oh, so that's your story now," she said. "You were quite satisfied with me back then."

"Well, yes, because I'm not a savant."

"I'd like to think I was pretty enough, though I cannot compare myself to the beauty at Jeannette. Yes, Monsieur, you should pay the estate a visit."

"You've almost given me a reason to wander there."

"Go ahead!" the husband encouraged. "Some people wander a long way just to see beauty in nature. Why shouldn't one do the same to see a beautiful girl?"

"Have you seen her lately?"

"Yes. She was recently in our little inn."

"Really? For a visit?"

"No, just for a short stopover."

"Was there was a problem with her carriage?"

"Indeed," he said. "She was on her way to visit relatives in Lüttich, but the axle on her carriage broke not far from here. Consequently, the ladies were forced to turn in here, unable to continue. Monsieur, an axle breakage could mean calamity!"

"Perhaps this mishap made her superstitious," the stranger said with a smile.

The proprietor sighed. "Then there were those Prussians. They had already advanced to Lüttich. We advised her not to go any farther, and so she wisely turned around."

"Surely, she must be the daughter of the baron who oversees the dairy operation."

"Oh no! She is visiting, that's all."

"What's her name?"

"I'm not sure," he said, giving the matter some thought. "She was with a lady, likely her mother, who called her by her first name, Margot."

"A pretty name."

"Yes. It fits her well! But too much beauty can be dangerous."

"Why do you say that?"

"Because her beauty has already claimed two lives."

"*Sapperlot!*"

The husband shrugged, "Just imagine how the garrison's soldiers at Sedan have sought to catch a glimpse of her. Many have desired just to be able to speak with the lady. Three duels have already occurred on her account. Twice it has cost an officer his life."

"Heavens! Does she prance about and make a spectacle of herself?"

"Not in the least! I've heard she's been invited to a ball or some festive occasion countless times and declines every invitation. If she does venture out, it's always in the company of her mother. No one can even boast to have kissed her fingertips."

"What about those duels?"

"As far as I can tell, her aloof manner is what drives men crazy!" the inn-keeper snickered. Then, he turned to his wife. "Well, old woman, just so you know, I wasn't crazy about you when we met," he teased.

"Serves you right for thinking I would have fallen for you on a whim," she retorted. She turned to face the stranger. "You must be tired after your long journey, Monsieur. We're going to turn in soon."

The old couple had warmed up, not showing any of their earlier mistrust that was so characteristic of rural folk. The stranger would have liked to stay up a little longer and hear more about the beautiful girl. She drew his interest more than the plundered strong box. He was, of course, very familiar with

Margot. He knew perfectly well why she acted withdrawn and lived in seclusion. After all, she was engaged to be married to him, Hugo von Löwenklau, the enterprising lieutenant, who had now been promoted to first lieutenant.

"Do you usually turn in so early?" Löwenklau asked.

"Yes, our chores necessitate that we get up early in the morning."

"Well then, I won't keep you from your rest. Please show me my lodging."

"It's not here, but rather out in the courtyard. Come, follow me." The innkeeper lit a torch and led the way across the small yard. As they walked, Löwenklau noticed a small structure that he supposed housed the goats.

"I have to close the hayloft," the old man explained, "or else strangers come and help themselves to the hay." He pointed to a ladder leading up. "Here's the ladder. Make sure to pull it up and keep it inside for the night. Especially now, during wartime, we find there are all sorts of rabble prowling about. With the ladder up in the loft, no one can climb up. Are your clothes dry enough, Monsieur?"

"As much as can be expected. I'm grateful for your hospitality."

"Should I come to wake you in the morning?"

"No, thanks. I'll awaken on my own."

"Then sleep well. I bid you a good night."

"Good night."

Löwenklau followed the old man's advice and climbed up into the loft. The hayloft consisted of a roof and a floor which was covered with straw. After he pulled the ladder up, he chuckled to himself. So, this small hayloft, that was barely three meters wide, was labeled first class, and the goat pen below was second class. He imagined some actually slept below in the muddy conditions. The old innkeeper must have been a very poor man indeed, not even owning a cow but instead settling for two goats that shared space with the lower class guests.

He prepared his accommodations, and in doing so woke up the goats below him, who responded with a quiet yet unhappy bleating. He could hear them clearly, a confirmation that the floor was very thin.

Löwenklau felt quite comfortable on the straw and the steady pelting of the rain had a calming, one could say even hypnotic, effect. Becoming drowsy, his thoughts returned ceaselessly to the pretty girl who stayed at Jeannette and the missing strong box until the two thoughts seemed intertwined with each other. Löwenklau had no idea how long he laid there. He wasn't even sure if he had slept or simply let his mind wander.

Suddenly, he heard a sound outside the loft and was instantly awake. He listened and made out a voice, barely audible, just below him.

"Did you check it out?"

"Uh-huh," a second voice answered.

"Have they already gone to bed?"

"Yes. All the lights are out in the house."

"Let's go into the pen."

"Hopefully, there's no one inside."

"Let's find out."

Löwenklau heard the gate open and the shuffling of steps that followed. The goats became restless, quieting down only after a few reassuring words.

"Come in," the first intruder whispered. "There's no one here."

"Good," replied the second man.

"It's warm here, much better than outside. I've slipped in here before on my way to the mountains."

"Secretly?"

"Yes. It's better this way. No one knows I've been here."

Löwenklau was able to catch every word. He remained motionless, aware that even the slightest movement would betray his presence. He asked himself who the two men were, remembering the innkeeper talking about the vagabonds who seemed now to be everywhere. Their presence suggested a planned meeting and their words conveyed a secrecy which went beyond the innkeeper.

"What would the old man say if he found us?"

"Nothing. We came in here because he was already asleep, not wanting to wake him. I don't believe he'd hold it against us. We'll have to give him a couple of francs for our overnight stay."

"It shouldn't be a problem, since you have more than enough."

"Of course I do," the other one laughed. "Still, it's best he doesn't know we're here."

"Do you think the pickaxes and spades will still be there?"

"Absolutely, we buried them!"

"If people only knew..."

"I made sure they wouldn't find out. I've wasted a lot of ammunition to keep it that way."

"Why then are you are willing to share your secret with me, and not the others?"

"Let me explain it to you. There were six of us at the beginning, and we all agreed to visit the chest together at a prescribed time. I was clever and left my marks at the site. When I noticed they had come individually to take coins as they pleased, I decided to get rid of them. I took care of four men, and you killed the fifth one yesterday. You didn't know it, but this was your test. Congratulations, you passed."

"Did you think it was my first killing?"

"Really, you've already...?"

"Six men all together."

"What? You've already disposed of six men?"

"That's what I just said."

"Hmm," one of them mumbled softly. "I guess you've done your bit. Tell me, are you really interested in my daughter?"

"Sure."

"Have you spoken to her?"

"Of course I have. We've made plans."

"Well, if that's the way things stand, then I can put my trust in my future son-in-law."

"Of course, you can. How did you make up your mind? I mean about going after the strong box. Planning the attack must have been difficult."

"It was more a matter of luck. I was making a living by selling wild game. Suddenly it seemed like everyone was trying the same thing. I didn't know how I was going to survive. One day, it came to me. The war left many either dead or badly wounded. All I had to do was take advantage of it by going through their pockets. If they offered any resistance, a quick thrust of my blade finished them off. A few men joined me in my little venture and we did all right together. We were nearby when the Prussians attacked Ligny. While we were lying low, we were able to observe a horse-drawn wagon, escorted by a small company of soldiers, leaving the area. It all looked very peculiar, so we concluded it had to be the war chest. Turned out we were right."

"What did you do next?"

"A few wanted to conduct an open attack," the voice continued, "but I prevailed upon them to reconsider, that it would be sheer suicide to do so. It was obvious the military company intended to bring the chest into the mountains. All we had to do was follow them. Picking the spots to ambush them was easy and we swiftly brushed them off, one by one, without any real danger to us. Well, you know the rest of the story. Not far from here, we killed the last four soldiers. We took charge of the wagon and drove it further into the mountains where we buried the strong box."

"What about the horses and wagon?"

"We broke up the wagon and burned the remains. Then, we rode the horses into the nearest village and sold them to local farmers."

"How much money was in the box?"

"I don't know. We couldn't count it all."

"Are you serious? That much?"

"Yes. It would have taken too much time to count it! Each one was allowed one thousand francs before we buried it."

"Did you go back often?"

"I went twice. However, when I realized the others were also helping themselves, I decided to get rid of them."

"So, where is the ravine?"

"It's easy to find, but the layout is harder to describe. Don't worry, you'll see it tomorrow."

"When do we leave?"

"With the morning light. That way, the old couple won't see us."

"What are your plans for the money?"

"I'm going to wait until the war has ended, then go to America."

"What about me? What should I do?"

"Don't be so dimwitted. You'll become my son-in-law, and naturally both of you will come with me. Enough for now, I'm tired and I need some rest."

"Wait a minute," the younger one said. "What if there's someone up in the hayloft?"

"Why would you think of that now?"

"I don't know, just a thought."

"Occasionally people have slept up there. You know, the ones with a higher class than ours."

"Dammit! What if there really is someone up there? He might have heard us talking."

"You're right. He would have heard everything."

"We would have to finish him off. We better make sure we're alone," he said, rising to have a better look.

Löwenklau had secured the latch. He wasn't afraid of them, and in any case he had two loaded pistols in his pockets. He considered himself lucky to have stowed the ladder, as the innkeeper had suggested.

"It's closed up there," one of the men pointed out.

"Then there's no one up there."

"Right, otherwise the ladder would still be leaning up against the frame."

"Good night."

"Sleep well."

The two vagabonds made some noise as they prepared their own straw beds, giving Löwenklau the opportunity to get comfortable without giving himself away. Unfortunately, having heard every word, he wasn't able to go back to sleep. *Who are those two?* he wondered. *Probably wartime deserters, hyenas who have chosen a life built on the misfortunes of others.*

He decided to wait where he was and follow the two men in the morning. Naturally, the thought of the fortune in the war chest didn't give him much rest. Eventually, sleep overtook him, allowing him a few hours of sleep. His slumber was shallow, waking him instantly when the two robbers started to stir below him.

"Are you still asleep?" one asked.

"No. I just woke up," replied the other.

"Me, too. What time would it be?"

"Let's find out," he said. As he opened the gate, he saw the dawn breaking in the mist. "It's almost light out. We'll leave shortly."

"At least the rain has let up."

"Damn. We're still going to get wet. It's not as heavy as yesterday, but it'll still penetrate our clothes. I would have preferred nicer weather!"

"I would rather have the poor weather. No one will be up in the mountains on a day like this."

"How long will we have to walk?"

"About two hours."

"We'll be soaked through by the time we get there."

"Stop your complaining. When you start counting the money, you won't be thinking about the rain. We'll make a fire in the nearby coal hut and dry out."

"Is it on our way there?"

"Sure."

"Is it occupied?"

"Not now. Don't worry, we'll be alone. Now stop asking questions and let's get going."

The second man walked out of the pen, closed the door, and stretched. "I'm ready. Which way, left or right?"

"To the right? What are you thinking? We're not going back into town. We have to start off to the left, along the river. When we get to the three alder trees, we turn toward the mountains."

They quickly departed, heading for the river.

Löwenklau, knowing their direction, didn't have to leave right away. He knew his task wouldn't be easy. He wanted to follow them, but not so closely that he would risk being seen. The rainy weather left the ground muddy and would make it easy to follow their footsteps.

He waited until he could no longer hear their footsteps, then slowly opened the loft door. He pushed the ladder out and climbed down. As he'd suspected, they left clear tracks behind to guide him. Hugo followed along the stream until he came to the three alder trees, where the track turned left. Had it been good weather, the day would have been bright, but today the rain swirled with the fog, making it difficult to see even ten steps in front of him.

The young officer continued for an hour, walking steadily uphill. As he neared the tree line, he became more cautious. He quickened his pace to close the distance. After some time, he could make out voices ahead. They spoke loudly so he could follow them in the trees without being spotted. The two were following a trail wide enough to allow a wagon passage. The path ended at a clearing where a small rundown shack stood. No doubt this was the coal hut they had mentioned earlier.

The two men didn't enter the hut, instead crossing to the far side of the clearing. He followed them from a safe distance, keeping under the cover of trees. Although the trail ended, a path continued further into the forest, where the trees were far enough apart to allow a cart or wagon to pass, albeit narrowly in places. The terrain slowly ascended until it came to a natural, wide depression that stretched upward toward a ravine.

Up ahead, the men turned into the ravine, with the lieutenant following at a distance. The edge of the gorge was covered with mature trees interspersed with wild brush. As they walked to the bottom, he was able to keep pace by remaining higher in the foliage.

Löwenklau finally spotted them out in the open and realized the one in the lead was older while the second was considerably younger. The older one had a full beard and carried himself like a forester. Perhaps he had once been employed as a warden or groundskeeper. He had a daring look about him, though he didn't seem particularly repulsive or unpleasant. The young man also had a full beard. He slouched and shuffled in his gait, while his face revealed a life riddled with debauchery and corruption. Löwenklau would not have been surprised to learn he had committed many crimes in his young life.

"Is it still far to go?" the younger one asked loudly.

"Hang on!" the older one called back, all the while scrutinizing the ground. "Walk twelve paces."

The young one obeyed.

"Stop there!"

"What? Why?"

"You're standing right on top of the strong box."

"How far down is it?"

"A little over a meter."

"Then it will be damned hard work!" he complained.

"Not at all. The ground is loose."

"What about the pickaxe and shovel?"

"Take another five paces ahead and stop!"

"They're buried here?"

"Yes, under your feet. All you need is your knife to loosen the earth around them."

"Should we start right away?"

"First, I need a little drink."

The older man produced a flask of whisky from his pocket, took a swig, and passed it to his partner. They started to work, first removing the pick and then the shovel.

"Tell me," the younger man asked the older one. "How should I dig the hole? Where is the border?"

"Listen up, it's roughly a square," the older one said. "Before we get at it with the pickaxes, we have to carefully cut and trim pieces of sod out with the shovel. Afterward, we replace it so no one's the wiser as to where we've been digging." He measured a square, carefully cutting around the edge. They lifted it out and laid it aside, then began the labor of digging the hole.

Löwenklau found a comfortable spot under the large branches of a spruce tree overlooking the 'worksite' and sat down to watch. The two men worked for about a half hour, alternating between the pickaxe and the shovel. Finally, one of them hit something that made a dull, echoing wooden sound.

"What was that?" asked the young one excitedly.

"You struck the wooden box."

"Ah! Is the money in the box?"

"No, in a metal box, which lies inside the wooden one."

"I have to admit," the young man said, "I've been skeptical until now."

"Fool!"

"I thought it was your idea to bring me along on account of your daughter."

"Don't be ridiculous! She can choose whomever she wants."

"Well, just so you know, I don't think she's the most desirable girl out there."

"If you're displeased with her, you can leave this very minute and find yourself another one."

"No! Far from it. Is the war chest really down there?" asked the younger man. He was in a delirious state, his eyes glowing with a strange, sinister luminescence.

"Well, where else would it be?"

The younger man reached for the pickaxe while the other one continued to shovel. When the older man bent forward, the young one took a mighty swing at his head. The impact fractured his victim's skull. The intended father-in-law fell into the newly dug pit without uttering a sound. The murderer threw the pickaxe to the side.

"Idiot!" he shouted. "You have your reward. You murdered all those people to get the war chest. Now you're dead and I'm the new owner. I'm rich, rich, rich! The devil can claim your ugly daughter. I, on the other hand, will find a much better looking one, perhaps even at Jeannette. After all, I can afford someone better!"

The horrible deed happened so fast that it would have been impossible for Löwenklau to intervene. He jumped up and pulled the pistols out of his coat. After he cocked the hammers, he carefully climbed down while the murderer stood fixated over his victim.

"Haven't I done a good job, Barchand!" he laughed to himself. "Come out of there! I've got to get the strong box out, and you're in my way!"

The murderer grabbed the legs of the corpse and pulled him out of the pit. He picked up the shovel to clear away the dirt.

Suddenly, he was wrought with fear and dropped the shovel, his eyes bulging open. He had finally noticed Löwenklau, standing not two paces in front of him, his pistols aimed directly at his chest.

"Murderer!" breathed Löwenklau with disgust.

The young man was speechless, as though the concept of speech was something foreign to him.

"See if he's still alive," the lieutenant said. "Hurry up, or I'll send this bullet into your head!"

The immediate threat brought the culprit out of his momentary shock. "Hell and damnation!" he blurted out. "Who are you?"

"You'll find that out soon enough." Löwenklau's tone and demeanor commanded respect, leaving no room for argument.

The man reluctantly bent down and examined the corpse. "He's completely dead. Why was he so stupid?"

"We'll determine who the stupid one is later. What's your name?"

The murderer recovered from his shock. "Why should it concern you?" he jeered.

"It concerns me in every way! Let me make something clear, perfectly clear," Löwenklau said. "If you give me one more stupid answer, I won't hesitate to shoot. Now, for the last time, what's your name?"

"Fabier."

"What do you do?"

"I'm a butcher in Raucourt."

"What's this one's name?" said Löwenklau, indicating the corpse.

"Barchand. He's also from Raucourt."

"What did he do?"

"He was a butcher, like me."

"Good. That's enough for now. Take the pickaxe and shovel and walk ahead."

"Where are we going?"

"You'll find out soon enough."

"Listen, Monsieur, do you know what's in the pit?"

"Yes. The war chest from Ligny."

The young man reacted with surprise. "Damn! How do you know that?"

"I'm an officer. That's all you need to know."

"An officer? Monsieur, we will split the money!"

"Ridiculous!"

"I only want a third!"

"Shut up and obey!"

"Only a quarter!"

"Are you going to pick up the tools or not?"

"I'll abide by what you say, but you have to listen to me!" Fabier said as he gathered up the tools.

Löwenklau, armed with pistols, followed him further into the gorge, careful to keep his distance from him. Pointing to a spot, he instructed. "Here, dig a hole for your companion."

"Gladly, Monsieur! Don't you want to discuss the strong box?"

"Later! First we'll lay the corpse to rest."

"Fine. I'll do as you ask." The murderer started to dig. No doubt it was the thought of money that spurred him into a frenzy. In a short time, he had dug a hole two meters long and one and a half meters wide. He looked inquiringly at the lieutenant.

"Make it twice as wide!" ordered Löwenklau.

"But why? This is wide enough."

"Don't question my order!"

With trepidation, Fabier continued digging to widen the grave.

When he finished, Löwenklau instructed him. "Now, fetch your former partner and put him in!"

Fabier became pale. He guessed why he'd been ordered to widen the grave. In spite of this, he complied, hoping to gain some time, perhaps convincing the officer to change his mind. "Now what?" he asked timidly, having laid the corpse into the ground.

Löwenklau caught the menacing look. He knew he had to be extra vigilant. It was now a matter of life and death. Each one was mindful of the other's actions. "You can cover the strong box, and fill in the pit with earth," he ordered.

"Cover it? Why?"

"No one is going to claim it. It's going to remain here."

"Monsieur—"

"Get back to work, or I'll send a bullet into your skull!"

"And afterward?"

"You'll find out."

"Monsieur, you shouldn't think the worst of me!"

"Of course not!" mocked Löwenklau. "You nicely eliminated six men and now you just added one more to your tally."

Fabier's face turned white from fright. His shock hardly diminished when his sordid instincts kicked in. "Well," he began with a hardened laugh, "if you know that much, you'll believe me when I say I'm only obeying you for a single reason."

"No doubt you fear my pistols."

"That's where you're wrong. Not every bullet hits its mark."

"I have every confidence in mine."

"Then give me a demonstration."

Löwenklau shrugged his shoulders. "Idiot!" he said. "Do you really think you can fool me? Pay heed to my instructions or you will soon feel the effects of my marksmanship!"

Fabier started to fill the pit. He replaced the sod and packed it into place. It would have been difficult for anyone to detect that a looming hole had existed just a few minutes ago. "So, Monsieur," Fabier said, "our secret is safe again. I hope we can come to an arrangement. How did you come to learn of the chest's location?"

Löwenklau felt that speaking the truth would drive home the culpability of his actions, and replied, "From the two of you."

"From us? What do you mean?"

"I mean from you and your companion, whom you murdered."

"How is that possible?"

"Last night, you spoke of it in the goat pen."

"In the goat pen?" he asked. "I thought we were alone."

"I was above you in the hayloft. I heard every word."

"But the enclosure was closed."

"I closed it from the inside."

"There wasn't any ladder."

"I lifted it up."

"Are you telling me the truth?"

"Of course! When the two of you finished your talk, you bid each other good night. After a while, you asked Barchand if someone was up in the hayloft. You decided then and there to have a look and finish him off. Isn't that right?"

"That's true! How stupid of us not to have checked further!"

"You mean how stupid of you not to have finished me off?"

"Damn, damn! We missed our opportunity!"

"This morning you discussed the way you intended to go," Löwenklau continued, "You left along the river, toward the alder trees. All I had to do was follow your tracks."

The man was stunned. "What idiots we were. We should have checked the loft. What did you intend to do?"

"I wanted to find the spot, and then later claim the strong box. Maybe I would have shot you both, just like you killed those before you. It would have been a fitting end."

"Kill me?" asked Fabier, shaking with fear.

"Most certainly," replied Löwenklau. He found himself filled with calm determination.

"But why? I didn't do anything to you, Monsieur!"

"Don't be a fool! You would have attacked me long ago if I was not in the possession of these pistols. You murdered your companion in cold blood, and now this place must remain secret. Those are two very good reasons to condemn you. You dug your own grave, and I suspect you'll rot next to your victim."

Fabier pretended to think about his heartless deeds, but in reality was deciding on a desperate move.

"Not if I can help it," he yelled. "Die, you bastard!" He lunged at his new adversary.

Löwenklau was not to be fooled, though. He saw Fabier brace himself and had expected just such an attack. He quickly stepped aside and lifted his pistol. "Go to hell, you devil!"

Löwenklau's shot hit the butcher in the head, stopping the man in his tracks. With this one shot, all the guardians of the war chest were finally avenged. The young officer felt no joy, no victory as in battle, and yet he was filled with deep conviction. Surely this murderer deserved death many times over for his crimes. However, the reality of his actions hit him hard, as he had unwittingly become both judge and executioner.

He laid the corpse in the freshly dug grave, the two former companions lying next to each other. Ironically, the two men, who had come to claim the treasure, were now resting just a short distance from the strong box. Löwenklau covered them with earth and distributed the remaining soil over the area so no one coming to the site would expect to unearth hidden treasure.

Löwenklau reasoned that the Prussians would probably win the war, at which time he would inform Blücher of the chest's location, not collecting it for himself but for the common good. All that remained was for him to bury the tools and ensure that he could find the correct spot. Taking out his notebook, he drew a detailed map, complete with distances, which he paced off. Once he was satisfied, he started his journey back to the farm.

When he reached the farmyard, he found the old couple occupied with their chores. They hadn't disturbed him, thinking he was still asleep. The lieutenant ate a simple breakfast and paid his bill. He received his passbook back and continued on his way, accompanied by the good wishes of the old couple.

CHAPTER FIFTEEN
Captain Sainte-Marie

I t was the beginning of June 1815. The French headquarters were situated at Laon, while the Prussian army was stationed near Thionville. Baron Daure, the French adjutant general, had arrived several days ago and the emperor's arrival was expected any day. He let it be known that he planned to go to Strasburg, intending to make an appearance before his beloved troops and rekindle their support. It was rumored that he might even appear at Thionville.

Some officers who knew their emperor well understood that he loved to show up where he was least expected. Although he had chosen the route which would later encompass his battle plans, he also liked to make unscheduled excursions to places which puzzled even his inner circle. Often the habits of the ruler found their way into the routines of his subordinates. Some of his marshals enjoyed a similar routine making unscheduled visits on their troops. Marshal Groucy liked to personally attend and conduct his own observations. The results were often attributed to his successful campaigns.

Löwenklau reached Sedan about midday, the same day he discovered the plundered war chest. Normally he would have skirted the city, but this time he was forced to walk through it since it was the only safe place to cross the Maas River. The river had risen considerably as a direct result of the pelting rain that had continued over several days, and crossing it had become a dangerous undertaking.

Sedan, the birthplace of the famous Turenne,[15.1] had often been heralded for its military importance. It was therefore no wonder that the city and its surrounding area were a beehive of activity for Napoleon's troops. Some of these belonged to Marshal Ney, the son of a tailor, who because of his wartime talents had managed to advance to the rank of Marshal of France, Duke of Elchingen, and Prince of Moskva. General Drouet served under him as *aide-de-camp* to the emperor. Drouet, however, had declined to live in Sedan, choosing instead to make his headquarters at Raucourt. He personally stayed at the Jeannette estate while his staff remained in the town.

On his arrival, Löwenklau was asked to present his identity papers. He showed them the same pass he had presented the previous evening to the innkeeper. Although it had been falsified by Blücher's headquarters, he knew it would satisfy the inspector's scrutiny.

Even though wartime regulations called for the close inspection of personal documents, Löwenklau felt he was getting more than the routine examination. He had fought against the French and spent some time in Paris. If he were to be recognized now as a spy, his escapades would come to a crashing halt. He breathed a sigh of relief when the pass was returned and he was allowed to proceed.

Raucourt, which lay to the south of Sedan, could be reached by foot in about two hours. Unfortunately, the roads between the two communities were in bad shape and the Argonne Forest, which encompassed much of the intervening area, had begun to take on a disreputable status. All sorts of rabble had made it their home, concealing themselves in the gorges and inaccessible parts of the forest. They only surfaced to conduct bold raids and acts of robbery on unsuspecting travelers.

For the time being, the road between Raucourt and Sedan was secure because of the large military presence, which most thieves tended to avoid. Further towards Laon, near Rethel, however, there were only traces of military activity, not enough to guarantee secure passage for civilians. As every war does, the revolution had introduced a new kind of vagabond to the French countryside. It was a part of the populace that had already been in contention with the law and seemed now to flourish by casting its 'lures' into the murky waters of the lonely highways between villages. Pockets of vagrants and drifters were everywhere, debasing themselves as common thieves and robbers, particularly in the wildernesses of the Ardennes and Argonnes, where travelers were most susceptible.

When Löwenklau reached Raucourt, he found it relatively easy to find his way to Jeannette. There, he found the military presence in a state of readiness. He even met a sentry at the gate performing his duty by blocking the way.

"You there, stranger," he called to Löwenklau. "Where are you going?"

"Inside, of course."

"To see the general?"

"No. Which general is in command here?"

"General Drouet. Whom do you wish to see then?"

"The proprietress of the estate."

The sentry almost smiled, as though the proprietress had frequent gentleman callers. "Oh, the Lady de Sainte-Marie?"

"Yes."

"She is absent, having departed early this morning."

"Then I would like to see her representative."

"That would be the young baron. Do you know him?"

"No, but I have business with him."

"Oh, that's different. You may enter," he said. "The baron, Roman de Sainte-Marie, resides on the main level." He pointed to a row of windows on the house.

Löwenklau thanked him for the information and proceeded to the front door. He knocked and was soon admitted into the foyer. Upon entering, he found himself in the office of a gentleman, likely unmarried, who had allowed the surroundings to fall into a semblance of disarray. It seemed an expected setting for a bachelor.

As the lieutenant closed the door, the young bachelor rose from the sofa and evaluated the newcomer. Roman's facial features possessed a softness that hinted at a younger age than his twenty-two years.

"Monsieur de Sainte-Marie?" inquired Löwenklau.

"Yes," he replied, continuing to examine him with probing eyes. "What do you want?"

"Would you be so kind as to advise me if Madame Richemonte is available for a visit?"

Roman's face revealed surprise, which an astute observer might have attributed to momentary concern. "Ah, Madame Richemonte?" he asked. "Do you have business with her?"

The question was understandable, as Löwenklau appeared in street clothes and gave the impression of being in common standing.

"It is a personal matter concerning the lady which brings me here," replied Löwenklau. "I am not sure if I have her permission to discuss it with a third party."

"I am solely interested in the welfare of the lady. Do you know her?"

"Yes, from my time in Paris."

The face of the young baron took on a darker shade. "Are you Captain Richemonte?"

"Certainly not!"

"An acquaintance then?"

"Yes," Löwenklau admitted.

"Then pray tell me, how do you know Madame Richemonte is lodging here at Jeannette?"

"I myself brought the lady and her companion to the estate."

"Do you mean as her coachman?"

"No," laughed Löwenklau. "As her companion."

Roman's expression held a peculiar look that implied either concern or delight, the lieutenant couldn't tell. Regardless, it prompted a quick response. "*Zounds!*" he exclaimed. "Then you must be the elusive Löwenklau."

"Indeed!"

"You dared to come here? Come in, come in!" He grabbed the lieutenant's arm, pulling him along through a side door and into his private chamber.

Roman looked him up and down, shaking his head in wonder. "My God, what a risk, coming to Raucourt!"

"Do you really consider it a risk?"

"First, you're a Prussian and, second, an officer under Blücher's command. Don't you know General Drouet is using the estate as his personal quarters?"

"I only learned of it this morning in Sedan."

"Still, you dared to show yourself. What if you'd been captured and treated as a spy?"

"I only came to see Madame and Mademoiselle Richemonte. That is all."

The young baron was at a loss for words. Looking around the room, he pointed to a chair. "Please Monsieur, take a seat," he said at last. "It's important that we understand each other. I take it you are a friend to Madame Richemonte?"

"Yes, one who is sincere in his devotion to her."

"I wasn't present when the ladies arrived. I was engaged at the time in Reims, helping a friend with the construction of a wine cellar. It shouldn't surprise you to learn I have a passion for winemaking. When I returned, I found the ladies residing on the estate. I was informed about a German fellow, named Löwenklau, who had accompanied them."

"I am one and the same."

"Exactly! Madame Richemonte also informed me she had cause for concern that her stay at Jeannette should not be revealed to outsiders. You seem to be held in high regard by the lady."

"I had the opportunity to be of service to both women. It would be a stretch to call it more than that."

Roman's face brightened. "Still, I am indebted to you. You must be aware that Madame Richemonte is my relative."

"Although she spoke of it, she did not elaborate."

"My mother and Madame Richemonte come from the same hometown. They are cousins and grew up together. When my father died, I naturally took on..." he trailed off, then finished with a cheerful and unassuming tone. "...the entire burden of administering the estate on my shoulders. It was very lonely here until the arrival of the ladies. A new life has come upon me for which I am grateful. Unfortunately, my easy and comfortable lifestyle has dramatically changed thanks to the arrival of the military. They throw everything into upheaval! On my mother's side, some German blood still runs through my veins. Consequently, I'm not too inclined to become a servant to the demands of an imminent war. However, all of my personal considerations were placed on hold when Drouet arrived with his entourage."

"I congratulate you on your loyalty," Löwenklau said politely.

"Thank you, although I'm not ready to jump on the French bandwagon just yet. Now, while you honor me with your presence, may I say: all these supporters of Napoleon can go to hell!"

"Please, pay no attention to my presence, Baron."

"If it were only that easy! Should I entreat you to leave?"

Löwenklau let out a brief laugh. "I certainly hope not!"

"Am I permitted to give lodging to a German officer?"

"Under the circumstances, yes. I'm not here as an officer in the Prussian army. I am in possession of identity papers which were scrutinized and accepted in Sedan."

"Well, that is different! I'll be honest with you. I do not long for the return of the war happy emperor. I would rather serve Louis XVIII. That said, I strive not to get all worked up over politics." He paused for a moment, as though remembering an important detail. "Actually, are you aware Madame Riche-monte is absent?"

"Where is she?"

"She and Mademoiselle took a trip with Mama to Vouziers."

"When do they plan to return?"

"Probably this very night."

A look of anguish passed over Löwenklau's face. "This evening?" he asked. "Not during the day? It's a journey of a full six hours."

"Of course, but because of the military presence, I need my mother back to assist me with all the preparations."

Löwenklau's thoughts turned to the danger of the roads through the Argonne forest and the risk of robbers. "I believe you. Consider, though, how dangerous a journey at night would be through the forest."

Roman took a step backward and tapped his forehead, contemplating the meaning of the Prussian's words. "Dear God, yes! We hadn't considered it at all. None of us!"

"The road goes through the forest, which is full of all sorts of trouble-makers."

"You're right! The devil! What are we going to do?" Roman possessed a carefree attitude, yet it was clear his concern for the ladies outweighed his usual nonchalance.

"Which route did the ladies take?"

"They drove through LeChesne and Boule aux Bois."

"Are they likely to return the same way?"

"Probably!" he said with mounting trepidation. "Oh God! If something happens to them! I should leave immediately and ride out, but this damned General Drouet is always after me to render him some sort of service."

Löwenklau had already made up his mind. "In that case, arrange a saddled horse for me."

"For you?" the young baron asked, half-surprised and half-relieved.

"Yes, for me, if I can impose upon you."

"Do you realize the danger?"

"*Pah!* Because of the thieves on the road?"

"Yes, and the fact that you are traveling as a German on French soil."

"I don't feel the danger. Here are my papers," he said, passing the man his false identification. "Please examine them so you can become familiar with my new identity."

Roman took a cursory glance at the pass. "I have a horse at your disposal. Do you have any weapons?" he asked.

"I have two pistols and a knife."

"That won't be enough. These thieves seldom work alone. I'll supply you with two more pistols. Do you know the road that you need to take?"

"Monsieur, I'm a German officer!" exclaimed Löwenklau, as though that information was enough to satisfy the question.

Roman nodded. "I do not doubt you, Monsieur," he replied. "I've heard the Germans have proven just how capable they are navigating with maps of France. Do you want to stop for a light meal?"

"Thank you, but I feel I don't have the time for it."

"Then I'll have something prepared for you and put it in your saddle bag. Please, excuse me." He left the room to make the necessary preparations.

Finding himself alone, Löwenklau was in the heart of the lion's den. He had been sent to learn as much as possible of the enemy's plans, knowing full well how difficult and dangerous the undertaking would be. If he were captured as a spy, he would face disgrace and the ultimate fate reserved for such criminals; namely, death by hanging. He weighed the risk against the prospect of seeing his betrothed again. As luck had it, he had already acquired one trump by discovering the location of the buried war chest.

Sitting alone in the room, he thought about the young baron, Roman. Löwenklau pictured him as an easygoing and good-natured man. *Did he suspect that he, Löwenklau, was actually engaged to Margot? Probably not, judging from their conversation.* His mind took him back to their arrival at the Jeannette estate the year before. Madame Richemonte hadn't introduced him as the lieutenant who was to become her future son-in-law, but merely as a friend. Löwenklau had been unaware of her reasons, though suspected she had chosen to exercise prudence even where her relatives were concerned.

Roman reappeared after a short interval, informing him that the horse was saddled and ready to go. He opened a trunk and removed two double pistols, handing them to Löwenklau.

"Are they loaded?" the lieutenant asked.

"No. I pride myself in being a man of peace, and I rarely have need of firearms. These weapons should do nicely, though. I inherited them from my father, who was an officer. Here is the ammunition." Roman produced powder, shot, and igniters.

"How will I recognize the carriage?" asked Löwenklau while loading the pistols.

"It is an old, stately looking carriage, from the era of Louis XV."

"What about the horses?"

"A white one and a brown one."

"Aside from the coachman, are servants traveling with the ladies?"

"Unfortunately not, even though there is sufficient space."

"I'm grateful for your help, Monsieur! I'm ready to depart now."

"Will you return to Jeannette?"

"I plan to accompany the ladies to the gate of the estate. However, the rest will be up to your mother, the baroness."

"Fine," Roman said. "I urge you to remain vigilant."

"Don't worry about me. I won't let them out of my sight."

They both walked to the courtyard, where a brown gelding awaited his new master. Löwenklau mounted the horse and, because the young baron had accompanied him, was allowed to depart without question. Löwenklau, attired in plain clothes, looked much like an ordinary servant instructed to deliver a message. Appearing somewhat unfamiliar on horseback, he rode out of the yard in a slow trot and waited to clear the perimeter of the estate. Once he was safely past Raucourt, he dug in his heels and took off like a shot from a gun.

The road led through the forest, closely following a stream to the left and nothing but trees to the right. Löwenklau rode on until he spotted a lonely little house, a rest stop for weary travelers. Needing to rest his horse, he decided to stop and make a few inquiries.

When he entered, he saw a young girl working at a spinning wheel. She stood up and, in a friendly tone, asked him what he wanted. Löwenklau nearly missed her glance, conveying a mixture of compassion and pity.

"May I have a glass of wine?" he asked, offering to shake her hand.

"Of course," she replied, barely touching his hand. She brought the drink out and placed it before him without making a sound. Wordlessly, she returned to her weaving.

He noticed her furtive glances in his direction, particularly her attempts in trying not to show it. "How far is it to LeChesne?" he asked.

"You will need a good hour," she replied.

"I intend to go that far, perhaps even as far as Vouziers."

"Oh dear!"

"Pardon me?"

She blushed and lowered her eyes. "Well, sir... it will be nightfall by then."

"Does this present a problem?"

"The night does not ingratiate itself to anyone. The forest is nearly endless," she said, lifting her eyes.

He decided to narrow his questioning and be more direct. "I was told that all sorts of things happen in the forest. Are these stories true, Mademoiselle?"

She looked at him inquiringly and asked a new question, rather than answering his. "Are you a stranger to these parts, Monsieur?"

"Yes."

"Yet you're riding a familiar horse!"

"Do you recognize it?"

She nodded. "It belongs to the Jeannette estate."

"That is true. Are you known there?"

"Oh, very well. I am the godchild of the baroness. My grandfather served under her belated husband."

"Ah! In that case, are you familiar with the baroness's carriage?"

"Of course. It came through here this morning."

"Well, dear girl, I want to meet the carriage halfway."

She nearly jumped out of her chair. "Meet her carriage? My God! Does the baroness plan to return at night?"

"It would seem so."

"But how will they recognize her carriage at night?"

Her admission had a two-fold meaning. Löwenklau noticed the implication and asked the girl. "Is it necessary for her carriage to stand out?"

"Well, yes!" she said without thinking. "Nothing should happen to her!"

"What could happen?"

The question brought her back to reality. She realized she had already said too much. A slight redness spread across her pretty face, which she tried to hide. "Oh, Monsieur," she said after a short pause. "You were right earlier when you asked me if the forest road is unsafe. At night, evil men are on the prowl."

"Do you know some of these men?" he asked with a penetrating glance.

Her long eyelashes concealed her thoughts behind her troubled eyes. "Monsieur, I live alone here with my mother. There are people who stop here whose identities I am not permitted to reveal. If I did, things would not go well for us."

"Dear girl, why don't you move away?"

"We thought about moving, but we cannot. When my father bought this house, the forest was safe and passable. Honest people came here and we enjoyed serving them. Then the war broke out, and soon the land was crawling with all sorts of rabble. My father died from a gunshot wound, and my grandfather was dismissed from the estate, dying shortly thereafter. We live alone and are not allowed to break confidence."

"Then sell the house."

"Who's going to buy it, Monsieur?"

"Plead with the baroness," he said. "She is a compassionate woman who will not refuse you."

"She already has."

"But why?"

She looked ashamed and hesitated to elaborate. "Because... well... she's mad at us."

"But why, dear girl? Perhaps I can help."

Suddenly, she covered her face, bowing her head. Löwenklau saw how a strand of her hair loosed itself, tears squeezing between her small fingers. The quiet sobs confirmed she was crying.

He waited for a while, then gently prodded her to continue. "Have I offended you?"

Slowly, she lifted her head and looked at him through her tears. "No, Monsieur. I know you're trying to help me. In fact, I've made up my mind to be honest with you. Do you know which way you have to ride?"

"The general direction, without the small twists and turns of the road."

"Well, it winds back and forth a few times. Are you familiar with the song, *Ma cherie est la belle Madeleine?*"

"Yes, I am."

"Good. When you reach the fifth bend, you will see a cross on the right-hand side. Some time ago, a traveler was murdered there. When you see the cross, start singing or whistling that tune."

"Why?"

"I'm not allowed to reveal the secret!"

"Then I will tell you," Löwenklau said. "Hidden behind the cross are those who sometimes come by here. They wait for the unassuming traveler. However, the one who sings or whistles your melody passes by unharmed, protected by it."

"Oh, dear God! I plead with you not to mention it to anyone."

"I won't tell a soul."

"But you have to tell at least one!"

"Who?"

"The coachman who drives the carriage for the baroness. He must be told. When he comes near the cross, he needs to hum or whistle the tune to escape the highwaymen. Ordinarily they wouldn't molest her entourage, but since she's traveling at night, they might not recognize the carriage."

"Don't worry about it, dear girl," Löwenklau said. "Don't you realize you'll be tainted with the same brush since you know the whereabouts of the highwaymen and fail to expose them?"

"I know, Monsieur, but if I did, they would kill both my mother and me. How could I bear the responsibility for the death of my mother?"

"You could flee until every last one is crushed or brought to justice."

"Crushed? Oh no! No sooner has one died than another rises up to take his place. That Fabier..." She stopped herself again, afraid to reveal too much. It was evident by her demeanor that she despised the man.

The name sparked the lieutenant's recent memory. "Please, go on, Mademoiselle," he said.

"No, I shouldn't have said anything."

"Yet you spoke a name."

"It escaped my lips by accident."

"Fabier? Mademoiselle, didn't you say Fabier?"

After a short hesitation, she lifted her head. "Yes, I did," she admitted.

"Then perhaps you know the name Barchand as well."

"Barchand? Do you know him, too?"

"I'm not sure. Were these two men part of the gang lurking in the forest?"

"Yes."

"Don't worry about them then. They won't trouble you anymore."

"How come?" she asked, surprised yet happy.

"They're both dead."

Her eyes widened. "Is it really true, Monsieur?"

"You can take my word for it."

"Where? Where did they die?"

"They killed each other," he said. "I saw their bodies for myself."

"When did this happen?"

"Just this morning."

She got up and slowly walked over to him, resting her small hands on his arm. "Is this really true?"

"Yes, of course."

"Are you willing to swear to it?"

"On my honor."

"Praise God! Had you guessed Barchand was one of the leaders? He was the one who threatened and oppressed my mother. Then there was Fabier..." She shuddered at her own mention of the name. "He was like a living nightmare."

"Really? Did he pursue you?"

"It's all too horrible to recall. He was here yesterday morning, proclaiming he would return as a rich man. I was supposed to become his wife, or die if I refused him."

"So, he deceived Barchand's daughter then!"

"Really? Did he tell her he loved her?"

"Yes, to gain her father's confidence."

The girl looked at him in amazement. "How do you know all this?"

"I overheard it by chance, before they died. I need to be honest with you: Fabier murdered Barchand to become rich, but I shot him in self-defense."

"You? You shot him?" she questioned, finding it hard to believe that her tormentors were finally gone and no longer a threat to her family.

"Yes, believe me. I even buried them."

"Where? This side of Sedan?"

He nodded. "Yes."

"Promise me they are not coming back to torment me!"

"I promise. They're never coming back."

Finally, she seemed to visibly relax. "Monsieur," she began, "don't regret what you've done." She took a deep breath. "You were God's chosen instrument and you've become not only my deliverer, but also one for many others. That cruel, repulsive Fabier, he would have been the end of me."

"I can tell," he said slowly, keeping his eyes on her. "Because you love another."

"Love another?" she asked blushing.

"Of course. You yourself revealed it just now."

"I did? Impossible!" she answered.

"It wasn't so much in your words, but in the way your face blushed with embarrassment." She wanted to turn away, but he firmly held her hands. "May I tell you whom you love, Mademoiselle?"

"How could you possibly know?" she countered.

"Perhaps I'm wrong, but I think I know his name. It's Roman, the young baron, who has captured your heart, isn't it?"

"Monsieur!" she whispered.

"This is why your grandfather was dismissed. It also explains why you lost favor with the baroness, my dear girl."

"Please, don't be cruel. You are mistaken, Monsieur!"

"I don't think so. I want to be your friend and my only desire is to help you in your plight. Did he reveal his love for you?"

She shook her head.

"Didn't his actions demonstrate his love for you?"

She nodded slowly. "Monsieur, I have no idea why I am disclosing all this to you. I find myself admitting truths I wouldn't have even considered revealing to a friend. I could he harmed for telling you this."

"Never, my dear girl. No one will find out without your permission. You see, even the most guarded heart can open itself under the right circumstances. An open and honest face can lead to becoming the recipient of unexpected news. My time is short and I must leave, yet I hope to see you again. Does the baroness's coach ever stop here?"

"Never."

"Does the young baron ever visit?"

"Occasionally," she admitted.

"Where is your mother?"

"She's occupied elsewhere. However, she will return shortly."

"May I know your name?"

"Berta Marmont."

"Thank you," he said graciously "Take care, Mademoiselle Berta! I am much obliged for your friendly warning. May God favor you with his blessing!"

He reached out to shake her hand. She held it tight and looked at him with new resolve. "Will you follow my warning exactly?"

"Certainly, I will whistle *Ma cherie est la belle Madeleine!* Is the way safe once the carriage is past the cross?"

"Yes, up to LeChesne. I can't speak for anything further than that."

"I take it you mean that it's not safe there."

"I've heard a number of sad stories. Please, watch yourself, Monsieur."

He dug into his pocket and gave her a gold coin for her hospitality. He then walked outside, declining to accept the change. She accompanied him to the door and watched as he mounted the gelding again. Her eyes followed him until he disappeared from view at the first bend in the road.

A good man! she thought wistfully. *His eyes spoke of truth and fidelity, even more so than the baron's. Though he wore simple clothing, he carried himself like a man of nobility. He rode like an officer and it's a shame I didn't get his name. I hope he remembers to whistle the tune!*

Löwenklau pondered similar thoughts as he rode further down the trail. *A pretty and courageous girl. So good and loyal, although she's been tarnished by those highwaymen. I bet some sort of romance will take place between her and the baron. I pray it turns out all right for all concerned in the end.*

CHAPTER SIXTEEN
A Resourceful Hussar

Löwenklau rode on and loosened his pistols so as to be ready at a moment's notice. As soon as he spotted the cross ahead, he started to whistle the popular tune. He looked ahead and sought to catch any sign of robbers in the brush. He was nearly abreast of the cross when he saw a slight movement in the trees. Two heads slowly retreated from underneath a branch.

He passed the infamous cross unmolested. *What if I could eavesdrop on the gang?* he asked himself. *I might even overhear something valuable. Why not risk it? I've got four double pistols, which means eight shots in total. And I'm actually under the protection of the girl's revelation.*

By the time Löwenklau reached the next bend in the road, he was out of sight of the highwaymen. He jumped from his horse and walked a ways into the forest. Finding a suitable spot, he tied the reins to a tree. Using the foliage as cover, he carefully crept back in the direction from where he had come.

Löwenklau worked his way deeper into the forest and made a plan to approach the robbers from the rear. He moved from tree to tree until he was back in view of the roadway. He got down on all fours and crept toward what he perceived to be their lookout point. He doubled his alertness and used every shrub to conceal his approach.

As he pressed closer, he could hear suppressed voices nearby. He could make out at least eight men seated in a small clearing. They were dressed in an assortment of clothes, which probably consisted of the loot of previous victims. What they lacked in attire, they made up for in their selection of weapons. Not one was without a rifle, and many had pistols. Situated near the cross, not far from the assembled group, Löwenklau spotted two more men, who were no doubt on sentry duty. They were probably the same two he had seen earlier. The two men whispered to each other conspiratorially while the others carried on a lively conversation, of which he could hear every word.

"You thought he was a servant?" one asked. "I think you're wrong."

"He had a military look about him. Didn't you see the way he carried himself?"

"What about his well-groomed beard?"

"Well, what are you arguing for? He's clear, and probably halfway to LeChesne."

"He didn't look like much. Probably didn't have much money!"

"He wasn't worth our while. Besides, he knew the signal."

"Who could have leaked it to him?"

"Maybe he just whistled it by chance?"

"More likely, he got it from Berta."

"Maybe he was an acquaintance or a lover!"

"Hang it all! Berta's a tasty morsel we won't give to just anyone."

"It's either one of us or nobody at all."

"Bloody hell!" one of the older men called. This one, who they called Curé looked well past his prime. Since Barchand hadn't returned, he had assumed temporary leadership over the bandits. "Stop arguing over her. A few of you tried and got your fingers burnt. I thought we all agreed to leave her alone since we couldn't decide who should get her. Why shouldn't she get a man she likes? Just drop it."

"I know the one she really likes, Curé."

"You mean the young Baron de Sainte-Marie?" one of the men asked jokingly.

"Yes."

"Impossible."

"Why impossible?"

"Well, he's a baron and she's a simple farm girl."

"*Pah!* Love knows no bounds."

"How would you know?"

"I've seen it for myself. Haven't you noticed how easily she turns red at the sound of his name? She's in love with him!"

"Is he fond of her?"

"Who knows?"

"She's head over heels in love. I can see her becoming a baroness someday."

"I've seen him at the wayside inn a few times."

"Does Fabier know about the baron?"

"Maybe he does."

"Perhaps the young baron should look over his shoulder! Fabier's likely to put a bullet into his head! He's crazy about her."

"We'll make sure he won't. It goes against what we've already decided."

"By the way," agreed another, "he's supposed to marry Barchand's daughter."

"Her? Not if he can help it."

"Why not? Fabier and Barchand are nearly best friends. They're always together, talking in whispers. Are they planning to cut us out of any future deals?"

"I wouldn't advise them to do that!"

"Be quiet. I didn't see you object when they left yesterday. They're supposed to be back tonight. What are those two up to anyway? I wonder if they're planning on striking out on their own..."

"I don't like the sound of that. We're in this together."

"Well, they're gone and they aren't the only ones. There's only ten of us left. What can we accomplish with such small numbers?"

"Had we been together this morning, we would have hit the big one. Imagine! Thirty soldiers guarding one wagon! What could have been the cargo? Probably a good catch."

"Maybe even a war chest?"

A hush fell over the group before the next man piped in. "It's all for naught," he said, "because the opportunity passed us by. If those two continue to fend for themselves, we'll have to bid them a swift farewell. Then another comes along whistling our tune, and all we can do is watch him ride past."

"Hold it! Have a little patience," laughed Curé. "Just wait until this evening."

"If only there was some truth to the story regarding the marshals," said another.

"I heard it quite clearly."

"Really, a marshal?"

"Two of them, actually."

"By God! Which ones?"

"What's it to you? What difference does the name make?" Curé asked.

"Nothing, as long as they have lots of money!"

"Do you really think a marshal would travel without his money purse?" laughed one.

"Without rings, watches, or diamonds?"

The old man smiled. "How true! They'll probably have an escort with them."

"We'll cut them down. When the rest of our boys show up, we should have twenty men. That'll be enough."

"Agreed. We're safe here in the trees. We won't emerge from our cover until we've downed each one."

Löwenklau frowned at the information. This was becoming serious. A holdup involving two marshals... should he wait to gather some more details? The longer he stayed, the riskier it would become.

Instead, the lieutenant decided to leave while they were still assembled in the dark. He slowly pulled himself back, careful not to reveal his presence by making any unnecessary noise. Once clear, he stood up and, remaining hidden behind the trees again, rushed back to his horse, which he found exactly the way he had left it. With reins in hand, he worked his way back to the road. He mounted the gelding and galloped away.

Löwenklau arrived at LeChesne about half an hour later. His first inclination was to ride through, but when he lent further thought to it, he decided to make a brief stop at the local inn. After all, he might learn something more to his advantage.

He led his horse to the back of the tavern and tied it up. When he stepped into the inn, he asked a slow moving innkeeper for a glass of wine. He feared he might have taxed the man to the limit with his first request, yet he dared to make the reluctant innkeeper a second request, if he could obtain a little hay for his horse.

"For your horse?" the innkeeper asked.

"Did you think it was for me?" he replied, laughing.

The man made a sour face, looking distressed. "I don't have any hay," he said. "However, if you go out into the garden, you'll see my servant girl cutting grass. It's just as good." Feeling he'd done his part, the innkeeper remained seated as though glued to his chair.

Löwenklau walked back outside and crossed the yard, opening the back gate and stepping under an arbor supported by crisscrossing grapevines. The vines covered the roof and led the way to the garden. As he walked under the covering, he heard the sound of distant voices. He stopped in his tracks upon hearing a familiar word: *Fabier*.

He listened intently and this time made out two distinct voices, one of them deep, belonging to a man, and another that of a woman, with an alto tone. Their voices sounded quite close. He crept forward to the garden entrance to eavesdrop.

"So, you're not interested in him?"

"No," she replied roughly.

"I thought he was your lover?" he remarked. "I saw it for myself. I saw you kissing him yesterday, by the fence."

"He kissed me, not the other way around."

"You didn't have to be so accommodating."

"He's stronger than I am."

"Well, you didn't have to go out to meet him."

"Idiot! How could I have known he was waiting for me?"

"Didn't you dance with him?"

"Yes, but also with other men."

"Why not with me, then?"

"Come on!" she argued playfully. "We're planning to be wed. I'm not worried about you."

"Oh, really? I wouldn't mind dancing with my bride."

"You'll just have to wait until we're married."

"And if I've changed my mind?"

The woman seemed to scoff at the idea. "You wouldn't! You'd forfeit becoming a rich man, one who can drink wine to his heart's content and smoke tobacco from the finest pipe money can buy, just to stay the way you've always been."

"It's fine for you to talk about riches," he said, "but what do you really own? One dress, two skirts, two stockings, an apron, a jacket, a handkerchief, and a pair of wooden shoes. This sums up your entire fortune."

Löwenklau heard contemptuous laughter.

"Where's it written that I have to carry my wealth around for all to see?"

"Where else would it be?"

"Well, you hide it, of course!"

"Ah, now I get your drift. You bury it."

"Exactly!"

"Perhaps a treasure?"

"Yes, a real buried treasure."

"And just what use is that?"

The woman paused, bewildered at her fiancé's idiocy. "What do you mean?"

"Well," he maintained, "if it's buried, what use is it to me?"

"Fool! You only dig it up when you actually require money."

"That's news to me. As if you only needed money occasionally!"

"I'm telling you the way it is."

"You? You buried money? That's a whale of a tale, even for you."

"Believe what you like," she said. "You'll find out once we're married."

"Do you expect me to believe it, just like that? At least tell me how much there is."

"Take a guess!"

"A thousand francs!"

"Guess again."

"Five thousand francs!"

"You're going to have to do a lot better than that," she said, needling him.

"Ten thousand, then!"

"Not even close."

He let out a long, confused sigh. "You're talking nonsense. You don't know what you're saying! I could buy myself a house or a small farm for ten thousand francs."

"What would I do with a house or a farm?" she asked. "I want a castle with turrets and large windows!"

There was a brief pause, probably because he was too flabbergasted for words. "You'd need at least a million!" the man replied, a little less sure of himself now.

"Well, yes. That's what I mean."

"Girl, you're crazy!"

"Idiot! How can I be crazy if I have over a million francs?"

"If you really have it," he said doubtfully. "Where is it?"

"It's buried."

"Where did it come from?"

"From my father."

"He's as poor as you are!"

"Don't you remember two weeks ago, how he gambled and lost about eighty francs."

"Yes, I remember. Where did he get the money?"

"I really shouldn't say."

"So," he began, "what you are saying is I have to marry you first in order to find out? Then, I'll surely become the fool you've always taken me for."

"So you don't believe me?"

"No!" he admitted. "You're just trying to rope me into marriage. Afterward, you'll be just as poor as ever, not having a single franc more, much less a million."

There was a long pause before the woman replied. "Aren't you pleased with me?"

"Not as long as you throw empty promises at me."

"I'm telling you the truth."

"Prove it!" he demanded.

"If I tell you the whole story," she said, "you'll blurt it out to all of your drinking buddies."

"Ridiculous! If I could get rich through you, I'd be stupid to tell anyone."

"What if the treasure belongs to another?"

"Serves them right, I'd say! Who would be stupid enough to bury his money?"

"It doesn't belong to any one person, but rather to the state."

He tried to wrap his mind around this interesting development. "The state? Well, that's entirely different. We can take their money. After all, they took it from us first! Is it a strong box then?"

"Yes."

"Who stole it?"

"It wasn't emptied. It was buried along with the crate."

"*Parbleu!*" he yelled. "Surely not the fabled war chest that disappeared without a trace?"

"Idiot! Don't shout!"

"Where is it?" he said, lowering his voice this time.

"You don't need to know that just yet. I've told you enough."

He shook his head emphatically. "No, it's not enough. You could have made it all up, like bait to catch me."

"What else do you want to know?"

"Where is it buried?"

"Up in the mountains, not far from Bouillon."

"Ah! You know the place?"

"No, but my father does."

"How does he know of its location?"

"Because it was he who buried it, of course! You never were very bright."

"What? Your father? So he was in on it. How do you know it lies near Bouillon?"

"My father told me."

"But what if he lied, just to throw you off?"

"I secretly followed him when he went to get more money," she explained. "I'm convinced he really knows the location."

"Did you see the place?"

"No. He was too fast for me and I lost sight of him. When he came home that night, though, his pockets were full of gold coins."

"Did you really follow him all the way to Bouillon?"

"Even further."

"Where to?"

"Past the river and up into the mountains."

"Go on."

"There's an old coal hut. That's where I lost sight of him."

"Well, we should follow him next time."

"That won't be necessary. He'll share the loot with you once we're married. He wants to let Fabier in on the secret, but I can't stand the man. He's clever enough, but has a terrible mean streak." She paused briefly to regard him. "You, on the other hand, are a simple and honest sort."

"Thanks," he replied irritably, not feeling the least bit complimented. "So that's why he always has money on him. Actually, did you know Fabier is planning to cheat you? He's after the girl who lives in the tavern in the woods."

"So you noticed it, too? I would have lost all my money and he would have brought it to her. Fortunately, I'm far smarter than he is! I'm not about to be cheated by any man, not even you!"

Löwenklau nearly burst out laughing. For a moment, he thought he might have given himself away, a fear that quickly dissipated when the other man, obviously offended, spoke loudly enough to cover his slip.

"You think you can cheat me?" he grumbled. "That day's a long ways off!"

"I'm not at all concerned with your vast cleverness," she said. "Anyway, I've taken up too much time already. We'll talk later, when my work is done. *Adieu!*"

"*Adieu!*" he replied.

Löwenklau heard the sound of a kiss and hurried steps plodding away through the yard. He carefully looked through the foliage and spotted the short, stocky girl, dirty and poorly dressed. Her hair was scraggly and her face was pockmarked and covered with freckles. So this was Barchand's daughter, the rival to the pretty Berta Marmont? What a difference between the two!

The man making a hasty departure was bow-legged and had a large, disproportionate head. He turned around one more time to smile at his lover. What he intended to be a smile unwittingly transformed into a grimace, altering his facial appearance into a mask-like caricature. The two seemed meant for each other.

As Löwenklau considered their conversation about the buried war chest, he felt uneasy, worried that the secret was compromised. At first, Barchand's daughter was going to present a problem. Fortunately, he was reassured by the news that she didn't know all the details.

Once he returned to the tavern, he was faced with an unpleasant thought. *Perhaps she does know the exact location of the chest and is only keeping it from her boyfriend to leverage her position. It's certainly possible, despite being unlikely. If that's the case, she wouldn't have told him she ran after her father only to return empty-handed.*

He decided to look after the horse himself, not bothering to inquire about the grass. He paid his bill for the wine and rode on.

CHAPTER SEVENTEEN
Napoleon's Last Love

Löwenklau's short stay at both taverns and his good fortune in over-hearing the robbers' plans had taken up more time than he had planned on. As he entered the forest road again, the day was rapidly coming to a close. He spurred his horse on and galloped onward.

Quietness engulfed the forest, enabling the rider to dwell on his inner-most thoughts. A picture, illustrating in detail the planned attack on the baroness's coach, formed in his head. He occupied himself with preparation for a possible attack by loosening his pistols and charging his horse to a faster pace. The shadows of nightfall faded ever lower, until he found himself riding in near darkness, barely able to make out the road. He trusted the trail to his horse, whose hooves made little noise on the grass.

Straining his ears, he heard a dull rumbling sound not far ahead. In the same instant, a shot rang out followed by several more. The sounds rever-berated through the forest culminating with what he feared the most—women's voices, gripped with terror and calling for help.

Löwenklau spurred his horse to a gallop. In the distance, he made out two faint lights, presumably coming from the lanterns of a carriage. Suddenly, an idea struck him. If he continued at this fast pace, the sound of hoof beats would betray his arrival to the highwaymen, enabling them to shoot at him while he was exposed. He decided to stop, tie the horse's reins to a nearby tree, and pull the young baron's pistols out of the saddlebag and insert them into his coat.

While running, he cocked the hammer of one pistol. He approached the scene, slowing his speed until he was creeping up to the swinging lanterns, searching for the culprits in the darkness.

He heard Madame Richemonte's pleading voice. "Really," she said, distressed, "we have no money with us."

Her reply was met by rough laughter.

"Distinguished ladies and no money?" laughed one man. "Since you claim you have no money, should there happen to be a pretty one among you, she can pay for all of you. We'll have to investigate this ourselves!"

The fear-stricken Madame was unceremoniously pulled out of the car-riage as one of the robbers shone his lantern inside.

"Well, well! What have we here?" he called out. "This one's pretty and alluring! Out with you, my pretty one!"

Löwenklau crept closer while the thieves were distracted by Margot. Surveying the scene, he spotted one of the horses, presumably dead, lying on the road. The second horse stood alone, snorting and shaking with fear. The coachman, on his bench, sat perfectly still, as though he had turned to stone, while nine foreboding shapes stood surrounding the carriage.

"By all means, out with her if she's good looking!" encouraged another robber.

"Finally, we'll have some fun again," replied yet another man, who reached inside for the unseen Margot. In defense, she cried out trying to fend him off.

"It won't do you any good, girl," he laughed. "Out you come and then we'll have a little wedding celebration... between nine grooms and one bride!"

"Here's my blessing, you reprobates!" Löwenklau shouted, jumping into their midst. The lieutenant fired his first shot and immediately followed it up with a second. The two men closest to the carriage fell dead in their tracks.

"Hugo, my Hugo! Is it possible?" Margot cried out. She recognized the voice of her betrothed, although she had no explanation for his timely intervention.

"Yes, it is I, my love," he said. "Hold on!"

With his reassuring words, he fired two additional shots. A third robber sank to the ground, mortally wounded. The fourth evaded the shot meant for him and only received a flesh wound. The bandits, completely caught off guard, failed to retaliate. It finally dawned on them that only one man was responsible for the sudden attack. Consequently, one of them grabbed his weapon and swung it around, intending to strike the lieutenant with the butt end of his rifle.

"You bastard! You'll pay for this! Your pistols are spent. Go to hell!"

"Come and find out if they're empty!" Löwenklau shouted back. Before he could connect, Löwenklau fired a bullet into his head.

A warning cry came from the carriage. "Hugo! Behind you!"

He quickly turned, heeding Margot's warning, and threw himself to the ground just in time. In haste, one of the highwaymen aimed and fired at Löwenklau's chest. The bullet missed its intended target. Instead, it struck his own companion in the chest, who was about to lunge at the lieutenant.

"Idiot!" was all he managed to say as he sank to the ground.

Löwenklau dispatched the unsuccessful shooter with a well-placed shot of his own. The coachman finally emerged from the shock that bound him to inaction and jumped from his lofty perch onto the few remaining bandits, grabbing one by his neck and choking him into submission. The robber fought wildly, but in the end succumbed to the other man's strength.

"This'll teach you to shoot at my horses, you vagabond!" The coachman threw him down, without letting up on his chokehold, and finished him off.

The very last highwayman tried in vain to get away, but he too was struck by the lieutenant's bullet. Löwenklau rushed over to help the coachman.

"It's not necessary, Monsieur!" the rider said. "This man's dead. He won't be taking part in any more robberies."

Löwenklau bent down and examined the body. "You're right," he replied. "Well done, friend. He was the last one."

"Is it true, Hugo? Is the battle over? Did we triumph over them?" Margot's voice called out.

"Yes," he said, walking quickly toward the coach.

"I'm truly grateful," she said, falling into his arms. Margot kissed him repeatedly. Suddenly, she stopped and called out with concern. "Where's Mama? She was forced out of the carriage."

Everything had happened so quickly, it hadn't occurred to him to locate the older woman. His attention had been so focused on the assailants that he had lost track of her.

"Here she is!" the coachman said, picking up one of the discarded torches and shone it on her. Madame was sprawled out on the ground.

"Dear God," Margot wondered. "Could she have been shot?"

The lieutenant bent over to examine the lady. "She's all right, just unconscious! But where is the baroness?"

"Over there, in the coach!"

As the coachman lit up the coach, they all watched as she slowly climbed out of the carriage. "Monsieur, we owe you our lives," she said regally. "Please take my hand and help us out of this horrid place."

While Margot was kneeling beside her mother, she couldn't help notice the dead bodies, strewn around them like mannequins. "My God, how awful!" she shuddered. "So many came against us?"

"Nine," replied Löwenklau.

"Did you down them all yourself?"

"Not all of them," he smiled. "The brave coachman took care of at least one. Look, your mother is coming around."

Madame Richemonte stirred and opened her eyes. She had lost consciousness out of fear for her daughter's safety. She slowly rose to her feet, aided by her daughter. "Are those evil men gone?" she asked, still frightened by the events of a few minutes ago.

"You don't have to worry about them anymore," laughed Margot. "Hugo defeated them."

"Which Hugo? Your Hugo? Where is he?"

"I'm right here, Mama! Do you want to try climbing back into the carriage?"

"Yes, let's try it," she said, her eyes brightening when she saw him for the first time. "Oh, how I'm indebted to you, my dear son! How did you ever come to this place? For a moment, I thought we were done for."

"I came to Raucourt for a visit, taking the road through Sedan. The young baron told me the three of you had gone on a trip to Vouziers, planning to return at night. He hadn't realized the road was unsafe anymore since the start of the war. Since he couldn't leave the estate, he loaned me his horse instead so I could ride out to you and warn you of the danger."

"You are a very perceptive young man!" the baroness exclaimed. "You have certainly demonstrated your courage. My dear Margot, I must say you surprise me."

"Why?" the lovely girl asked.

"Well, I've just noticed your relationship with Monsieur von Löwenklau is considerably more developed than you let on."

"Please forgive me, my dear," Madame replied for her daughter. "It's entirely my fault and I alone carry the burden since I couldn't openly announce Margot's engagement to the lieutenant. I'm sure you will understand my reasons once you hear them."

"I will not tattle on you. Monsieur, how else can I explain your presence in Raucourt? You will be my guest, of course."

"I would be honored, Madame, and pleased to escort you home," he replied. "If someone should ask for me, just call me Sainte-Marie!"

"Really? I have a relative by that name in Marseille. You can take his place."

"What is his occupation there?"

"He is a sea captain."

"In the navy?"

"No, in merchant shipping."

"Good, that should do. But look over there, Baroness! Your other horse just collapsed."

"Undoubtedly it has also been shot," the coachman said through gritted teeth. "Let's take a closer look."

They examined the animal and saw it had only a few minutes of life left. The mare had been shot in the chest and was bleeding profusely from the open wound. The other horse had been dead for some time.

"What can we do?" lamented the baroness. "I can't stand to be here much longer."

"My horse is nearby, Madame," Löwenklau said in an attempt to comfort her. "The coachman and I will remove the dead horses from their harnesses and replace them with my own. It should get us to LeChesne. If necessary, we will appropriate a second one there. In any case, we're obligated to stop there

198

and inform the authorities of the holdup." He retrieved his horse from where he had left it on the roadway.

In the poor light, it was a difficult task removing the harnesses from the dead horses. Both men were still occupied performing their difficult labor when they heard the sound of approaching wagons.

"Someone's coming," the coachman said. "The road is presently impassable because of the carnage. They'll have to wait a few minutes while we clear the roadway."

Löwenklau took it upon himself to make the announcement, calling out to the lead carriage to stop. He noticed there were three carriages, all accompanied by an armed escort.

"What do you mean, stop?" called out the first coachman.

"We have been attacked by highwaymen. Corpses and dead horses are blocking the roadway."

The door of the first coach opened and a commanding voice said, "A holdup? Get over there, Jan Hoorn! We need to have a look."

Margot perked up at the sound of the authoritative voice. "Dear God!" she said to the two ladies. "Jan Hoorn is the emperor's coachman!" As recognition settled over her face, she looked toward the dark carriages with amazement. "That voice belonged to Napoleon himself!"

The wagons approached slowly and came to a stop. A tall figure emerged from the coach, followed by another from the third coach. They walked toward Löwenklau, who was in the center of the road waiting for them.

"Monsieur, I hope this is a momentary delay. I'm Marshal Ney[17.1] and here comes Marshal Groucy.[17.2] May I have your names?"

"This lady is the Baroness de Sainte-Marie and I am her relative," Löwenklau began deceptively. "The other two are Madame and Mademoiselle Richemonte, here on a holiday from Paris. The other man is their coachman. They were accosted by nine highwaymen, who are now all dead. Unfortunately, they shot at the horses and they have succumbed to their wounds. The road is still blocked, Marshal. However, if you give us a few minutes, we will have the road cleared."

"Were they just highwaymen?" Marshal Ney asked, "or were they actual bandits?"

"I expect more experienced bandits would have approached us differently. However, I am not entirely sure about such things."

"So, they did not put up much of a fight?" Ney surmised in a superior tone.

"On the contrary," Löwenklau said. "They shot at us!"

Ney looked at him incredulously. "Are they all dead?"

"All nine of them."

"Who killed them?" Groucy asked.

"The coachman killed one, and in the course of the fight, another was inadvertently shot by his own companion. I took care of the rest."

Ney took the lantern from his coachman, lighting up Löwenklau's face. In doing so, he illuminated his own face. The marshal was tall in stature and possessed a muscular build. By Löwenklau's estimation, his domineering countenance conveyed an affinity for giving orders. The marshal evaluated the lieutenant with great interest.

"Were all the robbers armed?" he asked.

"Yes. There was no shortage of weapons."

Groucy joined him. "I heard you dispatched eight of them?" he asked in disbelief. "What weapons did you have?"

"Fortunately, I carried four double pistols."

"You seem to have been prepared for the attack."

"I had heard the ladies were intending to return at night. Knowing the road is unsafe, I took it upon myself to meet them."

The door of the first carriage opened and its occupant jumped out. He was short and squat, carrying a hat and a gray overcoat. His legs were covered in high buckskin boots.

"The Emperor!" Ney exclaimed for all to hear.

Napoleon came toward them. "Give me some light!" he ordered in his customary way.

The marshal took it upon himself to lift the lantern, revealing the faces of Löwenklau and the women. Napoleon carefully examined each of the corpses. It was rumored that once he had seen a soldier's face, he would remember it again.

"Highwaymen," Napoleon mumbled. "I recognize a few of them. They served under me once, and rather poorly at that."

He approached Löwenklau, who inadvertently stood at attention.

"Your name, Monsieur?" asked Napoleon.

"Sainte-Marie, Majesty."

"Are you an officer?"

"No, Sire."

"Just a soldier then?"

"No, Sire. I am a captain in the merchant marine."

"Pity. You are a brave young man! I heard you downed eight armed men in a short time. How long did it take you?"

"Everything happened so fast. It only took about a minute, Sire."

"Unbelievable! Do you have any desire to serve in the military?"

"I believe I can be of service to France in my current occupation."

"Well said," the emperor remarked. "You have been entrusted with a ship. Our country needs people like you. France's navy is still in its infancy. How are the ladies?"

Löwenklau introduced the ladies, beginning with the baroness, followed by Madame Richemonte, and lastly his bride, who bowed deeply before Bonaparte. He nodded briefly in his habitual quick way. However, when his eyes fell on Margot's lovely face, he tipped the brim of his cap. Her beauty seemed to captivate Napoleon.

"Mademoiselle Richemonte?" he inquired further. "What is your Christian name?"

"Margot, Majesty." Her clear, resonant voice had a wonderful pitch.

All those present noticed how he parted his lips, as though he intended to catch the delicacy of the sound with his tongue as well. "Margot?" he asked. "I believe the Germans would say Gretchen, or Margarethe. The rendering would be a pearl. You are certainly a pearl and we must give Captain Sainte-Marie our heartfelt thanks for rescuing such a jewel. Where do you live, Mademoiselle?"

"Sire, my mother and I are guests of the baroness at Jeannette, which lies near Raucourt."

Marshal Ney noticed how much pleasure the emperor had in conversing with the young lady. He thus allowed the light of the lantern to fully expose the lovely girl's features. Napoleon looked at her with admiration.

"Ah, Raucourt! Does the estate lie nearby?"

"Not too far away."

He quickly turned to Groucy and inquired, "Marshal, didn't you tell me Drouet has chosen his headquarters at Raucourt?"

"Yes, Sire," Groucy replied. "His headquarters are in Raucourt. His staff is sequestered there. I've heard he personally stays at Jeannette."

"Really? Does he stay with you, Baroness?" asked Napoleon quickly.

"Yes, Majesty. I have the honor of being the general's hostess."

Napoleon looked down at the ground, deep in thought, and then quickly glanced at Margot. "Is your estate of substantial size?" he continued.

"One could compare it to a castle with its surrounding estate, Sire," the baroness said.

"Are there are a number of apartments within?"

"Of course. The previous owner had a penchant for entertainment, and there are ample rooms for guests."

"Then one or two more guests would not be an encumbrance on you, Madame?"

"Of course not, Majesty."

"Even if I were to impose on your hospitality?"

The baroness wondered for a moment whether she should take his proposal in earnest or as a joke? The Corsican emperor wasn't known to be a prankster or for being particularly fond of jokes. He probably desired to pay her a compliment by asking to stay at her estate. However, such a visit also had its price. She was astute enough to recognize that his prevailing reason centered on Margot. But what could she say? She felt compelled to give in.

"Majesty," she carefully replied, "my house is very modest and without refinements, such as would not be pleasing for the ruler of France and the one who has conquered half the world."

A frown crossed Bonaparte's face. "Madame," he replied. "I have not had the pleasure of late to have been pampered as emperor, and I am certainly not inclined to make large demands on your hospitality. I am a soldier and enjoy the simple things. My plan was to make it as far as Sedan. You yourself have had the misfortune to be waylaid by brigands. Likewise, the emperor should avoid being attacked by a bunch of reckless bandits. I only ask you for temporary lodging at Jeannette."

The baroness bowed deeply. "All that I possess is at your disposal, Sire!"

"Very well, then it is settled," he said. "All that remains is to arrange for your transportation, seeing as both your horses are dead."

"We have a horse which can be used to move our carriage, Sire," the baroness added.

"Perhaps, Madame, but consider how your horse would have to pull the carriage now occupied by four persons, not including the coachman. It appears to be too much of a hardship. Captain Sainte-Marie can take care of your carriage and bring it safely back to LeChesne." Turning to face Ney, he said. "We have plenty of room for the three ladies in our carriages. What do you think, Marshal?"

It was clear he wished to have Margot's company in his carriage, but formality dictated he should make the first offer to his hostess. This is why he directed his last question at Ney, who, being familiar with his superior's habits, understood him right away.

"Sire, I am in complete agreement with you. We need to spare the ladies any further inconvenience. Baroness Sainte-Marie, may I offer you transport in my carriage?" His request was accompanied with a formal bow.

Marshal Groucy, who was perceptive enough to realize it was now his turn, bowed before Madame Richemonte. "Madame, may I likewise offer you a place in my carriage? It would be an honor to accompany you to LeChesne!"

She replied to the compliment with a bow.

"Ladies," Napoleon laughed, "you can see that your emperor has just been upstaged. When it comes to the small matter of conquests, my marshals often jump the gun. Mademoiselle, I regret to inform you that I am the only one left. May I persuade you to place your trust in me by accepting a place in my carriage?"

"I am at my emperor's command," she replied, bowing to Napoleon. Yet her eyes rested on Löwenklau. She wasn't blind to the fact that she'd been singled out by Napoleon and that the marshals had cleverly left her for him.

Although she would have much rather ridden in the old carriage with her betrothed, she knew she couldn't refuse the emperor of France. That's why, when she answered with a measured response to him, it was with an apologetic look to Hugo.

"Well then, shall we climb aboard and proceed on our journey?" Napoleon asked.

As the two marshals offered their arms to their respective escorts, the emperor likewise extended his to the lovely Margot. His previous companion, General Gourgard,[17.3] who had disembarked earlier, was now holding the carriage door open.

"The general will keep us company," was Napoleon's simple introduction.

Gourgaud, only thirty-two years old, was the famous officer who would later make Napoleon's three long years on St. Helena bearable. He would defend his regent and dispute with Sir Walter Scott about Napoleon's accomplishments.

The carriages' escort had a complement of twelve men. They were non-commissioned officers, but men of special standing who had been selected from the old guard. As the ladies took their seats, the coaches started the journey. They kept up a good pace and quickly reached LeChesne.

Margot sat beside the emperor with the adjutant general opposite them. Since it was dark, she couldn't see his facial expressions. However, Napoleon ensured there was no shortage of conversation. It was the kind of discussion usually conducted between men and women who weren't familiar with one another. Starting at a slow pace, it was marked with caution and politeness, extending to political events. Napoleon weighed each word, each inflection, and considered its meaning. Margot noticed he wanted to sound her out. Though unpretentious in her replies, she saw that he showed a great degree of interest in her affairs.

They arrived in LeChesne and stopped at the tavern. The innkeeper, who had been short and unaccommodating in his dealings with Löwenklau, was mesmerized by the appearance of the marshals. When he saw the arrival of the emperor, he was nearly beside himself. The glitter of the marshals' uniforms had no effect on him anymore; his only concern was for the little man who wore the cap and grey overcoat.

Napoleon escorted Margot to the door. While letting go of her hand, he asked for the proprietor. "Are you the innkeeper?"

"I am, my Emperor!" he replied exuberantly.

"Then, go find the mayor. Now!" came Napoleon's curt reply.

While their host hurried away to carry out the order, the officers entered the inn. Napoleon turned to Margot and helped her to remove her shawl and coat. She wore a wide-pleated skirt that was short enough to reveal her ornate shoes. Her bodice pressed her bosom together, revealing the top of her breasts over a low-cut front.

As the lovely Margot stood in front of Napoleon in the light, he gazed at her beauty. By the limited light of the coach's lantern, he had already noticed this was no ordinary girl in front of him. Inside the brightly lit parlor, he realized his earlier assessment had been correct. This realization left him at a loss for words, incapable of continuing the conversation. His gaze remained fixed on her face, as though he intended on studying her every feature. His eyes strayed to her wonderful bosoms, to her well-formed arms, and her small exquisite feet, which he glimpsed at the edge of her garment. The notion that Margot felt uncomfortable didn't deter him in the least.

Napoleon wasn't the sort of man to speak in frivolities, nor was he easily dissuaded from his objective. Bowing to her, he took her hand in his and pressed her fingers to his lips.

"But, Your Majesty!" she exclaimed, quickly withdrawing her hand.

"Forgive my boldness, Mademoiselle! I perform this little homage to you in the manner I would a queen."

She turned red from embarrassment. Fortunately, the innkeeper just returned and she was spared from having to answer. The emperor gave orders to provide refreshments for the ladies. They each received a glass of wine and some honey, the only thing palatable under the circumstances. The marshals continued in lively conversation with their ladies so the emperor could speak to Margot at his leisure.

Margot received a reprieve with the arrival of a man dressed in a formal coat, wearing a large, officious wig. He bowed reverently before Napoleon, nearly losing his head covering and causing a ludicrous scene.

"What is your name?" asked Napoleon.

"LeDuc, Sire. I have the honor of being the town's mayor," he stuttered nervously.

"...and doing a poor job!" the Corsican said, sounding irritated.

The mayor, facing Napoleon's penetrating glance, nearly lost his composure. "Your Majesty, I have no idea what I have done to deserve—"

"I am not at all satisfied with the performance of your office. Do you know of the road to Vouziers?"

"Yes, of course."

"Have you traveled on it?"

"Often, Sire."

"Also at night?"

"No, Sire. Only during the day."

"Why is that?"

"Because it is not safe to travel the forest road at night."

"And why not?"

"Because of the vagabonds and highwaymen."

"So your solution is to avoid traveling at night? Is this all you have accomplished?"

It finally dawned on the official why he had been summoned. "Sire, I had no choice. I have no authority beyond the town."

"You should have asked for troops!"

"I had made such a request, yet received not a single soldier for all my efforts."

"Really! Why not?"

"While the emperor was absent, the king was not able to rule adequately..." The official shrugged his shoulders to emphasize his frustration. He couldn't come up with a reasonable excuse on such short notice.

Nonetheless, the poor excuse struck a nerve with Napoleon. "Yes, I know!" he said with a dismissive hand gesture, implying nothing but contempt. "Did he furnish you with any military support?"

"None! He claimed that he had none to spare."

Bonaparte turned to Ney and chuckled. "What do you think about that, Marshal?"

Ney also shrugged his shoulders. "In order to command and to have influence over the military, you have to be foremost a soldier."

"Exactly!" Napoleon said. "This king is a civilian. He is not a soldier, and he will never become a field marshal, never mind a ruler. France only requires one ruler, such as myself, or else brigands will take over, subduing the nation. I was only away a short time and it will take me years to reestablish order." He faced the mayor again and continued. "These ladies were the victims of an attack."

"My God, can it be?" cried the official. Since Napoleon had taken up their cause, their plight had become considerably more serious.

"Do you recognize the ladies?"

"Yes, one of them. The Baroness de Sainte-Marie, Majesty!"

"Had a brave cavalier not arrived at the last minute, they surely would have been killed. A short distance from town, you will find the bodies of nine highwaymen and two dead horses. Look after it! Now, how many soldiers will you require to render the forest road safe?"

"At least a company, Sire."

"You will get them tomorrow. What else?"

"It will be necessary to record your instructions on paper, Sire."

"Do you have documents and ink?"

"Not with me, Sire."

"General Gourgaud, get my writing instruments."

The general left the room to collect Napoleon's papers and the required items from the carriage. When he returned, the emperor addressed the mayor. "All right. Sit down and start writing. I will dictate the orders myself."

It was Bonaparte's custom to take on various responsibilities. He wanted to demonstrate to his subordinates that he not only understood their tasks, but was fully capable of performing them himself. In doing so, he guaranteed for himself a high degree of respect and ensured his orders would be carried out in detail.

The mayor's pen flew across the page. It never occurred to him that the emperor himself would dictate the instructions. As he continued to labor, he began to sweat profusely. When he finally finished, Napoleon examined the documents, reading them through to the end. Before signing it in his own handwriting, he added his approval for a company of soldiers to be dispatched at this location.

"Done!" he said. "Tomorrow the soldiers will arrive. The day after tomorrow, I expect to hear that people will once again be able to travel these parts without being molested. Is this understood?"

"I am catching every word, Sire!" replied the mayor, taking a handkerchief out of his pocket to dab the sweat from his forehead.

"Then my business is completed!" Napoleon loudly proclaimed.

With these words, he declared he intended to resume their journey. He offered Margot her shawl and coat. Inadvertently, his fingertips touched her warm, irresistible skin, where he lingered a little longer than was customary. Finally, he escorted her to the carriage. Ney and Groucy followed suit with their ladies. Moments later, the carriages departed, accompanied by an escort of twelve armed Grenadiers.

CHAPTER EIGHTEEN
The Ambush

Shortly after the emperor had entered the inn, a dark figure appeared outside behind the tavern. He quietly stomped his feet and shifted his weight, giving the impression that he was waiting for someone. Suddenly, the rear door opened and Barchand's daughter crept out.

"Berrier, are you here?" she whispered.

The dark figure, presumably Berrier, stepped toward the door, out of the darkness. "Yes," he answered.

"Were you waiting long?"

"Longer than it suited me."

"Well, it couldn't be helped."

"Who were the gentlemen?"

"Berrier, you'll never believe who..."

"Don't exaggerate! I don't have time to listen. Were they the two marshals?"

"Yes, just like you said. Two marshals."

"Ney and Groucy?"

"I don't know them by name. They were there speaking to a general... and there was a fourth man. You'll never guess who he was—it was the emperor himself!"

"The emperor? Napoleon Bonaparte?" whispered the man. "Are you certain?"

"Yes, I'm sure."

"But you don't know him!"

"I've seen his picture a hundred times."

"How was he dressed?"

"He wore high boots, a gray overcoat, a white vest, and a small hat."

"Did he have a beard?"

She shook her head, trying to remember. "Not at all. I saw him through the kitchen window."

"It sounds like him. Of course, it's still possible you could be mistaken. This morning, I was told the emperor is still in Paris."

"But it was him! My employer, the old innkeeper, was completely certain."

"In that case, you're probably right."

"Besides, the emperor even called for the mayor of the town."

"What for?"

"I don't know. I'm sure I'll find out later when he shows up."

"That's great!" he said sarcastically. "We didn't count on him being here. What should we do?"

"Were you thinking of robbing just the marshals, and not the emperor?"

"No, too bold."

"Think of it," she said. "The emperor would command a greater ransom than the two marshals on their own."

"But what if he's shot?"

"No harm done. He'll likely have a lot of money and valuables with him."

"You may have something there, even though it's a devilish scheme to plunder the emperor. We can spare his life by shooting only at his horses. How many soldiers were with him?"

"I saw eight or ten riders."

"That's not too bad. There are nineteen of us."

"Is my father with you?"

"No," he said. "He hasn't returned yet."

"And what about Fabier?"

"I haven't seen him either."

She frowned, wrinkling her forehead. "Where could they be? By the way, there were also three ladies in his company."

"Who were they?"

"I don't know. Two of them sat in the corner where I couldn't see from the kitchen window. I didn't recognize the third one, but she was young and beautiful."

"That's good news. Often when ladies are present, men don't risk endangering them by starting a fight. Are you familiar with the Baroness de Sainte-Marie?"

"Of course!"

"Apparently she drove past here this morning. Did she stop here?"

Barchand's daughter shrugged. "Although I didn't see her, I heard that she passed by. It was her carriage and coachman."

"Has she returned?"

"We haven't seen her carriage yet."

"That's fine. We'll allow her passage. Do you have anything else to tell me?"

"No, that's all I know."

"I have to get back to the men," Berrier said.

"Will you attack the emperor as well?"

"I don't know yet. I'll have to discuss it with the others."

"You'll never make it on time," she implored him. "They'll be on their way while you're still walking back."

"What! Do you think that I'm that stupid?"

"You're all a bunch of dunderheads," she said. "What would the lot of you amount to if I didn't supply you with information about passersby? You should get yourself a horse."

He looked insulted. "I've got one!"

"Really? Where did you get it from?"

"Did you really think that I was going on foot while the marshals' coaches reach the ambush before me? We shot a lone rider out of the saddle this morning. He had a nice moneybag on him. We managed to corral his horse, too, which we decided to keep."

"So, did you ride over here?"

"Yes."

"Where's your horse?" she asked.

"It's behind a tree at the edge of the forest."

"Then it's high time you left and let the others know. You'll have to be in agreement before the carriages arrive."

"You're right!" he agreed. Then, hearing the scuffling of feet inside the inn, he turned to her again. "Listen! Someone just walked in."

"It's probably the mayor."

"So, are you really sure it's the emperor and no one else?"

"Yes," she repeated. "I'll swear to it."

"All right. Good night!"

"I hope to hear news tomorrow how the emperor and his marshals never reached Sedan. Tell my father to pay me a visit. Good night." With that, she returned to the kitchen, closing the door behind her.

Berrier hurried through the yard to the forest's edge. Once there, he mounted his horse and galloped toward Raucourt where a group of nineteen men lay well-concealed in the trees near the cross. They heard approaching hoof beats.

"A rider!" one of them exclaimed.

"Possibly Berrier."

"We'll find out soon enough," said the first.

He turned out to be right, because as the rider approached they all heard him whistling a familiar tune, *Ma cherie est la belle Madeleine*.

"Berrier?" called out the sentry.

"Yes, it's me," the rider replied, walking into view.

"How did it go?"

"Very well!" Berrier dismounted. He led his horse into the forest and tied the reins to a tree. Those that were present immediately accosted him with questions. "Hang it all! One at a time," he called out. "Listen, we have the chance for a good catch, assuming that you have enough courage."

"What! Not enough courage?" called out one man angrily. "I'll shoot anyone if he thinks I'm afraid."

"Me too! Me too!" was the unanimous outcry.

"All right!" Berrier said, trying to bring them back to order. "Stop yelling. I wanted to see if you were paying attention. Do you have any idea who's coming?"

"The marshals!"

"Yes, Ney and Groucy. But they're not alone. There's also a general."

"Which one?"

"I couldn't find out. What's more important, I've saved the best for last. The emperor is with them."

"The emperor?" they all shouted in unison.

"Yes," he confirmed. "There are three carriages. The emperor is in the first, Ney is in the second, and Groucy's coach is the last. A general is apparently riding with Bonaparte."

"Surely they have protection with them!"

"Only eight or ten riders from the old guard," replied Berrier.

"Dammit, then we'll have a fight on our hands."

Berrier remained unconcerned. "You think so? *Pah!* We'll conceal ourselves behind the trees, shooting at the horses and the escort. Once they're taken care of, we'll have the officers and the ladies all to ourselves."

"Really, ladies as well?" quipped two at once.

"Yes. There are three women traveling with them."

"Great! The men will avoid a fight to spare the ladies," said Curé.

"Exactly what I thought," Berrier said. "What do you all think?"

There was a long pause while they thought it over, considering their prospects. At first, the whole scheme seemed preposterous. The emperor had lost his luster due to his defeats in Russia and Prussia. He was no longer the undefeated champion.

"Do you think he'll have money with him?" asked one.

"Probably, and the marshals as well," Berrier said.

"It doesn't matter!" added another. "Just imagine the ransom we could demand for his release."

The older man spoke up. "You're all ignoring the biggest opportunity."

"Well, let's hear it!"

"I'll grant you that we'll capture him," Curé allowed. "But don't you realize who else might want to pay for him? Never mind his supporters. I mean, should he suddenly disappear, all the Bourbons, Orleanists, Republicans, Russians, Prussians, Austrians, English and others will gladly pay huge sums of money to dispose of him."

This implication elicited a variety of responses.

"Dammit, that's true!"

"We could earn millions with one shot!"

"Yes, there's no question of that," the old man said. "However, there are two things we'll need in order to accomplish this feat. First, we'll need a secure place where we don't have to worry about being discovered. Second, loyalty and secrecy from all of us are a must—without question."

"We're with you!"

"I hope so. When will the carriages arrive?"

Berrier considered that important bit of information. "The emperor sent for the mayor. I doubt he had much to discuss with him. Probably some minor issues. They could show up at any time."

"We have to come to a decision," Curé said.

"But what do we do with him and the marshals?"

The old man had to stop himself from laughing. "What a dumb question!" he said. "We'll deal with that later. We can debate it at our leisure once we have them in our hands. But we all have to be in agreement. There's no time to lose."

"Of course." The response was unanimous.

"We can demand so much money that we won't ever have to work again," the old man said, grinning.

"That goes without saying," agreed Berrier.

"Good," decided Curé. "We'll go after the emperor and the marshals."

"What about the Grenadiers?" asked one man.

"We'll shoot them!" replied Berrier.

"And the women?" he asked.

"The devil! They could get in the way and become cumbersome later. Maybe it would be best if we shot them, too," Berrier said.

"Wait! Not until we've had a little fun with them."

The old man rolled his eyes. "It makes no difference to me. We should find out who they are. Who knows? Perhaps they could bring in a nice little ransom of their own. We have to be careful. Are the ropes ready?"

"Yes, I have three."

"Excellent," he said. "One for each coach! We'll place them across the roadway at intervals. We'll fasten one end to a tree and keep it slack while we wait. We'll allow the carriages to pass until the first coach is just shy of the last rope, the second for the middle, and the first rope for the last carriage. At the right time, I'll give the order and we'll pull the ropes taut. The carriage horses will stumble on them, not to mention some of the riders."

"Yes, that should work," one of them said. "Quick, get the ropes."

"In the confusion that follows the attack, we can brush the soldiers aside with a single volley and corral the officers. The rest will be easy," Curé said. "Let's get a move on, boys!"

The men stood up and began attending to their preparations. It all went quickly and soon the three ropes lay stretched out across the roadway. Once they finished their tasks, they returned to their prescribed posts to await the arrival of the emperor's entourage.

Napoleon has no idea what is in store for him should this ambush succeed, Berrier pondered as he lay in the darkness.

The three ropes lying across the roadway were completely invisible in the blackness of night. At the opportune time, only one man was needed to pull each rope tight so the horses would stumble. In the resulting bedlam, the highwaymen would kill the entire escort, leaving the officers alone to defend themselves and the ladies.

The next fifteen minutes passed quickly. A noise, stemming from the rolling wheels of an approaching carriage, echoed from down the road, stirring the men to readiness.

"Here they come!" Curé whispered as he reached for his rifle.

"Could that be them already?" asked a nearby man.

"Let me have a look!" The old man moved out of the tree line, looking expectantly down the road toward the coming lights. "Yes, it's them!" he confirmed. "Three coaches with lanterns are only customary when trans-porting distinguished passengers. There's a gap between the coaches. Therefore, spread the ropes further apart so they'll accommodate the horses as well."

The men worked quickly to redistribute the snare. The rolling sound became more pronounced. The lanterns cast a bright light ahead of each car-riage. At the head of the procession rode two lancers, with the rest distributed on both sides of the coaches. First in line was the emperor's carriage, followed by Ney's and, lastly, Groucy's. The riders and the first carriage crossed the last rope. The horses of the second carriage were approaching the middle rope and the horses of the last carriage were approaching the first rope. In this instant, each rope posed the greatest danger to the horses.

"Now!" yelled the old highwayman. "Pull them tight!"

The three men holding the ropes pulled with all their might. Although each man was dragged a short distance, they were rewarded for their efforts. First, the horses stumbled, and some fell down. In the end, all were entangled in the ropes. They whinnied and stamped about angrily during the ensuing confusion.

"Fire! Aim at the lancers!" the leader of the bandits shouted.

The highwaymen were used to the darkness. They could see nearly as well at night as during the day. Shots rang out from the trees and many of the lancers fell from their mounts, mortally wounded, while others fell onto the carriage horses, adding to the chaos.

"Now, attack the rest!" Curé called again. Having fired his own rifle, the leader jumped from behind his cover, turned the gun around and in one swift motion swung it at the closest Grenadier, knocking him out of the saddle.

The plan seemed to go like clockwork for the robbers. Ultimately, they made one mistake. They had overlooked the fact they were dealing with experienced and seasoned soldiers. The ones who had received only flesh wounds defended themselves with unexpected fervor, downing a number of their attackers.

When the attack commenced, Marshal Groucy's carriage swayed and Madame Richemonte cried out in fear. "My God!" she cried. "What's going on?"

"*Pah*, it is nothing," he assured her. "Only two or three highwaymen. We will fix them." He threw the door open and jumped out with the drawn saber in his right hand and his pistol in his left. He waited for what seemed an eternity as his eyes became accustomed to the darkness.

A similar sequence of events occurred in Ney's carriage. "Dear God, we're all doomed!" the baroness said, unsure of what had occurred.

"Don't worry, Madame," the marshal said, smiling cold-bloodedly. "These few vagabonds picked the wrong men to revel with." He depressed the handle, threw the door open, and jumped out, coming to stand beside Groucy ready to defend himself. Just like his companion, though, he couldn't see much while his eyes adjusted to the shadows.

No cry or distress, however, emanated from inside Napoleon's coach. The horses, after having stumbled, rocked the carriage in near panic as the first shots were fired. Gourgaud was already on his guard and standing outside the coach.

"What's happening, General?" the emperor asked from the safety of the carriage.

"An ambush by bandits, Sire."

"Ah, charming! What audacity to take on the emperor's own coach!" Napoleon knew fully well that his men would defend him down to the last man, even to the last drop of blood. Still, his military prowess left him restless. "How many are there?" he asked as he leaned out the door.

"I cannot see anything yet, Sire, but the lancers are probably either wounded or dead."

"Then it is up to us." The emperor reached for his small dagger. He turned to faced Margot. "Are you afraid, Mademoiselle?" he asked.

"Not as long as I am with my emperor," she replied calmly.

"I am grateful for your confidence. You need not be afraid."

As he rose to disembark, Gourgaud pleaded with him. "Sire, please remain in your seat. The bandits are advancing!"

"Then it is my duty to defend the ladies. *Allons!*" With that, he pushed the general aside and jumped out of his carriage.

Ney and Groucy had already seen action. Both had fired their pistols and were doing their best with their sabers. Even Gourgaud was under attack. The half-mad horses struggled with each other. Several horses were able to get up off the ground, trying their best to free themselves from the confining harnesses. The coachmen had no choice but to dismount and attempt to calm them down. The neighing of the horses, the curses of the robbers, the blast from the odd shot, the clanking of the sabers, and the back and forth movement of the wagons created an eerie and surreal scene.

Most of the lancers were badly wounded or dead, leaving Napoleon and his officers alone to fend off a much larger force determined to overpower them. Jan Hoorn, the emperor's personal coachman, used his whip to hold off the onslaught, but he too had to contend with the half-mad horses.

The officers defended themselves with skill and courage. A few of the robbers were wounded but forged ahead regardless, redoubling their efforts under their leader's encouragement and the promise of riches. Napoleon himself fought two of them at once. His general did his best with his saber, fending off four at a time who were trying to hit him with their rifle butts. Although the officers fought valiantly, they began to tire.

The incessant voice of the old man droned on. "That's not the way, men! Take away their cover. Get at them from the back, and from underneath the carriages. If you have to kill, then do so... but spare the emperor!"

Ney, who was often called by Napoleon the bravest of the brave, called out. "By God, now's the time. Groucy, attack them while we still have strength!"

The wagon was still providing them adequate cover, but should the bandits gain the ground below the coach, the marshals would be exposed to further attack. Ney jumped into their midst, gaining a temporary reprieve. Groucy followed his example, and the two officers bravely held them off.

It was a ludicrous scene. Though they fought valiantly, they knew they would eventually succumb to the enemy due to sheer numbers. It was a frightful scene, not worthy of the emperor or his marshals. For the famous battle weary heroes, the battle was wrought with danger and an uncertain end.

CHAPTER NINETEEN
The Clever Coachman

After the emperor had departed with his marshals earlier, accompanied by the ladies, Löwenklau and the coachman, Florian, were left behind to look after the stranded carriage.

"Dammit!" Florian grumbled. "Now we've got the old box all to ourselves!"

"You think we should have kept the emperor back and harnessed him instead?" laughed Löwenklau.

The coachman cracked a smile. "Hmm! No harm in trying. Where he leads, the rest would surely follow. Are you going to help me with this rig, Monsieur?"

"It goes without saying."

"Are you going to Jeannette?"

"Yes."

"Will you be staying for a while?"

"That remains to be seen."

"Well said," Florian remarked. "The horse is almost harnessed. It should be strong enough to pull the coach to the next inn. What do you want to do with the corpses?"

Löwenklau looked out over the bodies strewn across the roadway. "We'll have to leave them," he said.

"All right, but what about their stuff? They've got a number of rifles we could make use of."

"They don't belong to us."

"Then who do they belong to? As victors, we've earned the right!"

"The emperor will stop at LeChesne and inform the government official of the holdup. The mayor will instruct a contingent of men to come here and take charge of the scene, as well as all their property."

"Others will come along before they get here, though. These bandits probably have other comrades lurking nearby, just waiting for us to leave."

"Do whatever you think best," Löwenklau said, not wanting to debate the matter. "I don't want to waste any more time. Neither would I want to find out later that the baroness's favorite coachman stooped to the level of plundering bandits."

"So, you think we should leave everything?"

"Yes. All of it."

"Well, I suppose so," he agreed reluctantly. "After all, I do have my honor to consider."

"Good! Now, let's finish harnessing the horse."

Once the coachman found the other lantern, the extra light allowed them to complete their work in less than fifteen minutes. "Monsieur, do you want to sit up here with me?" Florian asked as they were ready to leave the scene.

"If it suits you."

"If we travel together, we can keep our eyes on the road and keep each other company."

"Good point. Leave some room for me then." Löwenklau climbed up and the carriage started to roll towards LeChesne.

Both men were quiet, wrapped up in their own thoughts. While the coachman was occupied trying to sort out the night's events so he could properly inform the other servants back at the estate, Löwenklau was entirely consumed with thoughts of Margot, who was now riding with the emperor. Napoleon had paid her more than passing attention and had even made it clear he wanted to stay at the estate, a twist that seemed to allow ample opportunity for unforeseen problems to develop. The young officer intended to stay at Jeannette himself, even if only for a short time, but with the presence of the emperor, circumstances placed him in a precarious position. If his true identity were to be discovered, the consequences would be disastrous. Of course, he didn't consider for a moment the possibility of his betrothed being unfaithful to him—indeed, she was far too noble. Purely on the basis of his current assignment, however, the emperor's choice to remain at Jeannette brought rise to a number of potentially fruitful possibilities.

"Hmm," the coachman, absorbed in his thoughts, mumbled suddenly after some time had passed. "A strange story!"

"What do you mean?" asked Löwenklau.

"Well, I don't know if I should burden you with it..."

"Go on. Out with it."

"The whole affair of the ambush seemed clear enough," Florian began. "At first, I sat here on the buckboard, debating whether or not I should leave my post. I knew my first responsibility was to the horses and to safeguard the carriage. However, when those bastards started shooting at the horses, I made up my mind and jumped down to choke a little life out of the closest bandit. Doing so made complete sense to me in the moment. Yet you, Monsieur... you are a mystery I can't seem to solve."

"I'm not following you."

"I don't understand how it was possible for you to arrive just in time to dispatch those eight bandits, only with your pistols."

"I already explained it."

"Perhaps, but not to me."

"Then I will fill you in," Löwenklau said. "I came to the estate to pay the baroness a visit. When I arrived, I learned she was on an excursion to Vouziers. What she planned to do there was unknown to me."

"She cashed in some bonds."

"Fine. I informed the young baron that the road would not be safe, especially at night. He furnished me with a horse and I rode toward you, hoping to avert an attack by bandits. Mercifully, I arrived just in time."

"Yes, that makes more sense. But there's still one thing that isn't clear."

"What is it?"

"As I recall, you had already visited Jeannette once before, when you delivered the two Richemonte ladies. At that time, you called yourself Löwenklau and professed to be a German. Now, you call yourself Sainte-Marie and claim to be a Frenchman, a sea captain no less."

Löwenklau grinned. "And this is giving you a headache?"

"Yes," the other nodded.

"Tell me, honestly, which would be more acceptable to you, if I were German or French?"

"Well, which of the two are you?"

"You'll find out as soon as you answer my question."

"Well, that's easy. I would much rather have one German than all the Frenchmen put together."

Löwenklau's face registered shock at the man's unexpected answer. "Is this your idea of a joke or are you serious? Don't you hold any regards for your fellow countrymen?"

"Countrymen? I was not born here," Florian replied. "Don't you know my full name?"

"No, I don't."

"My name is Florian Rupprechtsberger."

"But that's a German name!"

"Of course it is. The name is German, as is its bearer!"

"Where were you born?"

"I come from the area of Weiskirchen and Metlach," he explained. "My parents had a position with the baroness. Since I proved to be an honest sort, her ladyship took me in as a youth and brought me to Raucourt many years ago. During my employment there, I've had the opportunity to master French."

"This is all very interesting."

"Will you have the courtesy then of telling me whether or not you're really a French sea captain?"

"You're right," Löwenklau admitted. "I'm not French."

"*Zounds!* Are you a German?"

"Yes, Prussian descent."

"Wonderful!" exclaimed Rupprechtsberger. "I can hardly tell you how pleased I am, Monsieur. I could bust at the seams.[19.1] Since we share the same background, I can rest easy and support you in your relationship with Margot."

"How did you come to that conclusion?"

Florian coughed, feeling a little sheepish. "Monsieur, do you think that a coachman is blind to the things going on around him?"

"I trust your eyes are on par with those of the French."

"Of course they are. Listen carefully, Monsieur. Margot is in a class all by herself, a girl who you would do anything for. I fell head over heels for her when you brought her to us."

"Really!"

"Well, as much as I could as an honest coachman without losing the high esteem of the baroness. I paid close attention, catching glances which no one was supposed to notice, and hearing those all too familiar sounds behind my back like lips coming together and then quickly separating."

"Florian!" the lieutenant managed, completely shocked.

"Don't worry. Since you're German, we can form a long and profitable friendship. I don't make these offers to just anyone. What should I call you?"

"I'm going by Sainte-Marie."

"That's fine, if it suits you. I can't force you to trust me, so I'll have to come by it another way. However, I want to show you I'm an honest sort and that you can depend on me. For starters, tell me first the real purpose of your visit."

"I came to see the baroness under the guise of a sea captain."

Florian squinted his eyes, inspecting his companion carefully. "Bless me, but I think you're fibbing, and I can prove it."

"Prove me wrong then."

"Your name is Löwenklau, not Sainte-Marie."

"Really!"

"You come from Berlin, not Marseille."

Löwenklau balked. "What?"

"And you're a Hussar lieutenant rather than a sea captain."

"Ridiculous!" Löwenklau was clearly taken aback by this revelation. How could this coachman have come to these conclusions? He resolved to tread more carefully in the future.

"Ridiculous?" the coachman asked. "This is not idle speculation. It's the truth. I heard it from both of them."

"Who are these two sources?"

"The first one is a 'she,' namely Mademoiselle Margot."

"Really? Did she talk about me?"

"No, it's not what you think," Florian said. "When my duties as coachman aren't required, I often head to the garden. One day, I saw her under the arbor with a letter in her hand. I saw how she kissed it repeatedly, probably because she assumed she was alone. She laid it aside on the bench and didn't realize it had fallen to the ground. When she left, she must have forgotten about the letter."

"Did you read it?"

"Of course."

"Dammit! That's deplorable."

Florian merely regarded him calmly. "Wait until you hear the rest."

"Why do I have to wait? You said you rushed to the arbor. Then what happened?"

"Yes. I hurried over."

"You retrieved the letter from under the bench..."

"Naturally."

"And you opened it...!"

"Of course, otherwise how could I have read it?"

"You read it? You actually read it?"

"Well, not in its entirety," Florian admitted. "I didn't have the opportunity. I only glanced at the cover and the signature."

"Scoundrel!"

"Don't be ignorant! I had my reasons. The cover read 'Berlin' and 'my passionate Margot' was the greeting. The signature was something like, 'Hugo von Löwenklau.' Did I read it correctly?"

"What possible reason could you have had to be so indiscreet?" Löwenklau's voice was stern, conveying frustration he was feeling. He was becoming visibly upset.

"What reason? Well, 'he' gave me a specific name to look for."

"He? Who is 'he'?"

"I'm not permitted to disclose that. Besides, you don't trust me, so why should I trust you?"

"Florian, I'm starting to get the feeling you're not the honest and trustworthy fellow I took you for. On the contrary, I now see someone who is cunning and deceptive."

"Then you misjudge me, Monsieur. I'm actually not as smart as I look, though I can be downright clever for those I care deeply about."

"Perhaps I could be included in this select company."

"But that is already the case."

Löwenklau paused. "Really?" he asked.

"Absolutely. I wanted you to join me on the buckboard so I could speak my mind."[19.2]

"It seems as though you haven't been entirely upfront."

"In what way?"

"Your reluctance to tell me about this 'he,' for one thing."

"I can only discuss this 'he' with a certain Lieutenant von Löwenklau."

"No one else?"

"Only with him," the coachman repeated.

"All right," Löwenklau said. "I want to trust you, and so I admit to being Löwenklau."

"Are you acquainted with the old Blücher?"

"Yes. But how do you know about him?"

Florian kept his eyes intent on the darkness ahead as he spoke. "We'll get to that shortly. Back then, you had intended to leave Mademoiselle Margot here secretly."

"How did you come to that conclusion?"

"Well, Madame Richemonte and her daughter had secretly left Paris."

"I don't see what you're getting at."

"You'll understand me shortly," Florian replied all-knowingly.

"Why would they have to leave secretly?"

"On account of a certain stepbrother, who is a captain in the army and goes by the name Richemonte."

"Heavens!"

"Not to mention a certain baron, who is the chief army supplier and goes by the name Reillac."

"Listen here, Monsieur. You've been spying on the ladies!"

"That couldn't be further from the truth."

"Then how do you know all this?" Löwenklau demanded.

"From 'him,' naturally."

"Who then is this 'him' person?"

"Captain Richemonte."

Had there been enough light on the buckboard, Florian would have seen Löwenklau's face turn white. The unexpected news hit the lieutenant hard. "From the captain?" he breathed. "Was he here, at Jeannette?"

"Yes. About a week ago."

"Dammit! Was he with the baroness?"

"No, I don't think so."

"Well," he said quietly, "was he with one of the other ladies?"

"No."

"How about Roman?"

"No, especially not him!"

"Hang it all! With whom was he then?"

The coachman took a deep breath before replying. After a moment, he answered. "With me."

"*Zounds!* How did he make your acquaintance?"

"He was recommended by Baron de Reillac."

"Do you know him, too?"

"Very well, actually."

"How is that possible?"

"Ah yes," Florian said. "That is the question. Didn't you know that he often comes to Raucourt?"

"To Raucourt? I didn't have a clue!"

"In fact, Reillac is stationed in Sedan!"

This next piece of news struck Löwenklau hard a second time. "Does he live there now? Is he in charge of army supplies again?"

"Indeed."

"That devil! It's starting all over again, the danger and the torment..."

"Don't worry, Lieutenant! Florian Rupprechtsberger is still here!"

"For God's sake, stop calling me 'Lieutenant.'"

"But no one can hear us."

"That may not always be the case. Refer to me as the sea captain. It's safer that way. Now, fill me in. How on earth did you get mixed up with those two?"

Florian loved to tell a good story and this was his opportunity. "One fine day, I drove the ladies to Sedan, where I dropped them off at their usual hotel," he began. "I drove the carriage toward the nearby stable when a well-dressed gentleman approached me. He inquired if I had just dropped off three ladies. I told him that I had and he asked me for their names. I gave him the information without a second thought: Baroness Sainte-Marie and her two guests, Madame and Mademoiselle Richemonte. He then asked me where they resided, and I told him about the Jeannette estate, which lies near Raucourt. He thanked me and pressed a gold *Napoleonder*[19.3] into my hand."

"No doubt it was Reillac," Löwenklau murmured.

"Some time passed and I was sent on another errand. I was near the estate when a rider approached me. He was the same friendly gentleman I had met earlier. Through our conversation, it seemed to me there was a purpose to his visit and that he was trying to gain my confidence. I decided to keep my guard up. At first, we just talked about general things and the operation of the farm, but at last he came to the point.

"Tell me," the gentleman asked, "did the two ladies named Richemonte come to Jeannette alone?"

"I don't know," I replied. "I was absent at the time."

"Did they have other visitors?"

"None that I have heard of."

"Then think carefully. Have you ever heard the name Löwenklau?"

"No, I don't think so."

I recall him looking at me closely, considering what to say next. "I previously gave you a Napoleonder. Would you like to earn more like it?"

"How many?"

"That depends entirely on you."

"Then I'm your man, Monsieur."

The baron smiled slightly before making his offer. "Well, can you start working for me?"

"Unfortunately, no."

"Why not?"

"I'm currently employed by the Baroness de Sainte-Marie," I explained.

"That is not a problem. You can serve both of us quite easily."

"At the same time?"

"Of course," he affirmed. "You can serve her openly, and me discreetly."

"What sort of service do you have in mind, Monsieur?"

"I'll fill you in as soon as you agree to our bargain."

"Then I'm at your service. What is the pay like?"

"I tell you what, I'll give you twenty-five francs for now, and if you continue to bring me good reports, I'll reward you accordingly."

"With pleasure, Monsieur."

"Good. Here are the agreed to twenty-five." He handed me the money. "Now, here is what I would like you to do," he continued. "I want to know everything which pertains to Mademoiselle Richemonte. I am her secret admirer, and naturally I would like to know if she is still available. For example, is she receiving any sort of correspondence from other gentlemen? In short, everything an admirer would like to know. Are you following me so far?"

"Completely, Monsieur. Where shall I write you?"

"You may write to my office at the military headquarters in Sedan. I am Baron de Reillac, the official supplier to the army. Tell me, can you be discreet?"

"I'll conduct myself without uttering a word about your affairs."

"I like the sound of that!" Reillac said. "It's vital the ladies remain ignorant of my interest in their affairs, which is why I will not come to Jeannette myself. Furthermore, our working relationship is to remain a secret. Pay particular attention to any letters that may come from Berlin, and if you can tell me whether they originated from a certain Hugo von Löwenklau, I will ensure you receive a bonus."

Löwenklau became more alarmed at each successive revelation, until he finally broke his silence. "Are you telling me you hired yourself out and supplied him with good information about me?"

"Actually, it was rather terrible information!"

"I'm not following you."

"In all honesty, I told him a lot of half-truths and stories I made up. I did, however, receive a gold piece for each report," the coachman snickered.

"You know, Florian, you're a real scoundrel."

"Compared to that character?" Florian asked incredulously. "I'm not offended at all. You see, he rubs me the wrong way. Still, good and honest people may see quite a different Florian."

"Have you been checking for letters from Berlin, the ones bearing my signature?"

"Yes, but not on behalf of the baron."

"Ah! For yourself, then."

He nodded good-naturedly. "Of course."

"What have you told the baron about my letters?"

"Absolutely nothing. I never mentioned having seen your 'Berlin' letter."

"Why then did you want to see it for yourself?"

"I wanted to satisfy my curiosity by finding out whether or not Mademoiselle Margot's friend was indeed a German. If that were the case, I could protect him from his enemies, since we would be countrymen. Did I do something wrong?"

"Wrong?" Löwenklau considered that for a moment. "Hmm, yes and no. I absolve you of any blame. Indeed, may I regard you as some sort of protector, Monsieur Florian?" He let out a quick laugh.

"Go ahead and laugh. It doesn't change my commitment to you both. A servant is often capable of rendering a significant service to his master. You can count on it!"

"I don't doubt you, and I've always been pleased with those in my employ," Löwenklau replied. "Have you met with Reillac often?"

"Quite often. Sometimes weekly. The last time I showed up, I fabricated some news so I could obtain my gold piece. Because his servant was absent, I entered through the unlocked door into the foyer. The baron was occupied in his study and I detected the sound of loud voices. As I sat down to wait for him, I heard every word spoken by the two gentlemen. The main topic of discussion seemed to be the old Blücher and, of course, you, Monsieur."

"Really!"

"They spoke of an attack in which you had worn some sort of a metal breastplate."

"Go on."

"Then they discussed Mademoiselle Margot, whom they had 'appropriated' and brought to the baron's residence. They also spoke about how you had come knocking with the field marshal..."

"Who was the man with the baron?"

"The same man who had stabbed you with the dagger and also shot at you."

223

"Captain Richemonte!"

"Yes. But I heard a lot more," Florian said.

"Fantastic! Please, go on."

"Next, the baron spoke about a dumb farm hand and how he had gained his confidence," he paused with that, making a face. "Evidently they meant me, but I'll show them a thing or two."

"I don't understand how the captain already knew Margot was at Jeannette," Löwenklau remarked.

"Yes. They already knew of it in Paris."

"I can't believe it!"

"I heard it in the course of their conversation."

"How could he possibly have known this? No one knew!"

"That's where you are mistaken, Monsieur," Florian said. "One other person knew... the banker from whom Madame Richemonte received her income."

"Ah! So that's how they found out."

"I learned the most important part at the end. Captain Richemonte had already visited the Jeannette estate."

"Did he visit the ladies?" Löwenklau asked.

"No. In fact, he saw General Drouet."

Löwenklau frowned. "What urgent business did he have that compelled him to make a personal appearance? Surely, it would have been wiser on his part to keep his distance from the ladies. It would be to his advantage not to reveal to them he knew of their whereabouts."

"He didn't do any such thing."

"But they should have been aware of his presence!"

"No, that's the point," Florian said. "He came at midnight."

"Was his visit primarily one of secrecy?"

"Of course! It was veiled in treachery."

"If you wouldn't mind answering another question, what did it entail?"

Florian paused for a moment, then asked, "Are you personally acquainted with the field marshal?"

"Of course."

"I don't want to pry into your affairs," he said. "I wish you were here in an official capacity."

"Do you assume I'm not in the army at the moment?"

"Naturally!"

"Why would you think that?"

"If you were in the military, then you would be with your regiment now, and not here."

"Florian, were you ever a soldier?"

"No, but my uncle on my grandfather's side was. That was a long time ago."

"I believe you," laughed Löwenklau. "It must have been around the time of the old crown prince and the Marshal Dorflinger. However, our strategy has changed somewhat since then."

"Yes, I recall now. He served under the prince. It would make more sense if I knew of your connection with His Excellency."

"Since you've been honest with me and given me your confidence, I should admit to you I am here in my capacity as an officer in the Prussian army."

"In Blücher's army? The one that's assembled at Lüttich?"

"Yes, the task before me is difficult and dangerous."

The coachman smacked his whip excitedly so that it echoed down the road. "Just as I thought, Monsieur sea captain! I'm your man. If you will, place your trust in me, the good old Florian. You won't be disappointed. Actually, Captain Richemonte is doing the same thing on the other side."

"Ah! Is he employed as a scout for Drouet?"

"A scout to be sure. More like a spy who would go so far as to commit murder."

"Murder? *Zounds!* What does that mean exactly?"

"Well, his objective seems to be murdering Blücher! I heard it with my own ears."

"How shallow and contemptible of him," Löwenklau said.

"I can confirm that he received his instructions from Paris."

"From whom?"

"Unless I'm mistaken, from General Drouet."

Löwenklau scrambled for words, finally giving up the attempt. "I'm speechless!"

"It's a different sort of warfare now. It's preferable to simply eliminate the leaders."

"But to engage in an assassination? Imagine how easy it would have been for me to have eliminated the emperor early along with two of his most famous marshals."

"True," Florian said, "but your self-respect stems from being a German officer. You would never stoop to that."

"Dear God! Captain Richemonte is far more dangerous than I imagined!" Löwenklau exclaimed.

"Evidently."

"And does Drouet support his actions?"

"It certainly seems that way."

"Inconceivable," the lieutenant whispered. "A general simply wouldn't stoop to such a level. The captain must have received secret instructions and either misinterpreted them or is handling it as a personal vendetta."

"I heard Richemonte's task is to remove Blücher and seek his revenge at the same time."

"By some chance, did he speak of an attempt?"

"He sounded disappointed that he had not succeeded in getting close to the old man."

Löwenklau drew in a long, deep breath. "This is serious. The field marshal is in great danger. How long ago did this conversation take place?"

"About eight days ago."

"Then my stay at Jeannette will be shorter than I hoped. I need to inform the field marshal as soon as possible."

"Right," Florian agreed. "That's why I decided to reveal the plot to you directly."

"Are you really a supporter of the Prussians?"

"Of course!"

"Are you an admirer of the famous Blücher?"

"Oh, if I only had the opportunity to shake his hand, even one time."

"But if that's true, why didn't you act yourself to prevent an attack?"

"Me?" the coachman asked. "What could I do? I waited patiently for your arrival. You would know what to do."

"But you didn't know I was coming."

"On the contrary. I noticed, for instance, how much Mademoiselle Margot likes to walk in the garden. Since she received your last letter, she expanded her walking tour and even ventured outside the farm estate. If a carriage came into the yard, she would rush to the window for a closer look."

"Florian!"

"Yes, Monsieur sea captain?" he asked, grinning.

"Aren't you the clever—"

"Not at all," he interrupted. "I'm just a good judge of character. If I come to trust someone, I'll do anything I can to help them out. I was convinced by Mademoiselle's mannerisms that she was expecting you. This is why I took it upon myself not to reveal the captain's plans until your arrival. I'm grateful for your faith in me. You've put your trust in the right man."

"Hmm," Löwenklau murmured, looking ahead down the dark road. "I see lights ahead. Could that be LeChesne?"

Florian nodded. "Yes, I think so. Do we go through the town?"

"No. We should stop at the inn for a glass of wine. Perhaps the emperor is still..." His voice trailed off, his eyes widening with a desperate realization. "Oh no! Florian, give the horse a smack with your whip. We have to hurry! I just remembered something vital!"

Startled, the coachman did as instructed, so that the carriage barreled along the road at twice the normal speed. "Really?" he asked. "Is it serious?"

"It is," Löwenklau confirmed. "The emperor and all those who are with him are in danger."

"What danger are you talking about?"

"Earlier in the day, I overheard two men talking down the road by the cross. They were plotting to ambush two marshals—the details, such as whom and where, weren't clear."

"You mean the cross toward Raucourt?"

"That's the one."

"Damn! That's a revolting place. Many have lost their lives there."

"Quickly, make your way to the tavern," the lieutenant said urgently. "The emperor said he would stop there. We have to catch him before he leaves."

"A dicey situation. My concern is not so much for Napoleon, but for our three ladies. I would rather whip the horse to death than let something happen to Mademoiselle Margot. Forward!" He used the whip to propel the wagon even faster.

"I was so absorbed with your story that I forgot to load my pistols." Löwenklau managed to load the pistols and finished just as they pulled up to the tavern. They both jumped down from the buckboard and walked through the entrance door.

"Was the emperor here?" asked Löwenklau abruptly.

The innkeeper was sitting at a table. The mayor was still at hand, preparing to leave just as the two men walked in.

"Yes," the mayor answered with an air of self-importance. "His Majesty gave me the honor of preparing an important—"

"Did all three carriages stop here?" Löwenklau interrupted.

"Why, yes. There were gentlemen and ladies, who allowed me to—"

"Fine. When did they leave?"

"Just now. I had the honor of writing a document—"

"Never mind all that. Answer me quickly and to the point. How many minutes have elapsed since they left?"

"Maybe two minutes. But young man, how dare you speak to me in this tone? Don't you know that, as mayor of LeChesne—"

"I notice you are holding a document. What are the contents?"

"It relates to an ambush on the forest road. The emperor himself dictated it."

"Well then," the lieutenant said, growing more impatient with each passing second, "you must be aware that one man appeared as their savior—"

"—who downed eight robbers," the mayor finished.

"Exactly. I am that man. The emperor himself is in great danger. Innkeeper, do you have a horse which could be saddled right away?"

"Yes. Why do you need one?"

"Just bring it out. Florian, you'll ride it!"

227

"What?" the innkeeper said, jumping out of his seat, taken aback by Löwenklau's suggestion. "Give you my horse? Think again! Who are you and what's your name?"

The mayor stood next to the innkeeper, equally upset and confused. "Yes, who are you, and where are you two from?" he said in his most convincing official tone. "If the emperor is in any kind of danger, then—"

"Your part is to act, and not to question me!" said Löwenklau, cutting him off. "Quickly, tell me if there was a mention of a sea captain in your protocol?"

"Yes, it was he who downed eight robbers. Evidently, he's related to the baroness, since the emperor referred to him as her cousin."

"Well, I am he. You will find a carriage outside which belongs to the baroness, yet with only one horse in the harness. We cannot catch up to the emperor in this fashion. Together, with his marshals, the whole entourage is headed to their demise. They're about to be attacked at the cross, unless we stop the bandits."

"At the cross?" the official asked, shuddering.

The innkeeper was aghast. "Their demise!"

"Yes. You have to act immediately or bear the consequences," Löwenklau intoned. "Not to mention the ire of Napoleon."

"For God's sake, not that!" moaned the mayor. "I am ready to walk, to run, to fly! What shall I do to save my emperor?"

"I want you to muster all those who are equipped with weapons and lead them to the cross!"

"Muster? Lead?" The mayor shook with fear. "I cannot lead or command. Actually, I'm hoarse and completely ineloquent."

"There's nothing wrong with your voice from what I've heard. Hurry up! All those who are not at the cross in fifteen minutes will be shot!"

"Dear God, I had better—" And with those words, the mayor ran out.

Löwenklau turned to the innkeeper. "Well, what about the horse? If it isn't ready in one minute, you won't be able to ride for a month!" Löwenklau pulled out his pistol to show he meant business.

"Right away, Monsieur," the terrified man said, already running for the door. "I'll have it out in half a minute."

"Don't bother to saddle it!" Löwenklau called after him.

"Are we both riding together?" asked Florian.

"Of course!"

"Then take the innkeeper's horse and I'll take the brown one," the coachman decided. Looking around the room, his eyes found an old cavalry saber hanging above the door. "Well, well! Here's a weapon I could use!" Florian pulled it down and ran outside, wielding the new weapon.

Löwenklau spotted a bunch of melted candles sitting on a nearby table. As he gazed at them, a thought struck him. It was already dark outside and the carriage lanterns would likely have been broken during the attack. By improvising, he could fashion a torch which could prove useful. Looking around some more, he spotted several wires hanging from the rafters. They ordinarily were used to support lamps, though they would be perfect for what he had in mind. He grabbed a walking stick and laid the candles at one end, taking the wires and winding them around the candles. It would have to do.

Grabbing a handful of gunpowder, he poured it around the tip of the torch. A pistol shot should suffice to ignite the contents. In total, it had only taken a few moments to put together. Faced with looming danger, he found himself able to accomplish more in a few seconds than many others could in a full hour. Löwenklau even remembered to leave a gold piece on the table as compensation for the supplies.

Meanwhile, Florian had removed the harness from the brown horse, climbed up onto his back, and now held the saber out with one hand. The innkeeper brought his horse out of the stable.

"Hold it," he called to the coachman when he spotted the familiar saber. "Where did you get that saber?"

"It was hanging above the door," Florian replied.

"It belongs to me. Give it back!"

"Come and get it then!" yelled the brave coachman as he galloped down the road in pursuit of the emperor's entourage.

"Do I get my horse back?" the innkeeper asked Löwenklau meekly as he stepped up to him.

"Of course!" the lieutenant assured him. "The men who've been summoned will bring it back." With that, he jumped onto the horse and flew off down the trail.

"Make sure you keep your word!" yelled the innkeeper after him.

Elsewhere, the mayor instructed the night watchman to assemble the 'troops' by blowing a horn for the emperor's rescue.

The innkeeper's horse was no champion runner, but it flew down the road like an Arabian under the Hussar's skillful guidance. He caught up to the coachman in a short time, encouraging him to press on.

"Forward, Florian, forward!" Löwenklau shouted.

"Monsieur," Florian warned. "You'll break your neck!"

"Not mine, but maybe the horse's," he replied determinedly.

The men rode like they were possessed. Florian tried his best to keep up with the Prussian, though he started falling behind.

Suddenly, Löwenklau heard gunshots in the distance. He dug his heels into the horse's flank and it shot forward. He couldn't judge his speed because of the darkness, but as the horse came around a bend, he saw a glimmer of light ahead, possibly from carriage lanterns. To his dismay, the lieutenant heard the unmistakable sounds of battle.

The officer approached without being detected and decided to employ his earlier strategy. He reined in his horse and jumped off, tying it to a tree. He ran the rest of the way, to the place where the coaches had stopped. Groucy, who was surrounded by four men, was managing to hold off the attackers, but the strength in his arm was starting to wane. Löwenklau appeared at his side. His first shot was to light his makeshift torch. The flame shot high, enabling him to see the surrounding area. He spotted Groucy, Ney, the emperor and the general, all under attack.

"Hold on, Sire!" he yelled, leaping forward. "Help is at hand!" He shot at a highwayman who was about to strike Groucy, and watched him collapse into a heap. Löwenklau used the spent pistol to strike another attacker in the face until he, too, was disabled.

"Dammit, you didn't come a moment too soon," Groucy said, relieved. The marshal downed the third man, then concentrated on finishing the fourth.

Löwenklau gave Ney some breathing room by downing two robbers with his double pistol. Dropping the spent weapon, he rushed to the emperor's side and drew his third pistol. Two more shots rang out and the emperor was out of danger.

"Any more shots left, my friend?" Gourgaud called to him.

"Two, Monsieur," was the reply.

"Then over here, please!"

It was as though Löwenklau had been preordained to rescue all four officers. He shot the last two bandits, who had been determined to kill the adjutant general.

Just then, he heard a loud menacing voice from the bushes. "If we can't get him," Curé shouted, "he can damn well go to hell!"

A shot rang out, one that was destined for the emperor. The flaming muzzle revealed the grimace on the face of the old leader, frustrated by the turn of the tide. Löwenklau, convinced the shot had found its mark, was overcome with rage. Armed only with the torch, he ran after the shooter.

"Stop there!" he called out. "I'm not through with you!"

The highwayman sought to flee deeper into the woods, but instead found himself fully illuminated by the lieutenant's torch. He stopped in his tracks, took a deep breath, and turned around. Löwenklau stood no more than three paces from him. Realizing he was unarmed, the robber threw his rifle into the woods and drew his knife to challenge him.

"Come on," the old robber growled. "Let's see what you're made of!"

He jumped at the officer like a panther, but Löwenklau was prepared for the attack. He countered the thrust by propelling the torch into the other man's face. The old man cried out in pain, blinded, and dropped his knife, clawing at his face to remove the hot, burning wax. Löwenklau forcibly dragged him back to the road, where the fighting had come to an end.

"Here's the emperor's murderer," he said, stepping out of the trees. The officers turned to look at him, bewildered.

"The emperor's murderer?" asked Ney.

"Yes. He deliberately took a shot at him."

Ney pointed to the side, smiling. There in the shadows stood the brave Florian, holding the bloody saber, and next to him was Napoleon.

"Ah! He lives," cried Löwenklau. He was still holding the torch in his left hand, the old man pinned with his knee while his right hand gripped his captive's throat.

Napoleon walked over to him. "No, my friend, I am not dead yet. The vagabond fired his last bullet at me, but fortunately missed his target."

"It was this man who fired at you, Sire," Löwenklau said.

"You alone fetched him?"

"Yes."

"Without a weapon?"

"I had this torch, Sire."

"Simply extraordinary!" Napoleon exclaimed. "Jan Hoorn, fetch a belt and tie him up. He will give me an account later."

Löwenklau finally stood up as the emperor extended his hand. "Here is my hand. You have been most enterprising—I owe you my life."

"As do I," Ney said, coming closer.

"Likewise," added Groucy.

Gourgaud nodded emphatically. "All of us!"

While the three men shook hands with him, a pale, though still pretty, face appeared in the open door of the first coach. Her eyes shimmered with tears of joy... or were they tears of pain?

"I have already spoken to the gallant coachman," continued Napoleon, pointing to Florian. "He came to our aid, brandishing a large saber. With it, he felled two robbers who had come at us from underneath the coach. What made you think to come to our aid, Captain?"

Löwenklau turned red, slightly embarrassed over the fact his negligence had nearly cost them all their lives.

"I overheard a conversation earlier regarding a holdup, money, and two marshals. It wasn't until I was on my way back to LeChesne that its significance dawned on me."

"Ah! I am beginning to understand you," Napoleon said. "Did you leave right away?"

"I procured a horse for our trusty Florian, removed the harnessed horse from the coach, and the two of us galloped after your entourage. That concludes my involvement, Sire."

The emperor simply smiled in his direction. "No, my good man, not by a long shot! That is where the story begins. We were in a bad state. You two arrived at just the right moment. Although the lancers had accompanied us, we were unprepared for the large number of highwaymen. Most of us only had one pistol and one saber, while the robbers had plenty of firepower. How many men succumbed to your prowess, Captain?"

"Seven, I believe, Sire."

"Remarkable. First you vanquished eight men on the road to Vouziers, and now you have dealt with seven more. You are a real bayard!"[19.4]

The sound of approaching horses drew their attention and all eyes turned back toward the road, where they detected a number of torches trotting toward them.

"Pardon, Sire," explained Löwenklau. "That would be the mayor of LeChesne."

"What could he possibly want now?" asked the emperor irritably.

"I talked him into assembling all the local men of the town and convinced him to hasten his 'troops' to the emperor's rescue. I also warned him that, should he fail to show up within fifteen minutes, he would be the first one shot."

Napoleon couldn't contain himself any longer and laughed out loud. It surprised Löwenklau, who had often heard of the Corsican's usually serious disposition. Even the officers joined in.

"*Merci!*" replied Napoleon, growing serious once again. "I am very impressed! I am convinced you could become a very capable officer. These riders could have proven their worth had they shown up earlier, when it really mattered."

"They can still be useful, Sire," Ney pointed out.

"In what way?"

"The coaches and horses are in disarray. Our wounded men need medical attention and our dead are lying about the place, not to mention the corpses of the bandits. We still have one prisoner—"

"Of course, Marshal," Napoleon quickly agreed. "Let them come!"

When the townspeople had come within earshot, the officers heard the brave mayor call out. "Stop in the name of the law!" he bellowed.

"What do you want?" replied Gourgaud, who, as the youngest of the officers, allowed himself a little latitude by replying before the emperor.

"Are you one of the robbers?" the official asked, a little less sure of himself.

"Certainly not!"

"Are you the emperor?"

"Of course not!"

"Then you must be... Captain de Sainte-Marie?"

"Wrong again," Gourgaud said. "I am His Majesty's adjutant general."

The mayor hesitated, surprised. "Oh! What is your name?"

"General Gourgaud."

"That fits with the report. Is the emperor with you?"

"Yes. He commands that you come closer!"

"Is there still a danger of shots being fired?"

"No."

"Will you give me your word on that?"

"Yes."

"Well, in that case, forward men!"

The small company advanced in the darkness. The mayor had found new courage when he learned the fighting had stopped, and bravely led the way. Löwenklau's torch was nearly spent, though it still gave off just enough light for the pompous mayor to recognize Napoleon. He guided his horse toward the emperor, intending to make his proclamation in his most dignified voice. He sat upright, his right hand on his hat and the left holding the reins.

"Sire, I wish to inform you that..." Just as he started to speak, his horse stumbled over a corpse, one of several blocking the roadway, and collapsed onto its knees. The brave man of the hour couldn't help but slide down the horse's neck, tumbling once head first, coming to rest on the part of his anatomy possessing the least presence of mind. Without missing a beat, he continued. "...I am at your service, and have brought twenty brave men."

The mayor's companions, considering the unusual dismount a requisite of formality, made a move to get down from their horses in like manner, even though they doubted inwardly they could pull it off as smoothly as their 'Battalion Chief.'

Biting his tongue so as not to explode with laughter, the adjutant general intervened just in time. "Dismount properly, Messieurs!" he called. "Dismount properly!"

Relieved, they followed Gourgaud's order rather than the example set by their superior, who had just risen and dusted himself off.

The emperor held him in his gaze without flinching a muscle. Those who knew him well understood that his seemingly serious exterior was a mask concealing mischievous thoughts.

"Monsieur," he began, "I will require you to write a second document."

"I am at His Majesty's service."

"Do you see what just occurred?"

"I see it, Sire." The mayor surveyed the carnage. Just then, he noticed a corpse lying face-up, its mute, grotesque eyes staring up at him, seemingly mocking him. The 'brave' mayor quickly sidestepped the body.

"They had the gall to holdup the emperor!" exclaimed Bonaparte.

"An offence punishable by death, Majesty!" the mayor blurted out.

"Yes, well, they *are* dead. All except one. Their leader is over there, bound and guarded by my coachman. He will need to be interrogated."

"I will have him strapped to a rack, Sire."

"They had concocted a plan to waylay my marshals. The ensuing examination must determine if it was a simple robbery or a deliberate act of treason."

The mayor looked at the emperor earnestly. "I will get to the bottom of it, Sire."

"You? You will not find out anything! You are neither gifted in the art of warfare, nor in matters of intellect. Just present yourself tomorrow morning at eight o'clock sharp with your prisoner at Jeannette, where you will receive further instructions."

"I will be there at a quarter to eight, Sire."

"I must, however, congratulate you for your quick response. Each of your men came equipped with a lantern. Who arranged that?"

"I myself, Sire," he said, thumping his chest for effect.

"Really? What for?"

"So we could better see where to strike at our enemy."

"An important point, my good man."

"Yes, Sire. Also to be able to confirm that they were actually dead."

"Who do you mean by that remark?" Napoleon asked.

"Those who counted themselves as our adversaries."

The marshals turned aside to hide their smiles, each of them on the verge of erupting with laughter at the mayor's ridiculous remark.

"Quite so!" continued Napoleon. "A superior has to demonstrate he can handle any situation, especially if it is a difficult and bloody affair, just like the task I assigned to you earlier. Do you know how to supervise the repair of carriages?"

"Completely!" the mayor replied.

"Then see to it that our coaches and horses are restored to proper order. Clean this place up and remove the corpses. Pay special attention to the prisoner, whom you will personally deliver tomorrow morning!"

The emperor turned away and approached Löwenklau, who was nearby and surrounded by well-wishers. "Are you injured, Captain?" he asked.

"No, Majesty."

"Wonderful! I believe we have all come out of the affair unscathed."

"Not one has been injured," confirmed Groucy.

"We have all been very fortunate," the emperor said gravely. "We must see to our ladies and reassure them."

Napoleon attended to his own carriage. Löwenklau watched enviously as the emperor stepped out of view, toward his beloved Margot. But it was not meant to be. As the two marshals likewise returned to their coaches, the lieutenant turned his attention to collecting the spent pistols.

CHAPTER TWENTY
An Emperor's Jealousy

When he climbed back into the carriage, Ney found the baroness bracing herself for the worst. Stricken with terror, she closed her eyes in preparation for what was to come. In another coach, Madame Richemonte fared about the same, also in a state of shock. The moment Groucy had left the coach, she slipped into unconsciousness, only to be revived in time to witness the tumult of fighting outside. It seemed to her that Löwenklau had appeared on the scene at the last possible minute, like a knight rescuing his damsel in medieval times. When the marshal inquired as to her wellbeing, she took the opportunity to ask after her daughter. Margot, as it turned out, was not faring well.

The emperor stepped up to the door of his coach. "Mademoiselle," he said apologetically. "This is all most regrettable. May I inquire as to your condition?"

"I am feeling very weak, Sire!" she managed in a whisper.

"Ah! Jan Hoorn, see if you can get a flask from one of the other ladies!"

"That will not be enough, Majesty," Margot said quietly.

"Why not, Mademoiselle?"

"I have been injured."

"My word! Is it possible? Jan Hoorn, get a lantern. Quickly!"

The coachman obtained a lantern and handed it to Gourgaud. He lit up the coach as Napoleon opened the door and stepped inside. Margot lay in the corner, white as a ghost. Blood flowed from her wounded shoulder, down her shawl, and onto her dress.

"Oh no! She's been shot!" exclaimed the Corsican. "When did this happen, Mademoiselle?"

"It must have been the last shot, the one meant for you, Sire," she replied softly.

"*Parbleu!* It missed me and headed into the carriage. What do we do, General?"

"Perhaps it would be best..." Gourgaud started, quickly interrupted by Margot.

"Please, send for my mother!" she whispered.

The emperor dispensed with calling for a servant and hurried to Groucy's coach. As the marshal was about to leave his carriage, the emperor made his hasty approach. Madame Richemonte, seeing him coming, wondered whether his presence meant bad news.

"Sire, did something happen?" the woman asked.

"Madame, now is not the time to be despondent," Napoleon blurted out. His intentions were to calm the lady's fears but, as many men do in such situations, he instead succeeded only in heightening her concern for her daughter.

"Of course I am upset. Did something happen to Margot?"

"Well, yes. It was a bullet meant for me—"

"A bullet? Meant for you? Dear God! Has my daughter been shot?"

"Yes, Madame," he acknowledged. "The inside of the coach is covered with blood, but it—"

"Oh my child! My daughter!" the mother wailed. She stormed out, simply pushing the emperor aside, hurrying toward the coach. Napoleon looked at Groucy in amazement.

"Did you see that, Marshal?" he asked, disconcerted.

"Of course, Sire," he replied with amusement.

"Did you see how I tried my best to carefully deliver the news?"

"Most carefully, Majesty."

"And yet she was near panic. Oh, these women. Especially the mothers!"

"Yes. Their daughters, however, strive to remain calmer."

The emperor nodded knowingly. "Certainly, my good Marshal. When I think about how tenderly Margot laid there, and how softly she whispered... she had been wounded! Then there are those mothers! They are lionesses. Look! Another one is about to escape from the coach." Both men looked on with concern as the baroness left her coach and followed her cousin. "Just as I surmised, she too has to have a look. I think one doctor would be better than ten mothers. Don't you think so, Marshal?" He turned to Ney, who had just come over.

"Of course, Sire," Ney said. "Is the young lady injured?"

"Unfortunately, yes. The last bullet, intended for me, found its way into the carriage. It must have struck her."

"Is it serious?"

"There is a steady blood flow!" the emperor confirmed.

"We should consider moving her to—"

"Yes, we should depart!" agreed Napoleon.

"Or send a messenger to a doctor," Groucy said.

"Yes, send a messenger for a surgeon. Right away!"

The decorated war heroes, so adept in warfare, were at a loss as to how to care for the wounded Mademoiselle.

"Jan Hoorn! Quickly! Send for a messenger!"

"Where to, Sire?"

"Anywhere. Someplace where we can quickly procure a doctor!"

"For God's sake, Sire," said Ney. "She will have bled to death before you can find a doctor. We must leave immediately for Jeannette."

"Jan Hoorn! Get ready to depart for Jeannette!" ordered the emperor. Napoleon, normally clear and decisive, was confused and preoccupied with Margot's condition. The coachman, debating whether or not to climb up to his seat, looked around and saw the open carriage door. He had no idea who was inside, or who would accompany them, or where the emperor was. Right at that moment, a savior appeared.

Löwenklau returned in the midst of the vacillation. With Florian's help, he had found his pistols and even retrieved the discarded rifle from the bush. He was walking to one of the carriages when he heard his name being called.

When Madame Richemonte saw her daughter covered in blood, she nearly lost her composure. She forced herself to remain calm while she reached for her daughter's hand.

"My dear child, is it serious?"

"I don't think so, Mama."

"No? Praise God! Where are you bleeding from?"

"Either from the front or from my shoulder. I'm not sure of the exact place."

"Are you in pain?"

"No, not at all. But I'm very tired. I want to sleep."

"Let me have a look!"

She entered the coach to examine the wound. The baroness arrived, now composed and ready to help. The blood was still flowing freely, making it difficult to pinpoint the source.

"Dear God, what should we do?" Madame asked. "Dear cousin, they're ready to depart."

"Where's Hugo?" whispered Margot.

"Hugo?" her mother asked absentmindedly.

"Yes, Hugo, Mama. He knows about wounds."

"But child—a man!" objected the baroness.

"He is my betrothed. I would rather have him examine the wound than the emperor." She spoke in a weak but determined voice.

The baroness stepped back and scanned the road for Löwenklau. When she saw him approach the carriage, she called him. "Dear nephew, hurry! We need your help."

"Help?" inquired Napoleon, turning to Ney. "Is the captain also a doctor?"

"It is very likely, Sire! A seaman must be competent in many things."

"Who needs my help?" asked Löwenklau.

"We have an injured lady," replied the baroness.

"An injured lady? Oh dear God! Not my dear…" He had nearly blurted out Margot's name, giving himself away. Instead he composed himself and walked up to the carriage. The mother hadn't thought of removing Margot's shawl, which still covered her shoulders, and so he quickly removed it while the baroness held the lantern. A feeling of dread struck him as he saw Margot's pale and weak condition. The blood was still flowing from the open wound.

"Oh, Margot," he said, taking her hand. "Are you in pain?"

"No, my dear Hugo," she whispered with a smile, slowly opening her tired eyes.

"The wound appears to be from a gunshot."

"Yes, the last one, meant for the emperor," the baroness said.

"Then it only just happened. Thank God. May I have a look?" asked Löwenklau.

"Yes," Margot managed. "Would you?"

He examined the wound carefully. "My dear ladies, your handkerchiefs please!" he said, turning to Madame and the baroness. The relief was evident in his voice. "The injury stems from a grazing shot, but the blood loss has weakened her considerably. I will render a makeshift bandage to stop the bleeding."

"Is it serious?" asked her mother.

"No," he replied, still examining the wound.

"It must be causing her some pain."

"I'm sure her strength will bear her up."

"Oh, I am so grateful, my dear Hu—er, captain," she said, correcting herself, nearly disclosing his true identity.

Meanwhile, the heroes and volunteers from LeChesne were not idle. They bound the broken poles and spliced the damaged harnesses to make them ready for the remainder of the journey to Jeannette. They exchanged their horses for those which had been wounded or killed and removed the dead bodies to the side of the road. Had it not been for the injured Mademoiselle, they could have departed.

At last, Löwenklau left the coach and approached the emperor.

"I see you have been blessed with many skills, Captain," Bonaparte observed. "Does this include those of a surgeon?"

"I am not a doctor, Sire," he replied modestly. "However, I have some experience in administering bandages."

"How is our victim? Is it serious?"

"Not at the moment, but we must guard against any further blood loss."

"Of course! What should we do next?"

"We cannot travel all the way to Jeannette. The wound must be cleaned and properly bandaged, which unfortunately we cannot do here."

"What do you recommend, Captain?"

"I know of a tavern not too far from here, Sire."

"Good. Are you suggesting we stop there?"

"Yes."

"What sort of a man is the proprietor?"

"There is only a woman and her daughter," Löwenklau said. "Yet they are quick and capable."

"Do you know them?"

"Not really. I was there only once. Earlier this day, actually."

"We should give the inn a try, Captain. How do we get there, gentlemen?"

"I will borrow the good mayor's horse," said Gourgaud.

"I will obtain one, too," added Marshal Ney. "This way, His Majesty can ride in my coach."

"What about our brave doctor, the captain?"

"I must remain with the injured lady, Sire."

"Rightly so!" the emperor exclaimed. "Always mindful of his duty for his patient. What about Madame Richemonte?"

"Why can't I stay with my daughter?" she asked, turning to face Löwenklau.

"Madame, think of all that blood!" Hugo reminded her.

"May I invite both ladies to ride with me in my coach?" offered Groucy.

Everyone had found a place except Florian. He approached the emperor's coach to speak to Jan Hoorn. "Tell me, comrade. You helped out in the fight, didn't you?"

"Of course. I made good use of my whip."

"Would you leave a fellow coachman sitting on the road?"

"Of course not! Climb up! Where are you from?"

"The Jeannette estate."

"Good. The emperor plans to stay there, and likely I will, too," Napoleon's coachman said. "Though, of course, you must already know this."

Florian nodded. "Yes, and I hope we can down a glass of wine together."

"Of course. I enjoy a good drink now and then, especially with a brave comrade. Listen up, the emperor is about to bid them farewell."

Napoleon walked over to address the 'heroes' of LeChesne. They formed a long line, holding the horses' reins in their left hands and a lantern in their right. They made quite the impression.

"Well, Messieurs," said the emperor. "You have certainly proved yourselves worthy in answering the call, and for that I am grateful. So long as I am emperor, not one of my subjects will be molested on this road again! Good night!"

"*Vive l'Empereur!*" yelled the mayor.

"*Vive l'Empereur!*" joined in his men.

"Raise your lanterns high!"

They whirled them, clanging them together noisily.

"He said good night, so wish him a good night!" encouraged the mayor.

"Good night!" they all bellowed.

The entourage resumed their journey accompanied by calls of "Good night," "*Vive l'Empereur*," and the clanging of lanterns. The mighty Napoleon and his marshals had eluded a great danger. There was only one unforeseen victim—Margot. She lay in the carriage, pale and weak, choosing not to rest on any of the abundant satin pillows around her. Instead, she chose the strong arms of her betrothed.

"Are you sleeping?" he whispered.

Her reply came weakly. "No, my love."

"Are you in pain?"

"Not at all."

"What about cold shivers?"

"No. I am blessed to be with you. Am I going to die, Hugo?"

"Oh no! You're going to live a long life of happiness."

"But only with you!" She leaned her head on his shoulder.

He softly caressed her cheek, allowing his hand to stroke her beautiful hair. He sat beside her, oblivious to the fact that he was sitting on the blood covered seat.

"Now we travel in an emperor's carriage," she whispered.

"Yet our future together is far brighter than his."

"Are you certain?"

"Yes," Löwenklau said. "I know our forces will triumph. His return was premature and our troops will capture the great eagle. They will trim his talons and clip his wings so he won't be able to subdue the world again."

"How terrible! After all, he is a man with feelings."

"Yes, a man with feelings—turned toward you."

"Hugo!"

"Margot!"

"Are you jealous?" she asked.

"No. I know I'm worth more to you than all the emperors in the world."

"Are you just saying this to comfort me?"

"No, I mean it."

"You make me so happy because you know the truth. I feel it in my heart."

"Then let's cling to this precious truth, just like when I hold you in my arms."

She cuddled up to him as closely as her waning strength would allow. Their lips found each other, enjoying a brief but happy interlude. Unfortunately, their time alone was short lived.

Florian interrupted them with an announcement from above. "We have reached the tavern belonging to the widow Marmont."

The three carriages stopped together. Hugo was just emerging from his coach when the emperor approached.

"How is she doing, Captain?" he asked.

"The temporary bandage is holding, Sire," said the young officer.

"Can you apply a better one here?"

"Yes, I believe so."

"Afterward then, we can proceed to Jeannette?"

"Yes," Löwenklau said. "As long as she is strong enough to travel."

"If she cannot travel, I will remain with her!" he blurted out.

"Your Majesty!"

"What?" asked the Corsican curtly.

"You are sacrificing a lot!"

"Sacrifice?" he mused. "What do you think? She became the recipient of a bullet meant for me. I owe her that much. Furthermore, she is very beautiful and that calls for no regrets."

"Sire, then permit the injured lady to be carried into the tavern."

"Who will do that?"

"I will assist the other two ladies."

"I will do it myself, Captain!" replied the emperor with a trace of jealousy in his voice. "But first, we need to speak to the innkeeper."

"I will hurry and arrange it, Sire."

"No! I will do it myself," Napoleon insisted. He walked alone to the door of the inn and entered the foyer. There he saw the mother sitting under the light. Her daughter had just risen to her feet, roused by the voices whom she supposed were new guests. Upon seeing the emperor, the girl stopped in her tracks with an outcry. Her mother looked up from her book and started to rise as Napoleon greeted them both with a slight bow.

"Why are you afraid of me, my child?" he asked the daughter.

She didn't reply.

"What is it?" he asked for the second time.

"Oh, mother," she replied, pointing to the emperor.

"Do you know me, my child?" he asked.

She held her hand to her bosom. "I don't know whether I am mistaken or not," she said.

"Well, who do you think I am?"

She pointed to a picture on the wall. It was a painting of General Bonaparte when he had fought at the famous battle at Lodi. "Is that really you?"

"Yes, it is really me."

She clasped her hands together. "Mother, oh mother, the emperor!"

"The emperor?" the older woman shook her head in disbelief. "That's not possible. The emperor would never come to our little tavern."

"And yet, I am here, mother!" he said kindly. "I am Napoleon, your emperor."

The woman slowly approached, looking closely at him. "Yes, Berta," she finally remarked. "It is he, our emperor. That is how your father described him."

"The father of this girl? Your husband? What is his name?"

"Oh! My emperor, you must know him. Surely you remember Jacques Marmont!"

"Marmont?" he asked. Napoleon's brow drew into a frown as he stared pensively ahead. It was the name of the armoire who had betrayed him in 1814, and whose defection had brought about his own abdication. Napoleon shook off the memory and composed himself. "There were many Marmonts," he replied evenly.

"He was there at the siege of Toulon," replied the widow proudly. "He had served under Desaix in the Rhine army. Then he fought at Lodi, Castiglione, St. Georges, in Egypt, at Marengo, Gastelnuovo and Ragosa, at Wagram, and finally in Spain. There he was wounded and was sent home."

"Ah! Was it by chance the same Marmont who saved the life of Soult at Badajoz?"

"Yes! Yes, Sire! That was he, my husband!"

"How did he fare?"

"Not too well," she said. "His scars caused him considerable discomfort. We had bought this little tavern so he could rest and regain his health, but instead he went to his eternal rest... he was murdered, Sire!"

"Murdered?" the emperor asked, raising his eyebrows. "By whom?"

"By robbers."

"Where did it happen?"

"In this very forest."

"Really? Another villainous act! They will pay for it! I will look after you. My very own entourage was attacked in this forest."

"You, Sire?"

"Yes, I! They were highwaymen!"

"My God! They dared to come against our emperor!"

"Their days are numbered," he said. "Many have died, and I will see to it that we will pursue them to the last man. A lady in our company was wounded by an errant shot. We need to arrange for a proper dressing. Will you permit me to bring the lady into your house?"

"My house and all I possess is yours, Sire. I will see to it myself and bring her inside. Come with me, Berta!" She walked out with her daughter.

As it turned out, Napoleon's help wasn't necessary after all. Hugo had already lifted Margot out of the carriage. The two ladies, assisted by the innkeeper and her daughter, carried Margot into the guest house.

"The lady seems to be doing better," said Napoleon gruffly as he approached Löwenklau.

The young officer had an idea of what Napoleon was after. "Sire," he replied evenly. "I believe that she will feel better after a proper dressing has been applied."

"Was she able to climb out of the coach herself?"

"No, Sire."

"Did someone assist her?"

"Of course, Majesty."

"Who was it?"

"It was I, Sire."

"You? Did I not expressly forbid you?"

"She asked me to, Sire."

"Young man, it is customary to obey your emperor's orders. Who will administer the dressing?"

"I will," replied the captain.

"Very well, Captain!" Napoleon allowed, his mounting jealousy growing ever more apparent. "However, I will observe. Come with me!" He led the way into the inn, with Löwenklau following him at a distance.

The officers also climbed out of the carriage, but didn't enter the small tavern. They knew better. It was as though a princess lived in the small house, whose threshold was off-limits to anyone else.

Margot's face brightened a little when Hugo entered, but quickly paled at the sight of the emperor. The carriage ride and the conversation with her betrothed had taken its toll on her, and she felt weak again. She lay on a simple bed and was attended to by her mother and the baroness. The innkeeper and her daughter stood at a distance, staring at the lovely girl. Berta's eyes shimmered with admiration and fear, compassion and hate.

The emperor held up Margot's hand. "How do you feel now, my dear?"

"Very weak, Sire."

"Should we not wait to administer a second dressing?"

"The first dressing was only temporary, Sire," replied Löwenklau. "It is not sufficient."

Bonaparte turned to face Löwenklau. Although his eyes conveyed a deep concern for Margot, he replied in a cool, unfriendly tone. "I was addressing Mademoiselle. I will carry out her request."

Löwenklau bowed out of respect.

The emperor turned to address Margot's mother, who was becoming quite alarmed at the developing tension between the two men. "Madame, are you in agreement that the dressing should be replaced with a new one?"

"If you please, Sire," she replied guardedly.

"Then the captain may proceed. Of course, I will oversee it."

It was clear to all those present that the emperor showed more than mere concern, and appeared resentful of the supposed captain's heroism. He crossed his arms and assumed a position of authority over the group. Löwenklau remained still, failing to move a muscle.

"You may commence, Captain!" ordered Napoleon.

Löwenklau shrugged his shoulders, but otherwise didn't move.

The emperor's nostrils flared angrily. "Did you not hear me?" he exclaimed autocratically.

Instead of responding to the emperor's challenge, Löwenklau turned to Margot. "Mademoiselle," he said deliberately. "Is it your intention to expose yourself to an outsider while I prepare the new dressing?"

"An outsider?" replied the emperor irritated. "Who do you mean by this remark?"

Löwenklau knew fully well what he was risking. "You, Sire," he replied evenly. Without wincing, he held the Corsican's fuming gaze.

Napoleon left his place and walked directly up to Löwenklau. "I am the emperor, do you understand me?" he challenged.

Löwenklau bowed before him. "Your Majesty," he replied, "may I remind you that it is customary that only the husband be present in such intimate circumstances. Or is it your intention to regard Mademoiselle Margot as one of those women whom one gapes at but cannot be bothered to later acknowledge?"

"Monsieur!" exclaimed the emperor, stomping his foot in anger.

In that instant, Madame Richemonte and the baroness turned pale, finding themselves speechless. Likewise, the innkeeper and her daughter gazed in amazement at the man who dared to confront the celebrated Corsican. Margot, who lay with her eyes closed, took on the appearance of a corpse rather than a patient.

Löwenklau's reply was another formal bow, accompanied by a faint smile. "Sire, I am well aware I have something majestic in front of me, yet the embodiment of purity lies before us. If I love a bride or a woman from the bottom of my heart, I would not uncover her in the presence of another man's lustful eye, waiting instead for the stranger to depart. It is only appropriate for her to be uncovered in front of a physician, or her lover. No man, not even an emperor, has the right to take something from a helpless being who, being in a position of disadvantage, would otherwise defend her honor, were she strong enough."

There was something in Löwenklau's tone and expression that left an impression on Napoleon. He took a step back and reconsidered. "Monsieur, you speak daringly to your emperor!"

"I acted in like manner when it was incumbent of me to defend your life, Sire!"

"Really!" was his singular response, a grating remark encompassed by a mixture of resentment and hostility that he could barely manage to contain from erupting into a violent outburst. "Monsieur! You have embarrassed me in front of these ladies, yet you stand here as a defiant subordinate. We are even now. You may leave us."

"I will leave as soon as I see that no one else requires my assistance."

"I command you to go!" replied the angry emperor, stomping his boot.

Löwenklau examined him from head to toe. "Majesty," he said with a smile, "do you have the right to rule over this lady? Is Mademoiselle Richemonte your wife or your betrothed? Even if she were, you would not have the right to place her life in danger. You are not here as the emperor, but as a man. And for the moment, I am here in the capacity as her doctor. If you are determined to cling to your high position, I will still outrank you as her doctor."

Napoleon threw him a damning look. "Then I will have you removed."

Löwenklau shook his head in a proud and contemptuous manner, reminiscent of a lion shaking his mane. "I will shoot anyone who dares to remove me before I have attended to my patient," he roared defiantly.

"Really! Does this include me?"

"Everyone, without exception!"

The emperor was surprised at the young man's stubbornness, deciding to change tactics. He stepped up to the bed and placed Margot's hand in his. "Then you tell him to leave, Mademoiselle," he whispered to her.

A shallow smile spread over her face. "He will not go. He is too proud!"

The innkeeper's daughter approached and whispered something into Margot's ear. She simply nodded, while Berta explained to the rest. "I have spent some time in a convent with the Sisters of Charity. I have learned the skill of dressing wounds and I possess a salve which, when applied, has wonderful healing properties."

"Child, shall I dress your wound?" Madame Richemonte asked, regarding her daughter tenderly.

They were all curious as to the answer Margot would give. "If the captain should allow it," she whispered.

"Mademoiselle alone knows what is best for her," Löwenklau said. "I will take my leave, sensing she is in capable hands. I know she will be the recipient of tender care." As he turned to leave, he gave the emperor a bow and departed the little house.

With nothing left for Napoleon to do, he too left the room. He met up with Jan Hoorn and quietly spoke to him. Jan Hoorn, in turn, approached Löwenklau.

"His Majesty has instructed me to tell you, Captain, that all the places in the carriages are spoken for."

Löwenklau simply nodded. He knew Napoleon was nearing his end, not only politically, but also militarily. He had clearly demonstrated this in the way he handled his passion for Margot by usurping his authority over him, the doctor. He walked to the side of the house and met up with Florian.

"Follow me," he whispered, "but don't let anyone see you."

He strolled a short distance, and then stopped. Florian appeared at his side shortly after.

"What is going on?" the coachman asked.

"Something unbelievable. The emperor is infatuated with Margot."

"That is obvious to all."

"He insisted on being present when I changed the dressing. I advised him to leave, out of respect for Mademoiselle, and then he turned on me. He even threatened to throw me out."

"Remarkable! A Prussian Hussar and the French emperor! Is that what you get for saving his life?" chuckled Florian.

"Well, at least Germany would be pleased with my efforts. However, here you will get the same thanks, whether from the emperor or the lowest farmhand. I was not counting on anything."

"But now you can count on his wrath!"

"Unfortunately," Löwenklau replied, nodding regretfully.

"Everything unappealing and unfavorable."

"It has already begun. I was just informed by Jan Hoorn that I will not be traveling with them the rest of the way to Jeannette."

"I expect this will include me as well," Florian said. "Well, so much for my nice ride on the coach. We will have to walk the rest of the way."

"It would appear so. However, I don't want to leave without informing the baroness. Could you do me a little favor?"

"Of course, Monsieur."

"The emperor will see to it that I am not admitted back into the tavern. See if you can approach it from the rear and enter through the back door. Simply tell the baroness or Madame Richemonte that the emperor has it in for me, and has instructed that I find my own transportation to the estate. They will give you instructions."

"Fine. Where do we meet?"

Löwenklau paused for a moment, considering a good location. "Let's meet back here."

"For a moment, I thought I might have to challenge the emperor to fisticuffs," Florian joked. "Now, that would have been a sight to behold! I'll be right back." He disappeared into the dark.

Some time elapsed before he returned. Löwenklau, waiting in the night, heard footsteps, with Florian finally emerging from the darkness.

"Well?" Löwenklau asked.

"I found both ladies and conveyed your plight."

"What did they instruct me to do?"

"You are to come to Jeannette."

"For what? I am not going to concede to that boisterous Frenchman when it comes to Margot's wellbeing."

"That doesn't concern her directly."

"Whom else then?"

"You probably think the emperor will accompany her," said the coachman.

"Of course, but don't make fun of me, Florian! I'm not at all jealous," he said. "Even if he were to sit alone with her in the carriage, I know she would rather die than allow him to go unpunished for the way he insulted her. I wanted him to understand that his authority didn't include him determining her future."

Florian smiled at him. "But that's not the case. The ladies will take Berta Marmont along."

"Is that feasible?"

"Why not?" the man asked. "The girl has a good understanding of the medicinal properties of plants and herbs. She will assume the role of her nurse and remain until the emperor leaves."

"Good. What about me?"

"I'm to bring you to the young baron, Roman, who will provide you with suitable lodging."

"What sort of accommodations?"

"It's a corner room, accessible by a winding staircase. A most suitable room, giving you access from above. Best of all, I can attend to your needs without being seen. The baroness purposely assigned you this room."

"Do you think so?"

"Yes," Florian answered. "We should go. I can fill you in on the details while we walk. We need to arrive before the emperor, and I know of a short-cut through the woods."

CHAPTER TWENTY-ONE
The Prussian Spy

Florian marched at a steady pace, leading the way ahead. Löwenklau followed him as he turned onto a narrow path through the woods just wide enough to accommodate two abreast.

"Are you afraid to take the forest shortcut?" laughed Florian.

"*Pah!* I have my pistols to deal with any surprises."

"Of course, but don't forget about me. Since nothing happens to old Florian, you're in good hands."

"I'm relieved to hear it," Löwenklau said. "Now, tell me more about this room I'll be staying in."

"To begin with, I can visit you there without anyone else knowing. You see, a winding staircase[16.1] makes the lofty perch accessible from the stable. Second, you'll be able to visit Mademoiselle Margot as often as you wish without detection. Third, and this is the most important part, all the credit goes to the baroness's craftiness."

"Now you're making me curious."

"Another winding staircase gives you access to the flat roof of the main building," Florian explained. "I'll supply you with the key to the access door. There's another entry, but it's always locked; I have been entrusted with the key. You see how much the gracious lady cares about you?"

"I have to admit I'm not following you. How could all this be possible?"

"I'll do my best to explain it, my dear sea captain."

"Would you please?"

"I have the key for the trap door, which leads to the flat roof. You'll have the second key, and since no one else has access you can rest assured that you won't be surprised by a third party."

"But why all the secrecy? Is the view up there so spectacular?"

"It is exceptional. The best part is that you can enjoy the spectacle without being seen."

Löwenklau was still trying to puzzle everything together. "Please," he said, "make yourself clear."

"I have to admit, it's to your great advantage that we met today. I'm the only servant who is privileged to know more than the others. The rooms on the second floor have small access holes, or shafts, embedded in the ceiling, which are covered with round inserts. The inserts can be removed without detection because of the camouflaged décor painted on the ceiling."

The lieutenant smiled, realizing the implication. "Ah, yes. I'm beginning to understand."

"Now, tell me. You are a sort of diplomat..."

"Yes, I suppose."

"I suspect diplomats like to be informed. If you happen to find yourself on the roof and remove one of the inserts, you will not only be able to overhear the conversations going on within, but also have a bird's eye view."

"Even quiet conversations?"

"Yes," Florian confirmed. "The rooms were constructed in such a way as to allow the sound to travel to the attic."

"That's very advantageous."

"Isn't it? But the best is yet to come. The baroness has determined that the emperor and his staff will be accommodated in these rooms."

"Really!" exclaimed Löwenklau, pleasantly surprised.

"Not bad isn't it, my dear sea captain? General Drouet is already there," the coachman said. Then, as though having almost forgotten it, he added, "One more thing. I will personally cater to all your needs. Now you know everything. Could that be beneficial to you?"

"It's more than I hoped for."

"If you require something, whether by day or night, you have only to pull on a bell cord located in your room. Unlike your typical noisy bell, it doesn't make a sound, but sends me a signal in the stable. Do you understand what the baroness had in mind?"

"Yes, I'm beginning to."

"She intends for you to spend as much time in the attic as you wish. She is of German heritage, and even Roman is partial to Prussian interests. They desire to give you every advantage, Monsieur," he said as they began to walk out from the cover of trees. "Ah, we're at the end of the forest. We just have to cross the field now and we'll be nearly home. Just follow me, Monsieur."

The trustworthy coachman jogged ahead while Löwenklau followed, keeping pace. In just a short time, they arrived at the estate, though not at the main gate but the back entrance. The only thing guarding the house from the rear was a long, tall fence.

"I trust you've learned to climb in your youth?" Florian joked.

Löwenklau let out a short laugh. "I'll try not to disappoint you."

They scaled the structure without difficulty, dropping to the ground on the other side. "We could have easily gone through the front gate," Florian admitted, "but it would have raised too many questions. Follow me to the stable."

"Are we not going to see Roman first?"

"You'll see him in good time."

They walked through a wide garden and arrived at the back wall of the stable. There, Florian opened a recessed door. They walked to a rear compartment that came to an end at a tall structure that resembled an old feeding trough. He pulled on the base and it slid forward, revealing a small entry door, barely visible in the poor light.

"Behind here is the winding staircase," said Florian.

"No one else knows about it?" Löwenklau asked. "What if another servant should stumble by accidentally?"

"Don't worry. This section of the stable is inaccessible from the main part of the house and requires a key. As long as it's locked, no one can enter. Please, Monsieur, wait here for a moment."

He walked to the front door and unlocked it. Once outside, he secured it again behind him and Löwenklau heard the sound of retreating footsteps. Florian returned a few minutes later, accompanied by Roman, who approached him with open arms.

"Welcome, sea captain!" the young baron said. "I just heard a small snippet from Florian about the events of late. Unfortunately, I also heard about the imminent arrival of some extraordinary guests who will keep me busy with preparations. I promise you, though, I'll pay you a visit as soon as I can to express my gratitude."

"That's not necessary, Baron!" said Löwenklau. "May I return your pistols? They certainly proved their worth!"

"Captain, I don't need them. You saved those who are dearest to me, far more so than these pistols. Please, keep them as a memento and sign of our friendship."

Löwenklau bowed slightly in gratitude. "Thank you," he said. Pocketing the two pistols, he took the key that Roman held out for him.

"Florian will show you to your accommodations," Roman said. "Will Mama arrive soon?"

"I hope so," replied the officer. He was mindful of his earlier conversation with the pretty Berta. "Are you aware that Mademoiselle Margot is suffering from a gunshot wound?"

"Dear God, yes! Florian just told me. Is it serious?"

"No, I don't think so. Actually, she'll be accompanied by a proper nurse."

"Hm, who could that be?"

"She appears to be an honest girl," Löwenklau said, "and very capable. She's the daughter of Marmont's widow, who lives in a small tavern in the forest."

Roman's face turned red. "What?" he called out. "Berta? Berta Marmont?"

"Yes, I believe that was her name."

"Extraordinary! How did she get mixed up in this?"

"We had to stop at the inn to change a dressing. When the young lady demonstrated her nursing ability, the baroness invited her to accompany the entourage back to Jeannette."

"Now there's a surprising twist," Roman commented. "But here I stand, wasting your time and mine, talking. Surely you understand that I'm faced with new commitments. Please don't resent me if I leave for now. I'll catch up with you later, when I have more time. *Adieu*, Captain."

"Take care, Baron."

The events that baffled the young man made perfect sense to Löwenklau. There had been no other way to keep the emperor from Margot's side but to instill the services of young Berta Marmont.

Florian let his master out and immediately locked up after him. He then returned to Löwenklau, lighting a lantern and motioning for Löwenklau to follow. They entered the steep and narrow staircase and began to climb. The steps ended in a small storage room, which was situated directly over the main stable. Löwenklau saw a small door, connected to the main building.

"Use your key," encouraged Florian.

The lieutenant did as instructed and inserted it into the lock. The key released the door, allowing them entry into an average sized room, complete with two windows. Opposite the entrance was another door.

"This will be your temporary residence," the coachman said as Löwenklau looked around, taking stock of the inventory: a sofa, four chairs, a table, a writing bureau, a mirror, and a small clothes closet. It was quite cozy and livable. He moved a curtain at the back, revealing a bed. At the foot of the bed he saw another winding staircase that connected to the upper level.

"This must lead to the roof," Löwenklau surmised.

"Yes. Your key also opens the door."

"What about this other door?" he asked, gesturing to the room's other door.

"Come with me and I'll show you!"

Florian unlocked and opened the door. It was another bedroom, which also served as a change room. From the faint trace of perfume, Hugo reasoned that it evidently belonged to a lady.

"Who lives here?" he asked.

The coachman laughed. "Do you want to take an educated guess?"

"Not Margot!"

"Of course, it belongs to Mademoiselle Margot," Florian said, watching the surprise on Löwenklau's face turn to pure joy. "She sleeps here, though her sitting room is next door. No doubt you realize your room could only be available under certain circumstances. These are not the usual accommodations an officer like you would come to expect. You're probably accustomed to finer comforts, but when you consider the advantages the winding staircase offers, you'll have to forgive the baroness for choosing these accommodations for you. I hope you're not displeased with us." Giving himself some of the credit, the coachman stood in front of him, the picture of loyalty, cunning, and courage.

"My God, Florian!" Löwenklau exclaimed, laughing.

"What is it, Captain?"

"How can anyone make sense of your ramblings?"

"I'm not worried about what others think, as long as I'm the better for it."

"I'm starting to realize how astute you really are. You purposely came across as slow on the uptake with Reillac, but if he could only hear you now! The master of this house could not express himself as eloquently. I now see a totally different man before me. Florian, Florian, you're not to be underestimated. You are a man to be reckoned with."

Florian nodded in agreement. "You're right, Monsieur. In the long run, it's far better to look dumber than one actually is. It doesn't do anything for the ego, but the rewards more than compensate in the end. Anyway, we should close up here and venture up onto the roof." He locked the door to Margot's quarters and turned toward the staircase.

Löwenklau grabbed his arm. "Florian, will you admit something to me?" he asked deliberately.

"What?"

"That I have you alone to thank for this room, the 'roommate' next door, and the priceless view port upstairs."

"*Only* me?" he grinned, stressing the word only. "No, that's where you're wrong. Let me be honest with you. I do count for something in this house, and the experienced coachman often has more to say than the young baron. I have to admit I took to you, and even more so to our Margot. You're both suited for each other, like no other pair I know. That's why I took it upon myself to be your guardian. Even the baroness has come to respect you. The way you handled yourself with the bandits was no small feat. According to the baroness, your defense of Margot's dignity and the ensuing challenge of the emperor was something to behold and may never again be repeated. Initially she was overwhelmed with fear, but because of your honorable conduct, she holds you in the highest regard. You know, we're partial to the Prussian cause and we want to be of service to you. I requested she provide you with this room and she agreed to it with pleasure. But the extraordinary thing she did was to permit Berta Marmont to accompany the ladies. There was no other way to keep the emperor out of the carriage."

"Is she still upset with Berta?"

"Yes," Florian said. "You see, Roman was head over heels in love with Berta. That subsided somewhat since Margot's arrival."

"Really?"

"Of course. Now he's smitten by Margot's beauty!" laughed Florian. "He has no idea you're her betrothed and is in full agreement that you should be given this particular room. He's convinced this door is always locked and you're only interested in politics, not in the girl."

"And when he learns the truth?"

"Oh, he'll blow off some steam and then laugh about it. He'll get over it with no hard feelings. The truth be known, he holds a good-natured and open-minded view of life. You can lay your fears to rest about the young baron. Now, permit me to get you acquainted with the layout of the roof."

The top of the staircase was covered with a cast-iron plate. It fit perfectly into the roof opening and the lock was accessible with the same key, now in Löwenklau's possession. The roof was flat and encompassed by a four-foot parapet.

"Take care that you don't bump into the base of the air holes," Florian warned him. "Here, let me show you." Florian took him by the hand and guided him to one of the covered holes. He showed Löwenklau how to open it. "I'm not sure how the guests will be allocated in the various rooms, but you'll figure that out later when you climb up to observe. You will have to be careful when you remove the covers, though."

"You mean because my presence above could easily be detected below?"

"Of course! You've been presented with a great opportunity. I trust you'll accomplish what you set out to do and keep the staircase our secret. I'll leave you now, as I need to attend to other matters. I'll make sure you don't lack for anything."

The coachman climbed back down from the roof, while Löwenklau replaced the iron plate and locked it behind him. He remained in his room for awhile after Florian returned to the stable. He extinguished the light, thereby minimizing the risk of being discovered. He opened the window for some air and sat down to observe the goings on in the courtyard below. Servants hurried back and forth in preparation for the arrival of the new guests.

A fair amount of time had passed before the carriages finally arrived. Servants hurried to facilitate the unloading of passengers and their belongings. The servants carried small lamps that suited their tasks, but shed little light beyond the coaches. Not being able to observe the small details as a result, Löwenklau decided to rest on his bed for a while. He reasoned that with all the unloading and room preparations happening, little opportunity would arise for gleaning something worthwhile.

Time passed and the young officer judged he would give it another try. He climbed to the roof and unlocked the metal access plate. He carefully made his way to the closest airshaft. As Florian had mentioned earlier, the opening was covered with a type of plug that allowed for easy removal. He carefully removed it and peered through the opening. What he saw moved him deeply.

He was situated directly over the bedroom of his betrothed. Margot lay on the bed, pale and tired, being comforted by her mother. A military doctor, who belonged to Drouet's headquarters and billeted at Jeannette, had been instructed to attend to her. He had examined the wound and applied a fresh dressing. He appeared to be on the verge of leaving.

"There is no need for concern, Madame," he uttered calmly. "Your daughter will recover quickly."

"I am very grateful, doctor!"

"Rest is the best advice I can give to Mademoiselle. The wound is not serious, but there is always concern should a fever arise." Turning to Margot, he added, "Avoid any exertion and you should be fine."

As he left the room, Madame Richemonte took her daughter's hand in hers.

"My poor girl," she said tenderly. "I'm relieved the injury isn't more serious. The bullet could have killed you. I find I'm still a little anxious."

"Because of me, Mama?"

"Yes, of course!"

"You don't need to worry. You heard what the doctor said. I, however, have other concerns."

"You have other concerns? For what?"

"For Hugo..." Margot whispered.

"Well, my cousin has reassured us that nothing can happen to him. He's well hidden, such that no Frenchman could find him."

"That's not what I meant," the young woman said. "Consider what will trouble him most."

"Do you think Hugo is afraid of discovery?"

Her tired eyes glowed with pride despite her current frailty.

"My Hugo, afraid?" she asked. "I don't think Hugo has ever felt afraid. He has proven himself time and time again. Rather, he'll be contemplating the emperor's next move."

"Do you think he'll be uncomfortable because of the emperor's attention toward you?"

"Naturally, my dear Mama. His interest in me is so obvious. It concerns even me."

"It's just a sudden rush of affection, my child," Madame said, trying her best to sound reassuring. "Nothing more."

"I don't believe it! Hugo saved his life and the lives of his marshals. If what you say is true, how can a momentary rush of affection impact his conduct to such an extent?"

"Dear God, I can't believe his interest in you is more than just a passing fancy!"

"I hope not, but I'm convinced Hugo will nevertheless entertain those thoughts. Even still, he can rest assured that my love and faithfulness are resolute."

Madame Richemonte looked down and fell into deep contemplation. Like all mothers of beautiful daughters, she sometimes entertained, even if only for a moment, those things that others found impossible. "Do you really love him with such passion?" she asked her daughter.

"Yes, Mama."

"There's nothing that can change your mind?"

"Nothing at all."

"Not even what the future may bring?"

"It's thoughts of the future that brings my love the most hope," Margot said. "Mama, your daughter is very, very happy." She drew her mother's hand to her bosom.

"We cannot dwell on our dreams," her mother said, "and keep wishing for castles in the sky. Life can be difficult, its prose mightier than its poetry, shedding light on everything in an unpredictable way. Suddenly, the light flares up in a bright and threatening manner only to quickly subside, with the darkness appearing deeper and sadder."

Margot looked at her uneasily. "Mama, I don't understand you."

"Dear child, I only mean that your lieutenant is a very young officer."

"Don't worry about that. He will advance in rank."

"But he'll never become an emperor."

A foreboding look crossed Margot's face like a dark cloud. "Mama!"

"Don't make a hasty decision, child! The emperor is showing you his favor. Do you know what that could mean?"

"I do, but my beauty is a gift from the Almighty. It has been entrusted to me for my betrothed's happiness."

"Would you repel the love of an emperor?"

"As soon as his affection crosses the line and becomes overbearing, yes, absolutely," she said. "Is it possible that you are considering different prospects for me?" Her voice was soft and innocent, though her words whispered a subtle reproach.

Madame Richemonte looked into her daughter's beautiful, faithful eyes. "My one and only desire is to see you happy, Margot!"

"Well, outward glitter and lavish parties will not make me happy."

"Are you saying that you place your hopes and trust with your Prussian officer?"

"Yes. In him alone, Mama."

"I sense you are almost ashamed of me, my dear child. I know you so well, and yet still I wonder if the aura which surrounds an emperor can have its influence on you."

"That glow is at the point of diminishing."

"So you think he will be defeated?"

"Yes," Margot said. "I'm convinced of it.

At that moment, the door opened quietly and Berta Marmont entered. "May I interrupt?" she asked respectfully.

"What is it, child?" replied Madame.

"Baron Roman de Sainte-Marie is waiting outside."

"Does he want to speak to me?"

"He asked for permission to pay his respects to Mademoiselle. He has not yet had the opportunity to do so. He has been occupied with his new guests."

Madame Richemonte turned to her daughter. "What do you think, Margot?" she asked.

A slight redness spread over Margot's pale face. She took a cursory glance at her room. "Roman is our host and relative," she reminded her mother. "We owe him our gratitude and respect."

"Do you wish to receive him?" Madame asked.

"Yes, please allow him to enter."

Berta nodded and started to bow out of the room.

"I will leave you two alone for a while," her mother said.

"No," Margot said quickly, stopping her before she left. "Mother, please stay with me."

"As you wish, dear Margot."

"I'm sure he won't object to find a mother caring for her daughter." Margot turned to Berta. "Please, allow him to enter."

The servant girl's face was marked with concern. For an instant, she appeared uncomfortable, then she left the room. A moment later, Roman entered. Although he had seen Margot daily around Jeannette, he hadn't ever observed her in such a weak state. Wearing a light-colored nightgown, she rested on a pillow, accenting her paleness and heightening his concern for her. He bowed politely before mother and daughter.

"Please forgive my boldness, dear aunt, for seeking your company so soon," he said addressing his aunt. "However, my concern for Margot's condition led me here to alleviate my fears." He spoke in a manner that ingratiated himself to the ladies, permitting him to enjoy an intimacy normally reserved for immediate relatives.

"Please, come closer, Roman," Madame Richemonte said in a friendly tone. "We gladly acknowledge your thoughtfulness toward us."

"How is Margot doing?"

"Much better than expected."

"Is she able to hold a conversation?"

"The doctor did not disallow it."

He approached the bed and picked up Margot's right hand, kissing it. "Dear Margot, you have no idea how worried I was when I learned you'd been injured," he said. "My first thought was that the bullet should have struck me instead."

Margot slowly pulled her hand back. "Was that really your first thought?"

"Yes, with God as my witness!"

"And afterward?"

All he could do was smile sheepishly in response.

"I'm flattered dear cousin," she whispered, "and I'm convinced you meant it."

His gaze had the quality of a dreamlike stare. Roman, unable to pull his eyes away from her beautiful face, made no effort to suppress his feelings. He reached for her hand again and pulled it to his lips.

"That moment, when I learned of your injury, has been etched in my memory forever. I can't forget it."

"How so, dear cousin?" Margot asked.

"It gave me an inkling of how much your life means to me."

"I certainly hope you value your cousin's life," Madame said, "and it should be of some consequence to you whether she is dead or alive, dear Baron." She was trying to make light of the conversation. With her years of experience, she knew precisely where he was headed, intending to declare his love for her daughter. He missed her intent entirely and blundered on.

"Oh please, dear aunt, let me explain," he stumbled further. "I meant it to be more than affection for a relative. I have suddenly realized that my whole heart belongs to Margot."

"Cousin!" she exclaimed in surprise.

"Yes," he replied. "I hope you believe me. I feel I can't live without you."

He purposed to kneel before her bed, but she beckoned him to remain standing. "You must be joking," she retorted.

"Joking? Oh, on the contrary, I am very serious."

She looked at his youthful, handsome face, suppressing a smile. "I feel sorry for you, dear cousin."

"Why?"

"Because you have chosen to die."

"Die? What do you mean by that?" he said, the color draining from his face. "Do I look sick to you?"

"No, not that way. Didn't you just say you couldn't live without me?"

"Yes, of course."

"Then, according to your own words, you'll have to die."

He simply stared and took a step back, unsure of her meaning. "Pardon me? Did I hear you right?" he asked.

"What did you hear?"

"Pardon? I don't understand you. Do you mean you don't love me?"

"Of course I love you. You are my cousin."

His face portrayed a childlike stubbornness. "I don't want your affection as a cousin, but as your betrothed, to be loved as your husband. This is what I desire."

"Then I'm afraid you will die," she repeated sadly.

Grief came over his face. "I'm falling as though from heaven," he whispered.[21.1]

"Please, cousin, don't harm yourself."

"Are you mocking me, Margot?"

"No, dear cousin. This whole scenario seemed like a foregone conclusion on your part. You should have asked yourself first if there were any obstacles toward a betrothal."

"What possible obstacles could there be?"

"Oh, the most obvious one—a bridegroom."

It was amusing to watch the awkward and surprised look appear on his face. "It certainly would prove to be a formidable obstacle," he replied dumbfounded.

"One which you are going to abide by, naturally."

"Wait a minute," he said, the turning of his thoughts evident in his bewildered eyes. "Are you already engaged, Margot?"

"For some time already, dear cousin."

"Dear God! I'll break his neck! Please, forgive my outburst! I really thought you were having a little fun at my expense."

She shook her head earnestly. "Don't take it to heart, cousin! You shouldn't have assumed I was free to marry, and perhaps treaded more carefully. As baron, you are wealthy and have a pleasant disposition, and women have always been friendly and accommodating in making your acquaintance. It's therefore quite commonplace for you to presume you would get whatever your heart desired. It's no wonder you haven't entertained the possibility of receiving a negative response. I regret having been so direct with you, but I pray you won't remain unhappy."

"But I am very unhappy!" he blurted out.

"Perhaps just in this moment?" she asked with a smile.

"Well, most likely forever."

"No," she said. "I imagine you'll change your mind quickly, due to your flexible disposition."

"My flexible disposition? Cousin, I assure you my heart has lost all feeling and has, in fact, nearly stopped beating."

She let out a hearty laugh, even though it was painful for her. "Your poor heart?" she teased, yet feeling sorry for him. "I hope it can be repaired."

He stepped back a pace, not knowing how he should take her last remark. "Margot, are you making fun of my circumstances?"

Madame Richemonte calmly placed a reassuring hand on his arm. "Please," she pleaded. "Don't view the circumstances so tragically."

"She didn't sound very sympathetic," he said. "Is it not insensitive to suggest my heart can be repaired so quickly?"

"It was not meant quite in that way, dear cousin."

"It almost sounded malicious!"

"Certainly not," Madame said in defense of her daughter. "I'm sure Margot is right in thinking your heart is more resilient than you might suppose."

"Well, that remains to be seen. Is Margot truly engaged?"

"Yes, for some time."

"While you were in Paris?"

"Yes."

The young man managed a slight smile. "Then I can find some comfort in that. If it concerned someone whom she had met here, I would have felt insulted. Since her heart was already spoken for prior to coming to Jeannette, I know I can handle the disappointment. It's a terrible shame, though. We could have been very happy together," he lamented. His last few words were spoken with such conviction that Madame Richemonte was amused.

"I'm convinced of it," she replied, a smile also growing on her face.

"Who is the bridegroom to be?"

The ladies looked at each other, wondering how best to answer the question. They shared the same thought, realizing it was not the best time to provide an honest answer. Even though Roman had taken the bad news good-naturedly, he was still under the influence of the recent disappointment. Madame Richemonte decided to tread carefully.

"Permit me to keep it a secret for the time being," replied Madame.

"But why?" he asked.

"Out of family considerations."

"Fine. But at least tell me what he does?"

"He's an officer in the military."

"Ah, I thought as much. French?"

"No," she answered. "He's of German descent."

"Even better. I thank you for your forthrightness. Does Mama know of the engagement?"

"Yes, she does."

He sighed heavily. "I find it hard to believe. I thought it would have been her wish to see Margot and I engaged."

"Did she speak of it openly?"

"No, she was not that specific," Roman said. "Although the inference was clear enough to me."

"Then if it's any consolation, nephew, she only learned of it today."

"And what was her response?"

"She gave her approval."

He scratched his head. "Are you implying that I should congratulate you as well?" he asked.

"Of course," replied Margot sweetly. "I expect nothing less from you."

His face conveyed an expression mixed evenly with joy and frustration. "Don't you think it's asking a little too much from me?"

"Not really. You're my cousin after all."

"Yes, well, the cousin who was handed a basket!21.2 Of course, I don't want to come across as impolite. I congratulate you, on your engagement, dear Margot."

"Thank you," she said.

He offered Margot his hand as a sign of acceptance and congratulations.

"Are you displeased with me, dear Roman?" she asked as she held his gaze.

"No," he said, even though I feel I should be." He smiled, finally coming to accept the news. "Well, I must leave you now. No doubt our guests will be looking for me."

"What is the emperor doing?" Margot asked.

"When I left him earlier, he had just left the supper table. He ate very little and asked that the marshals call on him later." Roman bowed to them once more and backed quietly out of the room.

Berta Marmont sat outside the door expectantly. She lifted her eyes to him as he walked out, her face filled with concern. He stopped near her, noticing her serious expression. "Why are you so somber?" he asked.

"Is a nurse permitted to be joyous, Baron?" she asked, rising to her feet.

"And why not, if the one cared for is doing well?"

"Really! Was Mademoiselle happy?"

"Very happy!"

She sighed inwardly. To be cheerful, one had to have a reason, and typically these feelings arose when love was involved.

"I envy Mademoiselle," she whimpered.

"In what way?"

"She has every reason to be joyous."

"Can't you find the same reason?" he asked her. He placed his fingertips under her chin, but she quickly stepped back out of his hand's reach.

"Do I have a reason to be happy?"

"Probably the same one as my cousin."

She looked at him questioningly.

"Can't you guess the object of her happiness?" he teased.

"No, Baron."

"Well," Roman said, "what does any girl hope for, but for a bridegroom?" He could tell he had shocked her with the words.

"Mademoiselle has a bridegroom?" she asked. "May I ask who it is?"

"Isn't that a little presumptuous of you?" he teased. "You probably thought it was me."

"Is that..." she began, her voice trailing off into a pregnant pause, "so unlikely?"

"Very unlikely. You see, she already has one."

She took a deep breath. "Then you're not the one?" she whispered.

"No, dear Berta, I certainly am not."

"I can hardly believe it."

"Why not?"

Berta's eyes opened wider. "It only makes sense for you to be the groom!"

"She may have the looks," he admitted, "but also an unyielding heart."

"Was she cold toward you?"

"I gave her no reason to feel that way. I've told you I find her attractive, yet she's no raving beauty. I know one who pleases me far more."

She remained quiet and blushed in turn.

"Well, are you going to ask me who it is?" he grinned.

"How can I ask about something that is none of my concern, Baron?"

"Why not?" he asked. "After all, you have every right. You see, it's you who pleases me."

He tried to put his arm around her. "Go on! Stop teasing me," she whispered, wiggling free. "It's not fair that you mock me about something like that."

"Mock you? Why would I do that? I'm serious when I tell you I favor you over my cousin. You're prettier and I'm sure you don't have a cold heart. Am I right?" He put his arm around her waist.

"Please, Baron, let me go," she pleaded quietly. "They will hear us."

"No, they won't," he said. "I'm going to kiss those lips so tenderly that no one will hear."

"Oh no, I can't allow it!"

"Why not?"

"Because you're the baron!"

"Well then, you will have to become my baroness."

"Who, me? A poor tavern girl?"

He nodded confidently. "Yes, you, and no other!" He took her face in his hands. He pressed his lips to hers and kissed her several times. He was too distracted to notice the door open behind him.

"*Bon appetit!*" was what they heard.

They broke their embrace, both calling out in unison. "The emperor!"

She rushed out of the room, leaving Roman alone with Napoleon. He, in turn, felt like a schoolboy caught in the act of committing a prank.

"Well, you do have good taste, Baron," the emperor mocked in his usual cutting style. "I hope you will forgive the intrusion."

"Your Majesty—" he stuttered.

"I certainly had no intention of disturbing your romantic interlude. I merely wanted to inquire as to the condition of our beautiful Mademoiselle. Where is the young lady?"

"Next door, Majesty."

"Is she alone?"

"No. Her mother is with her."

"Did you speak with her?"

"Yes. Just now, Majesty."

"Is a visit permitted?"

"I believe the ladies would be pleased to see Your Majesty."

"Then announce me!" The emperor's remark arrived in his usual short, curt style.

Roman obeyed, walking up to the door and opening it without knocking. "His Majesty!" he called to the occupants.

Both women were taken aback by the unexpected appearance of the emperor. Napoleon certainly had the ability to show his kind-hearted side when he chose. He bowed slightly.

"Pardon the intrusion, Mesdames," he said politely, "but I trust my intrusion will be overlooked because of my concern for Mademoiselle. I understand a visit is permitted."

Madame Richemonte bowed deeply and Margot tried to sit up slightly. The emperor searched Margot's face for a welcoming sign. She looked into his eyes and found they conveyed a mixture of emotions that made her blush.

Napoleon pulled up a chair next to the bed. "Was the doctor with you?" he asked.

"He left just a short time ago, Sire," Madame Richemonte replied for both of them.

"What is the prognosis?"

"He assured us there is no immediate danger, though cautioned she should not be exposed to any exertion."

"More or less what he told me," Napoleon confirmed. Once again, the emperor's eyes examined them, alternating between mother and daughter. It was as though he wanted to find out what sort of reception he was in for. He crossed his legs, getting more comfortable, and continued. "Mademoiselle was in the company of the emperor when she was injured. It therefore falls on my shoulders to express my sincere regret for such an act, and I wish to make amends. May I ask a few questions?"

Madame Richemonte bowed politely, encouraging him to proceed.

"Is Monsieur Richemonte still alive?" he asked the mother.

"No, Sire."

"Are you a widow then?"

"That is so, Sire."

"It is the duty of the emperor to care for orphans and widows. Are you with means?"

"We are poor, Sire."

"But on the contrary Madame, you are rich! One who has such a beautiful daughter is never poor. Is Mademoiselle engaged?"

"Yes, Majesty."

His eyebrows furrowed together. "To whom?" he inquired, displeased. To Napoleon, the great soldier, the notion that he might embarrass someone was of little consequence. Most considered themselves fortunate merely to be addressed by the emperor.

"To an officer," replied her mother.

"Ah!" he contemplated. "Is he a young officer?"

"Yes, Sire."

"Then he does not possess much wealth. Have you considered strengthening your daughter's position for her future? Mademoiselle is beautiful and has a spirited disposition. She could aspire to something higher and nobler. Would it give you pleasure to appear at court, Mademoiselle?" The question was directed at Margot. He expected her to accept quickly and full of gratitude.

"Sire, my desire is to be happy," Margot responded, sidestepping the purpose of his question.

"You could be very happy in those circles."

"I doubt that."

"Really! Why?" His glance was piercing.

She immediately realized his implication. "I favor a simple life, one devoid of glamour and pretence."

"One can still belong to the inner circle without standing out. We, too, recognize modesty and strive to live by the simpler things. You have suffered for my sake, and I find myself beholden to you. You will become the wife of a high ranking officer and achieve a higher social status."

"But, Sire, my mother has already informed you that I am engaged to be married."

"Well, yes, but to an officer of lower standing."

"I trust he will achieve a measure of success in the near future."

"Are you in love with him?"

"With all my heart."

He gazed into a corner of the room, debating how to respond. "Well, that is charming, is it not? I will make a point of getting to know him and reward him for his accomplishments. What is his name?"

An inner resolve gripped Margot. "There is nothing His Majesty can do for him," she replied simply.

No one had ever suggested such a thing to him before. To imply he was unable to do anything for a young officer was unthinkable. He had raised men of ordinary standing to the ranks of marshal, count, and even duke. "Why not, Mademoiselle?" he asked imperially.

"He is not in the army, Sire," she smiled.

"In the navy, then?"

"He is not a naval officer, but rather a captain in merchant shipping."

Astonished, the emperor looked at her. "Do you mean that sea captain, Monsieur de Sainte-Marie?" he exclaimed.

"None other, Sire."

"Well, he will not become your husband!" he said in a tone devoid of recourse.

Margot looked at him calmly. "From what does His Majesty draw that conclusion?"

"I forbid it!" he said curtly.

She moved her head and rested it in her hand for support. She looked at him sideways, as though she were addressing a servant. "Then you will encounter a most reluctant subject."

"And Mademoiselle will become familiar with a very stringent emperor. I have already determined your fate. I do not want to hear any more objections. Where is this captain now?"

"He was in His Majesty's company."

"I had him removed, however. Now I will send for him."

It was clear to the women that the emperor was insanely jealous. He stood stiffly. If he had any say in the matter, it was certain the beautiful Margot wouldn't end up with a lowly sea captain.

"I will give Mademoiselle until tomorrow morning to decide if she will become a compliant subject or not. This is the only hope of removing the captain from the predicament which he has placed himself in!"

"Sire, this latest predicament will not do him any harm!" Margot replied courageously.

"Mademoiselle is behaving very boldly!" He was clearly growing angry.

"I have no reason to act otherwise. My betrothed is already in a safe place. He will find an opportunity to send me word from outside of France and arrange for me to meet him."

The emperor was speechless. No one had ever spoken to him like that before. Stunned, he finally managed to find words for a suitable reply. "It seems to me Mademoiselle is considering a stay at a convent!" he replied coldly.

"Sire," she said, "I would certainly hope each of France's loyal subjects would be able to choose for themselves whom they would marry, and not have to forfeit that right."

He threw her a damning look. "*Pah!*" he called out. "Mademoiselle, you are very beautiful, but very unwise." And with that, he left the room, failing to acknowledge either one of them. His countenance was like granite, implying he arrived at an inward resolve.

"My God, what misfortune!" Madame Richemonte cried as soon as he was gone. "We're doomed!"

"On the contrary, mother. We have won!"

"How can you say that?"

"Simple. The emperor is prepared to love a girl, poor and lowly in stature, but he would never consider loving a stupid girl. If his intent is to draw me closer, then he has certainly given up on it."

"May it be as you say, or we're finished."

"I'm not worried about us Mama," Margot assured her, "but rather for Hugo. The emperor will vent his anger on him."

"I thought he was safe!"

"Probably not anymore. Please, Mama, go and tell the baroness right away what has just occurred so she can prepare herself."

Madame Richemonte left the room and hurried to find the baroness.

❧✠☙

Löwenklau lay prostrate on the roof in front of the open airshaft, following the entire scene as it unfolded beneath him. He closed the opening after the emperor left and worked his way along the roof, searching for another shaft. He found the right one and, after removing the outlet cover, realized he had an overview of Napoleon's room.

"Send for the baroness," he heard the emperor call out to his servant.

The servant retreated from the room hastily.

Well, well, Löwenklau thought, *now he's after me!*

The emperor sat on his divan and stared into space. When the baroness entered, he lifted his head and fixed his gaze upon her. "Madame, are you a loyal subject of France?"

"I certainly hope so, Sire," she replied, ignorant as to why she had been summoned to the emperor's chambers.

"I will give you an opportunity to validate your words. How long has it been since your relative, that sea captain, has been betrothed to Mademoiselle Richemonte?"

265

She froze momentarily. *How did he find out so quickly?* she thought. "A few months," she replied carefully.

"Where did he meet her?"

"In Paris, Sire."

"Is he a man of means?"

"I believe so," she answered with confidence.

"Ah! How long has he been here?"

"Only a few days, Majesty."

"Where is he at this moment?"

"I am afraid I do not know, Sire."

"You do know!" he bellowed. He stared into her eyes as though to penetrate her innermost thoughts.

"Sire, it is the truth," she replied steadily.

"You have no clue?"

"I can only surmise that he fled across the border as a result of the disagreement between His Majesty and himself, and the likely repercussions facing him."

"So, he is not on the estate then?"

"No. I would be aware of it if he was."

"I certainly hope so, because I intend to conduct a search of the estate. Is there anything you wish to convey to me?"

"No, Sire."

"Then you may leave."

As she left the room, the emperor didn't waste any time. He reached for the bell to summon the servant. "Get me General Drouet," he ordered.

Drouet came within two minutes of being summoned.

"Do you recall our conversation about the sea captain during our supper meal?" Napoleon asked.

"Of course, Sire."

"I want him captured. Please arrange for a search of the estate at once. If you cannot locate him here, then send out armed riders to search the immediate area. He must be in the vicinity." Although he dismissed Drouet, the general remained. "Is there something else, General?" inquired Napoleon.

"The captured highwayman just arrived," the man said.

"Excellent. We will interrogate him soon enough. Is that it?"

"I have news of the enemy, Sire."

"Ah!" exclaimed Napoleon with interest. "From which one? English or Prussian?"

"From both, Sire."

"Who brought the news?"

"Captain Richemonte, my best vanguard."

"Richemonte?" the emperor asked, mulling the name over in his head. "Is he per chance related to the family currently staying with the baroness?"

"Possibly," Drouet allowed, "although I am not certain."

"Where is this Captain Richemonte?"

"In my study."

"Instruct him to report immediately. Once you have carried out my previous order, have Groucy and Ney report to me!"

The general departed. After a short interval, the servant announced Captain Richemonte and led the newcomer into Napoleon's drawing room. The Corsican scrutinized his appearance closely, but couldn't find a resemblance between the captain and Margot.

"Where were you born, Captain?"

"In Paris, Sire."

"Where did you last reside?"

"Also in Paris."

"Were you in the army?"

"No, Sire."

"Why not?"

"I only wanted to serve my emperor, not the appointed foreign king."

Napoleon allowed himself a satisfied smirk. "That is commendable, Captain. We will see to it that such loyalty is rewarded. Do you have any relatives?"

Richemonte took notice of the emperor's deliberate line of inquiry. "Yes, Sire. I have a mother and a sister."

"Really? What is your sister's name?"

"Margot, Sire."

Napoleon nodded, inwardly satisfied. "I do not see the resemblance."

"She is my step-sister, Majesty."

"Really, how odd! Where would they both be now?"

"Here at Jeannette, I believe." It was the only suitable answer. Richemonte surmised that Napoleon had seen his sister earlier that day and had some peculiar reason for this line of questioning.

"Did you come here to report to Drouet, Captain?"

"Quite so, Sire."

"What news do you have?"

"News from Lüttich, Namur, and Brussels."

"When did you arrive?"

"About fifteen minutes ago."

"Have you spoken to your mother and sister, Captain?"

"No, Sire."

"Why not?"

"I have not had the opportunity," Richemonte said. "Actually, our relationship is strained and we are not on speaking terms."

The emperor took notice. "Was there a disagreement?"

"Yes, Sire. I am ashamed of their loyalty toward our country."

"Are you implying they are disloyal?" asked Napoleon quickly. "Explain yourself!"

"My sister is engaged to a Prussian officer."

Napoleon quickly rose from the divan and approached Richemonte. "You must be mistaken, Captain. It would seem you have been misinformed."

"Sire, I am convinced I speak the truth!" the captain attested.

"Your sister is betrothed to a sea captain in the merchant marine, based at Marseilles."

"That certainly is news to me, Sire."

"His name is Sainte-Marie and he is a relative of the baroness of this estate."

Richemonte could hardly hide his surprise at the emperor's information. "I was not aware of that either, Majesty."

"Perhaps because you are out of sorts with the ladies?"

"I have only been gone a short time, though I have maintained a sort of surveillance on them."

"Remarkable! What is the Prussian officer's name and rank?"

"Hugo von Löwenklau, lieutenant first grade with the Zieten Hussars."

"Are you personally acquainted with him?"

"Yes, Sire. Actually, he has special standing with Field Marshal von Blücher."

Napoleon narrowed his eyes dangerously. "Please, Captain, humor me and describe his physical appearance."

"He is fair, tall in stature, and has a muscular upper torso. He has blond hair and a well-trimmed moustache, blue eyes, a set of good teeth, and a small but distinctive birthmark on his right cheek."

Napoleon involuntarily stepped forward. "Are you absolutely certain of your description?" he exclaimed. "Could there be a mistake?"

"I am absolutely certain, Majesty."

"Well, well, not only have they dared to deceive me, but they willfully plotted behind my back. This so-called sea captain is none other than the previously mentioned Prussian officer, a favorite of Field Marshal Blücher. It seems obvious now that he came here to spy on us. We must do everything to capture him—and hang him! But first, I have another matter to deal with. Wait outside! I must see Drouet, but I will return shortly."

Löwenklau, who had followed the conversation word for word, became more and more alarmed as it progressed. The situation had escalated to the point that it could result in fatal consequences, not just for him, but for all concerned. He rushed down from the roof via the secret staircase to warn his loved ones. There was no time to lose. He had to speak to Margot.

CHAPTER TWENTY-TWO
The Relay Commander

The baroness left the emperor's room and immediately went to warn her relatives. She met Madame Richemonte outside Margot's room and persuaded her to step inside.

"I have to warn you, cousin," she began. "I just spoke to the emperor."

"That must mean unwelcome news," said Madame Richemonte.

"It's not as bad as it seems. The emperor has ordered a search of the estate for the 'missing' sea captain."

Madame looked horrified. "Dear God!" she exclaimed. "Will they find him?"

"Not likely."

"Where's he hiding?"

"Closer than you think."

"Really? Where could that be?"

"Here, Madame!" But it wasn't the baroness who had spoken, but rather Löwenklau himself, who was at that moment walking through the connecting door.

"Hugo!" cried Margot, relieved. "Were you next door this whole time?"

"Yes," he said. "For God's sake, we're all in danger!"

"We just heard. The baroness was about to explain."

"She can dispense with it. I just learned Captain Richemonte is here on the estate."

The mother and daughter reacted in perfect unison. "Albin, here?" they asked.

"Yes," he said. "He just arrived. I saw him for myself."

"Dear God, we've been found out! How did he learn of our whereabouts?"

"Through an employee of the bank, where Mama receives her money," Löwenklau said.

Margot's face fell. "Ah, we hadn't considered that possibility. Could you have been misinformed?"

"No," Hugo replied. "The captain was with the emperor just a few minutes ago and told him your betrothed is not the former French sea captain but an officer in the Prussian army."

"We're doomed!" Madame Richemonte wailed.

"Not yet!" Löwenklau said. "The captain was obliging enough to furnish the emperor with my physical description, right down to the small mole on my cheek. We may still have a way out. If you're questioned by the authority, just inform them that the engagement to Löwenklau was postponed and he has since been replaced by Captain Sainte-Marie."

"It's our only recourse," affirmed the baroness. "My servants are loyal to me. I will advise them right away, should they be questioned about Captain Sainte-Marie's visit."

"Then they'll need to be informed of my outward appearance," added Löwenklau.

"Naturally! I'll see to it. Where is the emperor?"

"He rushed to see Drouet, no doubt to expedite the search."

"Dear God," Margot exclaimed, "if they should find you!"

The baroness placed a comforting hand on the girl's shoulder. "They won't find him."

"I'm afraid the possibility still exists, though," said Löwenklau.

"How come?"

"No doubt they'll also search this bedroom and discover the connecting door to my room, which will lead them to the staircase and the way up to the roof. Then—"

"They will not get that far," the baroness interrupted. "They wouldn't dare enter the private chamber of a sick woman."

"And why not?" the lieutenant asked. "The emperor has already been in here, and didn't show you much courtesy. They still hope to catch me with my bride, which makes this room one of their most likely targets."

"All's not lost yet," she reminded him. "Please, go to your room and use the bell to alert Florian. Simply inform him that you wish to remove the stairs. That way, you'll remain undetected. But hurry! I already hear commotion outside."

Löwenklau left them and rang down to the stable. True to his word, Florian appeared shortly.

"You called for me, Monsieur?"

"Yes. You'll have to remove the stairs!"

"*Zounds!* How come?"

"Napoleon just learned that not only am I the infuriating Captain Sainte-Marie, but also the much sought after Prussian lieutenant. He ordered his troops to conduct a thorough house search."

"And you think they'll come in here as well?"

"I'm convinced of it."

"Fine. I'll remove the stairs."

"Is that a difficult job?"

"Not really. I just have to remove two bolts."

"What will you do with the steps?"

He pointed back down toward the stables. "I'll conceal them in the stables, near the dung trough."

"But won't they be able to discover the metal covering, even after the stairs have been removed?"

"No. Didn't you notice the cover plate is the same color as the ceiling?"

Löwenklau looked up and marveled that he'd missed that detail. "No, I hadn't. It's dark up there. Florian, we've got no time to lose."

"Then climb to the roof!"

"And should I stay up there?"

"Yes," Florian said. "Climb up and close the cover from above. You can't come down again until the danger of discovery has passed. I'll come back as soon as I'm able to keep you informed."

❧✠☙

While Löwenklau was concerned with concealing himself, Captain Riche-monte was waiting in the drawing room.

"The highwayman has just been sentenced and is scheduled to hang," said Napoleon upon returning to his quarters. "Now, let us deal with this German spy. The search has commenced, and he will not elude us if he is still on the estate. Would you recognize him, Captain?"

"Immediately," Richemonte said. "I also know of a second man who can readily identify him."

"Who?"

"Baron de Reillac."

"Is the baron here at Jeannette?"

"No, Sire. He is currently at Sedan."

"Perhaps he can be useful here. How is it possible that this Löwenklau, a Prussian officer, became acquainted with your sister?"

"I do not know, Majesty."

"Who gave the consent and blessing to the engagement?"

"My stepmother."

"Even though he is of German descent?"

"She also comes from a German lineage, Sire."

Napoleon was taken aback. "Really! You should have been more careful. Was there not a single Frenchman who could have captured your sister's heart?"

The captain realized there was something personal for Napoleon in all this business with his sister. Suspecting he could use this information to his own advantage, he began plotting ways to avenge himself on Löwenklau.

"This Hussar officer hindered one of my better plans, Majesty," Richemonte hinted.

"What kind of a plan?"

"Several years ago, when my father lay on his deathbed, he had decided Margot should become engaged to Baron de Reillac," Richemonte began, twisting the truth to serve his purposes.

"Baron de Reillac? You mean my supplier of military goods?"

"Yes, Sire."

"Was he able to win her approval?"

"Unfortunately, no."

A slow, knowing smile spread across the emperor's face. It revealed a measure of happiness, a hint of malicious enjoyment over another's misfortune. He stared at the floor for a moment and contemplated. "Did the baron abandon his plan?" he asked.

"No, my mother and sister disappeared. The baron not only helped me to find their trail, but I believe he is still bent on carrying out his plan."

"I have to admit he has good taste. Your sister would be an asset to him in social circles. I was prepared to open a way for her, but she declined my offer."

In that instant, it struck the captain that Napoleon was in love with Margot. "Heavens, how could that be?" a shocked Richemonte exclaimed with indignation. "To scuttle such an offer? If His Majesty would entrust me with this problem, I am certain I could bend my sister's will to reason."

"You would encounter a very energetic resistance, Captain."

"But with the full support of the emperor, I would not worry about a small roadblock."

"I am afraid you would also run into another barrier—her mother."

"I always thought my mother was knowledgeable enough in life to grasp what an advantage it would be to find favor with the emperor."

Napoleon laughed derisively. "We will have to give it some thought. First, we must see if we can capture that Prussian spy. It seems to me that Baron de Reillac is no longer in his prime to be courting a young lady."

"He is about fifty years old, Sire."

"Is he passionate about her?"

"Any time there is a mention of Margot, he carries on like a schoolboy."

"Ah, that surprises me. I thought his main motive in marrying Margot might be to show her off at social events and further the lineage of his house." Napoleon laughed to himself at its implication, knowing he had recently conferred nobility on Reillac. There hadn't been enough time for the baron to advance in his ambitions.

"Possibly, Sire."

"Let us see what comes of it. Have you given your consent to him?"

"Yes, some time ago."

"Will you see him shortly?"

"Yes, tomorrow," Richemonte said, "when I travel to Sedan."

"Then I will leave this in your capable hands."

The captain bowed before him. "Sire," he said, "my life belongs to the emperor."

"I am convinced of it... but you know, Captain, there are matters which are not openly discussed..."

Richemonte bowed again.

"Ones that are carried out without instruction..." the emperor continued, purposely flirting with indecision.

Richemonte's answer was another bow.

"I will say this much," Napoleon went on. "I am considered to be the guardian of all orphans."

"A bonus for one who holds the crown, Sire."

"Your sister is an orphan."

"Unfortunately, a rather independent orphan," Richemonte said.

The emperor ignored the remark. "It should be clear to you that I do not intend to abuse my authority in such matters. A lady might request certain considerations..."

"But it has its limits, Sire."

"I see that you understand me. This line can only be crossed under special circumstances, and only then in such a way as to mitigate our involvement. I will leave the details to your resourcefulness."

"I will endeavor to find the appropriate means, Majesty."

"Good," Napoleon said. "I think we understand each other. Please inform Baron de Reillac that I am inclined to consider him as the betrothed of your sister."

"I will see to it he receives the happy news tomorrow, Sire."

"However, I have one qualifier. I forbid him to approach her personally until I have granted him permission. Understood?"

"He will obey your wishes, even though compliance will be difficult."

"This is my will, Captain!"

"Majesty, I must inform you it will be difficult to carry it out."

"How come?"

The captain paused for a moment, then decided to stick with the truth. "Because I am not in good standing with my sister, and I must attend to other duties—"

"*Pah!*" interrupted the emperor. "I will reassign your other duties, arranging it so you can be in close proximity to your sister!"

"In that case, I am completely at your disposal, Sire, and will see to it that your instructions are carried out."

"I am counting on you. Shortly, my headquarters will be moved from Jeannette, but I will arrange for a contingent to remain here."

Richemonte made another deep bow, anticipating a favorable outcome.

"The best way to do that is to appoint you as relay commander.[22.1] You will assume temporary command of Jeannette," continued the emperor, "and I will advise General Drouet accordingly. Other than the usual military notifications, you will send me daily reports in regards to your sister. If something out of the ordinary should occur, inform me right away through a courier."

"Majesty, I am honored to accept this assignment, but I must state that, although I am familiar with the general responsibility, I would like you to clarify it."

"The edict is as follows: your sister and mother are to be placed in open custody, naturally in a discreet way. Both ladies are to remain at the estate and may not leave without my express permission."

Just then, the door opened and one of the servants admitted Drouet.

"Has he been captured?" Napoleon asked him.

"Unfortunately, not yet, Sire."

The emperor frowned disapprovingly. "I assumed your interruption indicated your success in capturing our fugitive."

"We have not found a trace."

"Then you conducted a poor search!"

"We have not yet searched the dwelling places of the ladies."

"Which ladies are you referring to?"

"The baroness and the Richemonte women."

"Well, search there as well!"

"Should we not take Mademoiselle's injury into account?"

Napoleon stared ahead while he considered. "I will allow it," he replied at last. "She will be spared the discomfort of having her belongings and rooms searched by a stranger. However," he continued, turning to regard Richemonte, "the captain will conduct a search."

Richemonte, who had been looking forward to causing the ladies a little discomfort, secretly believed this was the emperor's retribution for having been spurned.

"Captain," Bonaparte continued, "you will proceed directly to your relative's private chambers and conduct a thorough search."

Richemonte bowed again. "Permit me to say that all of our careful and diligent searching may not yield the desired result," he replied. "The German spy may still be hiding on the estate. No doubt Jeannette has many places where a spy could conceal himself. To be absolutely certain, we need to consult with someone who is well-acquainted with the layout of the estate."

"I doubt we could find someone who would be willing to expose the baroness," said Drouet.

"I know of one, General," Richemonte revealed.

"Who would that be?" asked Drouet.

"The old coachman, Florian."

"But I find him to be very loyal to them."

"He only appears to be, General. I have proof that he will be more forth-coming than the baroness or her son."

"Yes. The young baron strikes me as a little frivolous," said Napoleon.

The captain nodded in agreement. "True. He does come across as being somewhat fickle."

"Such people are weak and can easily be intimidated," the emperor observed. "If you come across a little heavy-handed, it might scare him into admitting the truth. General, I have promoted the captain to relay commander here at Jeannette. He will attend to the baroness's chamber, and also her son's quarters, informing them that they are under house arrest. The same goes for Mademoiselle and Madame Richemonte."

"But, Your Majesty, such strong measures—"

"Are well-founded," interrupted Napoleon. "Not only do they admit a Prussian spy to the estate, but they conceal him as well. This is an act of treason and worthy of an even more severe treatment than normal in war time. The law dictates death as a fitting punishment. Now, call for the coachman whom you spoke of earlier."

The instruction was meant for Richemonte, who relayed the order to a servant, who complied immediately. Within minutes, Florian entered with an air of timidity, just the way a low ranking man would behave toward a noble person. He understood the part he was to play. Napoleon didn't waste any time.

"Are you the baroness's coachman?"

"At your service, Majesty."

"Have you been in her employ for some time?"

"For many years, Sire."

"Are you satisfied?"

"Hmm," Florian murmured in consideration. He looked uncomfortable as he fumbled with his cap. "There are some things that have been lacking, Sire," he replied after a short pause.

"It is possible to improve your situation if you show yourself worthy."

The coachman's face beamed at the news. "Well, I have often contemplated leaving."

"Fine. Be forthright with me then, if you want to be shown favor. Tell me if you know of a certain German officer who is hidden on the estate?"

"I am not aware of one, Sire."

"Are you being truthful?"

"Of course, Sire."

"Perhaps you know him by another name?"

"He certainly would have stood out, Sire. Only relatives have visited of late."

Napoleon decided to change tactics. "Are you familiar then with an acquaintance of the baroness, a certain sea captain?"

"Yes, I know him."

"Did he come here for a visit?"

"Yes, he was here. He is also the same man who defeated the highwaymen."

"Was he here for a long time?"

"Only a few days, Sire."

"Did he spend much time with Mademoiselle Margot?"

Florian looked embarrassed for a moment. "Well, yes, come to think of it," he said with a laugh.

"What is so funny?"

"Well, Sire, they are lovers."

"Where is he now?"

"Absconded! Gone!"

"I doubt that. I believe he has concealed himself on the estate."

The coachman scoffed at the mere suggestion. "Hidden? Concealed himself? That would be the furthest thing from his mind. I know better, Sire."

"Really? How would you know of his plans?"

"Because he told me himself."

"Finally, a clue! What did he tell you?"

"That he needed to flee."

"Did he leave right away?"

"Right away, Sire."

"I find that hard to believe."

"He told me himself," Florian assured him. "We had stopped at the forest inn and he walked over to me. He told me it was not safe for him anymore and he had to get away, because..." The coachman feigned embarrassment.

"Continue!" the emperor demanded. "I command you to speak the whole truth. Why did he have to run?"

Florian continued in his slow speech, speckled with modesty. "He meant he had to leave because... er... because the emperor wanted Margot for himself, and an argument ensued over her."

"*Pah!*" exclaimed Napoleon with contempt. The coachman couldn't help but notice the man's pride.

"That is what he said," continued Florian. "He said if he came back to Jeannette, it would have been too risky, not only for him, but for the baroness and his betrothed. Then and there, he decided to head for the border."

"Where to?"

"I was supposed to notify the baroness that he was going first to Luxemburg, and then on to Cologne. He headed in the direction of Douzy."

"Is that true?"

"Why should I lie?"

"Did he say anything else?"

"Wait, yes... that he will come again."

"When?"

"When, er... when... I cannot say it."

"And why not?"

"Because His Majesty will get angry."

"I order you to tell me!" Napoleon thundered.

"He hoped to come again as soon as, well... as soon as the emperor gets thrashed by the Prussians."

A strange look came over the emperor's face, but he checked himself. "And that is all you know?"

"Almost all of it, Sire. There are two things that I almost forgot."

"And they are?"

"I was supposed to bring a thousand greetings to the young baron and the ladies, but a thousand kisses to Mademoiselle Margot."

Drouet laughed out loud. The emperor, for his part, maintained his composure. "And the second?"

"I am supposed to pay attention to all that goes on at Jeannette and report it to him later."

"Pay attention to what?"

"If the emperor spends a lot of time with Mademoiselle Margot, and if he kisses her."

"My word!" Napoleon said. "You are the outspoken one!"

"Well, yes. You can count on me," countered Florian in an attempt to puff himself up. It wasn't until afterward that he realized he had mistakenly taken the emperor's angry outburst for praise.

"Are you convinced he actually left the grounds?" Bonaparte questioned.

"Yes. I saw him leave."

"But he could have deceived you?"

"Deceived me? That would be the day. Not just anyone can get the better of old Florian!"

"I can see that," replied Napoleon sarcastically. "I think it is still possible that he did not go to Douzy, but secretly crept back and hid himself on the estate. Are there places he could use as a hideout?"

"Oh, there are many, Sire."

"Give me an example?"

"In the pigeon loft!"

"Ridiculous!"

"In the milk storage room. I have hidden there a time or two, when the baroness was displeased with me."

"Fine, fine!" called out Napoleon, pointing to the door. "You may leave now!"

Florian walked to the door and turned at the last moment. "Your Majesty," he said, "please do not forget me if there is an opening for employment." With that, he was gone.

The emperor shrugged his shoulders pitifully and turned to face Richemonte. "Well, you have recommended a most clever diplomat. Though he is of limited intelligence, I find his forthrightness believable."

If the emperor had had any idea the man he sought so desperately was watching through the airshaft at that very moment and was close at hand, he would have spoken very differently.

"It is still possible the Prussian spy is hiding on the premises," he continued. "The secret that envelops him must be resolved. We have to determine if the sea captain and the Hussar lieutenant are one and the same. I leave the entire matter in your capable hands, Captain. You may leave."

"I am not in uniform, General," replied Richemonte, turning toward Drouet. "May I request a guard of soldiers to accompany me, giving credence to my new authority?"

The general nodded. "Take as many as you deem necessary, Captain."

Richemonte turned and left the room jubilantly. For the first time in a long while, he saw himself as the master of his own destiny. His mother and sister had been placed in his charge and, should Margot become engaged to the emperor, soon all his worries would be over. Napoleon had given him a formidable weapon.

CHAPTER TWENTY-THREE
Richemonte Makes an Impression

Filled with self-importance, Captain Richemonte walked down the hall. The emperor's command had been explicit, in that Reillac was not to approach Margot. Reillac would have to concede that Richemonte was now under the protection of the emperor, and with this order, his hold on Richemonte waned considerably.

The captain descended the stairs and stepped into the guardroom, where he selected a few soldiers to accompany him. He made a few inquiries pertaining to the people he wanted to question. Once he decided the young baron should become the first victim of his newfound authority, he entered the man's room without bothering to knock.

"Monsieur, do you know me?" he asked Roman de Sainte-Marie.

"No," Roman replied curtly, surprised at the lack of formality used by the newcomer.

"I am Captain Richemonte, son and brother to the two ladies who are currently housed at this estate." He had hoped to surprise, perhaps even startle, the young baron.

His only reward was a look of distaste. "What do you want?"

"I come on behalf of the emperor. You are now in my custody!"

Roman seemed to have expected as much. "Your prisoner," he replied evenly. "Might I inquire as to the reason?"

"You are suspected of being implicated in matters of treason against the state. You are harboring a spy."

Roman shrugged his shoulders indifferently. "Do you really expect to find him here?"

"We will find him soon enough. If not in your rooms, then elsewhere on the estate. I might advise you that it is in your best interest to make a full confession."

"Do I also have to listen to your insults?" Roman asked curtly.

"I am leaving a guard at your door. He has been ordered to shoot, should you attempt to leave without permission."

"I have no intention of fleeing. Now, get out!"

Richemonte was disappointed, not appearing to have had the slightest influence on the young man. In fact, it irritated him. Since he had so little success with Roman, he reasoned he would have more success prying information from the man's unsuspecting mother.

The baroness had, of course, been advised of his planned visit, and yet managed to act as though she was ignorant of it. Without asking to be announced, he entered her drawing room. She had prepared herself ahead of time, intending to play her role well.

"Monsieur, it seems you have come to the wrong door. No doubt you are looking for one of my servants," said the baroness.

Taken aback, Richemonte smiled awkwardly at her rebuff. "Are you the Baroness de Sainte-Marie?"

"Of course."

"Well, it is you that I wish to see. I have come to the right place."

"Nevertheless, I'm disappointed you didn't consult first with my servant. I make a habit of only admitting those persons who can demonstrate by their conduct that they understand the rules of proper etiquette. This little meeting has come to an end, before it has even started." She turned to leave and was poised to walk into the adjoining room.

"Hold it!" he shouted at her. "You are staying." His tone was harsh and imperious.

She stopped momentarily and cast him a haughty look before replying. "What do you think you're doing? Are you aware that you're addressing the lady of this estate?"

"You had that position until a few moments ago."

"Really!" This one word invoked the entire scale of her vocal displeasure. It came out in a contemptuous tone, bordering on astonishment. "*Who* are you?" she asked coldly.

"My name is well known. I am a captain of the emperor's guard. My name is Richemonte."

"Richemonte? A captain?" she contemplated, shaking her head. "I have never heard of you."

"Then let me refresh your memory, Madame. Apparently there are two ladies residing here as your guests, also by the name of Richemonte."

"Yes, they are indeed. And your point?"

"I am the son of one, and the brother of the other."

The baroness feigned an expression of deep thought. "I recall Madame Richemonte once mentioning her stepson," she replied. "However, because of circumstances, their relationship has been strained to the point where his presence is completely unwelcome. No wonder, considering how he barges into a room unannounced and fails to abide by any semblance of decency."

"And yet you will have to put up with my presence," he said, emphasizing each word carefully. "You cannot do a single thing about it."

"Are you suggesting my authority doesn't extend to you?"

"That is exactly what I mean. I have come to your suite, acting on the emperor's explicit orders."

"Really? Perhaps you have accidentally exchanged your title of captain for that of a bottle washer. Your ill-mannered visit certainly lends some credence to the notion."

She realized immediately that she might have gone a little too far. He gritted his teeth angrily, suppressing his mounting rage in the hope of achieving his goal and soliciting some valuable information.

"I stand here as the empowered servant of the emperor," he continued, "and I implore you to treat me with more respect. To treat me otherwise would place your freedom in jeopardy."

"If you're here on the emperor's behalf, where's your authority?"

"I do not need a proclamation. My authority stands at your door." He swung the door open to reveal the soldiers.

"That should suffice," agreed the baroness. "I'm most curious to find out under what circumstances I have become the recipient of an honor guard."

"You are mistaken, Madame, if you consider them an honor guard. They are in place to ensure you will not leave without permission."

"Are you suggesting I'm a prisoner?"

"Yes," Richemonte said. "Without a doubt, Madame."

The look on her face was one of complete astonishment. "And what is the reason for such stringent measures?"

"The underlying cause is one of treason."

"Surely you're joking! Which country have I committed this treason against?"

"France!"

"Against France? You're making this up!" she said, breaking into a good-natured laugh.

Richemonte's eyebrows rose. "There is nothing to laugh about," he answered solemnly. "You are harboring an enemy of the state, an offense that is punishable by death."

"An enemy of the state? Who could that be?"

"A certain Hussar lieutenant who goes by the name of Löwenklau."

"At the risk of repeating myself," she said, "I must say this invention of yours is rather tasteless."

"*Pah!* This 'invention,' as you call it, could cost you your head. Where are you hiding him?"

"Your question is most disrespectful!"

"If you fail to give me an answer, I will be forced to conduct a search for him."

"Go ahead and search!"

"Well then, show me your rooms!"

She glared at him witheringly. "Pardon me? Surely you do not expect me to act the servant to a mere captain. Search for yourself!"

"Be careful, baroness. Your attitude may lead to consequences not at all in your favor. I am not used to that tone of voice, Madame." He paused, then turned to leave. "I will conduct the search now."

"And find nothing!" she added proudly.

"Do you expect me to believe this so-called deliverer of the emperor is a sea captain, and also your relative?"

"What you choose to believe or disbelieve is entirely inconsequential to me. My nephew did indeed save the emperor from certain death. Whatever gratitude befits him is not my concern, but that of the emperor!"

Richemonte moved through her apartment, going through each nook and cranny himself with the baroness firmly in tow. He thoroughly searched the lady's own quarters for any sign of the wanted man, but of course came up empty-handed.

"I should imagine it would be unthinkable for a Hussar lieutenant to conceal himself in the chambers of an older lady," he said spitefully. "Perhaps I'll find him with a younger one."

The baroness simply shrugged her shoulders, choosing not to dignify the taunt with a response.

"My impromptu visit has come to an end," remarked Richemonte.

"I'm glad to hear it!" she said.

"But I am not yet finished with you, Baroness," he continued in a superior tone. "I remind you that you are my prisoner."

"Are those His Majesty's instructions?"

"Of course."

"I find that such measures reflect rather poorly on His Majesty's hospitality."

"Well, it is your own fault. I forbid you to leave your room. I am leaving a sentry behind, with orders to shoot you should you decide to disobey my instructions."

"I'll comply," she said, "and retain my right to complain to a higher authority. Now, you may go."

"With great pleasure, Madame. A loyal officer takes no pleasure in the company of traitors."

The captain left, ordering one of the soldiers to remain with her. He then proceeded with the rest of the men to the rooms occupied by Madame Richemonte and her daughter. But this visit, too, was expected.

❧✠❧

After being dismissed by the emperor, Florian quickly dashed to the stable, removing the staircase leading to the roof, and went to work on removing the bottom half that rose up from the feed trough. He removed the stairs and brought hay and compost, spreading it about.

He left the top half of the stable ladder in place.

Now then, he thought to himself, *we'll soon find out how unexpectedly wrong a search up there can go, particularly if someone decides to stick his nose where it doesn't belong.* He closed the trough and remained on his guard.

❧✠☙

When he arrived, Richemonte found his stepmother's room empty. Instead he found her next door with her daughter when he made his sudden, unannounced entrance.

"Good evening, Mama," he greeted them with sarcasm. "A big surprise, isn't it?"

He had expected to see them upset and stricken, but to his astonishment could only find revulsion on their faces.

"What do you want?" his stepmother asked. Margot didn't even bother to acknowledge him, turning to face the wall instead, having already decided not to give him the satisfaction of answering his questions.

"Stop playing games!" Madame persisted. "Now, let me ask you again. What do you want?"

"Why, to see and greet you both!" He took a seat in close proximity to the ladies, giving the false impression that he was in good standing with them.

"Now that you've seen us, is there anything else?"

"Foremost, I would like to know the reason you left Paris in such a hurry."

"Very simply, it no longer suited us to stay."

"That's news to me! I thought you enjoyed the amenities that the capital city has to offer."

"Well, if you include attempted murder and kidnapping as a normal staple of life—"

"Of course!" he laughed. "Actually, I have no idea what you're referring to. By the way, what's the situation with the engagement of the renowned Lieutenant von Löwenklau?"

"That's Margot's affair and none of your concern."

"Evidently, since she is the one who left with him."

"Be quiet," she spat. "Your impertinence won't ingratiate you back to us. You know perfectly well the reason we left Paris."

"It was love, Mama. Love!" he said, laughing. "And it is love that brings me back to you. Love for my sibling and my mother."

Madame's face turned red with anger. "Don't you dare desecrate our view of love by your deplorable standards," she replied. "When did your heart ever respond with love?"

"Now for example, my dear Mama," he replied evenly. "My love for you drives me back to you. I came personally to warn you of a great danger, and to inform you of good fortune."

"If those are your words, I can assume the danger is good for us and your so-called good fortune a hindrance."

"You have it all wrong, Mama. I'm not here of my own accord, but at His Majesty's bidding."

"His Majesty does not have to resort to a subordinate."

"Really?" Richemonte asked. "Would a personal visit by him have been more pleasant?"

"Any visit would be considered more pleasant so long as you're not a part of it. But the matter you seem to represent has already been settled."

"How so?"

"Your question is too intrusive. We've cut our ties with you and aren't interested in your affairs. We expect you will govern yourself in like manner."

"You've certainly made things clear, but I'm speaking of different circumstances."

"And those are?"

"First, the will of the emperor."

"And second?"

"And the second, as of half an hour ago, I have been appointed relay commander of Jeannette."

"Really? And how did that occur?"

He pushed out his chest proudly. "Through the emperor's own edict," he replied.

"Don't be fooled into thinking you've been rewarded for your efforts," Madame said. "The emperor requires an instrument to do his bidding with personal matters and thinks you'll succeed where he failed. I'm afraid you'll encounter the same resistance as you did in Paris."

"Fine! I assume you're referring to my plans. Well then, let me tell you I'm man enough to admit that I have aspirations. Actually, ones that involve Margot. She's my sister and I expect she'll do her best to help me advance my career. The emperor holds her in his favor and I plan to see it also falls on me. If she resists him, I will use my brotherly influence. You can count on it!"

"I'm afraid it won't do you any good."

"You think not?" he asked. "Oh, my influence is greater and more prominent than you might think."

"You overestimate yourself! It is the emperor's duty to protect Margot."

"Of course," the captain said. "He recommended I personally address your safety."

She regarded him as though he were nothing more than a common servant. "We renounce anything that is remotely connected to you, Albin."

"I'd like to see how you plan to accomplish that, dear Mama. Are you perhaps counting on the help of a certain Löwenklau? *Pah!* He's a mere Prussian lieutenant compared to Napoleon, the mighty French emperor!"

"His throne is still on shaky ground!"

"Are you by chance hoping he'll go under?" the captain asked. "I give you my word that this simpleton, 'Marshall Forward,' will not march into Paris a second time. The campaign has already started, but the enemies of France will be mowed down. Actually, Löwenklau won't even take part in the battle. He'll be hung as a spy long before the first shot is heard."

"Ridiculous! I doubt you could bring it to pass."

"I'm telling you it's already happening. I'm here to search for him." He stopped for a moment, trying to read his mother's expressions. "Where did you hide him?"

"Who?"

"Löwenklau, Margot's Seladon."[23.1]

"Do you really think he's still here at Jeannette?"

"I know he is, and I'm going to find him. Do you really think you're smarter than I am?"

The woman shrugged dismissively. "Believe what you like."

"Fine. I'm convinced this sea captain from Marseille is none other than Löwenklau himself."

"Go and search if you're so convinced."

"Oh, I intend to. May I remind you, it would be in your best interest to deliver him to me now."

"We wouldn't do that, even if he was right here under your nose."

"Then I declare you confined to your rooms. In effect, my prisoners. I forbid you to leave without my express permission."

She laughed at him. "We find your regulations amusing!"

"Go ahead and laugh! To show you I mean business, I'll leave a guard at the door. He has orders to shoot anyone who tries to leave."

His mother coolly walked up to him, her eyes blazing. "Are you serious? Would you go that far?"

"Yes, if it comes down to it."

"Is it your desire to treat us, your relatives, as common prisoners?"

"You've forced me to!"

"God in heaven, may He punish you for your insolence. You're nothing but a coward masquerading as the emperor's servant. We'll pray that God deals

RICHEMONTE MAKES AN IMPRESSION

with your arrogance and renders you harmless. You won't escape the punishment reserved for you."

"You certainly have a flair for the dramatic, dear Mama," he said. "It was a nice performance. Too bad you weren't on stage. I doubt if your God will be able to do anything to me, though. I'm acting on behalf of the emperor, who at this moment has all the might in the world at his disposal."

Even his mother was taken aback by his heresy. "You godless heathen," she said. "God's justice will prevail."

"Leave that to me. I'll patiently wait to see who gets punished, but for now I think I'll have a little look around." He carefully searched both rooms, but to his frustration, he didn't find a faintest trace of the German officer. Just as he was about to give up, he noticed the door leading to Löwenklau's room.

"Where does this door lead?"

"I don't know," the mother replied.

"You'd like me to believe that. Don't you want to know what's behind it?"

"It was locked from the other side."

"Aha!" he proclaimed loudly. "A corner room, and you didn't think I would notice? I think I'm on the right track. They'll have to open up!" He knocked belligerently, but received no reply.

"Who's in there?" he demanded. His only response was deafening silence. He depressed the handle, and the door opened. "Well, not locked after all! You lied to me, dear mother."

He took a moment to study the open door. "Most unusual," he mused quietly, stepping into the doorway. Seeing the pitch darkness beyond, he called to one of the soldiers to fetch a lantern. When the man returned with the light, he pressed on into the room, encouraged by an intangible aroma of success.

The first things he noticed were the few pieces of furniture. As for occupants, however, he found no one. He completely missed the cover plate that blended so seamlessly into the ceiling.

"Empty!" he said through clenched teeth. Before turning back into Margot's chamber, his eyes spotted a second door. "Another room! Where could that lead?" He handed the soldier the lantern and put his hand to the door knob, turning it.

His eyes peered into the darkness, the light illuminating straw below them. "It looks like a straw floor," the captain observed. "We're situated over the stable, a perfect hiding place."

He let the lantern cast its light and discovered the small ladder, leading down to the trough. "There's a ladder here," he said to the soldier. "He must have climbed down. Quick, after him!"

With the soldier lighting the way, Richemonte climbed down the steps, counting them silently as he went. One... two... three... four... But that was all, for Florian had removed the rest. When Richemonte took his fifth downward step, his foot disappeared into the air below. Losing his balance, gravity took its hold on him.

"Dammit!" he cursed as he sailed down, trying in vain to grab onto something solid. He landed in a soft, viscous substance that oozed a strange, yet familiar, odor. *Where am I?* he asked himself. He looked up where the solider still stood waiting. "Shine the light down!" he called.

The soldier got onto his knees and held the light as far below him as possible.

"The bottom half of the ladder is missing and I fell into a manure pile," the captain said. "Tie the lantern to a belt and lower it down to me. I can't feel my way out."

The soldier obeyed, lowering the light. As Richemonte grabbed the lantern, he noticed the door leading out of the trough into the open area of the stable.

"I'm all right," he called up. "I can get out. Go back to your companions and wait until I come fetch you."

Good old Florian heard every word from nearby, where he had concealed himself into a dark corner of the stable. His hound, lying beside him, let out a low growl at the sound of the unfamiliar voice in the trough.

"Quiet!" the coachman whispered to the dog. "You'll spoil the fun, and yours too!"

Richemonte opened the door and stepped into the stable, failing to notice Florian and the large hound.

"Go," Florian whispered a second time. "Get him and make him comfortable."

Soundlessly, the dog shot toward the unsuspecting captain, knocking him over. Richemonte managed only a muffled cry for help. He didn't dare repeat it, feeling the dog's teeth at his throat.

Florian waited a moment longer to make sure his hound was master of the curious Frenchman. Satisfied that all was in order and the lantern had gone out, he quietly crept out of his corner, leaving the stable. He reached the yard through the garden without anyone realizing he had been there. He walked away, content in the knowledge that Richemonte had quite unexpectedly stopped his search and wouldn't be a hindrance for some time to come.

Chapter Twenty-Four
The Fugitives

N apoleon, unable to postpone his responsibilities, waited impatiently in his drawing room, eager to learn of good news pertaining to the search. He was occupied with General Drouet and both his marshals. An adjutant from Sedan had just arrived at Jeannette with important news and Napoleon immediately convened his war council, making preparations for deployment of his troops. Unknown to those assembled below, Löwenklau lay on the roof looking down, privy to their discussions. He became a witness to the upcoming campaign and observed Napoleon not only as the old strategist who was difficult to defeat in battle, but also as one who was knowledgeable even in the smallest details in the affairs of his subordinates.

"It is time to depart!" he commanded.

After taking a short rest, Napoleon was ready to get an early start toward Mauberge where his troops were gathering. Immediately after the war council concluded, Ney rode to Sedan to begin his preparations. Drouet and Groucy were also prepared for a quick departure. Messengers came and left throughout the night. One order followed another, with Jeannette becoming a beehive of activity. The previous day no one would have suspected that the plans being drafted at Jeannette would soon come to affect the fate of all Europe.

Despite the psychologically draining session of the war council, Napoleon's mind frequently drifted to Margot and his newly appointed staff officer, Captain Richemonte. Surprised not to have received any progress reports, he decided to call for him. A servant soon returned with the news that Captain Richemonte was nowhere to be found. A more diligent search was conducted for the absent captain, quickly informing the emperor that he was 'occupied' with a hound in the stable.

"Let me shoot the beast," one of the soldiers exclaimed, lifting his rifle.

"For God's sake, stop!" yelled a second man, one more prudent than his partner.

"Why?" asked the first. "How can we remove the dog? He won't obey our commands and I don't have any desire to tangle with him."

"What if you miss and hit the captain?" he asked, "What if the dog kills him, sensing danger. We have to find someone the dog will listen to."

A servant stepped forward out of the night, offering an explanation. "That dog belongs to the coachman, Florian."

"Go find him!" the first soldier instructed.

Within a few minutes, the clever Florian was alerted by a servant. When he approached the stable, he saw a crowd already gathering to watch the unfolding drama.

"What's going on?" he asked casually. "Someone told me my dog has cornered an intruder."

"Call off your dog!" was the curt reply.

"All in good time. We have to make sure it really is the captain, and not some vagabond."

"Look, man, why are you being so difficult?" asked the soldier who had wanted to shoot the dog. "Do you want the captain's throat ripped out?"

"Certainly not," Florian said, "but a captain wouldn't be sneaking around in my stable like a common thief."

"The dog will be shot as punishment for attacking an officer of our great emperor."

"Hold it! I'm sure my dog is only doing what he's been trained to do. Leave him to me. Don't you know he's a genuine Pyrenean mountain dog? He's strong like a bear, smart as a fox, and swift like a deer. Don't do anything foolish."

Florian took a lantern from a nearby servant and approached the group of onlookers. When the dog sensed his master's presence, he wagged his tail, keeping his fangs at the captain's throat.

"Hello Tiger, what have you caught?" Florian asked, bending down to examine the prostrate form. "Well, I'll be—it's true! Captain Richemonte! Back off, Tiger! This man is no rogue, but a capable fellow like you!"

The well-trained dog obeyed instantly and backed away from his prey. Richemonte tried to get up, still shaking from the experience. His face was ashen, the picture of a living ghost.

"Shoot the damn thing!" were his first words.

"I advise you to reconsider, Captain!" replied the coachman. "The dog is trained to respond to the smallest sign of aggression and will lunge at the threat. Monsieur, how is it you came to this part of the stable?"

"I was searching for the fugitive!"

"Down here? But I told the emperor he fled! Look at you, Captain!"

"I fell from up above, into this... this mess!"

"From where?"

"From that damned staircase above the trough."

"*Parbleu!*" Florian said. "But how did you get up there? There's only a remnant of a ladder there! Well, if they had only listened to me. Just look at your appearance, and that odor!"

A messenger arrived at that moment, interrupting them. "You are to report immediately to the emperor!" he announced to the captain.

"To the emperor?" Richemonte asked, horrified. "My God, looking like this?" He looked helpless as he examined his attire.

"Perhaps you can go to the guardhouse and quickly clean up!" the messenger suggested. "I'm sure one of the soldiers can loan you his jacket. In the meantime, I'll advise the emperor of your... er... accident, and why it's impossible for you to appear immediately."

Richemonte had no choice but to follow the advice. The curious crowd dispersed as the captain marched away, once again leaving Florian alone with his dog. He stroked his pet's thick fur lovingly.

"You've made me proud, Tiger," he commented. "He must have been scared half to death when you jumped him. With any luck it'll serve as a good reminder."

A short time later, Richemonte found himself standing in front of the emperor. Napoleon received him with his usual sarcastic smile, normally reserved for blundering subordinates. Bonaparte appraised him from head to toe.

"So, have you become a martyr on our account, Captain?" he asked mockingly.

"Evidently, Sire, but not in the religious context."

"I noticed you are not emanating a heavenly aroma. What results have your inquiries produced?"

"To this point, none I'm afraid. Unfortunately, I was detained by a minor mishap."

"Whom have you been with so far?"

"For starters, I was with Roman de Sainte-Marie."

Napoleon peered at him piercingly. "What did he say?"

"He lied to my face. I confined him to his room and left a sentry at the door."

"Good. Continue!"

"I sought out his mother and found her in her room. She too feigned ignorance of Löwenklau's whereabouts. I therefore confined her as well."

"Hmm," Napoleon murmured. "You should have consulted with me prior to making that decision. I am her guest, after all. Where did your inquiries take you next?"

"To my sister's apartment."

The emperor's face took on an animated expression. "How did you find the young lady?" he asked with interest.

"She was still confined to her bed. My mother was with her."

"What was her response to your inquiries?"

"Margot's complete silence was not unexpected."

The emperor seemed disappointed. "She certainly possesses a singular will," he mused. "The best characteristics a woman can possess are gentleness and geniality. What information did her mother give you?"

"Nothing at all. She would not admit to knowing anything about the Prussian's whereabouts. I feel certain she lied as well."

"Really? She is very proud, that woman. Could some of the blame lie with the messenger?"

"On me, Sire? Not at all!"

"Maybe your poor relationship with the ladies had something to do with it. This would make it difficult to elicit any worthwhile information."

Richemonte looked into the emperor's eyes with determination. "On my honor, Sire, I will get them to cooperate. All I have to do is to break the influence of the German perpetrator, and then my task will be easy."

"Do you still believe he is here?"

"I am a little confused on that point."

"How come?"

"If he was still here, I certainly would have noticed a measure of uneasiness from the ladies."

"And this was not the case?"

"Not in the least."

"Did you see any signs of apprehension?" Napoleon asked. "Embarrassment, turning pale, the twitching of the hand or movement of both limbs? Anything at all while they were questioned about his whereabouts?"

"No, nothing at all, Sire."

"Where did you go next?"

"There is a door that leads into a sort of storage room behind my sister's chamber. I searched it and found a staircase leading to the stable floor. It would have been an ideal hiding place, but, as His Majesty already knows, I became entangled with a guard dog."

The emperor listened to the captain's account attentively. "Your first attempt did not go according to plan," he commented. "I trust your future efforts will be more productive, Captain."

"Majesty, all my efforts are for the cause of France."

The emperor nodded. "Any other developments?"

"Yes. I just came from the guardroom and learned that General Drouet ordered the search of the entire estate buildings. This too has yielded no result."

"Then let us dispense with all these unfruitful inquiries," Napoleon said. "Your men did their best and the ladies are confined. I will leave it to you. You know my plans. In order to prepare for all possible contingencies, I think it best that we provide a means for the young lady to be married, and I mean sooner rather than later."

Richemonte bowed. "May I convey my request through a simple suggestion?" he asked.

"Are you referring to Baron de Reillac?"

"Yes, Majesty."

"Is he in love with your sister?"

"I have every reason to believe so."

The emperor placed his hands behind his back, as was his custom when considering a matter of importance, and slowly paced back and forth. After a while, he stopped in front of the captain and grasped the lapel of his coat.

"I trust I can depend on you, Captain!" he said forcefully.

"Implicitly, Your Majesty."

"Will you be able to accomplish your task, knowing you may only be able to exercise my authority if it is absolutely necessary?"

"Of course, Sire."

"Then I can tell you that your sister will become Reillac's wife in the course of the next few days," Napoleon revealed.

"I am at your service, Majesty, although I am convinced I will face a formidable obstacle."

"From which side?"

"First, from my sister."

"You will overcome it, since you are her brother. Anything else?"

"Also from the... authority," replied Richemonte haltingly.

Napoleon's brow furrowed. "I am the authority!" he said with conviction.

"I am convinced of it, Sire, but the outcome hinges on my sister's consent. I fear she will be vocal and not very cooperative."

"Then wait!" The emperor walked to his desk, produced a sheet of paper, and started to write. After a short interval, he handed the document to the captain. "Read this!"

Richemonte obeyed. He had barely glanced at its contents when his face began to shine with malevolence.

"Is that sufficient enough?" asked Napoleon.

"I have no doubt this order will be carried out to your complete satisfaction, Sire."

"I am sure of it. Anything else?"

"Only that I retain the favor of my emperor."

"That is entirely up to you," Napoleon said. "I know how to reward those who serve me well. The solution to your task will put a strain on your resources. I will give the order to furnish you with the necessary means. I expect to see you prior to my departure."

"May I take a ride to Sedan tomorrow and inform Baron de Reillac, Sire?"

"If you feel it is appropriate. But make sure all my instructions are carried out in your absence."

The emperor sat back down again at his desk while Richemonte took his leave with a bow, almost certain of his victory. He was in possession of an edict for which there was no recourse, one which all authorities would have to comply with and that the existing law was powerless to change.

Not a single word of the exchange escaped Löwenklau from his rooftop hiding place. He waited for a moment. When he realized the emperor was about to lie down, he quietly got up and stretched his cramped muscles. He nearly called out in surprise when he spotted a dark figure close to him.

"Psst," whispered the dark form. "Don't be alarmed!"

Löwenklau squinted his eyes in the blackness ahead. Finally, recognizing the form, he relaxed. "Ah! It's you, my good Florian. I thought you had removed the staircase."

"Yes, it's still absent and safely tucked away. Didn't I tell you I know of another access to the roof?"

"What luck that they didn't think of using it to climb up here for a look around," the lieutenant said wryly.

"Yes, my thoughts exactly. They somehow overlooked it. However, I have the key in my safe keeping."

"I would have been doomed without you."

"Not quite, my dear lieutenant. I was on my guard and had the means at my disposal to help you."

"What means?"

"Right here," Florian said as he stepped back to reveal a long narrow object. Löwenklau recognized it immediately, even in the dim light, as a ladder. "With the aid of this ladder, you could have climbed back into your room. Now, we still have to tread carefully. The emperor is stubborn and sometimes can be brutal in his dogged determination. Take, for instance, the condemned highwayman. His interrogation was swift and justice was meted out immediately. He's dangling over there, at the edge of the forest!"

"Brrrr!" Löwenklau shuddered.

"Yes, brrrr! By the way, have you been making good use of the ventilation shafts?"

"Yes, and I've been rewarded handsomely."

"Is it information you can use?"

Löwenklau nodded. "Yes, but I need to speak to Mademoiselle Margot and her mother. Should I risk it?"

"There's a guard posted outside her door."

"Right, but not in her room."

"If you carry on a quiet conversation, it should be fine. Actually, I could make my way down and get the guard involved in a bit of small talk. Tell me, are you planning to stay longer?"

"Unfortunately, I can't. I have to leave right away."

"You mean during the night?"

"Yes, tonight."

"That's a dangerous undertaking!"

"How come?"

"Drouet conducted a search and even sent riders out after you."

"I see, but that changes nothing. Everything depends on me getting through the lines and reporting my findings to Blücher."

"The necessity of the situation seems to speak for itself."

The lieutenant looked down at his clothes. "If I could only change my clothing!"

"Why not?" Florian asked. "I've got an idea."

"Well?"

"You know what attire would help the most? Simply dress yourself in a French officer's uniform."

"That's an excellent idea," he agreed. "But where could we procure one?"

"My specialty. We'll steal it!"

"Florian! Why steal it?"

"We pilfer it. How else would we obtain one? Were you considering making a formal visit to one of the generals and asking to borrow one?"

Löwenklau smiled at the suggestion. "You're right, but we'll have to choose one that's close to my size."

"I know of one. Its bearer just arrived tonight."

"Florian, explain yourself."

"If it suits you, you can ride dressed as a major."

"Of course!"

"You see, the adjutant who arrived earlier is a dragoon major. He retired to his room immediately after his report to the war council. He snores like a bear and won't wake up for some time. I'll sneak in and appropriate the whole uniform."

"What if he should wake up?"

Florian considered that for a moment, then snapped his fingers. "I'll tell him I was sent to clean it."

"Good, that will have to do. What about a horse?"

"I'll select one, and not an old nag either."

"Fine," Löwenklau said. "Now for the main thing. Margot has to come along, and her mother as well."

The coachman looked at him in disbelief. "Heavens!"

"Yes, Florian, it's absolutely necessary."

"May I ask why?"

"The emperor plans to marry her off, and to none other than Reillac."

"Reillac can go to hell! Mademoiselle Margot will never give her consent."

"They'll force her. Richemonte was given the emperor's absolute authority, even in writing."

"You're right, then. The ladies have to leave tonight. Can they ride?"

"Yes. Margot has told me she's comfortable in the saddle and Madame Richemonte used to ride often with her late husband."

"It's quite different for a lady to ride like a soldier or a servant, though," Florian pointed out.

Löwenklau nodded as the coachman's plan began to clarify itself. "Ah! Were you thinking the ladies should...?"

"Naturally! They have to be disguised to appear as your servants."

"Then we'll try to accommodate them in an unfamiliar saddle. What about their garments?"

"I'll pilfer those, too!"

"Florian, Florian! You're a downright scoundrel."

"I would steal Notre Dame Cathedral and drag it from Paris to Siberia out of my concern for you and Mademoiselle."

The lieutenant looked into his eyes and could tell he wasn't joking. "What about the horses?"

"I'll arrange for two trustworthy and quick-footed rides. How far do you expect to go?"

"I have to go to Lüttich or Namur."

"But the ladies won't hold out that long."

"I know," Löwenklau said. "The way is too far for them."

"Worst of all, the road is swarming with military activity. Sooner or later, they'll be discovered for who they are."

"I could take some back roads and hold to the forest trails, but that would take up too much time. I need to reach Blücher in time."

"What can we do?" asked the coachman thoughtfully. "Hmm, I have an idea that could work, but it all depends on your agreement."

"Explain it to me."

"I have a relative in Gedinne, a true and honest soul. He's old and lives by himself in a small cottage near the forest. He won't betray us."

"Are you suggesting we leave the ladies with him?"

"Yes. They should be fine. In fact, they could even pretend to be relatives on a visit."

"Do you trust him that much?"

"I'll vouch for him. He was born in Holland and despises the current regime."

Löwenklau wasn't convinced by the risky proposal. "But to leave the ladies all alone with him, and in a strange place! Overtones of the war could spread even to that area."

"It's even better if they do."

"Pardon me?"

"The Prussians are assured of a victory. When they occupy the area, our ladies will feel safe by their presence. If you like, I'll stay with them to make you more at ease."

"Will you get leave from the baroness?"

"I'm sure of it, but I don't plan on letting her or the young baron know."

"Why not?"

"I think it's best if they don't know about it. This way, they won't have to answer for us or shoulder any of the blame for our sudden departure."

"That's true." Löwenklau started moving toward the roof access. "I'm going down to speak with Margot. It remains to be seen if she's well enough to ride."

"Necessity breaks steel![24.1] I hope it works out."

"How long is the ride to Gedinne?"

"About five hours, but I don't know how well the ladies will hold up, especially if we're forced to use side roads. We need to go through Sedan and Bouillon, then turn into the mountains. You can backtrack later and regain the main road."

"Good," the lieutenant said. "Your idea is a good one. Our main objective is to ensure the ladies' removal from the captain's domain. Is this Gedinne a secluded place?"

"It's out of the way. My relative has a guestroom on the upper floor. The ladies can live there without fear of detection." He paused for a moment, taking a deep breath. "Now, I'll have to assume the role of thief again. Take the ladder, Monsieur, and pay Mademoiselle a visit." Quietly, Florian departed.

Löwenklau opened the metal covering to gain access to his room again. He lowered the ladder into the house and climbed down. Once at the bottom, he crept to the connecting door to Margot's room and listened. He could make out faint whispers, but couldn't distinguish any specific words.

After some time had passed, he felt reasonably safe in assuming no third parties were present. He knocked gingerly and heard the whispers subside at the quiet sound. He depressed the handle and cautiously opened the door a fraction of an inch. Margot was resting on her bed, her mother sitting by her side. No one else was in the room.

"Don't make any noise," he whispered, warning them. He opened the door fully and stepped in.

Margot's pale cheeks brightened instantly at the sight of her betrothed. "Hugo!" she called out in a whisper as she stretched her arms out to him.

He walked up to her and she wrapped her arms around his neck, pulling him close to her so his cheek rested on her bosom.

"Dear God, you risk too much!" her mother said softly, trying to maintain her composure. "There's a sentry outside the door."

"I know. Has he come in yet?"

"No, but he could at any moment."

"Well, let's make it a bit more difficult." Hugo freed himself from Margot's embrace, tiptoed to the door, and quietly slid the bolt into the doorpost.

"If they discover the door has been locked, they'll become suspicious."

"No harm done, Mama," the lieutenant said. "I'll be gone before they get curious."

"Where will you go?" asked Margot.

"Back on the roof."

"Are you safe up there, my Hugo?"

"Completely. Florian watches over me," he explained. "Tell me, my love, how are you?"

"I was quite weak, but I've regained some strength," she said with a smile.

"Are you in pain?"

"I don't feel the injury any more. I'm more concerned for you than anything else."

"For me? How come?"

"Well, you've faced all sorts of insults and animosity on my account. You were so strong, brave and, daring... and now they seek to capture you."

He took her hand and rested it on his chest. "All it takes is one word or one approving look from you and all is well," he replied intimately, looking deeply into her eyes.

"Do you really love me so much?"

"More than anyone or anything else."

"And I love you no less. If the emperor should catch you, though, he won't show you any mercy."

"Don't worry. He won't catch me."

"I pray you'll stay here until they leave."

"Unfortunately, that's no longer an option."

"Why? What's happened?"

He put a finger to his lips. "I have to leave this very night."

"Dear God, how dangerous! I won't let you leave," she said, holding him even tighter.

"You'll have to let me go, Margot. Duty is calling me."

"It's that single word, 'duty', that you men always defer to. Is it really duty that causes you to rush from one dangerous assignment to another?"

"At times, yes. No ordinary man can predict the things that are expected from him, much less from an officer. Besides, I have to bring important news to our friend."

"Which friend?"

"The field marshal."

"Ah, father Blücher! Is it for his sake that you have to go?"

"Yes," he said. "He sent me to scout out the situation and bring any pertinent information back to him. I have to leave right away."

"Were you able to find out anything of importance?"

"Indeed. Napoleon's plans for the upcoming campaign!"

"Heavens! It's understandable then that you have to report to the marshal. My love, your way is filled with danger." She nestled her head on his chest. "Oh, I wish I could share the experience with you, Hugo!"

"What if your wish should become a reality, my love?"

She quickly lifted her eyes to meet his. "What do you mean?"

"Do you have the courage and the strength to accompany me?"

"I know I do. I could watch the battle by your side without flinching. I have the strength within me. Do you believe me, Hugo?"

"I believe you. You've already proven yourself to me."

"Really?" she asked with a curious look in her eyes. "When did I do that?"

"In Paris," he answered. "You followed me out of concern for my safety on the night of the ambush. Was that not courageous of you, my love?"

"That wasn't courage. I was only following my heart."

"It proves you possess a courageous nature. Would you place yourself in danger alongside me?"

Her eyes seemed to glisten with the possibility. "Oh, how I would love to."

"Are you still weak?"

"I should be up to it, if it became necessary."

"It just might become necessary."

"You don't say!" Madame Richemonte interrupted. "Are you suggesting we might have to leave Jeannette?"

"Unfortunately, yes."

"For what possible reason?" she asked. Then, upon further thought, she seemed to answer her own question. "I think I can guess," she added with an air of disapproval.

"I'm convinced you're wrong about that!" Löwenklau said.

She looked at him persistently. "I'm sure I'm on the right track."

"Well, go ahead, but I think you underestimate me."

"You're a little jealous, my dear Monsieur von Löwenklau."

"Not at all!"

"Certainly! You think the emperor's influence might swing a young girl's heart."

"Perhaps another girl's heart, but not Margot's!" he insisted, shaking his head. "I suspect she would feel ashamed of me if I ever suggested such a thing."

"Thank you, my love," said Margot. "Is there another reason for your concern?"

"Ladies, a great danger awaits Margot, one which was ordained by the emperor himself."

"Then it still comes down to a form of jealousy," smiled Madame.

"No, Mama," he said. "I was fortunate enough to overhear a new plan. I'm sure you've heard the news that the emperor has proclaimed Captain Riche-monte a relay commander."

"Yes. He had the audacity to tell us himself."

"First, this title gives him considerable authority, one which can't easily be questioned. Second, the emperor ordered him to confine you to your room."

"Only because they suspect we have somehow harbored you."

"No," Löwenklau corrected, "because the emperor was rebuffed. I believe the real reason he wants to hand you over to another is one of spite."

"Really? Spite toward whom?"

"He intends that you marry Baron de Reillac."

Margot's mouth dropped open in disgust. "That horrible man?"

"Yes."

"How can they do this?"

"Through your brother. He now carries the emperor's authority."

"No emperor has that right!"

"That's where you're wrong, my dear Margot. I saw with my own eyes how Napoleon conferred his authority onto your brother for this singular purpose. He put it into writing to remove any doubt. All means are at your brother's disposal to bring it to pass and force you to marry Reillac."

"Dear God! Is that really the truth?"

"Sadly, yes. Richemonte is supposed to ride to Sedan tomorrow and inform Reillac of the happy news."

Margot turned pale. "Protect me, Hugo!"

"In every way I can, Margot, but I can only afford you that protection if you leave with me tonight."

"This very night, Hugo?"

"Yes, tonight!"

"Then I'm coming with you."

Now it was Madame Richemonte's turn to go pale. "But shouldn't we verify it?" she asked, hesitating. "I don't mean to doubt you, my son, but were those Napoleon's own words?"

"Yes, and the captain has it in writing!"

"Is there no other way?"

"I don't know of any other," Löwenklau said.

"Could we perhaps appeal to the emperor's mercy?"

"I'm afraid we've all experienced the breadth of his benevolence, Mama!"

She sighed deeply. "I suppose that's true. Is it possible for us to get away?"

"Yes, but only with a little help."

"We're confined to our rooms and are being watched," she reminded him.

"But this apartment has another exit."

"Am I supposed to accompany you, too?" asked Madame Richemonte.

"I wouldn't have it any other way."

She blanched, trying to come to terms with the sudden change in plans. "Where are you taking us? To Blücher's encampment?"

"That's not possible now," the lieutenant explained. "The emperor is making preparations to get underway tomorrow with his marshals and the troops currently deployed here. We wouldn't get far. Florian has recommended that you stay with an old friend of his, actually his relative. He was born in Holland, but now resides in a cottage just past Sedan. In fact, Florian will accompany us and remain with you while I carry on."

"Where is this place?"

"It's near Gedinne."

"That takes us through Givet and Sedan, both of which are swarming with troops. Isn't that too risky?"

"Not really. I'll be riding as a French major."

"And us?"

Löwenklau smiled. "As my servants."

Madame Richemonte, at first surprised, looked at him as though she had misheard. "As... your servants? You must be joking."

"No, Mama. It's no joke. You'll need to put on a man's uniform because as of tomorrow morning, all troops will be on the lookout for two ladies."

"You can't be serious!" Madame replied, exasperated.

"What an adventure!" exclaimed Margot. "To dress as your servant! How will we travel? By carriage?"

"No, unfortunately not. That would be too cumbersome and would give us away."

"But dressed in men's clothes?" complained Madame.

"Yes, Mama."

Convincing his future mother-in-law of the plan proved to be a great difficulty. Margot, on the other hand, was enthusiastic about it.

"When do we leave?" she asked.

"Florian will advise us. Are you well enough for such a long ride?"

"I feel strong enough."

"May God be merciful," he said. "I hope you're not wrong, my love."

"Is my cousin aware of your plan?" asked Madame Richemonte.

"No, none of your family knows. That way, they won't share in the blame for our escape."

The door through which Löwenklau had entered opened slowly. Florian emerged from the darkness, carrying a pack of clothes.

"There," he whispered. "This is everything we'll need."

"My major's uniform?" asked Löwenklau.

"Yes, and two for the ladies."

"Will they fit?" asked Margot.

Florian took a moment to look at the two women. "That's a good question. I grabbed them in the darkness and I wasn't able to judge their sizes."

"You grabbed them?" Madame Richemonte recoiled. "But why steal them?"

"It was the only way to get them."

"But we'll be blamed for the theft!"

"Don't cause yourself any extra grief, my dear Mama," pleaded Löwenklau. "We're leaving to escape the clutches of a sinister man who's determined to destroy me and appropriate Margot for his selfish purposes. What we do in times of war cannot be judged too strenuously."

"What do you have here? Women's clothes?" he asked Florian.

"Of course," replied Florian. "I brought a dress for each lady, as is customarily worn by women in the local area."

"Did you steal those also?" asked the downcast mother.

The coachman shook his head. "No, I'm not that kind of thief. I only borrowed them," he said grinning.

"From whom?"

"From the housekeeper."

"Is she aware of our plan?"

"No," Florian admitted. "I told her I needed them for a little wedding skit. Since I'm not usually known for engaging in pranks, she believed me."

"Why the women's clothing, Florian?"

"Simple. We're leaving during the night and the ladies will be more difficult to distinguish. But during the day, the uniforms could give them away. Once we clear Sedan, we can let them change into the dresses. Besides, they'll need to be wearing women's attire when we enter Gedinne." He turned back to the door, ready to leave again. "I need to go now and find the best way to move the horses out of the compound."

"Do you think it's possible that the captain will pay us another visit?" asked Madame Richemonte.

"I'm convinced of it," replied Florian.

"Won't he become suspicious when he spots the clothes?"

"No. I'll ask the lieutenant to take them up to the roof and wait for me there. I only brought them here so you could view them in the light."

Florian stepped out, followed by Löwenklau a few moments later, taking the clothes with him. He awaited the coachman's return. The officer understood him completely, appreciating his cunning ability to appropriate the items.

CHAPTER TWENTY-FIVE

Flight from Jeannette

I t was almost midnight when a solitary rider approached the estate's main gate.

"Who goes there?" inquired the sentry.

"Baron de Reillac," came the reply.

"In that case, you may enter."

The baron rode through the gate and into the yard, where he dismounted. He tied the reins to a post and walked over to the guardhouse, which was lit up for easy access. He stopped in his tracks halfway through the door.

"I didn't expect to find you here, Captain," Reillac said.

Even at this late hour, Captain Richemonte was not asleep in his quarters, choosing instead to stay awake. He was prepared to forfeit the night's rest if it meant capturing Löwenklau. After all, he could be lying low, looking for a suitable opportunity to leave.

"I'm just as surprised to find you here, Baron," replied Richemonte.

"Indeed! I just learned the emperor stopped here overnight. I rode by hoping to speak to him in the morning."

"Concerning supplies for the army?" asked Richemonte.

"Naturally."

"Are you hoping to procure a good deal on cattle at the slaughterhouse?" laughed Richemonte. "Or are you after a new shipment of military boots?"

"Go ahead and joke about things you don't understand," the baron said. "I've invested millions in this business. The order for troop deployment was announced earlier today. I came to receive further instructions from Drouet. Of course, I didn't expect to find you here, Captain."

"I make it a point to get around as well, especially when it comes to rendering you a service."

Reillac had a puzzled look on his face. "You, render me a favor?" It was usually the other way around.

"Yes, me on your behalf!"

"You must be joking. What could you do for me?"

"If you care to find out, follow me to my quarters."

"You have accommodations here?"

"Of course. Why should the relay commander not live on site?"

"Relay commander? For Jeannette?"

"Yes."

"I thought you would be out in the field."

"I just returned from there. But come!" Richemonte took the baron by the arm and led him up to the room that had been assigned to him. He lit a cigar and sat on the sofa, leaving the impression that his fortunes had much improved since their last meeting. "Have a seat, Baron!" he invited good-naturedly.

Reillac, the supplier of goods for Napoleon's army, sat down and examined the captain, all the while shaking his head. "Captain, I find you in the best of spirits. How is it you suddenly find yourself the relay commander?"

"*Pah!* How is it you're the supply chief?"

"Well, I have the means for the position."

"And I have the talent for mine."

"I can see you're quite pleased with yourself. How come?"

Richemonte smiled superiorly. "Perhaps I'll fill you in another time. May I ask you one question?"

"Go ahead."

"Could you loan me ten thousand francs?"

"No! Not even one franc."

"Don't you have any money?"

"Of course I do, but not for your exploits. You're nothing but a leech, one that sucks you dry and gives you nothing in return."

"Don't get too excited, Baron. I was only joking. It might surprise you to learn that I don't need your money anymore."

"What? You might convince the devil of that, but not me. I'm unaware of a single time when you didn't need my money!"

"Times have changed, my dear Baron."

Reillac regarded him scornfully. "What? A windfall from above?"

"Something like that," replied the captain calmly.

"I congratulate you, Captain."

"Thank you."

"Are you perhaps contemplating the notes which I still have in my possession?"

"I'm considering them now."

"My friend, you'll need a lot of money to redeem them."

"The emperor's purse is at my disposal."

"You're dreaming, Captain."

"And you are an idiot, dear Baron."

Reillac's reaction was sharp and spiteful. "Oho!" he exclaimed, offended. "Why the insult?"

"Because you don't trust me! At least give me the benefit of the doubt. My circumstances have changed. Do you really think I attained this position by chance?" asked Richemonte.

"You've made your point! You must have rendered the emperor some important service that goes beyond the everyday. May I know what it is?"

"I think I'll keep that to myself, for now. It will suffice to know I spent a few days gathering information in the area of the enemy encampment."

"You earned the staff position, but I'm not clear on the rest."

"Suit yourself. It doesn't matter to me whether you grasp the connection or not. Since you've accommodated me in the past, I want to return the favor and see if I can benefit you in some way."

The baron opened his mouth in disbelief. "Are you that influential?"

"I am indeed."

"Well then, shall we clear up the promissory notes?"

"I'm at your service."

"Perhaps I would rather have you..." Reillac trailed off in the middle of his sentence, another thought occurring to him.

Richemonte raised his eyebrows in curiosity. "Well? Go on, Baron."

"I mean it would suit me if you were finally able to accommodate my wishes."

"In what way?" asked Richemonte shrewdly.

"I'm talking about Margot, of course."

"Are you still interested in her?"

"Let's not play games, Captain!" the baron said. "You know my aspirations only too well!"

"Which at one time seemed hopeless. Thanks to me, they've suddenly become possible once again."

"What's that supposed to mean?"

"Wait and see," the captain said. "Let's review the facts. Are you still planning to marry my sister?"

"Heaven and hell! Are you trying to make fun of me? I can't get her out of my mind! If there was even the slightest chance—"

"What would you give me if I could make it happen?" interrupted the captain.

"I would rip up the notes," replied the baron.

"Aside from the usual considerations, how would the marriage benefit her?"

"Well, should I somehow die, she would benefit from a sizeable widow's pension."

The captain roared with laughter. "My dear Baron, what good is that? You could live to be a hundred! No, my friend, I insist she inherits everything in the event of your death."

"Captain, you demand a lot!"

"And do you demand less? My sister is worth a fortune."

"We'll discuss this more in the future."

"What more is there to discuss?" Richemonte asked. "No, dear baron, let me be perfectly honest with you. I'm not interested in mere words."

Reillac cocked his head to the side. "What then? Do you want specifics?"

"You will prepare a document, outlining how my sister will become the sole heir—"

"Agreed, but after the wedding."

"No!" the captain insisted. "Before the wedding. I want to be as certain as possible."

"Fine, go on. I can tell you're leading up to something."

"You rip up all the notes."

"Of course. After the wedding, naturally."

"No, Monsieur. Also before the wedding. There can be no deviation from my demands."

"I could say the same," Reillac pointed out. "What if I rip them up today and find out tomorrow the whole thing has been called off?"

"I'll provide you with an iron clad guarantee."

"What sort of guarantee?"

"Would a wedding decree endorsed by the emperor suffice?"

The baron's eyes widened uncharacteristically. "Dammit! Completely."

"Fine! Then rip up the notes."

"Are you implying that the emperor is inclined to issue such a decree?"

"He has already given his consent," Richemonte said with an air of deliberate certainty.

"Heaven and hell!" said Reillac as he jumped out of his chair. "Are you feeling all right? Are you in control of your faculties?"

"Of course I am!"

"I don't consider you a fool, only a man with a reckless streak."

"You think I'm making this up?"

"To be perfectly honest, yes, I do!"

"Then I'll prove to you I'm dead serious."

The baron's passion for Margot would not let him rest. "Ridiculous!" he exclaimed. "Indeed, you'll have to prove it."

"I'm prepared to show you the emperor's edict, which I have been empowered to act upon," Richemonte began. "But first, I have two qualifiers."

"And they are?"

"One, you'll sign a document to my satisfaction, thereby making my sister the sole heir. Second, you'll return to Sedan tonight to retrieve the promissory notes and make them available to me."

"Why are you in such a hurry?"

"The emperor will leave early in the morning. Don't you think I want to present you to him as my sister's betrothed?"

The baron's eyes gleamed with lecherous anticipation. "Is all this really true, Captain?"

"I give you my word as an officer!"

"All right," Reillac said, agreeing with the terms. "I'm prepared to sign your document, providing you show me the emperor's edict. I'll ride immediately to Sedan and, upon my return, furnish you with the notes."

"Can I count on you to keep your word?"

"On my honor!"

"Then have a look!"

The captain pulled out a dossier and handed it over to the disbelieving baron. Reillac grabbed it and devoured the contents with his eyes. He held the paper to the light as though to satisfy himself of its authenticity.

"It's real," he said, getting more excited the more he thought about it. "It's genuine all right! Margot will be mine! Finally! How long I've suffered, waiting for this moment to arrive." He let out a triumphant shout.

"Congratulations, Baron!"

Reillac's thoughts abruptly turned fondly to Margot. "Well," he said softly, "she'll experience heaven on earth."

"And your 'heavenly bliss' will turn into a living hell." He plucked the edict out of the baron's hand.

"Am I not permitted to keep it?"

"For what? You've just read that I've been given Napoleon's own authority to arrange for its implementation. Now I expect you to fulfill your part."

"Does it have to be right now?"

"Yes," the captain said. "I want to take advantage of the emperor's presence."

"Give me some paper then. How shall I detail the contents?"

"Keep them short. Simply write that you plan to marry my sister and intend to make her your sole heir."

The baron could hardly contain his excitement, reveling in the knowledge that his wish was about to come true. In his eager anticipation, though, he failed to contemplate the true meaning of the words being dictated to him. When he finished, he signed his name and added the date.

"So, is this sufficient?" he asked.

"Completely!" replied Richemonte as he collected the document nonchalantly, placing it neatly back in his dossier. Anyone watching closely could not have missed that momentary look, reminiscent of a predator keeping eyes on its prey.

"Have you already spoken to Margot?" asked the baron.

"Yes."

"Does she understand the implications of the emperor's will?"

"More or less."

"How did she respond?"

"More passively than actively."

"Then we're half way there!" Reillac crowed exultantly. "What about her mother?"

"She's easier to reason with than my sister. I simply told the emperor the truth."

"What truth are you talking about?"

"That both ladies have resisted your 'kindness' so far."

"Dammit!" he cursed, recalling Blücher's search of his home in Paris. "You don't have to remind me how embarrassing it was."

"Not at all. You're neither young nor handsome, so it shouldn't come as any great surprise that a youthful girl would prefer a young and dashing Hussar officer over you. One could hardly blame her."

"I find your forthrightness quite insulting, Captain."

Richemonte offered a small smile. "I simply tell it the way I see it."

"Yes, but your comments are bordering on discourtesy."

"Yes, my manners have often been described as being rude and tasteless."

"As they are now."

"I don't particularly care. Besides, friends don't scold each other too severely, and I have already demonstrated my friendship to you."

"You mean when it suits your interests," Reillac observed.

The captain shrugged his shoulders. "Why should I deny it? Of course, I hadn't counted on having to resort to harsher measures to keep Margot in line, such as keeping her tied to the rack."[25.1]

Reillac, once again, couldn't hide his surprise. "What are you saying? What happened?"

"Margot and her mother are currently in my custody," Richemonte explained.

"For God's sake, why?"

"It's all in an effort to restore her to reason. She'll have to consent willingly so that the wedding ceremony can be conducted openly and form-ally. If she refuses, she'll become your wife behind closed doors only, without pomp or fanfare. It's that simple."

"Would it hold up to scrutiny?"

"Who would dare to question the emperor's edict?"

"True enough! I would still like to know, in the interim—"

"*Pah!*" interrupted the captain. "I've been given the emperor's authority to act as necessary. I could easily arrange for her to appear to be sick... let's say, for instance, she suffered a small stroke and was incapable of speech. Don't worry, Baron. Just leave it to me."

"My dear Captain, you're an exceptional sort of man. Certainly, you're worthy of becoming my brother-in-law."

"Why, thank you! This compliment, although deserved, won't sway my actions. By the way, I should ask you, have you heard what happened to the emperor's coach today?" asked Richemonte.

"I heard about it in Sedan. His coach and entourage were held up."

"What did you hear about the rescue?"

"A most adventurous tale! I heard a young man saved them all—a real hero, a Goliath and a real Roland![25.2] He finished off the bandits like child's play."

"Do you know who that Goliath was?" Richemonte teased.

"Well?"

"You know him well. In fact, you've already dealt with him in Paris. He is none other than our dear Lieutenant Löwenklau!"

The baron opened his mouth in astonishment, though he couldn't seem to conjure the right words.

Captain Richemonte looked utterly triumphant over his co-conspirator, Baron de Reillac. As he continued, he contemplated the impact his words had on the military supply man. "Yes, indeed, I meant what I said. It really was Löwenklau," the captain confirmed, enunciating every word.

Reillac opened his mouth again and, this time, was able to utter a few words. "What! Him? Löw... en... klau? That mangy dog—impossible! I heard he was a sea captain from Marseille."

"And yet it was really Löwenklau. He masqueraded as a sea captain, his main purpose being to spy out the land. We've searched the whole estate for him."

"Was he actually here, at Jeannette?"

"Absolutely."

"Were you successful in capturing him?"

"Unfortunately, no."

"A real shame."

"I still think about it," Richemonte said. "The emperor personally instructed me to conduct the search. But despite my efforts, it went unrewarded. I did, however, make one important observation. You, of course, know the coachman, Florian."

"Yes. I found him myself."

"Do you feel you can trust him?"

"Of course."

"I want to warn you. I was the victim of a terrible prank this evening and I suspect he orchestrated it. He pretends to be harmless and not very bright, but I have my reservations about him."

"Really?" the baron asked. "He's served me well in the past, revealing much about what went on at Jeannette."

"Perhaps in doing so he found a way to further his own interests," Richemonte said. "I'm going to keep a close eye on him. I noticed he's been quite active tonight, sneaking around the estate. I'm sure he's planning something. Maybe he's even in cahoots with Löwenklau."

Reillac shook his head, unwilling to entertain that unlikely possibility. "Not possible, Captain!"

"I hope not, for his sake. But that's enough for now. I've taken up too much time already. It is time we parted company."

"What is so urgent that you have to leave?"

"I've decided to be more vigilant, and perchance net me a Prussian," he said. "I've been walking around the yard and its buildings, which is where I spotted Florian lurking about."

"Then I won't disturb you, Captain. It would be a memorable day if you should happen to catch Löwenklau. I'll leave right away for Sedan to gather up the promissory notes. I just want to remind you that I will deliver the notes into your hand only after we seek an audience with the emperor."

"It doesn't make any difference to me. If you hold the notes back, you forfeit your prize. That should be crystal clear to you."

"You're right," Reillac said. "Friends have to honor their commitments. I trust you still consider me as your friend. Until we meet again, Captain."

"*Adieu*, Baron."

"When does the emperor usually rise in the morning?"

"At daybreak."

"Then I must hurry. *Adieu*." He stood up hastily and left the captain's quarters.

Richemonte waited until the sound of footsteps diminished down the corridor, then took a deep breath. *Finally! I have him! Those damned notes will be ripped up at last. And the inheritance document? Ah, my dear baron, that's an entirely different matter! All I have to do is change the name and I'll be the sole heir. This affair could turn to my advantage on several fronts. The emperor has shown me his favor. In time, Margot will be tamed. I'll be rid of my debts and finally be able to breathe a sigh of relief. Of course, I'll dispense in telling the baron to keep his hands off Margot for now. The time is not yet right.*

He left the room himself, whistling a familiar tune, and resumed his patrol of the estate.

❧✠☙

Meanwhile, Florian climbed back to the roof, rejoining Löwenklau.

"Florian, I believe it's high time we left."

"I'm afraid we cannot!" countered the coachman. "I fear it's going to be very difficult to leave this night."

Löwenklau couldn't believe his words. "What possible reason could—"

Florian interrupted him. "Only one reason: Richemonte. He will not rest. He prowls about the courtyard and its buildings. It's as though he suspects you're still here."

"He will get tired of it. Let's be patient."

Another hour slid by as Löwenklau waited patiently. Florian eventually returned, suppressing a curse as he approached.

"What's going on?" asked Löwenklau.

"We had a short reprieve," he replied. "A lone rider appeared just before midnight and occupied Richemonte's time so I could get the horses out of the stable and into the garden. I managed to get three out, but the last one is still in there."

"Is the captain out and about?"

"Of course."

"He could spoil everything! How long will it take you to get the last horse into the garden?"

"Five minutes, at the most."

"Can we ride out of the garden without being heard?"

"Yes, but only when the main gate is open."

"Where's the captain most of the time?"

"I've seen him on the perimeter of the estate making his rounds."

"Couldn't you use your dog to distract him?"

"*Sapristi!* I hadn't thought of that."

"Your hound can occupy him until we're safely away!"

Florian nodded, smiling at the suggestion. "I'll see to it immediately. Please go get changed, Monsieur, and bring the uniforms to the ladies. I'll pack your belongings and the women's clothing, strapping them to the saddles. Unfortunately, the rest of their belongings will have to remain here. Do you have sufficient funds for the trip?"

"Yes, quite sufficient."

"Otherwise I could have made some available for you."

Florian retraced his steps back into the house, quickly jogging down to the stable where his dog was waiting. "Come on, Tiger!" he coaxed, untying him. "You'll have another chance to get at that troublemaker. Quietly now, I don't want any noise. Afterward, you'll come with us. Who knows, you might just come in handy."

The coachman crept out of the stable with his dog, finding a perfect spot to cower and hide near one of the smaller buildings. He waited a few minutes, until he heard soft footsteps approach. Florian pressed himself to the ground

312

to get a better look against the backdrop of the sky. Though there was minimal light, he could still discern Captain Richemonte's outline.

He let the captain walk past them. Then, to the dog, he whispered, "Hold him!"

The animal sprang at his quarry with a few measured leaps. The captain let out a muffled cry and fell to the ground as the premises grew quiet once more.

The clever coachman had solved his problem with one fell swoop. The cumbersome captain remained underfoot the best 'guard' at his disposal. Florian returned to the stable and quickly saddled the last horse. He led the horse out into the garden, joining the other three. He kept them together, leading them to the open field and tying their reins to a linden tree.

Florian returned to his room and packed the things he felt they might need on their journey. He then climbed to the roof, joining Löwenklau, who was already looking the part of a newly 'promoted' dragoon major.

"Did everything go well?" Löwenklau asked.

"Yes," Florian said. "My dog is keeping him company. How are the ladies doing?"

"They're ready. It went faster than I anticipated."

"Then I'll fetch them."

Florian descended down the ladder and returned soon with the disguised women. He pulled the ladder up and placed it next to the chimney, creating the impression that it had been left by a chimney sweep. He then closed the access to the stairway.

"Please, follow me!" he whispered. "But quietly. We can't afford to give ourselves away."

The three newly enlisted French soldiers followed him across the roof and came to a dark corridor, where they felt their way ahead until they came to a set of stairs. They climbed down the stairs into the courtyard. Once on the ground, they walked toward the rear gate and into the field without being noticed.

"Where are the horses?" asked Löwenklau. "Didn't you bring them to the garden?"

"I thought it would be best to bring them as far as the linden tree so they'd be out of sight."

Florian led his patrons to the tree and assigned each one a horse. "Please wait a moment! I need to go back and release the captain."

Löwenklau peered at him in the dark. "But why?"

"I want to bring my dog along. He could prove to be of some use to us."

He crept back into the garden. When he arrived at the place where Richemonte was being detained, he stood up straight and let his steps be heard as he walked around the corner of the building.

"*Holla!*" he cried. "What's this? Tiger, what do you have there? Let me see!" He bent down to have a closer look.

"Ah, you caught someone! Heigh day! Did you finally get that Löwenklau? I'm glad I let you keep watch with me." He turned his attention to the trapped Richemonte, deliberately pretending not to recognize him. "Just wait here, you scoundrel, until I turn you over to Captain Richemonte! I'm going to let you get up, but don't even think about taking off. My dog will grab you by the collar and finish you off. Let him up, Tiger, but watch him!"

The dog backed off, allowing the man to get up.

"Hang it all!" swore Richemonte. "That's the second time this has happened to me."

"What!" Florian exclaimed, perpetuating his lie. "Is that you, Captain?"

"Yes, of course it's me! Dammit, man, why do you allow that monster to roam free?"

"He was supposed to catch that Löwenklau fellow."

"Yet you yourself maintain he left!"

"Well, I had to keep looking. The emperor guessed he was here, after all. I'm still angry that the German managed to dupe me into believing his story. I couldn't simply give up, Captain!"

Richemonte got to his feet, dusting the dirt from his knees. "Keep that dammed beast on a chain and try to control your enthusiasm! I could have been killed."

"Yes," the coachman proclaimed proudly. "He's an exceptional dog."

"The devil can have him! As for you, go back to your quarters and resist the urge to put people in danger. And take that damn beast with you!"

"Psst, don't speak so brashly, Monsieur!"

"What! Don't you deserve the reprimand?"

"I don't know. If my dog senses you're about to attack me, though, he could turn on you in an instant."

"Damn that dog! Hold him tight. I'm leaving."

"Fine. I think it would be best if you turn in as well. After all, this German who's leading you around by the nose isn't worth the effort, Captain."[25.3]

Richemonte walked a few paces, then stopped abruptly. "What do you mean by that?"

"Nothing, Monsieur. I only meant you should be careful."

"Listen, I think you're mocking me. You better watch yourself, or else you might find your shenanigans catching up with you in your dealings with me!"

"Yes," Florian began, "and so far I've run into you each time you entangled yourself with my dog."

The captain's anger rose at the rebuke, though instead of furthering the discussion with the disrespectful coachman, he decided to resign to his quarters.

Once Florian was satisfied the captain was going to turn in, he sought out his three companions again, who had heard every word of the exchange.

"That was careless of you," chided Löwenklau. "It would have been better just to whistle for your dog rather than to have confronted Richemonte."

"The scoundrel will realize later who it was that got the better of him," Florian replied obstinately. "Otherwise, there wouldn't be any fun in it."

They climbed their mounts and started out on their journey. For all his efforts, Richemonte had unwittingly accomplished one thing. His constant vigilance had postponed their departure to the point that dawn was not far off. The two ladies, unaccustomed to saddles meant for men, consequently made slow progress. They were barely halfway to Sedan when the darkness gave way to a new day.

"We have to ride faster," Florian warned them, "or risk being detained in Sedan."

"True enough," Löwenklau agreed, his eyes moving instinctively to the horizon and the glowing sunrise. Then, his attention wandered to the figure of a rider approaching them from further up the road. "Look! A rider is coming toward us!"

Florian strained his eyes to catch a glimpse of the newcomer through the morning light. "Oh no!" he exclaimed in surprise. "Don't you see who it is?" he asked the lieutenant. "It's Baron de Reillac!"

"Dear God! This could prove to be a costly encounter! Isn't there a side road we could take?"

"Unfortunately, not!" Florian said regretfully.

"Then there's only one solution. We'll gallop past him and not pay him any heed. He won't easily make out our facial features."

Florian nodded his agreement. "I'll try to divert his attention as he rides by."

They brought the horses to a full gallop. When the baron rode closer, Florian allowed his horse to prance a little, giving the impression that he had difficulty in staying in the saddle. He succeeded in diverting his glance somewhat, but not entirely.

The baron gave them a fleeting glance and called out. "Florian? Where are you off to in such a hurry?"

"To Sedan, Monsieur," groaned the servant, attempting to control his horse. "I'm on an errand for the baroness."

"Who's the officer with the young soldiers?"

"I don't know."

"But you're riding with them!"

"No, Monsieur, they just caught up to me. Farewell, Baron." With that remark, he regained control of his mount and rode after them.

The little interlude allowed the ladies to get accustomed to the gallop. They maintained the pace even when they reached the outskirts of Sedan. A sentry stood at the gate and, upon seeing the uniform of the dragoon major, presented arms. Löwenklau saluted, but pressed them on.

They quickly crossed the city, finding themselves to be the unsolicited object of a number of curious onlookers, both officers and enlisted men. When they cleared Sedan, they rode on toward Bouillon. The closer they came to reaching their goal, the less they hurried. Now that Sedan, laden with military prowess, lay behind them, the two female riders started to show the first signs of fatigue.

Löwenklau looked at Margot with growing concern. She had turned pale and was starting to sway in the saddle as they entered Bouillon.

"It's too much for you, my love," he said, supporting her. "Does your wound cause you discomfort? Any pain?"

"No," she replied with a fragile smile. "I'm just weak from the ride."

"We should dismount and take a little rest. There's a roadside inn ahead," he said, pointing to the small cottage, "but the people know me there. Can you hold on for another two minutes until we're through?"

"Maybe," was her almost inaudible reply.

"Then I'll help you." He leaned over and braced her with his arm. It only delayed the inevitable. Her eyes suddenly closed, and she would have slid out of the saddle had he not been supporting her.

"Water!" was all she was able to say.

Löwenklau jumped from his mount and caught her just in time. He carried her to the nearby stream. He was too preoccupied with Margot to notice two elderly people working in the meadow. It was the old innkeeper and his wife, with whom he had spent the eventful night on his earlier journey.

"Look over there," the wife said, leaning on the rake. "That young soldier is feeling faint. Isn't it a shame that such a young boy has already enlisted in the army?"

"Yes," her husband observed thoughtfully. "Look, that officer seems like a good sort. He even helped the young man off the horse and carried him to the brook."

The old woman grabbed his arm. "Look closely at the officer, husband. Don't you recognize him?"

"Now that you mention it, he does look familiar."

"Of course, he does. He recently stayed with us!"

"We've never had the privilege of accommodating a major in our little abode," the man replied, rubbing his eyes.

The wife shook her head thoughtfully. "He wasn't dressed as a major at the time."

"What else then, woman?"

"He was that young musician. Don't you recall? We told him the story about the war chest."

"You're right, woman. Now he's an officer. He deceived us. Why did he stay with us and conceal his true identity?"

She grabbed his arm again, pressing firmly to get his full attention.

"What's wrong now?" he asked irritated.

"Don't you see? That young soldier's a girl!"

"Ridiculous!"

"No! Look! Don't you see the long, beautiful hair that just came undone?"

"Hmm," the man allowed. "That is unusual."

Margot's weakness faded quickly. Still unaware of the couple watching them, Löwenklau sprinkled water on her face and gave her some to drink. It refreshed her enough that she could stand on her own strength again.

"Thank you!" she whispered. "I feel much better."

"Can you ride again?"

"Let's give it a try. Help me into the saddle."

He gave her a leg up and she bravely hung on. Unfortunately, her mother was also starting to show signs of exhaustion. She tried to be brave and didn't complain, but it was clear that she needed to rest.

Up ahead, the lieutenant noticed Florian turn at the same place where, a day earlier, he had followed the two thieves bent on plundering the chest.

"Where are we heading, Florian?" he asked, surprised.

"Up into the mountains. We'll elude any watchers and deceive those that will surely follow us. We'll find a place where the ladies can dismount and get a little rest, rather than staying here on the open road."

Florian unknowingly followed the same path into the mountains that Löwenklau had taken earlier. After the uphill climb, they reached the abandoned coal hut.

"Please," pleaded Madame Richemonte. "Could we stop here for a short rest?"

Florian helped her out of the saddle and lowered her to the ground. She sat down in the soft moss, taking a deep breath. Watching them, a thought struck Löwenklau. Perhaps he could use this opportunity to show Margot where he had buried the war chest, while her mother and Florian rested.

"Which direction are we following, Florian?" he asked. "The path ends here."

"Straight ahead, over the mountain pass, there's a ravine that's situated on the right side of the mountain."

"Do you want to dismount as well, Margot?"

"No, Hugo."

"Then let's ride ahead toward the ravine. When Mama regains her strength, she can follow us with Florian."

"How come?"

"Let me explain it to you later, my dear."

They slowly rode off together, leaving the other two behind them. He remembered the way exactly and they quickly reached the entrance to the gorge.

"This looks like a good place to dismount," he said.

Margot watched him carefully, obviously aware that he was keeping something to himself. "You're being awfully secretive, Hugo."

"I've got good reason to be, dear Margot."

"Are you familiar with the area?"

"Yes," he revealed. "I was here only a day ago and witnessed events I won't soon forget. I'll tell you all about it when we get to the actual place. Come on!"

They dropped down from their horses and Löwenklau tied the reins to a nearby tree. Taking Margot's hand, he led his betrothed deeper into the ravine.

CHAPTER TWENTY-SIX
Unfruitful Inquiries

T he baron watched the coachman gallop after the others. He shook his head, disappointed by the way Florian had answered him. He pondered the encounter as he whipped his horse into a trot. *Something is up at Jeannette,* he thought. *But what? That officer seemed familiar, not to mention the fact that he looked too young to hold the rank of a major. I could swear I've seen those two soldiers before.*

He concentrated as he rode, trying to remember where he had seen them. *Ah well! Why should I trouble myself with such things?* Then, as though he had some company with him, he said out loud, "I'll make inquiries later when I've reached Jeannette!" The silent horse, his only companion, picked up its pace as though on cue.

Reillac couldn't shake the strange feeling that he was on the verge of solving a puzzle. He continued riding and, when he came within sight of the estate, the solution suddenly dawned on him. He abruptly stopped his horse. "Heaven and hell!" he called out into the open air. *What a thought! Could it really be? Richemonte was right not to trust that Florian. This could be a huge blow to our plans... I'll have to act quickly to set this right.*

The baron dug in his heels so the horse flew toward Jeannette. He didn't let up until he rode into the courtyard. He dismounted with a jump and rushed up to Richemonte's quarters. He found the captain awake, reclining on the sofa. Upon catching a glimpse of Reillac, Richemonte slowly stood up.

"Back so soon?" he asked lightly.

"Just as I promised."

"Did you bring the promissory notes?"

"Of course. However, it remains to be seen whether I'll hand them over to you."

"What? Why the uncertainty?" Richemonte took a closer look at the baron and, to his chagrin, noticed the man's restless state, bordering on anxiety. "What is it?" asked the captain. "Did something happen?"

"Perhaps something very significant. Please, just answer my questions without interruption."

"Go ahead."

"Did you discover any signs of Löwenklau's presence?"

"None whatsoever."

"Are your mother and sister still here?" asked the baron.

"Of course."

"Are they still confined to their rooms?"

"There's a guard at their door."

Reillac frowned, trying to reconcile that information with his theory. "Then it's a mystery to me. What about Florian, is he still at hand?"

"I have no reason to think otherwise. I spoke to him only a short time ago."

"He is no longer here," the baron informed him. "I met him on the road coming back."

"Really? Where was that?"

"Between Jeannette and Sedan. A dragoon major and two lads were with him. I'm positive it was Florian because we exchanged a few words."

"Did he ride out from Jeannette?"

"Yes."

"Well, there's only one dragoon officer here," Richemonte said. "He came late at night with important dispatches, and should be sound asleep in his quarters."

"I don't doubt that he's asleep, because the major whom I saw is none other than Löwenklau himself."

Richemonte looked uncomfortable, trying to conceal his emotions. "Baron, it just can't be! Are you sure?"

"I'm telling you it was Löwenklau. Florian betrayed us!"

"Could you be mistaken?"

"I wasn't sure at first. I didn't recognize his face, because I only glanced at him in passing. All the way here, I strained to remember where I had seen him before. The answer came to me as I rode into the courtyard."

"Damn! You could have pursued him had you realized the deception sooner. Now he's gone."

"There were two lads with him," the baron continued. "I can only hope I'm mistaken, but they had an uncanny resemblance to your mother and sister."

Richemonte's face turned pale as a sick feeling crept into his stomach. "You don't mean to suggest, that..." he stammered, finding himself moment-arily speechless.

"...that damned Prussian had the gall to conceal himself in the very same building where the emperor resided," Reillac interrupted. "Then he had the nerve to abduct my bride! Yes, that's exactly what I mean."

"It's impossible! If it were really true, the shame of it all might compel me to shoot myself."

"Then do your best to prove me wrong!"

Captain Richemonte jumped up. "Yes," he said. "Come with me now!"

Both men hurried out of the room and rushed to Margot's chambers, where they found the sentry still guarding the door dutifully.

"Did anything happen?" Richemonte asked.

"No, Captain."

"Any noises?"

"None at all."

Both men looked at each other bewildered and it seemed as though their fears were unfounded. Perhaps the ladies had simply fallen asleep. Richemonte continued in his inquiries. "Did you hear any conversation? Did they make any requests?"

"None, Captain," reported the soldier.

"Let's see for ourselves!" decided the captain. Without wasting any more time, he opened the door impulsively. He was able to do so only because Margot had slid back the bolt prior to her departure.

"There's no one here," Richemonte said loudly. "But, of course, there's another door." He entered the room that had once been assigned to Löwenklau, but he was disappointed with the results. He examined the ladder carefully that led down to the stable, the source of his earlier embarrassment. "They must have climbed down here!" he called. "That miserable Florian helped them escape and undoubtedly concealed the German somewhere. We have to determine if the baroness and her son were accomplices."

He rushed next to the baroness's chamber, Reillac right behind him. The sentry here was still in place as well. "Is our prisoner still inside?" asked Richemonte.

"Yes, Captain."

"Did you overhear any conversation?"

"I just spoke to the baroness."

"About what?"

"She came to the door and demanded that I send for her maid."

"Is the girl with her now?"

"She just went in."

"Let's go find out."

The captain forced himself into the room without knocking. The baroness, attired only in her dressing gown, sat in front of her mirror. Upon seeing the two men, she quickly rose to her feet.

"Excuse me, Messieurs," she exclaimed, "but I resent—"

"Madame, did you at any time leave your room?" Richemonte demanded without the courtesy of a greeting.

She looked at him contemptuously. "Monsieur, since when has it become customary for gentlemen to enter a lady's dwelling, much less her private dressing chamber, without an announcement or greeting of any kind?"

"Since the lady has become my prisoner. You heard my question, and now I expect you to answer me."

"Why should I answer you?" she asked, shrugging her shoulders. "I only communicate with people who appreciate how to conduct themselves in the presence of a lady. However, I see the whole concept of etiquette is lost on you."

"Really!" he replied in anger. "Don't forget that you're still under my authority!"

"Certainly, under the authority of the emperor, who has appointed you to be his jailer and ruffian.[26.1] You may leave."

Richemonte, however, stood his ground. "I'm not leaving until you answer my question. I must inform you that my mother and sister have departed during the night..." The baroness's face showed a trace of surprise at the revelation, but otherwise maintained her silence. "...and you are suspected of aiding in their escape."

She kept her composure and remained silent.

The baroness's defiance stirred up anger within him and caused him to step closer. "Madame, have you forgotten how to speak?" he shouted. "I'll find a way to make you talk!"

This last threat still failed to produce the desired results. Reillac decided to take matters into his own hands and took Richemonte by the arm.

"This room has only one exit," he said. "The sentry said that Madame has not left it. I think we can accept that."

"Perhaps!" replied the captain. "Dammit! I'm used to obtaining answers to my questions."

"We should leave now. We're wasting precious time. The young baron is probably involved."

"I think it's quite likely. Let's head for his room, and if we find him responsible he will have to answer to me."

They left her room and attended to Roman's residence. The guard at the door proclaimed the same message the others had, confirming that the room's occupant had not left at all. Even so, both men barged in without knocking or announcing themselves.

They found Roman reclining on the sofa, where he appeared to have spent a sleepless night. When he spotted the unwelcome guests, he rose from his sedentary position.

"Baron de Sainte-Marie," announced the captain, "you are accused of being an accomplice in this plot, which carries serious consequences. Therefore, I trust you will come to your senses and make a confession. I want to put a few questions before you and I hope you will answer me truthfully."

Roman was genuinely puzzled, not understanding what the captain was implying.

"Confess?" he asked. "I am not aware of having done anything requiring a confession!"

"I will come to that in a moment. But first, did you at any time during the night leave your room?"

"No!"

"Have you conspired with anyone or in some way communicated with an outsider?"

"Certainly not!"

"Why are you trying to deceive me?"

"I am not lying."

"Do you know what has happened this very night?"

Roman merely glanced at the book sitting on the table at the end of the sofa. "The only thing I am certain of," he said slowly, "is that I managed to finish reading my book."

"You could convince someone else of your ignorance, but not me. Are you implying that you have been awake all night?"

"Of course."

"Well, this only gives me more proof to support the theory that you were an accomplice."

"You are not making any sense, Richemonte. An accomplice to what?"

"I will fill you in, even though you probably knew about it before I did. Madame and Mademoiselle Richemonte have escaped!"

Roman's face conveyed total shock. "Did you say escaped? Impossible!"

"Dammit! They have escaped!"

"For what reason?"

"I am sure you know the reason."

"Where would they have gone to in the middle of the night?" Roman asked.

"I am sure you know the answer to that as well."

"On my honor, I have no knowledge of it."

Richemonte simply glared at the man. "Even the fact that your own coachman left with them?"

"Florian? How would I know that? A sentry has been outside my door all night. I have been completely cloistered in here."

"I don't believe you."

"Monsieur, don't you place any worth on my honor? Do you know what this means?"

"As the investigator," Richemonte continued, "it doesn't mean anything to me. I don't place much value in the answers of a guilty party. In fact, it could be perceived as a careless act to believe anything you say."

"So, in effect, you are calling me a liar."

"Take it any way you want," replied the captain matter-of-factly.

"Then, as an officer of the emperor's guard, you know your responsibility. I will be seeking satisfaction, whether as a formal apology or by way of a duel."

"Don't be ridiculous! You are my detainee, nothing more!"

Roman picked up a walking stick and wielded it at him. "*Pah!*" he shouted. "You're not the man to dictate whether I am a detainee or a defendant. Don't you realize I am a cavalier and a nobleman? I simply want to know if you will give me satisfaction."

"I can't be bothered!" replied Richemonte. "You are neither one at the moment. You are my prisoner."

"Well, I am going to demand that you comply!"

Roman advanced, holding the stick in front of him. Richemonte backed up, so his attacker could see the guard behind him. "Stop! Not another step," the captain warned him, "or I will order him to shoot!"

The young baron stopped and threw away the stick with disgust. "Monsieur, you are a coward, one without honor! However, I know of someone who will ensure I get satisfaction from you."

Just then, he looked out the window and spotted Napoleon walking through the courtyard. As expected, the emperor had risen early in the morning. Before he could be hindered, Roman thrust open the window.

"Your Majesty!" he called out in a voice that carried through the estate grounds. The young baron was too agitated to realize this was hardly an acceptable way to gain an audience with the emperor.

Napoleon turned around, his eyes searching for the one who'd had the audacity to address him so brazenly. He looked to the window sternly, intending to chastise the impetuous caller, when he recognized Sainte-Marie. "Ah," he said, his voice already softening. "It is you, Baron. What do you want?"

"I want justice, Sire!"

"Then you will get it!" He made a move to turn around and resume his walk, but was held in place by Sainte-Marie's plea.

"Your Majesty, I am being detained for no valid reason and it is deplorable how people gain admittance to my quarters. First, they accuse me of wrongdoing and covert activity and, lastly, they dishonor my name by refusing to give me satisfaction. I plead with His Majesty to hear me out."

The emperor's eyebrows rose at the implication. "Young man, your manner is very bold," he said, but quickly relented to the young man's request. "I will come myself." He left the courtyard and returned to the building, intending to call on Roman at the earliest opportunity.

In the same instant, an angry Richemonte forcibly removed Roman from the open window, naturally too late.

"Are you insane?" Reillac asked. "You will get us all incarcerated!"

"Dammit! Here comes the emperor!" Obvious though the statement was, it was all Richemonte could manage as he turned deathly pale. He had assumed all responsibility for watching his detainees and now felt he was losing his grip on the situation. The news concerning his mother's and sister's flight would not be well received by the emperor, and would most likely result in the direst consequences.

"Yes, he is coming," Roman said. "I have no reason to be fearful."

"Go to hell!" Richemonte said through clenched teeth. "Just be prepared for the worst, should the slightest blame fall on you."

The sentry presented arms as the emperor approached. Napoleon entered the room slowly, taking in the scene and all those present.

"Captain Richemonte, what has transpired?" he demanded.

"Sire, something has occurred, the relevance of which would be best discussed in private," replied Richemonte.

"Never mind that now. I will dispense with protocol. Tell me now!"

The captain, trying to conceal his growing anxiety, cleared his throat and replied, "The prisoners have absconded, Sire."

"Which prisoners?"

"My mother and sister."

Instantly, the emperor's tanned face took on an even darker shade. He quickly stepped to the window and glanced out, as though noticing something suddenly. However, he only did so to mask his feelings and control his facial expression. When he turned to face them again, any sign of agitation had vanished.

"When did they leave?"

"With the break of dawn."

"How did this happen?"

"I came here to seek clarity in the matter, Majesty. An escape would have been impossible without outside help."

"When did you discover their absence?"

"Baron de Reillac came across them."

"Ah! Why did he not detain them?"

"He did not recognize them, since they were disguised as soldiers."

"Were they alone?"

"No," Richemonte said. "The coachman Florian was their companion. However, their leader was none other than Lieutenant von Löwenklau himself."

The emperor tried to hide his disappointment by biting his lower lip. It was a while before he mastered his feelings again. "Did you not arrange for a sentry, Captain?" he asked loudly, weighing the word 'Captain' with scorn for good measure.

"Of course, Sire!"

"Then he must have fallen asleep."

"Apparently not. With the coachman's help, the prisoners managed to get to the stable and then into the clear."

"That leads to the one obvious conclusion, that there was a second exit."

"Unfortunately, there was, Sire."

"Was it unguarded?"

Richemonte hung his head in embarrassment. "I'm afraid so, Majesty."

"Did you know about the second door?"

The emperor's questions came with such rapidity that the captain had trouble keeping up with his answers. He tried to formulate a response in his defense and hesitated.

"Well! Answer me!" ordered Napoleon.

"Yes, I was aware of it," Richemonte replied despondently.

"Then why did you not assign a second guard?"

"I considered it inaccessible. It led to the same ladder from which I had fallen onto the stable floor."

"Why are you here then, and not after the escapees?"

"I naturally came to interrogate the young baron, having just come from his mother's room."

"Ah! What did the baroness have to say?"

"She claimed to have no knowledge of their escape."

"And you, Baron?" asked Napoleon, turning to face Roman.

"I was completely in the dark, Sire," he replied. "I assured Captain Richemonte of my ignorance by giving him my word as a cavalier and a nobleman. He scorned my words and called me a liar. When I demanded satisfaction, he ridiculed me and turned a deaf ear to my pleas. He refused to comply, stating I did not merit it as an accused."

The emperor looked at Richemonte with a singular, penetrating glance, which was anything but favorable. He continued in his inquiry. "What you are saying is that the guards performed their duty."

"Yes, Majesty," was Richemonte's embarrassed reply.

"The baroness's room has only one exit, which was guarded?"

"Yes, Sire."

"And this one as well?"

"Yes, as His Majesty can verify."

"Since you failed to secure their only means of escape, then you alone are to blame for their departure. I should punish you severely!" He hesitated for a moment, allowing the captain to feel the brunt of his words and to contemplate his failure. "This entire affair, a most peculiar one to be sure, does not merit my concern. I will abstain from any further involvement. In any event, these individuals chose to leave because of personal reasons, for which I will not hold them accountable. Baron Roman de Sainte-Marie and the baroness are not implicated in the escape and are hence free of any blame." His eyes turned to Roman. "You and the baroness are no longer confined to your rooms. You may resume your usual schedule."

"Majesty, I am grateful for your decision!" the young man exclaimed. "I knew the emperor would vindicate us!"

Napoleon barely acknowledged his remarks and instead turned back to address Richemonte. "This matter has been concluded. Cancel the sentry duty and return to your quarters, but leave yourself at my disposal. Baron de Reillac will accompany you." He turned around and left the room.

The two men followed shortly. When they arrived at the captain's quarters, Richemonte could hardly contain his frustration.

"What do you make of that, Baron?"

"A most unfortunate turn of events!"

"I'm angry that the emperor chose to chastise me in front of Roman! We've lost our advantage, and I fear the women will get away."

"Do you really think so? I, for one, doubt it."

"Why?"

"I'm convinced the emperor feigned his indifference," Reillac said. "Further, I think his intent was to lull the young baron and his mother into a false sense of security. I wouldn't be surprised if he called for us in the next few minutes."

"Dammit! You might have something there."

"Of course I do. We were instructed to return to your room and remain at his disposal. What other reason could he have but to send for us privately?"

"I'm so full of rage, I could—" Richemonte's rant, however, was interrupted by a soft knock at the door. When the door swung open, the emperor himself entered. The two men, taken completely by surprise, jumped out of their seats like two schoolboys.

Napoleon closed the door behind him and fixed his stare on Reillac. "Baron de Reillac, it has come to my attention that you are in love with Margot Richemonte." The baron made a formal bow. "Is she your betrothed?"

"Not yet, Sire."

Napoleon's voice took on a sharp and cutting tone. "She already is! Your emperor has declared it and Captain Richemonte carries the written proof!" He was holding a folded document in his right hand. He gave it to the baron and continued, "Your bride has fled. What is your responsibility?"

"To follow her, Majesty," replied Reillac quickly.

"Exactly! I trust you will bring it to pass."

"I will gladly do it, Majesty! However, I have responsibilities and duties here that—"

"Which ones are you referring to?" Napoleon interrupted.

"I am the chief supplier of army provisions, Majesty."

"Do you not have any subordinates?"

"My business is set up in such a way that I can permit myself a short absence without causing any harm to my financial affairs."

"Then arrange for an assistant to relieve you of your immediate duties," Napoleon instructed. "I hope you will be able to overtake the fugitives. Quickly, though, tell me how and where you met them!"

The baron supplied him with a brief, yet thorough report, which the emperor followed with considerable interest. Satisfied with the update, Napoleon turned his attention to Richemonte. "Captain!" he barked, employing his fiercest tone.

"Sire!" replied Richemonte, nearly shaking.

"A man demanded satisfaction from you!"

Richemonte made a short bow, confirming the obvious.

"Not just *any* man, but a nobleman!" Napoleon said. "And you chose to refuse him!"

Another bow. The captain, unable to escape his embarrassment, and terrified at the inquisition, felt his heart beat like a drum.

"Through your carelessness, you permitted the escape of people whom I had entrusted into your care. Do you know what this means?"

Drops of sweat formed on the captain's brow.

"As I indicated earlier, I have forgiven your failure. Baron Roman de Sainte-Marie's presence left me little choice. However, I will not tolerate your incompetence, and I no longer consider you an officer and a gentleman. I suggest you pursue the fugitives with a renewed fervor. Should you fail in your attempt to bring them back, there is nothing you could accomplish that will bring you back into my good graces. In the event that happens, I do not want to see your face again. Only when you are successful in capturing them will you receive any hope of milder judgment. Now, are you still convinced the German Hussar lieutenant is with the ladies?"

"Yes, Majesty," Richemonte said, relieved the inquiry had changed direction.

"You can bring him back to me alive," Napoleon said, "or simply shoot him when you find him. Either way, take great care to bring the ladies back to me unharmed."

"We will depart immediately."

"Where will you start the search?"

"First, we will follow the trail to Sedan," the captain began, "where we should be able to ascertain the direction they took. With your permission, Sire, we will procure the necessary soldiers to accompany us."

"Perish the thought!" Napoleon scolded him. "Are you actually considering the enlistment of an entire regiment to capture two women? Do you wish to draw the attention of the whole world to your unusual plight?

Three, at most four, soldiers should be sufficient. If you ride hard, you can catch them in a short time. Do not disappoint me again, Captain!" He made an about turn and left them alone to ponder their task.

Reillac didn't bother to conceal his satisfaction with the way the conversation had gone. "Now you can see I was right!" he said. "He came by himself instead of sending for us. What a beastly mess! First, I need to become familiar with the contents of this document."

"No, not now! You can do it once we're underway. We need to leave right away, because the emperor is watching us closely."

"If we're unsuccessful in our attempt to recapture the ladies, then our careers are finished. How can we get even with the elusive Löwenklau and that traitorous Florian? If only we had more soldiers at our disposal."

"*Pah!* We can handle it with a little luck. If we have no other choice, we can ambush them. The important thing is that we leave right away and bring this miserable tale to a successful conclusion!"

About the same time, Napoleon made his way back through the corridor to his room. Before he arrived, a door opened suddenly, striking him square on the forehead.

"What a pigsty!"[26.2] an angry voice called from inside the room. "Who had the audacity..." A bearded man appeared in the doorway, clad only in a nightshirt. He was none other than the dragoon major, whose uniform had fallen victim to the enterprising Florian. Napoleon stopped, gently probing his forehead with his hands.

"*Mon dieu!* How can anyone be so careless?" complained Napoleon.

The half-clad major realized whom he had unintentionally hit with the door and bowed deeply. "Hang it all! The emperor!"

"Yes, it is I, your emperor! I have a good mind to instruct you, in the future... Ah!" he interrupted himself, only then recognizing the man he was addressing. "Major Marbeille!"

"A thousand pardons, Majesty!" the undressed man stammered. "I was looking for my uniform, which seems to have been removed for some reason..."

Napoleon, however, had already deduced the event's significance. "You are the victim of a robbery," he said, trying to keep himself from smiling at the pathetic-looking major.

"Stolen? By God, if I catch that thief, I will hang him from the rafters!"

"The question remains, can he be caught?"

"But what should I do?"

"Borrow another uniform in the interim and close the door!"

As the emperor walked away, only then did the major grasp the severity of the encounter in the hall. *"Zounds!"* he cursed loudly. *He saw me in my nightshirt! I'll have to call for another uniform right away and start inquiries about the thief. If I manage to catch up with him, I'm going to hang him, or simply shoot him, as revenge for all the embarrassment he's caused me.*

He closed the door just in time so he wouldn't be seen by Richemonte and Reillac, who were just then walking past.

CHAPTER TWENTY-SEVEN
Reillac's Reward

The baron and captain left the estate a few minutes later, accompanied by three Grenadiers. They spurred their horses to a gallop, following the road to Sedan. When they arrived, they quickly learned that the fugitives had crossed and exited the city, taking the road toward Bouillon. They continued on that road, pursuing their quarry and making much better progress. They had nothing to slow them down, while Löwenklau had to contend with the two ladies, a vice of combined injury and inexperience. As a result, the pursuers reached Bouillon in a relatively short time.

In a field near the town, they spotted two elderly workers. The men stopped nearby to rest the horses, while Richemonte dismounted his horse and walked toward the old couple.

"Are you from this area?" Richemonte asked, calling to them.

"Yes, Monsieur," the man answered.

"Who are you?"

"I am the innkeeper and this is my wife."

The captain took a moment to regard the old woman, who had also stopped her work to listen in. "How long have you been working outside?" he asked.

"About two hours."

"Did any riders come this way?"

"Yes, a few."

"How many?"

"Four, Monsieur."

"Were they soldiers?"

"Yes, three soldiers, one officer and two subordinates."

"What about the fourth one?"

"He looked like a servant."

"Did something stand out about any them?"

The husband exchanged glances with his wife. "Should we tell him?" he whispered to her.

"Who knows what's right," she replied quietly.

Richemonte, noticing their reluctant whispering, shot them a clear warning. "I am here in the service of the emperor. I implore you to tell the truth or be prepared to face the consequences. So, was there something unusual?"

"Well actually," the man hesitated. "One of the soldiers was a woman."

"Really? How do you know?"

"The major helped her from the horse and her hair fell from under the cap."

"Why did he lift her from the horse?"

"Probably because she felt queasy. He carried her to the brook and gave her water to drink."

"Did they stay a long time?"

"No," the man said. "They rode on after a short rest."

"Which way? Probably towards Paliseul?"

"No, they turned left and headed into the mountains."

"*Zounds!* What could they want up there?" he called out to Reillac. "I suppose that's a good way to elude pursuers."

The baron nodded. "Right," he agreed. "It'll be more difficult to pick up their trail in the forest covered mountains. Of course, we still have to make an attempt."

"That goes without saying," Richemonte agreed. He faced the innkeeper again and asked, "Did they ride fast?"

"Very slowly, actually."

"Did they talk to you?"

"Not a word. However, we recognized the major."

"How come? What is his name?"

"That I don't know. He spent the night with us two days ago."

"As a guest?"

"Yes."

"Was he in uniform?"

"Oh no. He told us he was a musician from Paris."

Richemonte pursed his lips irritably. "That was a lie. I will let you in on a little secret. He is a Prussian spy whom we have been pursuing. Where does that path lead?"

"Into the forest to an old coal hut."

"Not further? Does it lead to a town or a village?"

"No."

"That's no good. How long since they left?"

"Perhaps half an hour."

Richemonte turned to his companion. "Maybe we can still catch them before they reach the forest!"

"If you leave right away and exert your horses, you might get there before they reach the coal hut."

"Then let's go!"

They dug in their heels and shot up the small mountain path, the soldiers following close behind them. It was difficult to remain in the saddle going uphill, but they had no intention of sparing their horses. In fact, they pushed them faster than ever, gaining as much ground as possible on their escapees. Richemonte was fixated on the task and kept all his attention ahead. Just as they were about to circumvent a bush, he suddenly pulled in his horse's reins, signaling a stop.

"What do you see?" asked Reillac, following his lead.

"Over there! Look!" The captain pointed ahead. Reillac's eyes followed the movement of his hand.

"Dammit!" he said. "That must be the hut."

"Of course! Look at those two sitting there in the moss... they look familiar, don't they?"

"It's that damned Florian."

"What about the fellow beside him? He's looking the other way."

Reillac narrowed his eyes, focusing on the person in question. "Ah, he just turned around..." His voice trailed away, his eyes turning to Richemonte, wide with surprise. "Albin, I can't believe it. It's your mother!"

"Unbelievable. Who would have thought this woman was capable of donning a soldier's uniform! Where are the other two?"

"Löwenklau and Margot? Probably inside the hut."

"I doubt it!" replied the captain, shaking his head. "I don't see their horses."

"You're right! Did they split up to confuse us?"

"Not likely. They probably rode a little ahead. They're lovers, after all. They probably wanted some time alone."

The baron's eyes glowered dangerously. "Damn them! What should we do now?"

"We couldn't have asked for anything better. We'll surprise them so Florian won't have a chance to put up a fight. Then we'll go after Margot and Löwenklau."

"The best option is to ride circumspectly around to the back of the shack, dismount, and approach them from the forest side," Reillac suggested. "We'll catch them by surprise and have an easy time of it."

"Right! Let's go!"

They rode in a big circle to get to the far side of the clearing and approach the hut from the rear without being seen. They dismounted and crept closer. Florian was talking to Margot's mother, completely unaware of the looming danger. Even Tiger, his loyal dog, didn't warn them of their approach, since the wind favored the pursuers.

"Will you be able to continue, Madame?" asked Florian.

"I hope so," she replied. "I've managed to get a little rest, and am ready to continue. Will we find them?"

"Without a doubt," said Florian.

"Will they be waiting in the ravine?" she asked.

"Yes. I know the way. May I help you to mount your horse?"

"Yes, please."

She rose to her feet. Florian intended to do the same, but was pressed into the moss by six strong arms. In the same instant, a powerful rifle butt struck Tiger on the head, taking him out of commission. Madame Richemonte was easily subdued. Before she knew it, her eyes were gazing at the face of her stepson, as though it were a dream.

"So, we've finally caught up to you," Albin said, catching his breath.

"Albin! Dear God, it's Albin!" she exclaimed in a terrified voice. Her face went pale as she sank to the ground and drifted into unconsciousness.

"Dammit, let me go!" exclaimed Florian, trying to free himself. It was a valiant but futile attempt against two prepared and determined adversaries.

"You bastard," Richemonte said. "Cooperate or you'll pay for it! You're nothing but a liar and a traitor!"

"Don't be ridiculous!" said Florian. "I can go on excursions with whomever I wish."

"Yes, but your current outing will not fair well. Where's Monsieur Löwenklau?" asked Reillac.

"I don't know!"

"And Margot?"

"Likely with him." Florian hoped Löwenklau had enough of a head start to elude his pursuers.

"Look here, Florian, you're going to have to do better than that," Richemonte demanded. "Give me something to go on or else you'll get a smack on the head. Where are they now?"

"I don't know. Go ahead and hit me!"

"We'll have time for that later. By the way, you're mistaken if you don't think we'll find them," Reillac said. "The ravine you talked about earlier is not that remote."

"This is where they rode," interrupted Richemonte, pointing to the tracks on the ground. "You can clearly make out fresh tracks."

"Right!" replied Reillac. "It shouldn't be difficult to follow them."

"It looks like they rode slowly, perhaps so Mama and Florian could meet up with them. We may as well take our time and follow on foot."

"That's probably the best," the baron agreed. "It's too cumbersome by horse. First, we have to make sure these two accomplices won't be tempted to escape."

They quickly tied up Florian and the unconscious mother and gave the soldiers orders to stand guard over them. Led by Richemonte, the two men followed the fresh tracks made by Löwenklau. The soft forest floor left deep imprints, making it child's play for them to follow. Before long, they reached the tree where Löwenklau had tied up the horses. Richemonte spotted the horses first and held Reillac back.

"Hold on!" he whispered. "Do you see the horses?"

"Of course! Where are the riders?"

"Close by, I'm sure."

"Should we wait here until they return?"

"No," the captain said. "I think I know why they didn't wait at the entrance to the ravine."

"You think they left the others behind on purpose?"

"Something like that. We might be able to get a glimpse if we follow them carefully, but we have to remain on the upper edge of the ravine."

They crept forward and spotted the two lovers, alone in a small clearing. Löwenklau was standing while Margot sat on a nearby boulder.

"He must be talking about something important, judging from his animated gestures."

"Yes," confirmed Reillac. "If we get closer, we'll be able to overhear their conversation."

"There's a large bush near them," Richemonte said, pointing it out to the baron. "If we get behind it, we'll be able to listen without being detected."

"What if they spot us?"

"Then we'll attack him! I doubt that Margot would put up much of a fight."

"Maybe we should just shoot him," Reillac suggested.

"I've thought of that. It would be a much too easy end for the bastard. If we can manage it, we'll let him live for now so he can dangle from a rope later."

They succeeded in concealing themselves behind the overgrown bush. Not only were they close enough to observe the couple, but they could also hear every word of the private conversation. Reillac was mesmerized with Margot's beauty, even though she was still clad as a common soldier.

"Is this the same strong box the old innkeeper talked about?" asked Margot.

"Yes, there's no mistake."

"Do you know how much is inside?"

Löwenklau paused, considering the question. "No, but judging from its size, probably millions."

"Who else knows of the plundered war chest?"

"Only a few people. No one knows of its exact location, though. Except for me, of course."

"How will you make use of it?"

"First, I'm going to see how events are affected by the outcome of the war. Then I'll know how to act."

"Oh, please, show me the spot, Hugo! I would love to know how one feels while standing on buried treasure."

"You'll see soon enough. Come on!" He took her by the hand and led her to the place where the chest was buried. "This is it, Margot. You're standing on a great treasure. This place is guarded by the spirits of the two dead robbers." He turned as he spoke to point out the graves of the two murderers. By chance, he glanced quickly at the nearby bush concealing the two eaves-droppers.

"Dammit!" Richemonte whispered. "I think he saw us."

"I've got the same feeling," replied Reillac quietly.

"Still, we don't know for sure. Just when I thought he spotted us, he continued talking to Margot, as though he didn't have a care in the world. The idiot is captivated by his newfound fortune and blinded by its allure."

Richemonte couldn't have been more wrong. Löwenklau had not only detected him, but his companion as well. His initial reaction was one of utter shock, yet he had the fortitude not to show it and continued talking to Margot.

"Actually, my love, this is not the only treasure I know of."

"What? You know of others?" she asked incredulously.

"Yes. That was an incredible day for me. I learned the thieves had also conducted a daring raid and made off with a chest of diamonds. The stones are buried near here."

"Really? Where?"

"Not far from the entrance to the ravine."

"This is wonderful!" she cried. "What do you plan to do with this new find?"

"I'll take the necessary steps to return them to their rightful owners."

She smiled at him lovingly. "I'm blessed to have you Hugo, and I would have expected no less. Many would have been tempted to keep the spoils for themselves."

"Not me! I know my responsibility is to ensure the victims of this world are looked after. I fear they could easily be discovered. Therefore, I need to move them to a safer location, which is why I've brought you here."

"Move them where?"

"I thought of moving them beside the strong box. This way, no one will suspect there's a treasure around here. Are you with me, Margot?"

"Of course! What shall I do?"

"Wait here until I return and retrieve the diamonds."

"How long will you be?"

"Maybe ten or fifteen minutes."

"That's too long, Hugo. What if someone has followed us?"

"No one knows we headed into the mountains. We're safe here."

"But I'm afraid of my brother."

"I'm not. I don't think he can measure up to me."

Her eyes pleaded with him. "I still don't want to wait here all alone with the dead men. Please, take me with you!"

"All right. We'll be back in no time at all to bury the diamonds alongside the strong box. Then we can head back to the coal hut." He took Margot by the hand and walked back with her to the ravine entrance, where they had left their horses.

Richemonte and Reillac looked at each other, not believing what they had just heard.

"Quick, after them!" whispered Reillac. He was about to leap from their cover when the captain reached a hand to hold him back.

"Hold it! That would be a big mistake, Baron!" warned the captain. "We must remain here."

"I don't understand."

"Well, to begin with, if he spots us, he'll lead us somewhere else and we'll never discover the location of the diamonds."

Reillac settled himself back into position. "Yes," he acknowledged. "You're right."

"The better way is to have a little patience and await their return. This way, we'll find out the location of the strong box and be assured of success."

"Hmm. Are you sure he'll come back?"

"Of course! You heard what he said."

"Yes, every word!" the baron said, his eyes beginning to glitter with the prospect of the treasure. "My God! A military strong box and diamonds!"

"So, what do you think?" asked the captain. His own eyes held a sinister glow, full of desire for affluence and riches. Of the two men, he was the poorest, who had risked so much for wealth. Now, he found himself on the threshold of acquiring a fortune so immense it would solve all his financial problems.

Richemonte looked over at his companion, realizing that he stood with another man before this stream of wealth. Should he allow Reillac to become a partaker and enjoy a portion of the treasure? Wasn't he the same man who still carried those dreaded promissory notes in his pocket, the ones that had condemned him to so many sleepless nights and unfulfilled prospects? Hadn't Reillac committed himself to retaining only one heir, his sister Margot? The whole matter rested on one critical point. Margot could only exercise her right as heir if he were actually dead! An ominous thought worked its way through Richemonte's mind, taking root.

337

"Wonderful!" Reillac said, not even bothering to contain his excitement. "Imagine, there's a war chest buried in this ravine."

"And thanks to Löwenklau," Richemonte added, "we're partakers of that knowledge!"

"Extraordinary, Captain! Simply extraordinary! How do you think he came to learn of this secret?"

"Who knows! If we arrived a moment sooner, we might have found out, but that's beside the point. We need to decide what to do now."

The baron paused, collecting himself again. "Well, it's quite simple."

"What do you have in mind?"

"We'll brush Löwenklau aside with one good shot. The others don't need to know what we overheard. We'll bring them back to the emperor, and then—"

"Then what?"

"We'll return to claim the chest."

"Fine, but if we want to carry out the plan, we can't arrest them now."

"Why not?"

"Because it'll reveal to them we've been spying the whole time. The chest could so easily be lost."

"That's true," Reillac allowed. "It would be best to wait until they buried the diamonds. That way, we'll be witnesses to the actual site of the treasure. From there, we can decide what to do."

"I suppose you're right. We should conceal ourselves deeper in the brush, so they won't see us."

"Yes, come on!"

As Reillac crept ahead, Richemonte followed him, although slightly behind him and to the side, so he could carry out his newly formed plan. He reached into his pocket and, unseen by Reillac, removed a hunting knife. "Once we have the war chest, then what?" he asked Reillac to distract him.

"We'll divide the spoils!" the baron replied enthusiastically. "Today's my lucky day!"

"I don't think so."

"No? I don't understand you. Are you thinking of leaving some of it behind?"

"Would that bother you?"

"Well, why shouldn't we keep it all? Were you thinking of leaving it for the state?"

"Of course not! However, I don't have to worry about dividing anything. In fact, I'll take the money for myself."

"What?" Reillac asked, surprised. "Do you think I'll turn it over to you, Captain?"

"Why not?"

"For one thing, I'm not that stupid—Oh!"

Reillac only managed to let out a single gasp before collapsing to the ground, for in that same instant Richemonte's knife plunged deep into his back. His body shuddered and convulsed one final time, then was completely still. Reillac, the wealthy businessman and supplier to Napoleon's army, was dead.

"Well, well, my dear Baron!" the captain said quietly, grinning. "This is indeed our lucky day. Now you can share the spoils with whomever you wish. You deceived my father and brought nothing but misery to me. You alone are to blame for what I've become, and this is your reward. Fitting, isn't it? I'll fabricate a story and tell the emperor you fought with Löwenklau, later succumbing to your injuries. The war chest, the diamonds, the notes... all will be mine for the taking."

He unfastened the dead man's jacket and rifled through its pockets. He found a purse full of money, a large billfold, containing various documents, and the long sought after promissory notes.

"I've finally won!" he cried out jubilantly. *He made Margot his sole heir, and when I have her under my control, I'll have access to his entire fortune. Now, all I have to do is wait for Löwenklau to return. As soon as he buries the stones, I'll finish him off before he has a chance to mount his horse."*

While he waited for Löwenklau's return, he pocketed the stolen items in his jacket. He had barely finished when a shot rang out.

What was that? he asked himself. *It sounded like a gun shot, and nearby too. Dammit!* Another one sounded loudly, and then another—three shots in total! *They seem to be coming from the vicinity of the coal hut! Could they have anything to do with the three Grenadiers?* He ventured toward the sound of gunfire, anxious to have a look for himself.

Richemonte crawled out of his hiding spot and ran to the edge of the ravine. He stopped for a moment to collect his thoughts.

The horses are gone! he thought to himself, smacking his forehead with his hand in disgust. *Damn! That's the second time Löwenklau got the better of me.* Then, an unwelcome thought dawned on him. *I'm sure the strong box is here, somewhere close, but perhaps he made up the story about the diamonds to distract us.* Suddenly, he was convinced that Löwenklau had spotted him earlier in the bush.

"Well, I'm not through with you yet, Monsieur Löwenklau," he whispered under his breath. "I have a score to settle with you!"

He drew his pistols and held them out in front of him, ready for action. He rushed forward to the hut, using the trees as cover. His instinct didn't betray him. The horses were gone, as well as his captives.

Meanwhile, Löwenklau and Margot had reached their horses. He untied them in a rush and called out to Margot. "Quickly, get on your horse!"

"Why?" she asked surprised, seeing the sudden and urgent change in his expression.

"I'll tell you in a minute," he replied, helping her into the saddle. He was on his mount in no time. He grabbed the reins and led both horses in a roundabout way back to the hut.

"Why are we going back?" she asked.

"To rescue Mama," Hugo replied. "I fear she's in great danger."

"Rescue her? What kind of danger?"

"I suspect Florian and Mama have been captured."

Sheer terror seemed to come over her. "Dear God," she managed. "How do you know that?"

"It came to me in an instant. You'll be shocked when I tell you who I saw lurking in the bushes back there."

"Who?" she asked frightened.

"Your brother. He was hiding in that large bush behind us. A second man was with him, but I couldn't see his face. They must have followed our trail and overheard our conversation about the strong box. I'm sure they would have shot me if it weren't for that story about the diamonds."

"Did you make that up, Hugo?"

"It was the only way to save us. They allowed us to leave unmolested, thinking we would return with the diamonds and reveal the treasure's location."

"You holy saints!²⁷·¹ What about my Mama? Hugo, what can we do?"

"I can only surmise the following. The fact that our pursuers are already in the ravine only suggests that those we left behind are now under their control."

"Then we're doomed!"

"Not yet! It all depends on how many we have to deal with. I'm going to leave you here, Margot. You have to trust me."

They came to a dense cropping of fir trees and dismounted.

"For God's sake!" she cried. "Don't leave me alone."

"Don't worry, my love," Hugo said, trying to reassure her. "You're safe here. Watch the horses and I'll return as soon as possible."

"Will you promise me?"

"Yes, my love."

"Then hurry, Hugo. I'll pray for you."

He crept toward the hut, moving slowly so as not to arouse attention from those inside. As he approached, he spotted something on the ground near the hut. With heightened awareness, he crept closer. What he saw next both surprised and reassured him at the same time. Madame Richemonte sat on the ground, unmoving. Florian lay next to her, tied up with a rope. His dog lay on the ground a few paces to the side, unconscious, having sustained a fractured skull. Three armed soldiers stood guard over them.

Poor devils! said Löwenklau to himself. *But I can't afford to spare their lives.* He crept to the far side of the hut, which was shielded by brush. He pulled the pistols from his coat and cocked the hammers. Even though he was careful, one of the soldiers heard the sound.

"Who's there?" he called out and walked around the corner. He was struck by Löwenklau's bullet, killing him instantly. The other two soldiers met the same fate before they could mount a defense.

"Lieutenant!" Florian shouted in gratitude.

Madame Richemonte also roused at his approach. "My dear son!"

"At last!" called out Hugo and concentrated on freeing them from their restraints. "We have to act quickly," Hugo reminded them. "Are there any others?"

"Just the captain and Reillac," replied Florian.

"Then fetch the horses. We have to leave before they get back."

They quickly mounted and rode to the place where he had left Margot. It was clear she was frightened, though her face lit up when she spotted her mother unharmed.

"I heard shots," she said with uncertainty. "What happened?"

"Later, later!" Hugo said. "Now's not the time for explanations. Follow me!" He led the way back to the ravine, this time using the longer way so he could avoid the remaining two pursuers.

Florian was surprised as they entered the ravine. "Why in here?" he asked.

"No questions," the lieutenant said again. "Just follow me! We have to return and allow our horses to beat the ground, creating more tracks, and making our presence more difficult to detect." He led his horse near the area where he had spotted the concealed captain earlier. Suddenly, he noticed a pool of blood on the ground.

"Blood!" he said aloud. "What could this mean? Those two should be long gone! They must have heard the shots at the coal hut and rushed to the aid of their subordinates."

Florian jumped from his horse and carefully approached the bush. "Dear God! A corpse!" he exclaimed.

Horrified, the two ladies turned away. Löwenklau dismounted and joined Florian. They pulled the body from the underbrush and turned him over.

"Reillac!" exclaimed a shocked Florian.

"Yes, Reillac," Löwenklau said more quietly in confirmation. He bent down and examined the dead man. "He's dead, but still warm. There's a deep wound in his back which has penetrated the heart. It seems as though he's been stabbed from behind. His watch, billfold, and personal papers are all missing." He paused, coming slowly to the natural conclusion. "Obviously, Captain Richemonte is the murderer!"

Madame Richemonte screamed in horror at the latest revelation about Albin. "Dear God, it just can't be!"

"Yes, it was Albin," replied Hugo. "No one else was with the baron. I believe I know the reason why he was murdered, too, but that's for later. We must leave this place. The captain could return at any time. We'll have to leave the body behind!" He allowed his horse to prance about, making new hoof prints and disguising the location of the buried chest. They rode up the embankment of the ravine, heading away from the tragic scene.

By the time Richemonte had reached the hut, his prisoners were gone and he was left with the corpses of the three Grenadiers. "Hell and damnation!" he cursed. *He shot the guards and freed the captives. Where could they have gone? He must have seen me in the gorge while I spoke to Reillac and now he's gone back to settle the score with me. But that's where he's wrong! My bullet will find its mark before he sees me.*

He climbed onto his mount and let the other horses run free. They would only have been a burden to him. He rode back to the ravine only to find it abandoned. Still, Richemonte rode in, continuing his search. He spotted the hoof prints and examined them carefully.

Damn, they were here all right, he thought, clenching his teeth. *They let their horses stomp the grass, probably in an effort to disguise the location of the chest. No bother, I'm still going to find it, and then... Dammit! The baron's corpse! Well, they probably suspect I'm the murderer, which could prove awkward for me. I have to go after them and finish them off! I don't have to worry about mother and daughter, just the men!*

CHAPTER TWENTY-EIGHT
A Deadly Encounter

It was the fourteenth of June when a young man dressed in civilian clothes rode like the devil on the road from Lüttich to Namur. Though not in uniform, many officers on the busy highway greeted him as he flew by. Upon his arrival in Namur, he immediately inquired about the location of Field Marshal von Blücher's headquarters. He reported to the adjutant, who arranged for his immediate admittance. The marshal was occupied with several officers, including General Gleisenau, Major-General Grolman, and Major von Drigalski.

Despite the presence of the high profile personalities, Blücher invited in the newcomer with open arms. "Löwenklau, my boy!" he called out. "Did the devil bring you back so soon?[28.1] Were you looking for me in Lüttich?"

"Yes, Excellency, I was not informed until my arrival that your headquarters had been relocated."

"It was necessary, my son. All hell will soon break loose! There's going to be a thrashing like you've never seen, a terrible time for everybody. It hasn't been determined yet which side will be its recipient. Can you guess, my boy?"

"I don't know, but I do know you've been singled out, Excellency!"

"What! Me?" asked the old warrior, a little perturbed. "Am I supposed to get a thrashing? Who said that?"

"The emperor himself."

"Really, Napoleon? That only proves he's half-mad, something I've known for a long time already. Who did he tell?"

"Ney, Groucy, and Drouet."

"Ah! A formidable bunch which I'll no doubt have to contend with. Are you perchance on friendly terms with one of them?"

"Thanks for that honor, Excellency!" he said sarcastically.

"Well, I just assumed it, since you seem to know exactly what was discussed with Napoleon."

"I was able to overhear their plans."

"Where?"

"At Jeannette, near Raucourt."

Blücher reflected on that for a moment, quickly recognizing the name of the place. "Over there? Isn't that where you kept your girl? Was Napoleon there, too?"

"Yes, Excellency!"

"What on earth did he want?"

"I had the distinct impression he wanted to take my bride for himself."

The old marshal stared at him, dumbfounded. "You're putting me on, my boy!"

"Not in the least. In fact, he openly declared his affection for her."

"*Zounds!* He should have been more concerned about a pair of warm mitts and a blissful end to his reign.[28.2] Let me hear all about it!"

"Excellency, if I may, a lot has occurred at Jeannette, much of which is of a personal nature. It would take a considerable amount of time to relay. May I defer that for another time and instead deal with Napoleon's plans for the upcoming battle, which will require immediate preparation?"

"Of course. Will he make the first move and attack our forces?"

"Yes," Löwenklau said. "I believe so."

"When?"

"Tomorrow, or the day after tomorrow at the latest."

"Excellent! The sooner the better! But against whom?"

"Against you, Excellency!"

"Not Wellington?"

The lieutenant shook his head. "No, and I know the reason why he singled you out."

"What is it?"

"He stated to his staff that Your Excellency is impetuous and hot-tempered, while Wellington weighs matters carefully and doesn't act on impulse. If he were to attack Wellington, then Blücher would rush to his side—"

"That's true," Blücher interrupted. "We would make short work of him."

"However, if he were to attack Your Excellency, then your forces would be defeated by the time Wellington made up his mind to deploy his forces."

"Listen, my boy, that Corsican is not as crazy as I first thought. We need to be more cautious."

Löwenklau continued to explain in detail what he gleaned from his lofty observation post at Jeannette. It was clear that, with the revelation of Napoleon's plans, new measures were in order.

Blücher was so occupied with issuing new orders that he only had time for Löwenklau later in the evening. They sat together, each one with a pipe in his hand and their boots propped up on a chair. The lieutenant spoke of his experiences of the last few days, and was often interrupted by a curse, question or comical retort, all proof of the interest the old Blücher had in the young man's affairs.

"Do you think Richemonte was still watching you both?"

"I would swear to it."

"So," Blücher pried, "is Margot still safe in Gedinne?"

"No, even though the trusty Florian is guarding her."

"Hmm! It's like reading a romantic novel. But unlike the novel, we can do something about the outcome."

"Will His Excellency allow me the opportunity to look after my interests?"

"Right away, my son. Do you know what you have to do?"

"I trust His Excellency will advise me."

Blücher paused for a moment, allowing the young man's anticipation to build. "You have to look after your girl."

"Excellency!"

"Don't worry! I know what you want to say. I want you to render a service for your country, yet at the same time look out for your personal interests. Do you know what I'm referring to?"

"The strong box?"

"Yes. Are you convinced Richemonte will make every attempt to discover the location of the chest?"

"Absolutely."

"Well then, it's up us to beat him to it! But how? After all, the chest is located in enemy territory."

"That may be the case for now," Löwenklau began, "but our forces will soon occupy that land."

Blücher nodded, then added, "But our friend Richemonte might help himself to the treasure in the meantime. We should at least consider guarding the spot until we get there."

"I fear it would be too cumbersome, Excellency."

"I suppose you have a better idea?"

"I think it would be appropriate for us to remove the strong box altogether and find a better location. Then we can wait for the right time and Richemonte will be none the wiser."

"Yes, that's probably best, my boy! Do you want to be assigned to the task?"

"Yes, with all my heart!"

"Then why didn't you already do it?"

"I didn't have the resources. I will need men whom I can trust."

"Right!" the marshal said. "I'll provide you with discreet men. How many will you need?"

"Ten should do it."

"Good, you'll get them. You can choose them yourself and I'll leave the rest to your ingenuity. Furthermore, I'll ensure that the news of Richemonte's cowardly attack on his companion doesn't fall between the cracks. In fact, I'll make sure it comes to the attention of the French authorities!"

A few days later, a man dressed in tattered clothes entered the little town of Gedinne. Not only did his disheveled appearance suggest he had been through a hard time, but he also wore a bandage wrapped around his head, which in itself made a convincing argument. He stopped in front of the local inn and considered persuading the innkeeper to give him a drink. His musings, however, were interrupted by a knock on the window.

"Come on in, poor fellow," a voice called to him from inside. "Are you hungry?" The sojourner didn't have to be asked twice. He entered through the front door and walked into the parlor. A few men were seated at the table, all seemingly town's folk save one. It was he who had invited the vagrant to enter.

All eyes were on the stranger as he stepped in. They shook their heads in disapproval. The innkeeper at least felt he should address him. "Man, what business do you have in here?" he asked.

"I'm not sure. This monsieur called me inside."

The innkeeper turned to face the inviter. "Monsieur, why did you call him in? He doesn't belong in here."

The man being questioned was younger than the innkeeper and dressed in decent clothes. He looked at him reproachfully. "Proprietor, do you know who I am?"

"No, Monsieur."

"Then I will forgive your indiscretion. I trust you are a loyal Frenchman."

The innkeeper seemed indignant to even be asked such a thing. "Of course, Monsieur!"

"And these gentlemen?"

"They are as well."

"Have you heard of the army supplier, Baron de Reillac?"

"The millionaire? We've all seen him."

"Well then, he's suddenly disappeared, vanished without a trace. I have been instructed by the emperor to search for him, as he's likely fallen into trouble, maybe even treachery."

"Are you a procurator?"

"Yes, I have just come from Paris. So, if I show this poor soul, who's obviously hungry and thirsty, a little charity, then leave that to me. I can well afford it!"

"You're right, Monsieur. Do what pleases you. Just make sure he has proper identity papers!"

"Of course," he replied, turning to the vagrant. "What do you do for a living?" he asked.

"I had a monkey and a marmot in my act," replied the stranger in a southern dialect. "I would go from village to village and amuse the townsfolk for a few pennies. Then I ran into the Prussian army and lost it all, including my animals. I'm forced to beg so I can get home!"

"Then have a meal and put it on my account, you poor devil. Come sit here!"

The southerner accepted the invitation, showing his satisfaction with a big grin on his face. While the vagrant dug into his meal, the procurator made small talk.

"Are they all together?" he whispered when no one was within earshot.

"All of them," replied the southerner.

"What about the tools?"

"They're concealed in the forest, Corporal."

The procurator put a finger to his lips. "Don't mention my rank. By the way, I'm impressed with your role playing."

"It's not difficult. Where do I meet the lieutenant?"

"At the isolated cottage, near the forest's edge."

"What name is he going by?"

"Just ask for Florian. The rest will unfold. Follow his directions and it'll lead you to the meeting place. I'm going now. Don't hang around here too long."

The disguised procurator paid his bill and left the guesthouse. The southerner, having consumed his meal, left a few minutes later.

He had only been gone a short time when a new guest entered. The newcomer looked around and addressed the innkeeper in an authoritative tone.

"I am Captain Richemonte," he said. "I am looking for the mayor. I was told he was here."

One of the men stood up. "I am the mayor, Monsieur," he said. "What do you want?"

"A little information."

"Then I am at your service," the mayor replied politely.

"Tell me," Richemonte said, "did the population of your little hamlet increase recently?"

"Yes, indeed. We had a birth two weeks ago."

"Amusing!" laughed the captain. "That's not what I meant. Are you aware of any strangers who may have recently settled in the area?"

The mayor thought about it for a moment, then shook his head. "No, I can't think of any."

"Are visitors obligated to register with your office?"

"Of course."

"Have there been any such registrations?"

"Not recently."

"Fine," Richemonte said. "I'm looking for three people, two ladies and their servant. The ladies are refined and are actually mother and daughter. They're in hiding somewhere in your district. I'm prepared to offer a reward to anyone who can supply me with information on their whereabouts."

"Can you give me a description of the three people?" the mayor asked.

"A full description is not necessary. The daughter is supposed to be very beautiful."

"How curious? You're the second man today making inquiries in our little village. A procurator from Paris has just left. He was also looking for someone who had disappeared."

"Ah! Who was he looking for?"

"A certain Baron de Reillac," the mayor answered, "the army supplier and millionaire."

The captain felt the blood drain from his face. "Where did the solicitor go from here?"

"I don't know, Monsieur."

"Is there still a military presence in town?"

"No, not since the emperor won the battle at Ligny.[28.3] The troops have been redeployed. Is there anything else I can do for you?"

"Just a glass of burgundy from the innkeeper," Richemonte said, deep in thought. He sat down with his wine but had no further conversation with the mayor. Later, he paid his bill and quietly left, taking the road to Paliseul. He carried on a loud conversation with himself as he walked.

"Damn lousy luck!" he grumbled as he came to an abrupt halt. "The army has won some major battles, but I can't show my face to the emperor. And on top of that, I lost the trail of those tiresome women! If only I could catch that meddling Löwenklau!" He resumed his walk, only to come to another stop a few steps later. "That war chest is the solution to all my problems," he continued, his voice echoing across the lonely road. "If I could only believe it's really buried in that ravine. Why don't I look for it myself, rather than running after Margot and Mama? Reillac's body is probably still there, just as I left him. What if someone were to stumble across him? Are the three Grenadiers actually dead? What if one of them survived and reported the incident to his commander? I should have satisfied myself that they were actually dead." He shook his head at his own apparent imprudence. "I'll stay in Paliseul tonight and head for the ravine in the morning so I can bring everything in order."

As he walked, the captain didn't realize he was passing by the very ones he had been seeking after the most. He heard something in the distance, like a rumbling or thunder. "The sound of another battle," he remarked. "*Pah!* Let them kill each other. Just leave me the plundered strong box!"

He was right in his prediction, as much killing was going on at the source of the noise. It was the infamous battle of Waterloo on the eighteenth of June 1815, the one that was characterized so intensely by the embittered conflict between the armies of a defeated emperor and those of a determined Blücher.

❧✠☙

A fine-looking cottage stood on the edge of the forest. Its appearance was far from lush, yet it had a clean and charming look about it. The owner was a relative of Florian's, who had been willing to receive and later conceal his charges. This had, of course, proved difficult in the last few days. The area was bristling with military activity and he had been forced to accommodate several officers for a couple of nights. This necessitated the concealing of the two women in the cellar. Once the army had moved on, he was able to relocate the ladies back to more suitable quarters. They made themselves as comfortable as possible under the circumstances, finding their small gable room to their liking.

In the meantime, Florian sat with his host in the garden, content to talk about anything and everything. A distant rumbling interrupted their talk on this particular day.

"Did you hear that, Florian?" the landlord asked.

"Yes, a few times already."

"It sounds like an earthquake."

"More like muffled thunder. I noticed it at midday."

"Do you think it could be another offensive?"

"Quite likely."

The landlord looked sidelong at Florian. "It could mean bad news for the Prussian forces," he said, expecting a reply.

The coachman didn't disappoint. "Why would you think the Prussians are getting trounced?"

"Just a hunch."

"Would you be glad if this were the case?"

"No. You know I'm not in league with the French, and I never have been. Since you've chosen to be secretive with me, I'm permitted to keep my thoughts to myself."

"Really?" Florian wondered. "I know you to be a loyal and trustworthy man, uncle."

"All right. But why don't you trust me?"

"What! Not trust you? I don't follow. You've got nothing to complain about."

"I do have a legitimate complaint," the uncle pointed out. "You can't pretend not to notice those strangers who've hidden themselves in the forest and keep looking at my cottage."

"Really?" Florian said again coyly. "I haven't noticed."

"Tell me, who was the gentleman that came with you and the ladies?"

"I'm not supposed to disclose that, but I suppose I can trust you. He's a German officer."

"You mean a Prussian? One of Blücher's men? Ah! He risked a lot by coming here!"

Florian nodded in wholehearted agreement. "Indeed, but that was only a small part of it. He risked far more than you know. I'll fill you in, uncle." Florian proceeded to give him an overview of the circumstances while his host listened attentively.

"That's a remarkable story," his uncle replied. "It was as though I read it in a book. Look! Here comes someone now, probably a peddler. Let's see what he has on him."

The slowly approaching man had red hair and matching beard. He was shabbily dressed and pulled a cart behind him. When he reached the little garden, he removed his hat and greeted them.

"What are you trading in?" asked the landlord. "Do you have something to sell?"

"No," replied the stranger. "I'm here to make purchases. Do you have old scraps of iron, zinc, or anything like that?"

Florian listened and found a familiarity in the voice. He looked closely at the man, and slapped his hands together. "Is it really you, Monsieur? What a disguise. I almost didn't recognize you."

"Who is it?" his uncle asked.

Florian quickly grabbed the stranger's cap and removed the man's wig. "Look for yourself!"

There stood... Löwenklau.

"Please forgive my deception," he said. "I assume Florian has already told you that I'm of German descent."

Before the host could reply, the gable window opened and Margot's voice emanated from up above. "Hugo, my Hugo! Can I come down?"

He looked up at her with a huge grin forming on his face. "No, stay where you are! I'll come up." He was through the door in no time and flew up the stairs.

She opened the door and fell into his arms. "I saw you coming," she said.

"Was your heart beating with heavenly bliss?" he teased.

"I didn't recognize you at first. Oh, what ghastly red hair!"

"If you only knew whom I just encountered on the road but escaped without detection."

"Who was it?"

Löwenklau entered the small room and greeted her mother. He then pointed out the window. "Do you see that man walking towards Paliseul?" he asked.

"Yes."

"That's none other than your stepbrother, Albin!"

"The captain?" she gasped. "Didn't he recognize you?"

"No. He probably felt he had seen me somewhere before. He kept looking at me as I walked away. He didn't make the connection, though."

"It could have been catastrophic for all of us if he had. The landlord told us he's been everywhere, asking for news of two women and a servant. But, my love, there must be extraordinary circumstances to bring you back here."

"The field marshal sent me back to move the war chest to a more secure location, far away from the prying eyes of the captain. I'm meeting men here tonight who will assist me in moving it."

"Is it true that the Prussians lost an important battle?"

"Yes," Löwenklau confirmed. "At Ligny. But we'll win a more important one today. Did you hear the sounds of fighting?"

"Yes. Where is the main battle?"

"In the south of Brussels, in the area of Waterloo."

"What if the allies fail to win?"

"They will triumph. I'm convinced of it."

"Tell me about the marshal and how he received you."

Hugo sat down and started to tell her about his meeting with Blücher. He became so absorbed in his account that he missed the approach of the southerner. The latter came up to the two men in the garden and greeted them politely.

"Pardon me! Does a Monsieur Florian live here?"

"Yes," Florian replied. "You've found him."

The stranger looked at him closely. "I'm supposed to make an inquiry."

"About what?"

The man leaned forward and whispered something into his ear.

"Ah," the coachman said, nodding. "Then you're part of it. You mean first Lieutenant von Löwenklau."

"Yes. Is he here?"

"He just arrived. Do you need to see him?"

"Yes, right away."

Florian left the garden and fetched Löwenklau from the upper room. When Löwenklau returned to the yard and spotted the supposed southerner, he laughed out loud.

"Splendid, Kunze!" he said as though greeting an old friend. "No one would ever think you were a German. What's your message?"

"We're all assembled, sir," Corporal Kunze said.

"Good. I have the tools."

"Can you tell us what this is all about?"

"Not yet." Löwenklau turned back to face his host. "Can I leave my cart with you?" he asked.

"Of course."

"I've concealed rifles and ammunition under the old iron. By the sounds of it, we'll need them sooner rather than later. Listen to the canon fire!"

"God, give the Prussians the victory!" Florian pledged.

"He's heard our prayers and our triumph will come sooner than the last time," Florian's uncle said.

With that vote of confidence, Löwenklau held a brief conversation with him and was assured that he could trust him completely. He returned once more to speak with the ladies, who received him as a more welcome sight than ever. Margot, who had completely recovered from the injury she had sustained during the holdup, rejoiced inwardly that Hugo was with her and not on the battlefield.

"What will Napoleon do if he wins?" she asked.

"He'll be proclaimed emperor over Rheins."

"And if we triumph?"

"Then we'll march toward Paris, arriving within the week. We'll dictate terms for a lasting peace, which won't be easily broken. Do you know what will happen after that, my dear Margot?"

"What?" she asked, her face turning red.

"We can finally embark on our festive trip to Berlin."

"Under your banner and coat of arms, my love?"

She put her arms around his neck. "Do you know your love means more to me than anything the emperor could have ever offered?" she whispered.

"Yes," he said, "and I'll never forget it."

❧✠❧

The first lieutenant arrived at the prearranged meeting place close to midnight and met Kunze and his nine companions. He had chosen them because they were physically well-built and itching to participate in an adventure behind enemy lines. The men collected the cart, along with the weapons, and started their journey. They reached the foothills at daybreak and commenced their climb. The forest trail was quiet and devoid of people, allowing them to arrive at the ravine without being seen.

"This is it," Löwenklau said as they approached the ravine. "Keep a lookout until I return! I'm going to look for a suitable place nearby where we can safely bury the chest."

Any passersby wouldn't ever suspect they were dealing with German soldiers. They were all clad in peasants' clothing and Löwenklau had once again donned his wig and red beard. After he left, his men took a break and camped in the nearby bushes, awaiting his return.

"What's that awful smell?" asked one of the men.

"God, there's a body behind this bush!" exclaimed another.

They gathered around the place and, to their surprise, came across Reillac's corpse.

"This must be the body of the French baron the lieutenant told us about," Kunze said. "He intends to submit a full report on the incident."

After a short time, Löwenklau returned to his men and began directing them on how to proceed. "Start digging!" he ordered, gesturing to the secret location of the strong box. The job went quickly with the aid of so many willing hands, and they had no difficulty in removing the chest from the ground. They fashioned a wooden litter out of sturdy branches and lifted the chest with it, transporting it to its new underground location.

Löwenklau made a small sketch, one useful enough to help refresh his memory but not sufficient to lead someone to the buried chest should the drawing fall into the wrong hands. The men worked quickly and finished the job near midday. He allowed them time for a short lunch before they all made their way back to the open trough so they could fill the cavity with earth and head for home.

Captain Richemonte, who had not been idle, had made his own plans. Armed with a spade, he too ventured into the mountains. His plan was to bury Reillac's body and then conduct a thorough search for the strong box. Not suspecting that anyone had been there, he arrived in the gulch and walked to the prescribed spot. He came to an abrupt halt, not believing what he saw. He gazed at the empty pit, the flat sides of which suggested it had once encompassed a large object.

"No, it can't be! It's gone!" he cried out. "*Mon dieu!* I came too late!" He couldn't move, paralyzed as though all his strength had suddenly left him.

"But wait! Someone must have been here just before me," he considered softly. "The earth looks as though it's been recently disturbed. But who was here?" He looked around for some sign that might lend him an explanation. He stamped his foot in frustration. "My last hope is gone! It must have been that damned Löwenklau! How I wish I could meet up with him one last time and make him pay for all I've been through!"

At about that same time, Löwenklau returned to the ravine with his men behind him. He had considered the possibility that someone could stumble across the open pit, but he was nonetheless shocked to see a man standing right at its edge. He motioned for his men to follow him quietly. They crept closer, not making a sound. Recognizing the captain, he surprised him from behind by grabbing his arm.

"Who are you talking to, Monsieur Richemonte?" he asked.

Richemonte spun around at the sound of the voice and turned white as a ghost.

"Who... who... are you?" he stammered.

"Isn't it obvious?" Löwenklau asked. "Treasure hunters like you, of course, though somewhat more successful, I might add. The timing couldn't have been better. Why don't you do us a favor and come over here." He led Richemonte toward Reillac's corpse. "Now, look at this body and tell me if you recognize it!"

Richemonte regained his composure and looked intently at the man with the red beard. "Dammit!" he cursed. "Löwenklau, it's you!"

"Yes, it's me! But don't worry, I'm not here as your judge. After all, you're still the stepbrother of my future wife. I would rather not personally deal with your indiscretions. I only want to witness one thing: your admission and complicity in Reillac's murder!"

"I would rather deal with the devil himself!" Richemonte hissed, trying in vain to free himself from Löwenklau's grasp.

"Can't you at least admit to us that this is the corpse of your good friend, Baron de Reillac?"

"What concern is it of mine?" evaded the captain.

"Fine with me," Löwenklau said with a shrug. "But I think we should at least have a look into the captain's pockets. Hold him!" he instructed his men. Four strong arms grabbed him. Despite struggling, he could not prevent them from conducting a thorough search. Löwenklau quickly found the items he suspected had been taken from Reillac's body. He found the stolen purse and the billfold, both bearing the insignia of the dead man.

"Just as I thought," said a somber Löwenklau. "This is all the proof I require. I'll appropriate these items for now, and turn them over later to the authorities." He looked over at his men. "Remove his weapons and send him packing with a good kick in the *derriere*. We owe him nothing more."

The lieutenant's men carried out his orders to the letter. Löwenklau examined the corpse after Richemonte's departure and instructed his men to bury it. He prepared a detailed report and ensured his men signed it, becoming witnesses to the final resting place of one Baron de Reillac. Only then did they commence their homeward march.

Alone again, Richemonte couldn't grasp what had happened to him. It was as though he were living in a bad dream. He hadn't dared to speak to his tormentors, and even received the kick as though it meant nothing.

After several hours of walking, he reached the foot of the mountain. He finally snapped out of his trance, coming to a halt. "Vengeance!" he cried futilely. "I want revenge!"

And then, a thought occurred to him which calmed his spirits somewhat. *It all makes sense to me now. That disguised vagrant is the same man I saw yesterday near that out of the way cottage. That's where I'll find him and his Dulzinea!*[28.4] Deliberations of revenge and his hatred for Löwenklau left him no peace, propelling him down the winding path. He arrived in Gedinne just as the night gave way to a new dawn. Surprisingly, he found that nearly everyone in the little village was awake.

A troop of soldiers arrived with the bad news that the emperor had been defeated at Waterloo and all was lost. The small gathering did not take the news well. There was much crying and lamenting. The development was welcome news to the captain, however. He approached the townspeople and explained that he could deliver eleven German spies into the hands of the brave patriots of Gedinne. Furthermore, the bride of the leader was concealed in the little cottage at the forest's edge.

The villagers were skeptical at first, but the defeated soldiers jumped at the opportunity for a little retribution. Led by Richemonte, they quickly made their way to the cottage and encircled it. They forced their way in and had little difficulty in taking the sleeping occupants captive. A few soldiers stayed behind as guards, while the remainder headed back up the mountain path to capture the German spies.

Löwenklau had decided his men should go back together as a single unit. As a result, they came down the hill, pulling the cart, completely unaware of the danger. A salvo of gunfire rang out and ten men fell down, dead in their tracks. Richemonte walked over and examined the bodies himself. "Their leader isn't among them," he said. "I expect he'll be coming after them. We can't allow him to escape!" Despite his efforts, however, he was greatly mistaken in this assumption.

While the men were en route to Gedinne, a thought struck Löwenklau. He recalled that Richemonte had seen him earlier that day near the cottage and could conceivably deduce that Margot was inside. He decided to forge ahead and prepare himself.

He didn't choose the path which his men had taken, instead forcing his way through the underbrush, taking a more direct way. In doing so, he missed the ambush and wasn't detected by Richemonte. As he came close to the cottage, he spotted the soldiers and instantly reasoned what must have happened. Fortunately, the remnant of the troop left to guard the cottage was small in number. His gaze was fixed on the cottage, and in his single-mindedness, he missed the arrival of a Hussar patrol, which had just emerged from the woods. Still dressed in his vagrant garb, he casually walked up to the cottage.

The sentry at the door tried to bar his way, but Löwenklau pushed him aside when he heard Margot scream. With pistols drawn, he ran into the cottage to witness a horrific scene. The landlord and Florian were bound, lying on the floor. Madame Richemonte had collapsed and lay in a corner, while Margot struggled in vain against four soldiers. He wasted no time and his four shots rang out, dispatching the four attackers. Löwenklau was too absorbed with the scene in front of him to pay attention to the sentry, who had followed him inside. Margot, seeing the danger, cried out in desperation, her shrill warning resounding off the walls. Heeding her warning, Löwenklau spun around, though not in time. The Frenchman's saber whistled through the air and struck him on the head. He collapsed to the floor, with Margot falling into unconsciousness beside him.

The Prussian Hussars on patrol had just broken out of the forest as their commander surveyed the area. At the sound of several shots, followed by a woman's screams emanating from the little cottage, they began to make their way to the source of the disturbance.

"Did you hear that, men?" called out the officer. "It sounds like a fight! Perhaps we can come to their aid. Forward, men!" They galloped the short distance to the cottage, dismounted, and stormed inside.

The sentry who had dealt Löwenklau the near-fatal blow sought to escape by jumping out the window. The Hussar commander summed up the scene at once and fired a shot after him, which didn't miss its mark.

In the aftermath, Florian and his uncle were freed from their ropes just in time to learn of a larger troop of Prussian infantry on its way into town. With reinforcements coming, they were relatively safe from any further reprisals by the French. Florian identified Löwenklau to the officer, ensuring he received immediate aid for his wound. Unfortunately, because no doctor was on hand, only a temporary bandage could be affixed to the lieutenant's wound. Florian gave a quick account of the recent events and then, acting on the officer's instructions, arranged for the two women to be carried upstairs.

Löwenklau's injury was particularly grave, but any further medical aid had to wait for the arrival of the military surgeon accompanying the advancing regiment.

When the doctor, experienced with such injuries, arrived, he simply shook his head, promising to do what he could for the young lieutenant. Later, when Margot had somewhat recovered, she received a measure of comfort from him, although he didn't permit her to see Hugo in his present state.

On the outskirts of town, Richemonte decided not to return to the cottage. He waited in vain for Löwenklau to show up, and reluctantly dismissed the soldiers. Once he realized the Prussians had control of the surrounding area, he didn't want to risk being apprehended and so headed back into the mountains. But in doing so, he didn't hear about the events at the little cottage or his sworn enemy's brush with death.

CHAPTER TWENTY-NINE
Forging New Plans

The old Marshal Forward had once again managed to subdue the proud French nation, a campaign that culminated with the Battle of Waterloo. Paris had capitulated and a new lasting peace enveloped all of France. Napoleon had been stripped of his throne, as well as his freedom, and was banished to St. Helena, an isolated island in the South Atlantic. Prudence dictated it would have been far more difficult for him to rally his supporters from this remote habitat than that of his former exile, the Island of Elba.

Unfortunately, Hugo von Löwenklau was unable to participate in the fight to bring the Corsican's cohorts in line, and ultimately to submission. The consequence of his dreadful blow, which would have proved fatal for many, confined him to his bed for months. In his unconscious state, his mind was detached and seemingly unresponsive. For the most part, progress was slow and his consciousness often swayed from passive indifference to bordering on dreamlike incoherence. Only much later did he show signs of becoming more cognitive by distinguishing the faces of his faithful caregivers, Margot and Madame Richemonte. Löwenklau slowly recognized them for who they were and his recollection of past events gradually improved. His memory reached back to the point where Florian had brought Margot safely to the isolated cottage. However, try as he might, his recollection of further events drew blanks. Even much later, when his doctors had given him a clean bill of health, he still lacked the memory of those events that had affected his life so dramatically.

Hugo knew perfectly well that he had returned to the cottage for the express purpose of moving the strong box to a safer location. Although he still carried the little diagram that outlined the general details, he didn't know how to interpret it. He was in possession of the detailed account, signed by all those present, explaining how he and his fellow soldiers had found Reillac's corpse. But what had happened after he returned to retrieve the strong box? He knew all the names of those who had accompanied him to the ravine and had been engaged in the removal and relocation of the strong box, but little else.

His first task after being released by doctors was to travel to the ravine where the war chest had at first been buried. He easily located the graves of the two robbers, but it was impossible for him to recall what had occurred in those fateful hours prior to his injury. Löwenklau methodically sought to remember the events of that night. He tried to determine what had happened to the ten man detachment that had been placed at his disposal to recover the chest. All he could learn was that none of the men had ever reappeared. He had no choice but to eventually return to Berlin and report his findings, such as they were.

Blücher had also just returned to Berlin, Prussia's capital, in time for Christmas. Löwenklau sought to pay him a long overdue visit and was naturally welcomed by the old man in his usual coarse yet friendly manner.

"Good morning, my boy!" said the marshal. "I heard you received a horrible gash to your head, one which even caught the attention of the grim reaper!"

"Yes," he said. "It was a very memorable gash, Excellency."

"But as I can see, the reaper had to hold off. Well, that pleases me to no end and it's about time you got back to your life."

"It's certainly been one peculiar story, Excellency!"

"I can well-imagine," Blücher said. "Such a saber strike would have thrown me flat on my face. They probably tried to embalm you with Russian ointment, Weiermüllers universal dressing, or even Schwarzburger ointment,[29.1] and all that medicinal stuff. If you ask me, all these ministrations actually make you sicker. Sometimes the best thing you can do is pull up your socks![29.2] I wouldn't have let them near me. When I breathe my last, my boy, I want to arrive in front of St. Peter without smelling like a cadaver."

Löwenklau smiled at the man's off-color sense of humor. "Of course, Excellency. Yet the injury itself, frustrating though it was, was not entirely to blame for my disappointment."

"No? What was it then?"

"It's two-fold."

"I'm all ears, my boy!"

"First," Löwenklau began, "is the fact that I had to abstain from participating in the battles and missed critical opportunities for advancement."

"I know. Every brave man who was sidelined wishes he was back in the thick of things. One has to find a way to overcome that."

"There certainly are things which would make it more bearable."

"What things?" Blücher asked.

"Well," Löwenklau said modestly, "the overlooked promotion, for example."

The old man coughed and nodded to himself, pleased there was an opportunity to rectify an earlier omission. "Hmm, yes, you have something there," he replied. "It's a real shame, everything you've been through, but I think there's something I can do about it. You've accomplished much for our cause. Your adventure at Jeannette and the resultant information you obtained was of more use to us than if you had been present to fight in every battle. I'll look after it, my boy. Old Blücher can keep his word, wouldn't you agree?"

"Completely, Excellency!"

"Well then! I wouldn't suggest they ignore my recommendation for your promotion a second time. If they did, they'd see a totally different side of me." He paused then, remembering that the lieutenant's disappointment had been two-fold. "What else is bothering you?"

"The war chest, Excellency!"

"The war chest? Heavens, yes! Now I remember. I had sent you, along with a bunch of good fellows, to secure the old piggy bank and relocate it. Since you didn't return, I had to keep pace with that old *Bonaschwarte* and show him how we Germans can dish out blows. Later, of course, I found out you had been injured and were unable to return. So, what happened to the strong box?"

"That's what I don't know, Excellency."

"You don't know?" asked Blücher, surprised. "Were you injured before you secured it?"

"No, that was later."

"Yet you must know if you found it!"

"Certainly, I found it."

"Did you bury it elsewhere?"

Löwenklau hesitated. "I think so."

"You think so? What's that supposed to mean? There's nothing to ponder here, my boy!"

"Of course not, Excellency! I hate to admit it, but I've forgotten."

"Forgotten? You mean this business with the strong box? *Sapperlot!* Are you a mere child to forget something so important?"

Löwenklau pointed to the discolored scar that extended from the top of his head to his nose. "It's not my fault, Excellency. This is what I have to contend with."

"Your injury? Heavens! Are you saying the aftereffects of the blow are playing havoc with your memory?"

"Unfortunately, yes. I just can't seem to recollect those fateful hours prior to my injury."

"You probably haven't given it much effort, my boy!"

"On the contrary! I've spent entire days, and sometimes nights, in deep thought. I have mused, contemplated, meditated, and brooded—all for nothing! The memory has completely eluded me thus far!"

"Remarkable!" Blücher mused. "It's as though a gear skipped and the blow somehow damaged part of your brain. You simply can't patch that, or put ointment on it. I expect you attended the place where it was first buried. Were your lads with you?"

"Of course."

"Did you instruct them to remove the chest?"

"I think so. When I had recovered sufficiently from my ordeal, I traveled back to see for myself. Even though the box is gone, a big hole still serves as a reminder of its earlier presence."

"Hmm. Another person could have discovered its location and retrieved the chest."

"It's possible, though not likely."

"Why do you say that?"

"Because I don't trust Captain Richemonte!"

Blücher made a face at the merest mention of the man's name. "Ah! Him again. Was he up there, in the ravine?"

Löwenklau's expression changed to one of embarrassment. He simply shrugged his shoulders. "Very likely," he replied.

"What? Very likely! *Zounds!* I'm not at all pleased with you. What good is probable, possible, or maybe. I want certainty!"

"I can only give you a measure of that, Excellency. You see, I can say with a degree of certainty that I removed the strong box and then found a suitable location and reburied it. I even fashioned a diagram to refresh my memory. Here it is, Excellency."

Blücher took the paper and studied it carefully. "Your sketch is well-drawn and easy to follow—a birch tree, a pine tree, some spruce, and there a cross, probably the burial place. Listen, my son, it's no wonder you couldn't find the location from the way these trees extend to the edge of the forest."

"I spent several days searching for the site, but I came up empty."

"What about the birch, pine, and spruce trees?"

"They were of no help. I cannot remember the direction we took that day."

"That's a sorry tale if I have ever heard one," Blücher said. "Now, look! Even my pipe went out." The old marshal laid it aside even though he had just stuffed it and lit the contents. Pacing back and forth in his room, he held the sketch in his hands. He abruptly stopped and threw it on the table. "I know it's not your fault. We can lay the blame on that dastardly blow, but we can't change the outcome. What happened to the men whom I had assigned to the task? They would certainly have some recollection."

"I made inquiries, Excellency, but they are all dead."

"Hang it all! Did they die in the subsequent battles?"

"No, apparently they all died on the same fateful day. The isolated cottage where I received my injury was used as a sort of gathering point. A small contingent of French troops had attacked the cottage. A roaming Prussian patrol arrived just in time, and prevented any further aggression. They later discovered ten bodies, the exact number of men which I had with me, a short distance away. My men had all been shot and their bodies plundered."

"Then your Grenadiers are of no help to us. Well, we can take some comfort in knowing the Frenchmen didn't discover the box's location. How do you know Captain Richemonte was up in the mountains?"

This part, at least, Löwenklau was sure about. "I made notes that outline the tragic scene where he murdered Baron de Reillac. I witnessed the recovery of his body myself. This document makes it clear that we found Reillac's corpse and that Richemonte was also present. We found personal items on him which had belonged to the baron."

"Did you take them from Richemonte? If so, where are they now?"

"I later found them in my possession. I still have them."

"It seems the captain has disappeared," Blücher noted.

"Perhaps he slipped through our lines, Excellency. Or worse, we actually allowed him to walk away."

"That wasn't very smart of you."

"Pardon me, Excellency, but I wouldn't put it that way!"

"No? Why not?"

"You need to remember that we were in enemy-occupied territory."

Blücher snapped his fingers, nodding. "Right. Hmm! You were just 'observers' behind enemy lines. Yes, you may have run into trouble if you had tried to snatch Richemonte."

"It's still possible to track him down and turn him over to the French authorities."

"Still? I suppose that's true. Would you be able to locate Reillac's body again?"

"Without a doubt."

"Then that's not a bad idea. We have the proof, namely the entire story and your signatures. Also, the artifacts you found on Richemonte himself and safeguarded for later."

"Actually, I have more proof, Excellency!"

"What further proof?"

"Margot has received correspondence from him, wherein he states—"

Blücher interrupted him with a gesture. "Margot! Ah! I almost forgot about her. How stupid of me. Where is she now?"

"Right here in Berlin, with her mother."

"Well then, I must pay them a visit, my boy."

Löwenklau cleared his throat. "It's my intention to invite His Excellency for just such an occasion."

"Really? Is there something special being planned?"

"Naturally, Excellency—a wedding!"

"A wedding? A million hailstones!²⁹·³ Of course, your wedding, and you really want to marry this girl? When? Out with it!"

Löwenklau started to laugh. "The ceremony is the day after tomorrow."

"What! So soon?" he asked. "How can I possibly acquire an appropriate wedding gift so quickly? I might be able to obtain a coal shovel, a fruit basket, or a bouquet of wildflowers. Why the short notice?"

"Well, Your Excellency has only just arrived in Berlin."

"True enough. Listen, have you chosen a best man yet?"

"Yes. Lieutenant von Wilmersdorf."

"Him? Wilmersdorf?" asked the marshal. "Blast! Why him?"

"He's a good friend of mine."

"Ridiculous," Blücher said, unimpressed. "There are plenty of friends to go around. Not everyone has what it takes to be the best man, though. Have you looked at him closely?"

"Quite often," replied Hugo with a knowing smile.

"What about his thin and crooked legs?"

"Hmm! I don't find them that thin or crooked."

"Well, he has a blunt nose!"

"Just a little bit blunt, Excellency."

"I noticed he only has three hairs in his moustache."

"There may be a few more than three present."

"Really?" Blücher murmured. "Well, forget about him and fix your attention on me." He stood up and spun himself around several times, giving Löwenklau ample opportunity to view him from all sides.

"Do I have thin or crooked legs?"

"No, Excellency," smiled Löwenklau.

"Does my nose have an irregular appearance?"

"Not in the least."

"Do I need to rub some *Melissengeist*²⁹·⁴ into my moustache?"

"His Excellency's moustache has no need for ointments."

"Well, is this Lieutenant von Wilmersdorf a more genial man than I?"

"I don't believe so."

"You don't believe so? Oh, I see! You're not convinced, is that it? Look here, my son, and quit joking. I'm telling you, I would have given you some stiff competition if I were only fifteen years younger. Since I'm as old as Methusalem, I'll withdraw my aspirations to become the bridegroom. You'll have to take my place, with the promise that you'll at least grant an old man one last hurrah, namely the privilege of being your best man. Understood?"

"At your command, Excellency!"

"Command? Hang it all! To the cuckoo with orders!²⁹·⁵ I'm not ordering you to accommodate me through army regulations. Don't put too much stock in orders!"

Löwenklau dropped his smile and became instantly serious. "Excellency," he said, "not only would this be a great honor, but it would give Margot and me great pleasure..."

"Well then! That's more like it! You have finally come to your senses. And now, that Lieutenant Wilmersdorf can run his dogs all the way to Bautzen.[29.6] He can escort Madame Richemonte if he likes." Suddenly Blücher remembered a detail from earlier in their conversation. "Didn't you tell me Richemonte had written to Margot?"

"Yes. Three times already, though she hasn't responded."

"Where is that braggart now?"

"He's been holed up in Strassburg for two weeks."

"Do you have his address?"

"Of course. He's expecting a reply."

"That's good. Now we know where to find that reprobate. What does he say in his letter?"

Löwenklau grimaced. "He had the audacity to tell Margot she should leave me and meet up with him."

"He's mad. She'll never give you up!"

"Oh, but he's very persuasive."

"You're making me curious."

"He had the nerve to point out her poor circumstances," the lieutenant continued. "If she consented to join him, he promised to make her wealthy beyond measure."

"*Sapperlot!* What rich old crone has suddenly died, allowing Richemonte to make such outlandish claims?"

"Why, Reillac, of course!"

Blücher stepped back, astonished.

"Is His Excellency aware how extensive Reillac's holdings are?"

"Yes, I heard. He became rich because of his crooked deals. He acted like a high-priced chicken catcher and amassed millions as the supplier for Napoleon's army while his soldiers starved, clad only in rags. Reillac!" The name came out distastefully. "Of course! He's dead. Now she's supposed to inherit all that he acquired? Hang it all! How is this possible?"

"Excellency, do you recall one of my reports concerning Napoleon and Margot?"

"Yes," the marshal said. "You mentioned that he had cast his eye on her, or maybe both of them."

"Well, the emperor's plan had been for Reillac to marry Margot. In turn, she would have gained admittance to the inner circles as Baroness de Reillac."

"Ah! Now I understand. That way Napoleon would have seen her at court, giving him the opportunity to have his way with her. Just as well, because he'll have lots of time to grate cheese on St. Helena.[29.7] Fortunately, our Margot is safely out of his grasp."

"Anyway, Richemonte had his dirty hands all over it. He wrote Margot that Reillac had died suddenly, leaving no close relatives."

Blücher narrowed his eyes. "How does that concern Margot?"

"He claims to possess a document which had been written by the emperor himself. Apparently the decree orders that Margot be betrothed to Reillac without reservations."

"Ah! This amounts to an arranged marriage!" declared Blücher. "Is it still valid today?"

"Perhaps," replied Löwenklau. "It would be a matter for interpretation. I'm not a lawyer. Actually, Reillac left his last will and testament behind."

"This implies there are heirs to his fortune. How many could there be?"

"Only one—Margot!"

"Explain yourself. Why only her?"

"Reillac had attained the emperor's proclamation by agreeing to recognize Margot as sole heir without reservations or restrictions," explained the lieutenant.

"What luck! Or should I say, what a disgrace for you," said Blücher, his voice dripping with sarcasm.

"Luck has nothing to do with it! It's disgraceful for Margot to accept."

"Of course, my boy. You're an honorable man and you can look after her. Where could his last testament be?"

"Richemonte has it."

"Is it genuine?"

"It would have to be examined."

Blücher thumped his hand on his desk. "Hang it all! I wouldn't put it past him! But he's still a fool, a big fool!"

"In what way, Excellency?"

"You said he intends to lure Margot with the will, right?"

"Yes, as I have already told you."

"So, if she happens to decline his offer...?"

"She would not be entitled to any of the benefits."

"Far from it! It should be relatively easy to separate the will from him. We could enlist the long arm of the law and force him to hand it over."

"I doubt it would be that easy," Löwenklau said. "He could lie about the will and say he fabricated the whole story. He could offer a plausible explanation for wanting to meet with Margot through deception."

"That's certainly true. What does Margot say about it?"

"She wants nothing to do with him."

"Very commendable," Blücher praised. "I know you both don't have a fortune, but I'll make sure you advance in rank and not be in need."

Löwenklau's face looked crestfallen for a moment. "Excellency, I'm afraid any advancement is out of the question."

"What?" asked Blücher. "How come?"

Löwenklau pointed to his scar for a second time. "This is the reason!"

"Dammit! Since when does a war wound present itself as an insurmountable blemish?"

Löwenklau smiled bitterly. "Excellency, didn't you yourself just say that a gear had skipped, that something in my head had failed?"

"*Papperlappap!* I was making a joke."

"I know that, but it doesn't change the outcome. My memory has suffered and is no longer reliable."

"Only in this one singular instance."

"Up until now, yes," he allowed, "but it's possible it could fail me without warning, especially when it comes to military matters."

"Donner and Doria! Who would dare say such a thing?"

"The doctors."

"Which doctors?"

"The experts, who have been entrusted with my care, will determine my future in the military."

Blücher looked at him in a peculiar way. "Experts?" he asked. "Decide about your future?"

"Yes."

"I don't understand what this is all about."

"At first, I didn't understand it either. Once it was explained in terms I could understand, though, I realized I had no choice. I'm afraid I'll have to resign my commission."

"Resign? Are you insane?"

"They have already informed me."

Blücher walked over to the window and stared outside. Once he had mastered his emotions again, he turned around to face the young officer who showed so much promise. The marshal's cheeks had a red glow and his eyes shimmered with a softness Löwenklau had never seen. In a measured, seemingly even tone, Blücher continued in his candid manner. "Have they recommended that it would be in your best interest to resign?"

"Yes."

"What have you decided?"

"I've chosen to take their advice," the lieutenant revealed.

"Even if I counsel you not to?"

"Even then, Excellency."

"Dammit! For God's sake, why?"

"Because I'll receive an honorable discharge if I don't make a fuss."

"I can still step in and make the long and short of it."[29.8]

"Of course, I'm indebted to his Excellency," Löwenklau said respectfully. "May I speak freely and openly?"

"Tell me exactly what's on your mind, my boy!"

"Your intervention would certainly postpone my dismissal," he said, "and yet I fear I would have to go through it all over again with the next superior."

"Those all knowing superiors can go to hell!"

"It would not happen right away, Excellency. There would be instances where—"

"Yes, yes," interrupted Blücher quickly. "I know what you intend to say. The next marshal would look at it differently, and my influence may not be sufficient to sway his mind. I understand your dilemma, my boy."

"What if the doctors' prognosis is correct?"

"Are you referring to that loose gear of yours?"

Löwenklau shook his head, a smile returning to his face for just an instant. "Not in that respect, Excellency. My intellect and decision-making ability haven't suffered in the least, or so I've been led to believe. What if this isn't really the case, though? On occasion I still suffer from bouts of pain and discomfort as a result of the injury. If I'm really honest with myself, I would have to concede such a serious head injury could still present unforeseen difficulties. It could seriously hamper my welfare, and possibly those under my command."

"Listen, my boy, you sound like a pessimist!"

"Not at all! I merely need to point out my condition's potentially serious repercussions."

"Perhaps! But it's still a damn shame! Is your mind made up? Are you certain this is what you want?"

"Absolutely certain!"

"Well then, go ahead," Blücher relented. "How soon?"

"As soon as possible."

"Not likely, my boy. With your loose gear, it could take a few months to accomplish."

"Not necessarily," replied Löwenklau laughing. "What should I do then?"

"I suggest you write it today!"

"Excellency, if I may be so bold as to—"

"Enough!" the marshal thundered. "Hold your tongue! Who has the higher authority? You or I? Keep it short! There's a quill, ink, and of course writing paper on the bureau. Sit down and prepare your proposal. Or have you forgotten how to write during your convalescence? I'll fetch another pipe while you prepare yourself!"

Löwenklau obeyed. He sharpened a quill and began to write his letter.

"Hold it!" called out the marshal again. "Do you think better with or without a pipe?"

"With one!"

"Then get one before you start your scribbling." He plucked one up and tossed it to the lieutenant. "Here, take this one."

The lieutenant brought the pipe up to look at it. It was an exquisite Dutch piece. He filled it with the marshal's best tobacco and lit the contents.

"Hold it!" yelled the old man again. "To whom are you addressing this?"

"According to regulations, it should be delivered to the regimental commander."

"Don't be ridiculous! You're no longer bound to such regulations. Since the regimental body wants to cut their ties with you, we'll accommodate them. There's no need for you to address your commander."

"To whom then should I write this important correspondence?"

"What? Can't you figure it out?"

"No."

"I can't believe what I just heard? Do I have to lead you by the nose, or what? You'll address your farewell letter to me, the old codger! It's the smartest thing that you can do!"

"And pass over the chain of command?"

"Exactly!"

"I will do as His Excellency instructs," he said.

"I wouldn't have it any other way! Now, it's high time you started writing. First, push your tobacco down a bit. You wouldn't want it to fall on that nice little document of course."

Löwenklau put his head down and started to write. Despite being rushed, he took the utmost care with it. After twenty minutes, he laid the quill aside, and looked expectantly at Blücher.

"Read it out loud!" the marshal commanded.

Löwenklau stood up and commenced to read. "To his most noble Excellency, Field Marshal von—"

"Stop!" his superior said. "Is this the preamble?"

"Of course."

"Listen, my boy! If a certain subordinate decides to write to his superior, he better employ all the rightful titles: Sovereign, Gebhard Leberecht, Field Marshal, His Excellency, the old Blücher, Your Highness and Your Grace. Woe to him who omits one iota! But if you, the about to be released officer, write to your superior, this being I, then it's not necessary to go through all that. I want to show them you count for something. How many lines are there in your manuscript?"

"About fifty-two," said Löwenklau.

"Dear God! Fifty-two? Are all those chicken scratches really necessary? Sit down and get some more paper. I'll dictate something more appropriate and to the point!"

Löwenklau obeyed. Blücher relit his pipe and paced back and forth for a few minutes. He then interrupted the young officer in his typical manner. "What is today's date?"

"The twenty-third of December," he answered.

"Right," Blücher remembered. "The day after tomorrow is Christmas. So, you decided to get married on Christmas? I like your way of thinking. Are you ready with your quill?"

"Yes."

"Then write... 'Berlin, the twenty-third of December, 1815. To: My friend and patron, Gebhard Leberecht von Blücher!'... done?" When he saw Löwenklau was ready to move on, he said, "Then continue... 'Dear friend and fellow soldier. During the course of battle, I received a miserable gash to my head, one which nearly cost me my life. I have been instructed to tender my resignation as an officer. I will do it forthright, and through you. You know I fulfilled my obligations and performed my duties for my country. I remain your faithful, Hugo von Löwenklau, First Lieutenant.' There," he said after a short pause. "Are you done?"

"Yes," replied Hugo.

"Well, now you know how to write a resignation letter."

"Excellency, I barely managed to write the words down on paper."

"How come?

"This little joke is certainly proof of your singular way of—"

"What! A joke? Don't be ridiculous! This is no joke, my boy! Let me see, I'll just use a little ash in place of the blotting paper. There, that should do it!" Blücher examined the paper in his hand. "Hmm, you have a pretty good writing style. It's more legible than mine. Can you guess who is going to read it?"

"I have no idea, Excellency."

"What, no idea? You're hopeless. Who else, but the king himself!"

Löwenklau's jaw dropped as he looked helplessly at Blücher. He had considered such a possibility, though the words still came as a shock. "Your Excellency," he replied haltingly, "in this case it would seem to me that more appropriate words would be in order."

Blücher raised his eyebrows. "Change the words?" he asked. "Löwenklau, what's gotten into you? Perhaps you thought I could not come up with a worthwhile document? It'll even be placed in a proper envelope."

Hugo had to laugh. "Excellency," he started to say. "I am convinced that..."

"...that I can't write a simple declaration," asked Blücher, interrupting him. "This edict is nothing less than a literary masterpiece, and the king will see it. Count on it! Now, back to where we were. What's our position with this Richemonte? Should we pursue him?"

"I'm not sure if it's still possible," Löwenklau said. "Strassburg is in French territory."

"This amounts to a hill of beans. What's the French title for chief public prosecutor?"

"Attorney General."

"Well then, he's the one whom we'll address. I will send the information to the attorney general's office, ensuring they deal with old Blücher's request in an expedient way. Now, what items did you say were removed from Reillac's corpse?"

"His purse and billfold," Löwenklau answered. "His name and insignia are embossed on them."

"That should be more than enough. You said you ordered the body to be buried there. I believe you said you could find its location again?"

"Absolutely!"

"After all, it's possible they'll request your presence during their examination of the case. Did you witness the murder with your own eyes?"

"No."

Blücher led out a small sigh. "That's too bad. Then he can lie about his complicity."

"I don't think so. I had seen them together just before. I returned to the same spot within minutes, finding Reillac lying dead in the bushes, stabbed in the back, and Richemonte nowhere to be found. The baron's body was still warm. Those things that I later obtained from Richemonte had been removed from the corpse."

"That should be enough then. How could Reillac's last will and testament have ended up in Richemonte's possession?"

"It could be a forgery. If it were genuine, Reillac must have had a reason to deliver it into the captain's hands."

"That's true," Blücher said. "Is Richemonte wealthy?"

"No, on the contrary. He has many debts, as Your Excellency already knows."

"Now I see how desperate his situation has become. The will, which represents a fortune, is only accessible through his sister, now the sole heir."

"That's why he wants to lure Margot to Strassburg."

The marshal nodded knowingly. "It's clear he wants to facilitate the inheritance for her. He'll somehow swindle her out of it and disappear with his newfound fortune. We have to make sure he won't succeed. We'll speak again the day after tomorrow and deal with it then. You can take your leave, my boy. Give my regards to your Margot and her mother. We have dealt with your farewell letter, and now, *adieu!*"

Löwenklau left the marshal's residence. If the events of late placed him in a turbid mood, and his letter of resignation only compounded that bleak outlook, then the conversation with the old marshal picked up his spirits. He returned to his own home, uplifted and optimistic. It was true he wasn't rich, but the small estate he called his own should bring him enough income to afford them a modest living. When he imagined Margot looking at him with those happy and trustworthy eyes, everything else seemed less important.

"How did father Blücher receive you?" she asked as he sat down beside her on the sofa.

"Very well," he said. "He still has more than a passing interest in our affairs. Let me tell you all about it."

Margot smiled at him, taking in the warm expression in his eyes. They shimmered with joy and pleasure, a stark contrast to the events of the last few months.

"Blücher is not the man to abandon something once he's made up his mind," Margot added in a reassuring tone once he finished his report. "You can believe he'll do his utmost to ensure you receive the compensation for your war efforts. He's not going to stand idly by while the general view is to give you a quiet dismissal."

Of course, she was absolutely right in her prediction.

CHAPTER THIRTY
Blücher's Last Hurrah

Christmas Day arrived, with Hugo receiving the most precious gift he had ever dreamed off. She was a woman of such beauty and charm that she had no equal. Even though Margot was dressed in an ordinary wedding gown, she still took his breath away. She had the appearance of a heavenly being. Having dispensed with all earthly refinements of fancy clothing and jewelry, she opted to adorn herself with only natural beauty.

The guests were gathered at the church, anticipating the marshal's arrival. In honor of his two special friends, he showed up in his best dress uniform. Despite his advancing age, he still managed to demonstrate his quick step. His youthful vigor quickly spread to all those present, a characteristic often applied to extraordinary people who take interest in the simpler things in life.

"Good day to one and all!" he said cheerfully as he gazed out at the guests. "Heavens, what a Christmas celebration this has turned out to be! The Christ child has blessed us with a bride and bridegroom. If only I could have experienced this once more myself. But of course I'm just reminiscing! Where's this *Mossjeh*, the Lieutenant von Wilmersdorf?"

"Here, Excellency!" Wilmersdorf replied by stepping forward and clicking his heels.

Blücher surveyed him from top to bottom. "So, this is the *urian*, the upstart who tried to assume my rightful place as best man. What would be more fitting than for three teams of horses to abscond, leaving him high and dry?"[30.1]

Wilmersdorf, who understood Blücher's mannerisms, was momentarily taken aback by them. He quickly recovered his composure. "Forgive me, your Excellency!" he apologized. "I had no idea I was infringing on my marshal's right. I respectfully decline and offer the honor to my lord."

"Well, that's more like it!" Blücher said. "Let's not wrangle about who does what. I'm allowed a little pleasure now and then, right? But to show you, my dear lieutenant, that I have no desire to rob you of all responsibility, I'll give you the opportunity to escort the bride. Where might Fräulein Margot be?"

"Next door, Excellency!"

"I'm supposed to fetch her, but I'll leave that honor to you. It would only be fitting."

While the young lieutenant left on his errand, Blücher greeted Löwenklau and those nearby. A few minutes later, Margot appeared with her escort. The sight of her produced a remarkable announcement from Blücher. "Heavens, bless me!" he called. "Could this be our dear Margot?"

The brave and trustworthy girl had been transformed into a beautiful bride, second to none, including those of the higher class. The marshal approached her in a manner befitting royalty. He raised her hand to his lips and looked into her radiant face, as though he were her father.

"Fräulein," he started, "did you know the old Blücher doesn't have many years left? Even though I don't let it show, I'm sure the old grim reaper is slowly reaching his morbid hand out for me.[30.2] Therefore, I wanted you to know how much you've enriched my life and that I'm truly delighted to be a part of this ceremony." The old man's words struck her solemnly, even though he'd peppered them with his customary wisecracks.

By this time, the word had slipped out that Blücher would be passing himself off as best man. It was therefore little wonder that the church was packed to capacity, as though an important church service was about to commence.

Many of the young men present envied Lieutenant Löwenklau, who had captured the heart of such a ravishing beauty, and a Frenchwoman no less. Despite his scar, the ladies cast admiring stares at the tall and handsome lieutenant, with no one begrudging him his recent accomplishments. All of them, without exception, were inwardly glad the famous field marshal had circumvented the formality of his elevated position and simply followed his heart by appearing at the wedding.

After the couple recited their vows and were blessed by the priest, Blücher took Löwenklau's hand. "Well, my boy, she's your wife at last," he proclaimed. "Hold her in high esteem, as you would the most exquisite gemstone. Do it for me!"

He gave Margot a kiss on her forehead. "My child," he said as he held her hand. "You know he is a very capable man. Don't be too hard on him if life denies him what he strives for. The approving gaze of a loving wife wipes away all disappointment and frustration!" As was his custom, he had unwittingly spoken so loudly that his voice carried to the rest of the church. His modest speech brought about a solemn moment, one he hadn't intended. There wasn't a single couple among them who could have been more worthy of Blücher's special recognition.

Later at the reception meal, many a joke escaped the jovial man, who still possessed the heart of a child and gaiety of a younger man. Despite over-hearing the odd political comment he couldn't completely agree with, he remained on his best behavior.

As the evening drew to a close, Blücher finally stood up and clinked his glass. The conversations quickly subsided as all eyes became fixed on the old marshal.

"All right children," he began. "We witnessed many toasts today, as is fitting on such an occasion. What I would like to propose now is not so much a toast, but a plea. Come here, Löwenklau, my boy, and fill my glass one more time!" As the lieutenant complied, the marshal continued. "And now, my good people, give me your attention! The old Blücher has become quite famous, but it will eventually pass. They will talk about his accomplishments and his cont-emporaries will come up with all sorts of stories, many true and some fabricated. Perhaps his name will be read all over and even appear in school books. But what good is that? He knows fully well what he accomplished with his saber, with God's help and that of his soldiers. Yet the historians will spoil it with their accounts. When the madness of war recedes, a time of lucidity will enter in, since a season of moderation always follows a time of exuberance. Likely the same will come to pass now. What we paid for with our own blood will dissipate with the ink. They won't stand behind all their promises. But let me remind you that our loving God is still in charge. The blood of a nation is a costly commodity and will once again come to fruition. And so it will be throughout Germany, who will harvest much fruit from her labors. I will not be here to see it, but you will be here to witness its growth and triumph. When you look at that spectacular tree, the one that bears the fruit of our noble deeds, and you see it start to show signs of rot due to politikers and diplomats, just turn your thoughts to your old Blücher! Don't forget to tell your children's children: when the German nation comes once again to the forefront just as we have now experienced, simply raise your glass in a toast to the old Marshal Forward. He would have cut a decisive path through the entire Vienna convention, just as he did through the French lines on the other side of the Rhine!" He paused, looking out contentedly over the crowd of people. "This is likely the last toast you will share in this lifetime with the old Gebhard Leberecht!"

The effect of his words was indescribable and gripped the entire gathering. The old man, embittered by war, shared from his heart and cleared the air. He spoke like a prophet of old, through whom God had given his people a glimpse of the future. His last desire was that his legacy be passed from generation to generation. It truly was a spectacular moment, solemn in itself and one rarely seen in a lifetime. Those present quietly lifted their glasses and emptied the contents without saying a word, afraid their words would tarnish the dignity of the moment.

Following the somber toast, it fell to Blücher to reinstate the joyous tone of the evening. "Now, my children," he said, pointing to the side table bearing the wedding gifts. "Look over there. What do you think? You probably thought the old Blücher still remembered how to make a speech, but had forgotten the main thing! That's where you're wrong! I am not a rich man, and many of you know how wine and gambling have cost me more than I would like to admit. Were it not for the king's intervention, I would have fallen on hard times. I can't give you what I don't have, but I still managed to bring a present. Here Margot, take it and give it to your husband. Don't open it until I have left the celebration, though. That's all I ask."

He removed a large envelope from his tunic and handed it to Margot. She took it reluctantly and started to open her mouth to express her gratitude, but he wouldn't hear of it. "Hold it!" he said. "Be quiet, my little mouthpiece! I don't want to hear a word of it. I'll only admit to one thing. The king had a good chuckle when he read a certain letter, penned by a certain first lieutenant, giving rise to an opportunity for a certain marshal to expound on a certain tragic story to His Majesty. That's all you need to know. And now, may God grant you a long and happy life. Do me a favor and don't forget me too soon!"

He sidestepped her and, before anyone could stop him, he rushed out the door. Hugo went after him, but the old man eluded him with unexpected quickness, a residual bit of strength left over from his youth. In no time, Blücher had climbed into his waiting carriage, which he had arranged to arrive at a prescribed time, and was whisked away.

Löwenklau had no choice but to return to his guests, who were all fixed with curiosity at the envelope's contents. Back at his wife's side, he opened it and found two royal edicts contained inside. He read the first one through, and then handed it to Margot.

"My discharge papers!" he smiled, conveying a mixture of joy and sorrow. She looked at him with concern.

"Go and read it for yourself, my love," he nodded in encouragement.

She complied and, having finished, remarked with unmistakable satisfaction. "It's certainly a discharge, my love, but in a most honorable way!"

"A promotion, no less!" he added. "It gives me permission to assume the title of cavalry master, with the rank of captain and all its obligations and privileges. That certainly is worthwhile, despite my discharge."

"And now open the other letter, my son!" encouraged Madame Richemonte.

Löwenklau opened the second document. As he scanned the contents, his face brightened instantly. "Listen, my dear Margot!" he said. "This is thanks to our good, old marshal!"

She took the letter and read it quickly. "Is this really possible?" she asked, overjoyed.

"What? What?" their friends asked all at once.

"A gift," she explained. "A kingly gift, one you could only dream about! His Majesty proclaims that, in lieu of the extraordinary service Hugo von Löwenklau performed for his country, he will be given the estate of Breiten-heim!"

This news created quite a stir throughout the room as their guests all milled around them, asking Löwenklau what important service he had carried out. Hugo was forced to explain how he had come to learn of Napoleon's plans and was able to advise Blücher and Wellington accordingly.

"This is an extraordinary gift," he said at last, "that will free us from worry about the future. We'll have to give our heartfelt thanks to the king. I certainly didn't deserve all this. Good old Blücher took up my cause and exaggerated my contributions." He turned to Margot. "Do you know, my love, that this gift has a special significance?"

"Really, what is it?"

"It just so happens that Breitenheim borders on my own estate," Löwenklau explained. "I believe both the king and marshal must have been aware of the close proximity. I didn't let on that my discharge affected me deeper than it showed, but I'm more than satisfied with the final outcome. I'm now in possession of an estate that I can use not only for our blessing, but also for others."

❧✠☙

What followed was a confirmation that the new couple had indeed been blessed by the king's edict. They gained an audience with the king in the next few days to express their gratitude. They naturally took the opportunity to also visit their benefactor, affectionately known to Margot as Father Blücher.

Blücher enlightened them in regards to Richemonte's indictment. He could have elaborated about it at the wedding, but had wisely saved it for a later, more private, time. "Should we pursue him to the full extent of the law?" he asked.

"He certainly deserves it tenfold," answered Löwenklau.

"What about your thoughts, Madame von Löwenklau? He is your brother, after all."

Margot contemplated the issue carefully before responding. "Would it be perceived as heartless if I condemned him?"

"Not in the least," the marshal said. "How does your mother feel about it?"

"The same as I do. He was our nemesis for many years and we still fear him to this day. I'm convinced he'll look for an opportunity to rob us of our joy."

"Fine. Then we need to ensure he'll be powerless to inflict further harm. I plan to travel by carriage this very day to meet with the French minister and present him with the case."

He was good to his word and was informed by the minister's subordinate a short time later that the entire matter would be a priority in light of its serious nature. But the results to come were quite different than either man could have anticipated.

Löwenklau was invited by the French court to a preliminary hearing, one that was carried out with true French protocol. He was required to turn over the purse and billfold, as well as the report he had written pursuant to the discovery of Reillac's corpse.

"Where is Richemonte now?" inquired Löwenklau.

"He's in custody in Strassburg," the court's magistrate replied.

"Is it secure custody?"

"Of course! We treat the matter of murder very seriously."

"The allegation stems from outside of France in this case, and I fear this matter may not be treated with the same severity."

"You may be right, though I'm not officially allowed to confirm that," replied the magistrate. "Is it your wish that I include a relevant report?"

"If you would! Please Monsieur, advise the magistrate in Strassburg that Richemonte is a dangerous and most resourceful man, one who would exploit anyone to gain his freedom."

"I'll accommodate your request, Monsieur Löwenklau, even though I don't think he'll resort to that."

"Do you feel the authority there will release him?"

The magistrate paused, giving the matter some thought. "I can only surmise that in light of this romantic situation, anything is possible!"

Löwenklau's fears and the official's prediction were not entirely without merit. He heard an escort had taken Richemonte to the mountainous area where the chest had been buried. Hugo had fully expected he would be asked to accompany the excursion, but such was not the case. The magistrate in Berlin was advised that the French detail was quite capable of finding Reillac's grave on their own.

A short time later, Löwenklau presented himself before the French court. He was advised that Richemonte had in fact been very cooperative. He had pointed out the place where he had last seen Reillac's body. Then the unthinkable occurred, a development that deeply disturbed Löwenklau. Richemonte had maintained his innocence, and turned the spit around.[30.3] He advised the court that Löwenklau had been enlisted as a spy during the war. It was he who had murdered the baron, out of fear of exposure, then plundered the body and left it to rot. They said it was Richemonte who had returned to bury his friend, only to be accosted by Löwenklau. In short, Richemonte had turned everything around.

Finally, under oath, having accused Löwenklau, he demanded that he, not Richemonte, should be taken into custody and that they make a short process of the German at his trial. What could Hugo say to refute Richemonte's lies? He had been present at the time the murder was committed and was in possession of the dead man's belongings. He had even buried Reillac. He thought about the ten soldiers who could have exonerated him, but like Reillac, had met an untimely death and could not answer to the court. His own version sounded more like a fable. And lastly, should he mention anything about the buried war chest?

But unlike Richemonte, he was not alone. Margot and her mother gave a full account of the story, including their relationship with Albin. Likewise, the coachman Florian, who was now in Löwenklau's employ, came forward in his defense. The whole story sounded preposterous, and yet would have cast a shadow on Löwenklau had it not been for Blücher's intervention. The marshal's version of events endowed a measure of credence to Löwenklau's story, to the point that the court was not going to cause him any further embarrassment. The French authorities, having taken all relevant information into account, rendered the following judgment:

'Arising out of the most peculiar circumstances that led to the demise of Baron de Reillac, two suspects have come to the attention of the authorities. One German, who resides in Berlin, and one Frenchman, who resides in Strassburg. Both have accused the other of wrongdoing and murder. The German, although facing a more severe incrimination, is not being charged by his government. Consequently, no accusation can befall the French procurator if he abandons Richemonte's prosecution. Without the testimony from independent witnesses, the supporting evidence is inconclusive, and the matter, though serious in its entirety, remains unsolvable.'

Their verdict was succinct and to the point. Such was the bizarre outcome of Löwenklau's pursuit of justice. Reillac's fortune, unclaimed by Margot for obvious reasons, was dispersed among distant relatives, much to the chagrin of Richemonte. And the captain? Although not exonerated, he was released from custody. A careful search of his property and residence did not reveal the slightest trace of Reillac's will, nor the emperor's edict, whereby Margot would have become Reillac's wife.

It seemed that Richemonte had an answer for every conceivable situation. When presented with the three letters he had written to Margot himself, he retorted in an impudent manner that he had concocted the whole story to save his sister from a horrible fate. He hadn't wanted her to marry the murderer of his friend, Baron de Reillac. The captain disappeared shortly after the inquiry, leaving no trace of his whereabouts.

Shortly thereafter, Hugo and Margot, now settled in their new estate, received a surprise visit from the Baron Roman de Sainte-Marie. Berta Marmont, now married to the young baron, accompanied him on the visit. She had borne him a son, and it was only natural that Hugo and Margot, along with Madame Richemonte, stepped forward to be the godparents. The only blemish, which pointed to the fact Berta was not of noble descent, was that the Baroness de Sainte-Marie still looked unfavorably on their union. Hugo and Margot were relieved when they realized that the baroness, who now had to face the fact she had a grandson, had made provision for her son Roman, so he would not be without funds.

As time passed, Margot conceived and bore a son, who they named Gebhard Leberecht, much to the delight of her husband, and nearly as great a delight to the old Blücher himself! He, of course, insisted he be proclaimed as one of the godparents, not wanting to miss out on the joy of being the boy's benefactor.

It was to be his last joy, however. Blücher died at the ripe old age of seventy-seven, on the twelfth of September 1819. He was mourned by all of Germany, but even more so by Hugo and Margot von Löwenklau.

TRANSLATION NOTES

I have taken the utmost care to render the original German text into a coherent and legible English format. Some of the passages were difficult to translate in the way they were presented, whether because of the sentence structure or by their sheer length. Karl May seemed to enjoy enveloping his readers with a series of interwoven thoughts, all in the same paragraph, or plunging them deeper into the story through long sentences. You may read it in its entirety in German, all the while trying to catch your breath, but it just doesn't translate well in English.

In some cases, May employed old idioms or outdated sayings that I've coined as "Blücherisms." Although they heighten the dramatic moments, rendering the literal expressions into English would have modern readers shaking their heads. One example, taken from Chapter 21:

Original:	"Mein Himmel, da falle ich ja wie aus den Wolken!"
Literal:	"My Heaven, I'm falling as though from the clouds!"
Interpretation:	"I'm losing my composure."

The final translation has to be faithful to the original, as much as possible, while remaining an enjoyable read for anyone unfamiliar with the original German text. The editor affixed parentheses to outline where changes had to be made, and notes were created to explain the deviations. In some cases, a further explanation of a word or phrase was necessary.

1.1   Montmarte
"Mountain of the martyr." A hill, about 130 meters in height on the north side of Paris. Saint Denis, Bishop of Paris, was martyred on the hill in 250 A.D. Eventually an abbey was built to commemorate the site, which was expanded into a full-fledged monastery in the 12th century by the Benedictine monks. Often used as a meeting place, the Montmarte became the center of the Commune in 1871 and housed many forms of artistic life in the 19th century.

1.2   Warmbeer
Warm was the only way to drink beer in the days before refrigeration. Since the dawn of civilization, beer was served at room temperature. Later it was cellared, so that it could cool, but for the

most part warm or hot was the preferred temperature for consumption. It was relatively easy to find *warmbeer* in any tavern. Called "mulled," meaning heated, it was the fashion of the day and enthusiasts lapped it up in staggering quantities. Not only did they prefer it hot, but they were convinced it was good for them. Mulled beer was considered an aid to healthy living. The brief text "Panala Alacatholica," dated 1623 (author unknown), was one of many sources that praised the virtues of warm beer, explaining that it "doth by its succulencie much nourish and corroborate the Corporall, and comfort the Animall powers."

| 1.3 | L'Hombre |

L'Hombre is a fast moving card game. It follows the general rules of winning a hand by the taking of "tricks" and was played by three or four players. In the 1800s, it held a prominence among serious players similar to the game of bridge in the modern world.

| 1.4 | Zieten Hussar |

A mounted soldier in a light or heavy cavalry regiment. Originally, the term Hussar emanated from the Serbian "Huszar", and later the Russian "Hussar", meaning *highwayman*. The Hungarians were so successful that the term became synonymous with a Hungarian cavalry soldier in the 15th century. In 1741, an Austrian major, H. von Zieten, adopted the model of the Hussar and implemented it with great success in upcoming Austrian campaigns. The uniform consisted of a busby (upright fur hat with a plume), a jacket with heavy braiding, and a dolman (loose coat) worn over one shoulder.

| 1.5 | Gottfried |

Of Germanic origin, combining the words for God (Gott) and peace (fried). In 2 Kings of the Old Testament, Elijah's mantle was a symbol of God's power, a spiritual covering to embrace. The term Gottfried was an extension of this thought and afforded the bearer the natural covering from the wind and cold, but also implied a form of protection in the spiritual context.

| 1.6 | "Feder fuchser" |

Literal: Feather pusher.
Interpretation: To "fuchsen" is to vex or annoy. "Feder" is a feather or quill. A "schreiberling," or penpusher, is an endearing term referring to a clerk who was steeped in bureaucracy and engaged in writing boring reports. However, in this context, I believe Karl May was showing Blücher's frustration with the interim governing body by

referring to them as "penpushers."

1.7 "Wegen diesen verdammten Franzmännern schmore ich mir nicht mein Fleisch von den Knochen."
Literal: "Because of these damned Frenchmen, I'm not going to braise my flesh from my bones."
Interpretation: "They're not going to get under my skin."

1.8 "Aus dem Regen in die Traufe kommen."
Literal: "Out of the rain, and under the eavestrough."
Explanation: The implication is that it was favorable to stand under the eaves during a storm, thus not getting wet from the deluge. However, a sudden downpour could overflow the gutters and drench the unsuspecting traveler. Therefore, Karl May implies that perhaps by leaving one bad situation, you could end up in a worse predicament.

3.1 Dante's Hell
A reference to Dante Alighieri's masterful depiction of hell. Alighieri was an Italian poet (1265-1321) who also spent time in France. In the story, he outlined an unusual journey that carried the reader through hell, purgatory, and finally into paradise. Although referred to as a comedy, it is a progression from the pilgrim's moral confusion, culminating with a vision of God.

3.2 Brunhilde
A mighty female warrior, one of the *Valkyries*; a heroine from the *Niebelungenlied*, revered as an Icelandic princess. The story grew in folklore during the 1200s and became a German epic over time.

3.3 Bonapartists and Orleanists
Bonapartists were monarchists who desired to restore the French Empire under the house of Bonaparte. They had a strong following throughout the early 1800s and continued even after Napoleon's defeat at Waterloo. They competed with the Orleanists, who favored the restoration of the House of Louis-Phillipe, and the Legitimists, who favored the House of Bourbon, the traditional royal family. The strength of these three factions was probably greater in influence than those of the Republicans. However, public sentiment stayed with the Republic as the other three could not choose one candidate to further the monarchy.

4.1 "Donnerwetter"
Literal: Thunder weather.
Explanation: An old idiom used in place of a swear word, such as

zounds ("By God's wounds" or "For Heaven's sake"). Karl May employed the use of minced oaths since they were more accepted in his time. They were derivatives of holy terms (cross, church, saint, heaven) and the result was such expressions as *Kreuzmillionensternhagel*, *Millionendonnerhagel*, and *Donnerwetter*.

4.2   **"Plaudertasche"**
Literal: Gossip bag.
Interpretation: A gossiper who "spilled his guts"; a chatterbox. A term reserved for those who can't keep a confidence and blabber it to anyone who will listen; one who has loose lips.

4.3   **Sodom** and **Gomorrah**
Sodom, from the Hebrew *Sedom* (meaning "burnt") and Gomorrah, from the Hebrew *Amorah* (meaning "buried"). A biblical reference to the destruction of the two cities (Genesis 19:24-25), apparently destroyed by fire and brimstone. Flavius Josephus, a respected Roman historian, indicated that the occupants of the cities were not only deviant in their behavior, but were known to be arrogant, insolent, and boasters of their wealth.

4.4   **Methusalem**
Methusalem, son of Enoch, has been referred to as the oldest man that ever lived. According to the book of Genesis, Methusalem, also known as "Man of the Dart," lived to be 969 years old.

4.5   **Pharaoh** and **Biribi**
Since the revolution of 1789, the Palais Royal in Paris had become a glittering attraction to many gamblers in Europe. Five main gaming clubs operated from noon until midnight. It was rumored that the famous Marshal Blücher visited the Palais Royal on several occasions after the Battle of Waterloo, losing on one count nearly 1,500,000 francs. *Pharaoh*, or *Faro*, was a favorite card game consisting of forty-eight or fifty-four cards. Players bet against a banker (dealer), who drew two cards. Bets were placed on one or both cards. *Biribi*, or *Cavagnole*, was played on a board containing numbers from one to seventy. Players bet on their desired number on the board. The dealer would select from a bag a "ticket" bearing a number and calling it out. The successful holder of that number was rewarded sixty-four times his wager.

4.6   **"Man hate Mich ganz gehörig gerupft."**
Literal: "Man, they sure plucked me thoroughly."
Explanation: A reference to the pulling of feathers from fowl, as in

plucking a chicken.
Translation: "I lost my shirt."

6.1   Papperlappap
       Rubbish, poppycock, or balderdash. An endearing term referring to
       useless blubbering.

6.2   "Panzer"
       A flak jacket or cuirass, from the old French *cuirasse*. A device worn
       over the torso as protective armor. It usually comprised both breast
       and back pieces. It was quite often made of leather, but was also
       sometimes fashioned out of sheet bronze or a thin iron plate. A *panzer*
       was used extensively by the French and Prussian cavalries.

6.3   Arabic gum
       The ancient Greeks chewed a type of resin called mastic gum, *mastiche*
       (pronounced 'mas-tee-ka'). The resin originated from the mastic tree
       and was also combined at times with beeswax. It was a favorite in
       Eastern Europe, Turkey, and Greece.

6.4   "Auf den Leim gehen."
       Literal: "Going on the lime."
       Explanation: This idiom suggests that a person has been tricked or
       cheated. The implication here, according to Blücher, is that anyone
       agreeing to enter into marriage has been coerced and therefore does
       not understand the full implications of his actions.
       Interpretation: "How I got caught."

6.5   Bramarbas
       A loudmouth, or outspoken braggart. Bramarbas is the main char-
       acter from a German composition entitled "Jacob of Tyboe," written
       in 1741 by the Danish poet and historian Ludwig von Holberg.

8.1   "Auf die Folter spannen."
       Literal: "Stretch out on the rack."
       Explanation: Karl May introduces the reader to a concept very
       familiar to those who lived in medieval times: the ancient torture
       method of being stretched out on a rack. This was a very painful way
       of extricating information from an unwilling subject. The unfort-
       unate person was strapped onto a rectangular board with leather
       straps while the limbs were systematically "stretched" by means of a
       roller.
       Interpretation: Stretching one's "time" or one's interest, so the
       "captive" recipient will be more interested, even curious about the

outcome of the story.

8.2 **"Blendlaterne"**
Literal: Burning lamp.
Explanation: Oil burning lamps were used extensively in Europe in the 1800s. They burned with paraffin lamp oil or oil made from animal fats. The brass base housed a simple burner with a flat wick. They were durable and dependable.

8.3 **"Der Stab gebrochen über das Haupt"**
Literal: Staff broke over his head.
Explanation: One of the ways to place a curse on someone in medieval times was to "break a staff over his head." This symbolic act was often depicted at a public trial. As the staff was broken, it signified that the perpetrator's folly had come to and end and justice had prevailed.

9.1 **"Schwarzwalder perpendikel."**
Literal: Black Forest pendulum.
Explanation: "No lover will pay attention to a clock keeping time." A reference to the pendulum of an old clock, and in particular a clock from the Black Forest region.

9.2 **"Ein X fur ein U."**
Literal: "An X for a U," or to replace an X for a U."
Explanation: This old idiom dealt with the idea of being deceived or cheated. In the middle ages, money lenders tried to insert the Latin X instead of the Latin V on loan documents, so as to receive higher repayment. V, for the number 5, was of lower value than X, for the number 10.

9.3 **"Das ihr alle blau und rot anlaufen sollt, wie die altweiber Nasen um Weihnachten herum."**
Literal: "You're going to see blue and red, like old women's noses at Christmas time."
Translation: "I'll fix it so that you'll get pummeled, and look like an old woman's nose at Christmas time."

9.4 **Pince-Nez**
Literal: Pinched nose.
Explanation: A style of spectacles used in Europe as early as the 1500s. The C-bridge on earlier models used a flexible piece of metal to provide tension against the nose, keeping the spectacles in place.

9.5 **"Achtgroschen stuck"**
Literal: An eight groschen piece.
Explanation: The Groschen, from the latin *denarius turnosus*, meaning "big penny on tour." In German, the name adopted was "big-little". It was first minted in the 1300s and, in subsequent years, many forms of the coin emerged, ranging from the *onegroschen* to the *eightgroschen*. The silver content and quality of the coins varied as a result of the many wars. In the 1800s, a new currency was introduced in Prussia: 1 groschen = 1/30 thaler.

9.6 **"Sonst soll Euch der Teufel Purzelbäume schlagen."**
Literal: "The devil will make summersaults around you."
Interpretation: One who pushes himself to extremes while daring others to follow; a daredevil.

9.7 **"Auge und Beine machen."**
Literal: "Make eyes and legs."
Translation: "Get going and have a good look around."

9.8 **"Jetzt aber lege Dich mit dem Ohre wieder auf Deine Pritsche."**
Literal: "But now lie down with your ear on the bunk. "
Interpretation: "Lie down and get some rest."

9.9 **"Wenn ich wüßte, wer der Flegel ist, so ließ ich ihn citiren und hieb ihm seine Schaftsandalen mit sammt den Struppen höchst eigenhändig um die Nase herum!"**
Literal: "If I knew who this lout is, I would let him recite something whilst singlehandedly slapping him about his nose with his high sandals and laces."
Interpretation: "I'll beat him over the head with his own boots until he gets the message."

9.10 Urian
In German folklore, the term *Urian* also referred to Satan. See *Tragedy of Faust*, by Johann Wolfgang von Göethe:

> Now to the Brocken the witches hie,
> The stubble is yellow, the corn is green;
> Thither the gathering legions fly,
> And sitting aloft is Sir Urian seen:
> O`er stick and o`er stone they go whirling along,
> Witches and he-goats, a motley throng.

"Sir Urian" was an unwelcome guest whose presence or untimely visit implied that trouble or bad news wasn't too far off.

10.1   "Du bist das größte Kameel, was in der Wüste Sahara Datteln und Radieschen frißt!"
Literal: "You're the biggest camel that feeds on dates and radishes in the Sahara Desert."
Interpretation: "You're as gullible as a camel that wanders the Sahara."
Explanation: Camels, if hungry enough, were known for devouring anything and everything. Blücher is poking fun at August, suggesting he's like a naive camel, "eating up" (believing) anything.

10.2   **Donner** and **Doria**
Literal: Thunder and Doria.
Explanation: This minced oath, or expletive, was taken from Friedrich Schiller's story, "The Conspiracy of Fiesko of Geona."
Interpretation: Thunderclap or lightning. A modern rendering would be, "By Jove!"

10.3   "Es leidet mich zu hause nicht, wenn mich nicht der Knaster und die Nase brennt."
Literal: "It doesn't bother me at home, if the aroma of tobacco smoke burns up my noise."
Explanation: Blücher was an avid pipe smoker. He was referring to the smoke not irritating him as it entered the nostrils.
Interpretation: "I'm quite comfortable at home, so long as it burns properly."

10.4   "Latten arrest."
Explanation: Various forms of discipline and corporal punishment existed in the Prussian army geared toward bringing a disobedient soldier "back in line." At times, punishment was brutal and carried to excess. One such form was the use of "latten arrest." The soldier was housed in a structure, or stockade, made out of latten strip (of crisscrossing wooden planks). The prisoner, confined in this small enclosure and exposed to the elements, was visible to all.

10.5   "Rebecca also heaped burning coals on the head of Herodes."
Explanation: Is there a connection here between Rebecca and Herodes? This seems to be a reference to Herod, probably Herod Antipas. The suggestion is that Rebecca (likely Herodias) heaped burning coals onto Herod's head. In Scripture, Herod Antipas was incited by his wife Herodias to behead John the Baptist to appease her guilty conscience. Karl May certainly knew his scriptures and likely wanted the reader to see Blücher's fallibility by allowing him to mix up his 'femmes fatales' (Herodias instead of Rebecca).

11.1 "Das Du nicht auf die Nase gefallen bist."
Literal: "You have not fallen onto your nose."
Interpretation: That you have not taken a misstep and landed on your nose. Also: "I can see that you know your way around."

11.2 Bonahomier
Another Blücherism, coined to express Blucher's displeasure of having to deal with the imminent return of Napoleon.

11.3 "Tausend Sapperlotter."
Literal: "A thousand *Sapperlots*."
Explanation: Derived from *Sapperlot* ("Upon my soul.") Another expression for *Zounds!*

12.1 Changeur
Money changer. Many common people were loathe to use banks, and resorted to money lenders out of convenience. The lenders were always "enterprising." ensuring they always made money. Because there was always an underlying sense of being "stiffed" by the Changeur, they were looked upon with disfavor.

12.2 "In Gold fassen"
Literal: "Cast in gold."
Explanation: Blücher was pleased with the Grenadier's watchfulness, so he was willing to compensate him for his efforts rather extravagantly, and probably with money.
Interpretation: "Worth his weight in gold."

12.3 Laubtaler
The *taler* (or *thaler*) was also known as the *lorbeertaler* or *franzgeld*. It became the standard for commerce in Europe during the 1500s and was used in France as the *ecu aux laurier* from 1726-1790. In the 1700s, the *kronenthaler* was issued in Germany, weighing 29.44 grams, which was valued at one Cologne mark of silver. It gave way to the Maria Theresa *taler*, a silver coin widely adopted in most European countries. It was named after the Empress of Austria, Hungary, and Bohemia, who reigned from 1740 to 1780.

13.1 "Maulheld"
Literal: Hero of the mouth.
Translation: Big talker, braggart.

Kriegskasse
14.1 A military war chest used in transporting coins or valuable goods.

15.1   **Henri de la tour d'Auverge**
Vicomte de Turenne, Marshal Turenne, Marshal of France (1611-1675).

17.1   **Marshal Ney**
Marshal Michel Ney (1769-1815), Duke of Elchingen, Prince of Moskowa. Ney, known to his men as 'the bravest of the brave,' supported Louis XVIII after Napoleon's defeat in 1814 in an attempt to stabilize a fragile postwar France. He later changed his allegiance to Napoleon, much to the chagrin of the ruling party (the Bourbons). After Napoleon's second defeat in 1815, Ney was arrested and tried for treason. He was executed by firing squad in December 1815, an event that deeply divided the French Republic.

17.2   **Marshal Groucy**
Emmanuel, Marquis de Grouchy (1766-1847), was born in Paris into an aristocratic family. He was a leader who often placed himself near the front, explaining why he was often wounded. In 1815, he joined Napoleon on his return from Elba and was made Marshal and Peer of France.

17.3   **General Gourgaud**
Gaspar, Baron Gourgaud (1783-1852). During the campaign of 1813 in Saxony, he showed courage and prowess. During a battle near Brienne, he killed the leader of a small band of Kossacs, thereby saving the emperor's life. He was *aide-de-campe* to the emperor and fought at Waterloo.

19.1   **"Freude die Bulle Platzen."**
Literal: "Happily burst at the seams."
Interpretation: "I'm so happy, I could explode."

19.2   **"Auf die Leber."**
Literal: "Open the liver."
Explanation: In medieval times, an attack to the unexposed lower body (i.e. the solar plexus, kidneys, and liver) could prove serious, or even fatal. To stand up and not worry about exposure was inherently risky.
Interpretation: To stand up and not worry about being heard, or "verbally" attacked, was akin to being *auf die Leber*.

19.3   **Napoleonder**
This gold coin was in wide circulation in the 1800s and was also called the "Napoleon d'or." It was worth 20 francs.

19.4   **Bayard**
Pierre Terrail, Seigneur de Bayard (1473-1524). He was generally referred to as the 'chavalier de Bayard.' A descendant of nobility, he proved himself to be a fearless and valiant knight in battle.

21.1   **"Mein Himmel, da falle ich ja wie aus den Wolken!"**
Literal: "My Heaven, I'm falling as though from the clouds!"
Explanation: An old expression, implying a sense of losing peace of mind. In the context of the story, however, Karl May introduces some dark humor, that cannot be omitted. Though one might render the above as "I'm shocked!" the subsequent reply of "Please cousin, do yourself no harm" would be meaningless.
Interpretation: "I'm losing my compsure."

21.2   **"Da soeben einen Korb erhalten"**
Literal: Just handed a basket.
Explanation: Tradition stated that when a young suitor wished to announce his love for a girl, he would get a wooden pitchfork, a "flachsgabel," and present himself with the instrument at his lover's house. If the maiden saw him coming and wished to show that she was not interested in his proposal, she would quickly place a hand basket in front of her door.

22.1   **Staffelbefehlshaber**
Literal: Relay Commander.
Explanation: During war time, the timely and steady supply of information, as well as seeing that orders were being carried out, was vital to any campaign. The task of overseeing this important assignment often fell on the "Staffelbefehlshaber," or relay commander.

23.1   **Seladon**
The verdant lover The term *Seladon* appears in a poem by Thomas Swartwout (1631):

> And be ye faithful to each other, like Seladon,
> Who found not his spouse on the beach his heart to gladden,
> But in the hands of pirates, who many did appear;
> One made a doleful cry and to deprive him of cheer.
> Allow'd her time enough to say: Love, take me with you.
> They bound and cropp'd him with many pains and aches anew.

24.1 **"Die Not bricht Eisen."**
Literal: "Necessity breaks steel."
Interpretation: "Need will always find a way."

25.1 **"Auf die Folter spannen."**
Literal: "Stretch out on the rack."
Explanation: Margot was confined, like on a rack (see 8.1 above).
Interpetation: "To restrict her movements."

25.2 **Roland**
This was likely a reference to the Song of Roland, a poem from the Renaissance period that embellishes its hero, a knight who fought under Charlemagne (778 AD) against the Muslim forces. In the song, Roland is portrayed as an exceptional fighter, equipped with an "Olifant", a magnificent horn, and a "Durendal" (an unbreakable sword). Roland was 'adopted' by various European countries as their hero, including the French, German, and even Italians, where he was known as Orlando.

25.3 **"Von Ihnen an der Nase herumfuhren last."**
Literal: "You're being led around by the nose."
Interpretation: "The German is playing games with you, making you look like a fool."

26.1 **Büttel**
Literal: Ruffian.
Explanation: This is a loose reference to a Hungarian sheep herder from the early 1800s. A Büttel was later known as a ruffian or high-wayman, feared for daring raids on unsuspecting travelers in South-eastern Europe.

26.2 **"Verfluchte Schweinerei."**
Literal: "Dammed pig's mess."
Explanation: An old expression implying annoyance and abhorrence.

27.1 **"O Ihr Heiligen!"**
Literal: "Oh, you saints!"
Translation: In May's time, expressions depicting something holy had to be "minced", or curtailed so as not to offend the populace.

28.1 **"Bringt Dich der Teufel schon wieder zurück?"**
Literal: "Did the devil bring you back already?"
Interpretation: "You returned with such supernatural speed that you must be in league with the devil."

28.2   "Der sollte sich doch lieber um ein Paar warme Filzschuhe und um ein seliges Ende bekümmern!"
Literal: "He should rather worry about a warm pair of felt shoes and a blissful end to his career."
Interpretation: "He should have been more focused on the matters at hand."

28.3   Battle of Ligny
The famous battle of Ligny (June 16, 1815). Blücher, counting on Wellington's troops, lost to Napoleon. According to historian Sir Herbert Maxwell, Wellington was at a cricket match on June 13. He dismissed news of French troop movements as overblown. He downplayed other reports and even attended a ball given by the Dutchess of Richmond. A final plea from General Dornberg on June 14, brought his army to Quatre-Bras, but they were too late to sway the outcome.

28.4   Dulzinea
Miguel de Cervantes Saavedra entitled his famous novel *Don Quixote de la Marche* and penned it during the Spanish Golden Age (1605). The protagonist, Don Quixote, sets out in search of adventure to impress his imaginary lover, Dulzinea del Toboso. The illusion-struck "knight" conjured up the image from observing a neighborhood farmgirl.

29.1   "Russisches Seifenplaster" (or "Weiermuller's Universalplaster," "Schwartzburger Zugpflaster").
Explanation: A reference to the many kinds of ointments and dressings available, each one having its own history and proven value.

29.2   "Anstatt ihm auf die Socken zu helfen."
Literal: "Instead of helping with his socks."
Interpretation: "Leaving the sick man worse for wear."

29.3   "Kreuzmillionsternhagel"
Literal: "A crossed million hail from the sky."
Explanation: A minced oath, implying "Holy crap!" It is similar to *Milliondonnerhagel* and *Donnerwetter*. These are oaths that cannot be translated with the same intensity. "Dammit" almost sounds benign in comparison.

29.4   "Melissengeist"
Explanation: A special ointment or preparation, to be used by gentlemen for moustache grooming.

29.5   "Lauf zum Kukuk mit Deinem Befehl!"
Literal: "Run to the cuckoo with your order."
Interpretation: "To hell with your order!"

29.6   "Er mag die Hunde führen bis Bautzen."
Literal: "Let him lead his dogs all the way to Bautzen."
Interpretation: He should let his dogs run all the way to Bautzen, a city in eastern Soxony. The implication is that it would be better if the lieutenant left Blucher's sight by going to Bautzen than to remain behind, usurping his rightful place.

29.7   "Jetzt mag er auf St. Helena Käse reiben,"
Literal: "May he now grate cheese on the island of St. Helena."
Interpretation: "Now that he's in exile on St. Helena, he can occupy his time with mundane household matters, like grating cheese."

29.8   "Ich werde mich doch in der lange und der breite legen."
Literal: "I'm going to lie down, lengthwise."
Interpretation: "I can still get involved, resolving it to my satisfaction."

30.1   "Mit ihm sollen doch gleich drei Schock Schulpferde durchbrennen!"
Literal: "He and nine score of training horses should stampede out of here at once."
Explanation: Clearly in this case, Blücher is having some fun at the young lieutenant's expense, and is suggesting that it would be better if he just went away, leaving all the honor to Blücher himself.

30.2   "Daß dieser armselige Klapperbein doch so langsam seine Hand nach mir ausstreckt."
Literal: "That this wretched rattle bone slowly stretches out his hand toward me."
Interpretation: "Death is slowly coming to get me." This is a reference to the grim reaper, stretching his hands toward his next victim.

30.3   "den Spieß umgedreht"
Literal: "Turned the spear around."
Explanation: The circumstances have changed, or the roles have been reversed. The implication, especially in warfare, is that the enemy's plans have been thwarted and are now being used against him
Interpretation: "The tide has turned."

What follows is an exclusive peak
from *The Marabout's Secret*, the next volume
in *The Hussar's Love* series.

CHAPTER ONE
Countess Rallion

D uring the first half of the nineteenth century, few Europeans managed to visit the infamous Timbuktu.[1.1] Countless researchers and scientists would have gladly given half their wealth to be able to reach the small city on the border of the Sahara and Sudan. Only a lucky few ever succeeded in the attempt, some of whom went at it alone, while others participated in larger, better equipped expeditions, choosing to approach it from the north or the west.

To the north, the desert posed a number of dangers in the form of pervasive robbers who lived in the shadow of the Atlas Mountains. The elusive Tuareg[1.2] tribes that dwelt in the innermost region were unfriendly to the looks of curious Europeans and posed no less of a threat. To the south lived the followers of Islam, a group that already held a seasoned mistrust of any newcomer. The Muslims, acutely aware of their penchant for proselytizing heathens, steadfastly resisted any attempts toward religious conversion.

In 1848, the Berlin Society for Exploration, having been entrusted with the commission of exploring the vast Sahara, came up with plans for a thorough expedition into the desert and, if the conditions proved suitable, a further push toward Timbuktu, though not at the expense of the team's safety. The society made inquiries to secure the most capable, enterprising, and knowledgeable team of adventurers they could find with scientific backgrounds.

The unanimous decision was to select First Lieutenant von Löwenklau for the task of leading the expedition. The young officer enthusiastically jumped at the opportunity, though his parents were forced to overcome their natural reservations over sending their son on such a perilous journey. After all, Gebhard was the only child of Cavalry Master Hugo von Löwenklau and his wife Margot (née Richemonte). The young man's special benefactor and godfather remained none other than the irrepressible Field Marshall von Blücher himself.

Gebhard, the spitting image of his father, had barely reached young adulthood when news reached the Löwenklau family that the Baroness de Sainte-Marie had died and had providently made him the sole heir of the Jeannette estate. The story of the Sainte-Marie family had unfolded tragically.

Baron Roman, having disregarded his mother's objections to marrying Berta Marmont, had fallen out of grace with the baroness. Consequently, he had been forced to leave the estate and relocate to Berlin with his new wife.

Shortly after his wedding, Hugo von Löwenklau had moved to his own estate at Breitenheim, accompanied by his new bride. Occupied with his new business holdings, he was unaware when the young baron's marriage to Berta began to dissolve. He received a letter from Roman outlining how Berta had fled in the company of Captain Albin Richemonte, and that he was pursuing them both. After all this time, it seemed Richemonte hadn't gone far after all. He might have exercised his own revenge on the Löwenklaus had it not been for Berta's intervention.

Some time later, Madame Richemonte received a letter from the Baroness de Sainte-Marie, describing how she had not only lost her son's heart but his mental faculties as well. She learned that Berta had been killed in Marseille, at the hands of her own son.

Since that time, Baron de Sainte-Marie and Captain Richemonte had disappeared without a trace. Richemonte, implicated as an accomplice in Baron de Reillac's murder, had ultimately been discharged from the army for undisclosed reasons.

Choosing to focus on the present and prepare themselves for the future, Hugo and Margot von Löwenklau had decided to distance themselves from the past as much as possible. It was Hugo's wish that his son enlist in the military, resulting in Gebhard's enrolment in the officer's academy. The young man excelled in his studies and distinguished himself among his peers. Only one other cadet, Kunz von Goldberg, proved to be his equal and their common interests formed the foundation of a lasting friendship.

Young people often dream of the future and the promise of accomplishments, and these two friends were no exception. Determined not to fall behind their peers, both men fulfilled the necessary military requirements and received their commissions as officers. After the initial service, Kunz von Goldberg was seconded to the Paris legation. He had already been residing in Paris for several years when Gebhard von Löwenklau received the invitation to lead the expedition to Timbuktu.

Gebhard requested a short holiday so he could make the necessary preparations for such a lengthy trip. There was much to accomplish. He had to procure maps and check the availability of instruments and other scientific items, many of which were only available in Paris. It was thus decided to make the French capital the meeting place for the expedition participants.

Having concluded his business in Berlin, Gebhard took his leave and traveled to Paris. Upon arrival, his first order of business was to surprise his good friend Kunz with a visit. As they greeted each other warmly, Kunz was the first to speak.

"What a surprise to find you in Paris!" he exclaimed. "Are you here on leave?"

"Yes, a holiday that will take me into the Sahara."

"The Sahara? You intend to travel to the desert?"

"Travel to it, yes," Gebhard began, "but my plan is to march right through."

"Gebhard, don't talk in riddles."

"It's really quite simple. I've been fortunate enough to be included in an expedition to Timbuktu."

"All the way to Timbuktu? It sounds like a dream, almost impossible to believe."

"That's how it seemed to me when I accepted."

"Tell me all about this expedition," Kunz encouraged. "How did you manage to take part in it? Who are the participants and what goals have you set?"

Kunz listened in amazement as his friend launched into the story. When Gebhard finished, he heartily shook his hand.

"I congratulate you," he said. "My God! Gebhard, I'm so glad that finally one of us can follow that boyhood dream we had so long ago. You'll see the vastness of the Sahara firsthand!"

"No doubt," Gebhard replied, seemingly in jest. "Not only firsthand, my friend, I'll be up to my elbows in sand while you continue to study and expand your influence in Parisian society. You'll revel in the finer things while I roast under relentless heat. When I return, you'll have been promoted to the rank of major while I'll have been converted to a *Moor*."[1.3]

"Despite all those refinements, I wish we could trade places. What an adventure awaits you, my friend. You'll live with the Bedouins, fight with the Tuareg, and shoot hyenas, jackals, and maybe even tangle with a lion. Heavens, a lioness! Somehow, that reminds me of Hedwig."

"Hedwig?" asked Gebhard. "Hyenas, jackals, lions, a lioness, and lastly... Hedwig. Together, they seem to form a progression toward wild ferocity."

"Hmm, you're not that far off. Hedwig isn't tame at all."

"Ah!" Gebhard laughed. "Is this Hedwig perchance a wild and unfettered tigress? Perhaps she should be confined to a zoo! Or a menagerie."

Although Kunz shook his head, he cast his friend a glance that conveyed a hint of the mysterious. "No, my friend. Hedwig is a wonderful being who unfortunately possesses a measure of the untamable. She isn't confined to a tiger's cage, but rather to a palace on *Rue de Grenelle*."

"Is she young and beautiful?"

"A beauty whose looks could drive a man to madness."

"Is she rich?"

"Destined to inherit a fortune. She lives with a wealthy aunt."

"*Zounds!* Then take your Hedwig and leave the aunt for me."

Kunz laughed. "With pleasure! Though you might think about Hedwig's younger sister, a far sweeter choice. Together, we could divide the spoils as brothers-in-law!"

"You don't say! So, your Hedwig has a sister? May I solicit you for a description of her outward appearance?"

"Yes, though I wouldn't do it for just anyone."

"Thank you," Gebhard said. "Now then, how old is she?"

"About seventeen."

"And the color of her hair?"

"Blonde."

"Hmm, my favorite color. What about her eyes?"

"Hazel," Kunz said. "They shine like the stars."

"Are they more like a distant planet or a blazing comet?"

"They're so soft and tender, likely to melt your heart at first glance."

"What about her figure?"

"She's slim and, despite her youth, has an appealing shape."

"What's her voice like?"

"Like the golden voice of a nightingale."

Gebhard let out a low whistle. "She sounds almost too good to be true. Does she already have an interested suitor, like your Hedwig?"

"No, not yet."

"How convenient. Tell me, what's her name?"

"Ida."

"That doesn't sound too bad. Does she have any parents?"

"No," Kunz said. "They're both dead."

"Really? She must be nearly ready for marriage."

"Unfortunately not. There is a large obstacle, a *Cerberus*."[1.4]

"Does this obstacle come in the form of an old, rich aunt? We could overpower the dinosaur with a good club," Gebhard suggested. "Or better yet, with our charm, whichever proves more effective."

"I hate to be the bearer of bad news," sighed Kunz mockingly, "but in this instance, you can't wield a weapon. Nor can you rely on your skills as the consummate socialite."

"I believe you," replied Gebhard. "Perhaps I'll have more luck than others."

Kunz's eyes sparkled tenaciously. "I'll endeavor to pray for your success."

"You're too kind," Gebhard said. "Now, here's what you can do for me. Take me with you to *Rue de Grenelle* and facilitate the introduction."

"As long as she doesn't snarl, howl, or bite," Kunz mused.

"Do you think I'm afraid of an old woman? Don't forget, my name is Gebhard and Blücher is my fearless protector. My motto is *Go forward!*" Just then, another thought occurred to him. "You spoke of howling and biting. Where on the rungs of the social ladder might I find this old aunt?"

"She's the Countess of Rallion."

"I take it she's not friendly."

"My friend, she's positively set against anyone of German extraction. What's worse is that she doesn't seem like any newcomers at all."

"Yet you managed to get close enough to become infatuated with her niece."

"Well, yes," Kunz admitted after a brief hesitation. "I should add that I did so despite a few obstacles."

"What might those be? There's more than just a disagreeable aunt, I presume."

"First, of course, is the aunt. Second, Hedwig herself. The third comes in the form of a bad-tempered nephew, Count Rallion, who's always getting in my way."

"Does the aunt favor him over you?"

Kunz shook his head. "Not in the least. It's as though the old lady has no desire whatsoever in welcoming any suitor for her nieces."

"Stop exaggerating, Kunz," Gebhard jibed. "I wouldn't mind getting to know this family. That's where you come into the picture. Since they're already familiar with your finer qualities, it shouldn't be too difficult for you to introduce me."

"Then you want an introduction?"

"If it's not asking too much."

"How long will you be in Paris?"

"No more than two weeks."

"That's good!" Kunz exclaimed. "You won't have enough time to cause too many problems for me. I'll do my best."

Gebhard narrowed his eyes at his friend. "You think I would cause you some embarrassment?"

"Well, you are taller. And stronger. And have more sex appeal. I have a lot at stake here, my boy!"

"But you forget that I'm also your friend. Don't worry. I'll be gentle and do my best to conform to etiquette. Believe me, you have nothing to worry about. I'm not a fan of boisterous women – you can keep Hedwig all for yourself."

"Heaven knows she's feisty," Kunz said. "Ida on the other hand is quite compliant. I'm convinced you'll be impressed with her, if only you were staying a little longer."

"Two weeks is long enough," Gebhard laughed. "Tell me, does the aunt have a weakness or preference by which we could work our way into her good graces?"

"A weakness?" Kunz asked, thinking about it. At last, he snapped his fingers. "Of course! I nearly forgot. That's what I wanted to talk to you about. Certainly, she has a weakness."

"A weakness for what?"

"Have you ever heard of Gérard?"[1.5]

"Gérard? Which Gérard? The general?"

"No, the famous lion hunter."

"Oh, you mean Gérard from the Sahara," Gebhard said. "His exploits are legendary. Of course I've heard of him!"

"Hedwig and her aunt are infatuated with his adventures."

"There's a curiosity," Gebhard said. "I suppose it's understandable. They are women, after all."

Kunz nodded. "Uncomfortable for me, though," he said, gaining a faraway look. "Especially since I'm no lion tamer."

About the Author

Robert Stermscheg was born in Maribor, Yugoslavia in 1956. His parents were of Austrian descent, and due to his father's profession as an electrical engineer, moved to various countries in his early childhood. His father kept a steady supply of Karl May books to broaden his education and exposure to the developing world. The family moved to Canada in 1967, and settled in Manitoba. Robert was involved in hockey, chess, skiing, and flying, but always kept up his interest in the German language.

His repertoire included about forty Karl May books, which he read over and over again. He developed a passion for sharing his love for these books, and turned to searching for English translations.

Robert retired from the Winnipeg police service in 2006, and now had the time and opportunity to pursue his dream of writing. His wife Toni suggested that he consider a translation project. She supported him with encouragement and volunteered to be a proofreader. Robert began his translation work with this volume, *The Prussian Lieutenant*, a classic tale of conflict between the French and German peoples during the Napoleonic War of 1814.